DANCE THE MOON DOWN

by

R.L. Bartram

An Authors OnLine Book

Text Copyright © R.L. Bartram 2011

Cover design by Siobhan Smith ©

All rights reserved. No part of this publication may be reproduced, stored in a retrieval system, or transmitted in any form or by any means, electronic, mechanical, photocopy, recording or otherwise, without prior written permission of the copyright owner. Nor can it be circulated in any form of binding or cover other than that in which it is published and without similar condition including this condition being imposed on a subsequent purchaser.

British Library Cataloguing Publication Data.
A catalogue record for this book is available from the British Library

ISBN 978-0-7552-0682-7

Authors OnLine Ltd
19 The Cinques
Gamlingay, Sandy
Bedfordshire SG19 3NU
England

This book is also available in e-book format, details of which are available at www.authorsonline.co.uk

For Miranda.

For my mother
Bessie Bartram
17/12/22 to 26/1/08
A true rose of England

Hope you enjoy the book
Regards Robert
R Bartram

About The Author

Having first put pen to paper at the age of 17. He has now been writing for a number of years and many of his short stories have appeared in various national periodicals and magazines. His two main passions in life are writing and the the history of the early twentieth century, which made 'Dance the Moon Down' a logical choice for his first full length work of fiction.

He is single and lives and works in Hertfordshire.

Author's Note

Extensive research into this genre led me to conclude that whilst a great deal has been written about the First World War, very little had been done about civilian life, particularly that of women, on Britain's home front during those times. Whilst being historically accurate, 'Dance the Moon Down' remains entirely a work of fiction. However, many of the situations portrayed in the book are based on actual events.

R.L.Bartram

Chapter One

It was during the spring of 1910 that it became the subject of heated debate between Victoria's parents as to whether or not she should attend university and continue her education. Her father had been a staunch advocate of the idea, whilst her mother had vigorously opposed it.

Eventually, her father had prevailed, but in spite of their differences, both had their daughter's best interests at heart. However, it was scarcely possible that either of them could have foreseen that this innocuous decision would be the catalyst for a sequence of events that would ultimately propel Victoria from her staid suburban life into a world she was totally unprepared for.

*

The village green was barely visible beneath a thin veil of autumn mist that had rolled inexorably along the valley, shrouding buildings, fields and fences, frosting the grass and blanching the bare trees into grey spectral silhouettes. At the end of the green, still distinct despite the fog, stood the Staunton Gifford war memorial, its stone cross stark against the pale disc of the winter sun, its solid form tall and hard against the vaporous air of the chill November morning.

The names of those it honoured, the fallen of the parish, had been incised deeply into the stone so that they might stand the test of time, and yet perhaps it was its very permanence that had relegated it, in the modern age, from the status of sacred memorial to the lesser degree of landmark. It stood year in, year out, obvious and unseen, useful these days as little more than a point of reference.

At its base lay a wreath or two of sombre laurels threaded with black ribbon and adorned with poppies cut from scarlet cloth. Victoria noted with resignation that now there were but few, where once there had been many. She had been here on that day, more than forty years ago, when the cross had first been unveiled. She recalled that hundreds had gathered to honour the heroes of the Great War but as time had passed, they had passed, until only she and the memorial remained.

Occasionally there were some new faces, but invariably they came not to pay tribute, but merely to observe a piece of history, something not of their time, something outside of their experience that they had read about, but did not quite understand. They would stare idly at the weathered stone, the eroded names half-obscured by cushions of moss and bright patches of orange and yellow lichen that grew imperceptibly, irresistibly erasing one identity after another before consigning it back to the distant past.

No matter, Victoria knew all the names by heart, and there were others who had died but did not appear on this monument. They'd once had faces, lives, they'd laughed and loved. Many had been close friends.

"Are you sure it's this one?" a woman's voice enquired peevishly.

"Yes, I think so," a man replied. "This is Staunton Gifford, isn't it?"

"Oh God, don't tell me you've driven us all the way out here, and you're not sure!"

"Well, it's this damn fog. I could have missed the sign, but now we're here we may as well look."

Victoria suspected that the couple who had lately arrived were just 'new faces'. They were both young. The girl had waist length blonde hair that flowed from beneath a navy blue plastic cap, which fitted snugly on her head and matched the colour of her boots. She wore a short suede jacket trimmed with imitation fur, and a floral mini dress which frankly left more thigh exposed to the elements than seemed healthy on a day like this.

The man, his hair almost as long as the girl's, his beard thick and unkempt, wore a similar cap, a bizarrely patterned waistcoat over a red shirt, and black flared trousers. He began to stalk around the monument, squinting at the weather-beaten names until, at length, he gave a shout of triumph.

"Ah, there it is!" He jabbed a pointing finger at the stone. "I told you. Gerald Avery, second lieutenant. Can you see?"

"Where?" The girl leaned forward.

"There!" he continued to point. "Gerald Avery. One of the foremost English poets of his time. I read him in my third year at Cambridge. Look, there at the bottom."

"Oh yes!" The girl leaned closer and as she did so, her dress rose higher and higher, leaving little to the imagination.

Victoria spared herself a philosophical shrug. It was, after all, the swinging sixties. Free love, sex, drugs and wild music and all of them behaving as if they'd just invented it. In the twenties, they'd roared; now in the sixties, they swung. So much had changed. So little was different.

In her day, it had been considered indecent for a woman to wear trousers in public. God only knows what they would have thought of this immodest young lady.

So, Victoria mused, returning her attention to the young man; this student of literature considered her husband to have been one of the foremost poets of his time. That was most gratifying. It was a pity, she recalled, that her mother hadn't been equally as enthusiastic on that Easter break of 1913, but so much had already happened, even before then.

As the only child of middle class parents, it had never occurred to Victoria to expect anything beyond that which was provided by her sheltered Edwardian existence. She had been born into an era that clung doggedly to the aging Victorian ethos that a woman's place was in the home. The new century was already a decade old and yet the majority of women were still condemned to be the lesser half of an unequal partnership in which they had no voice, no hand in current affairs, not even the right to vote. They passed from father to husband with nothing in between but the vague and misguided belief that they'd fulfilled some unspoken obligation. Most could read and write, cook and sew; other than that, nothing was expected of them beyond the role of homemaker. A gradual change in attitude was beginning to emerge, but as yet it did little more than divide opinion and split the population into antagonistic factions.

At the age of sixteen, the only indication Victoria had of the circumstances surrounding her life was the continuing debate between her parents as to whether or not she should attend university. She'd already enjoyed an expensive formal education, similar to many girls of her class. Having clearly demonstrated her ability to go beyond that, the question now was whether she should be allowed to take it a step further and experience a degree of learning generally reserved for men.

Her father was a distinguished physician, well respected in his field, who could have made a lucrative profession out of prescribing placebos to the wealthy upper classes. However, he was also a man of ethics who believed that medicine should be made available to everyone including the poor. He was a man of vision, an ardent reformist and a progressive thinker. Whilst he ensured that his family enjoyed a relatively affluent lifestyle at their home in the suburbs of Chelsea, he divided his time between his visits to the less fortunate in the East End, and his private practice in central London. For him, the desire to see Victoria advance was not merely the manifestation of his egalitarian zeal, but simply the next logical step in his daughter's development.

Her mother, on the other hand, was a diehard Victorian whose unswerving patriotism had extended to the naming of her only child after the great Queen-Empress herself. She did not care to see her daughter vulgarly over-educated. A girl of Victoria's class would never be expected to make her own living, let alone pursue anything so masculine as a career. She should be concentrating her efforts on making a propitious marriage. In her opinion, she needed no further education beyond that required by an accomplished wife and mother. A duty to one's country, husband and family and a strict observance of the proprieties; these were the rigid principles she'd been brought up to believe in, and she fully expected her daughter to do the same.

Indeed, it was these very principles that had compelled her mother, against her better judgement, to concede to her husband's wishes, and Victoria was subsequently enrolled at Caufields, a residential ladies' college in the centre of Cambridge that specialised in higher education for women. In spite of a few misgivings Victoria harboured concerning her attendance at the college – she'd never stayed away from home before – the prospect of an adventure had tweaked her curiosity. She tried to imagine what it would be like, without ever really anticipating the sudden deluge of new ideas that would assault her senses. However, as the days passed into weeks, the most significant change she began to experience was the hitherto undreamed of sense of freedom that, at one and the same time, both terrified and exhilarated her.

At home, she came under the control of her parents. At Caufields, she was bound by the influence of her tutors, but it was the spaces in between, the little fragments of unsupervised time that allowed her the opportunity to be entirely herself. It was during these moments that she began to acquire an extracurricular education, a new and more diverse experience of the world at large than she'd ever thought possible. It was something that she endeavoured to keep secret from her parents whenever she came home at the weekends or on one of the seasonal breaks, but an occasional slip of the tongue, a hint of mischief, would incur a glare of disapproval and her mother's favourite chastisement.

"It's that college I blame!"

Victoria made many friends among the other girls who attended Caufields. One in particular, with whom she shared a room in the dormitory block which constituted part of the college building, was a tall willowy redhead named Beryl Whittacker. Beryl was an irrepressibly forthright young lady whose opinions on women's rights and their position in society were always radical and very often alarming. She had lately become involved with an organisation calling itself 'The Women's Social and Political Union'. At the risk of being expelled, she would smuggle their pamphlets onto the grounds and distribute them among the other girls. Victoria read them without completely understanding what they meant, but she didn't dare keep any for fear of being discovered. Instead, she tore them into little pieces and scattered them, like confetti, behind the bushes in the park when out on walks.

"I had to threaten I'd jump from a window before my parents would send me here," Beryl confided, as she and Victoria strolled in the forecourt one lunchtime. "My mother beat me for it, but I got my way."

"Wasn't that a little drastic?" Victoria frowned.

"Drastic measures are what's needed, if we're to change anything," Beryl informed her stiffly. "I don't see why, just because we're women, we have to conform to the expectations of an archaic social order. I want to live my life on my own terms, without constantly having to defer to a man!"

"Does that mean you're against marriage?" Victoria asked, wondering if Beryl's drastic measures extended that far.

"You're missing the point," Beryl replied patiently. "I'm not against marriage as an institution. I'm against it being offered to women as their only option in life."

"It seems to me," Victoria told her, "that the fault lays with the society of the day, which itself has been conditioned by past generations, which conditions us, setting a standard to the way we think and behave, whilst for some, inadvertently placing a limit on their aspirations."

"The fault is theirs," Beryl pointed a disdainful finger out into the courtyard where other girls were milling about. "Look at them all," she sighed contemptuously. "Modern educated young women, with a world of opportunities before them. Even if they have been indoctrinated to accept whatever their parents or society tells them, they do so without ever once questioning the validity of it. Consequently, in spite of a superior education, most still believe that the best they can achieve is to become some man's wife. God, have they no more ambition than that?"

"What about love?" Victoria asked.

Beryl stopped and looked at her friend as if she'd expected better from her.

"Love is an illusion," she told her flatly. "Romance is the sugary bait in the snare." She gestured once more at the occupants of the courtyard, offering them up, yet again, as a typical example. "I doubt if there's one of them who in spite of their intellect, doesn't have their heads stuffed full of silly romantic nonsense, who hasn't gone into raptures every time some brute male looks in their direction. One admiring glance and they're ready to surrender their independence and discard every opportunity."

"But surely it's natural to be attracted to the opposite sex?" Victoria suggested.

Beryl studied her for a moment, wondering if her friend had her priorities quite in order. "I don't consider the subjugation of one half of society by the other to be in any way natural. Besides," she concluded, "I believe that we should always strive to rise above our baser instincts."

Victoria felt that it was probably wiser not to pursue the subject. They were best friends. Beryl trusted her, whilst assuming that she thought as she did. Because of that, Victoria didn't dare mention that she'd also indulged herself in a romantic notion or two before now, and had often enjoyed the admiring glances of young men as they'd passed by. She couldn't help but feel a delicious tingle of excitement when they looked at her in that certain way, beyond formal acknowledgement. Occasionally, she'd offered a coy smile of appreciation in return, whenever she could, whenever Beryl wasn't watching. As for sugary bait, she fancied she might be developing a sweet tooth.

Beryl had also received her share of admiring glances from men, but she'd always made a point of deliberately snubbing them, as if they'd offered the gravest offence. She seemed to have laid all the faults of society firmly at the feet of any man she met, viewing every member of the male sex as the personification of her unequal existence. She made no secret of the fact that she considered any female who thought otherwise to be a traitor to the cause of women's suffrage.

Victoria decided that it would be safer to return to the topic of ambition.

"What would you be, Beryl?" she asked. "If you had the chance"

Beryl squinted, pursing her lips in thought. Then thrusting back her shoulders and tilting her chin at a haughty angle, replied, "I would be Prime Minister."

"Beryl, you're the limit!" Victoria gasped. "A woman as Prime Minister, that's impossible!"

Beryl leaned closer, narrowing her eyes at Victoria. "Nothing is impossible for those who try."

*

By the time Victoria was eighteen, the circumstances surrounding her life, those that would ultimately affect the shape of her future, began to gather momentum. Her father died of influenza which he'd contracted from the patients he'd been treating at the clinic he ran for the destitute. Devastated by the loss, she was also fearful that her mother might remove her from Caufields which she'd for so long considered to be a bad influence on her daughter. Fortunately, in the end, she'd allowed her to remain and complete her final year, in deference to her late husband's wishes.

Inexplicably, German was dropped from the curriculum whilst all the senior girls, including Victoria, who were already fluent in the language, were advised to refrain from speaking it in public. Victoria could see little reason for their caution. After all, no one seemed to believe that there would be a war with Germany. The rumours had been circulating for years, but nothing had ever happened. Yet they persisted; rumours of what was being called the 'European War'.

There was mention of international treaties and of far flung Serbia, of Austria-Hungary and the Archduke Franz Ferdinand, none of which might have affected Victoria directly, had she not met and fallen passionately in love with Gerald Avery.

She'd merely accepted a general invitation, as had many other girls from the college, to attend a literary afternoon at a neighbouring university. After about thirty minutes of a less than engaging programme, Gerald stood up to recite one of his own poems. Victoria was instantly attracted to him. He was tall and slim with broad shoulders, which gave him a tendency to stoop slightly. As he stepped onto the rostrum, his very presence seemed to fill the hall. It was as if a veil had been drawn over the lamps, casting all else into shadow, until only he and she remained. For a moment, he shuffled the papers before him, pausing only to drag a hand through his shock of blonde hair, a vagrant curl falling back upon his brow. Then, having arranged the manuscript to his satisfaction, he looked up. The pale dancing lamplight banished the shadows from his face, leaving his features as smooth and well defined as those of a marble statue. His voice, as she listened entranced, was strong and deep, filled with eloquence and grace. It fell like music on her ears. Even after he'd finished and sat down, she couldn't take her eyes off him. So much so that Beryl eventually gave her a sharp nudge.

"Careful," she warned in a hissed whisper. "You'll stare a hole in him!"

For his part, Gerald Avery could hardly fail to notice the trim brunette who occupied the centre seat in the row opposite him. She sat, her chin perched lightly on her fingertips, the delicate curve of her rose-tinted lips parted in a dazzling smile that dimpled her pale cheeks. Her large eyes, intent upon him, flashed like polished emeralds each time he looked in her direction. Intrigued, he sought her out at the end of the recital.

They talked at great length, discovering to their mutual delight that they had much in common, whilst both realising that it had little or nothing to do with their desire to meet. Victoria was captivated by this man, this gentle poet, his boyish good looks, whose natural charm and ready wit she found irresistible. As for Gerald, he was fascinated by this beautiful stranger, this enchanting young woman, whose vivacious personality and guileless innocence had besieged his senses and taken his heart by storm.

It was only after a discreet cough from a college chaperone that they looked up to discover that the rest of the audience had drifted away, leaving the hall empty except for themselves and Beryl, who remained at the back of the room skulking moodily in the shadows.

Finally, reluctantly, they parted, but not before they'd agreed to meet again.

Beryl was immediately suspicious. "What was all that about?" she demanded as they made their way back to Caufields, with the chaperone bringing up the rear.

"Nothing really," Victoria lied shamelessly. "I'm just interested in his work."

"Well, as long as that's all you're interested in," Beryl responded, sounding less than convinced.

From that moment on, both she and Gerald took advantage of any opportunity that arose to attend any function, no matter how boring, just so they could go on meeting. Whilst all around them rumours of war abounded.

Rumours, and surely that was all they were, which had persisted for so long now lacked any credibility. The idea that the political unrest in a place like Serbia, a small and relatively minor country, could somehow plunge the whole of Europe into war was frankly ludicrous. It was utterly inconceivable that superior nations like Britain and Germany would come to blows over nothing more than an unpopular Archduke and an insignificant blot on the map. Even the 'Irish troubles' had been overshadowed by what was now considered to be the tedious and quite unnecessary speculation concerning this European war.

All but oblivious to the weight of opinion that circulated around them, Victoria and Gerald had continued to meet whenever possible. They'd become very close very quickly, but Victoria was beginning to feel, as doubtless Gerald was, that their relationship was being stifled in public places amongst large crowds and the constant attendance of a chaperone. As a man, Gerald was free to come and go as he pleased, but as a young middle class spinster, Victoria came under certain restrictions that were imposed by society and administered by every institution in the land, including Caufields.

Whilst it was perfectly acceptable for a young woman of Victoria's class to make the acquaintance of a young man, it was considered entirely inappropriate for her to do so unchaperoned. To Victoria, young and in love, this archaic custom seemed so unfair, so unjust and she would not be bound by it. Her feelings for Gerald were so intense that she didn't intend to share him with the rest of the world. This was her secret, or as good as. Now that she'd found him, she wanted to keep him all to herself. In defiance of convention and all the rigid rules of conduct, she was prepared to risk her reputation and the condemnation of her peers just to be alone with him. That was the plan, but how to achieve it presented a problem.

The policy of the college reflected the attitudes of the day. Whilst it permitted groups, or even pairs of girls to go out unescorted, no single individual was allowed off the grounds without supervision. The rules were very clear and very strict and there was the eagle-eyed Mrs Adams, who presided over the hall of residence, and her army of equally vigilant assistants always ready to enforce them. Getting past them on her own wouldn't be easy. She was left with no choice. She'd have to enlist Beryl's help, which meant she'd have to explain her reasons for wanting it. That wasn't going to be easy either.

Beryl reacted to the news as if she'd been told that Victoria had contracted an incurable disease which, in a way, she had.

"No, not you. You of all people!" she cried in dismay. "Do you realise that you could be taking the first step towards a lifetime of male domination?"

"That's not the way I see it," Victoria informed her calmly.

Beryl was anything but calm. "So," she assumed, "all those pamphlets I gave you went to waste."

"Not at all," Victoria disagreed. "I'm well aware of the inequality suffered by women in this society. I also know," she continued, pointing out a fact that Beryl had always refused to admit to, "that whilst all men do not think alike, those that accept our situation have themselves been indoctrinated by convention into believing they are right. We should be demonstrating our ability to be equal, not inciting division."

"That kind of thinking is ineffectual and naive," Beryl objected.

"So is breaking windows and knocking politicians' hats off," Victoria retorted.

"It got their attention," Beryl glowered.

"Yes," Victoria continued to argue, "but what kind of attention? The suffragettes are seen as criminals. Their organisation is viewed as subversive. Their actions gain them no political ground, only prison sentences."

"If that's your opinion," Beryl challenged, "then why did you join?"

Victoria was taken unaware. She'd completely forgotten she'd allowed Beryl to persuade her into becoming a member of the movement some years ago. Now she regretted it.

"I can't imagine what I was thinking to let you talk me into that," she admitted. "That room full of women all calling me 'sister'. I wasn't related to any of them."

"A sister in the cause," Beryl was stung by her flippant remarks, "as you well know."

So far, Beryl's scepticism had been sustained by her unassailable belief that her friend's invulnerability to the devices of men was equal to her own. Now, unable to convince Victoria to abandon what she considered to be a disastrous course of action, she began to suspect foul play.

"What on earth has he done to you?"

"He's stolen my heart," Victoria confessed poetically.

Beryl remained impervious to the sentiment, feeling disappointed and betrayed when she heard Victoria admit to being a willing victim. "Is that all he's stolen?" she enquired bluntly.

"Beryl, really!" Victoria protested against the vile innuendo. "How could you say such a thing? My virtue is quite intact."

"Yes, but for how long?" Beryl sneered, possibly a little jealous. "I've seen the way you look at him. It's positively indecent. I can almost read your mind." She paused, then added waspishly, "Let's hope he can't."

"That's cruel and unfair!" Victoria objected vehemently, both shocked and surprised by her friend's malicious insinuations. "What I think and what I do are two entirely different things. But if that's the way you feel, perhaps we shouldn't be friends anymore." With that, she stalked off in a huff.

Her statement took Beryl totally by surprise. Suddenly, she realised that she'd gone too far. After all, Victoria was her best friend, even if she had strayed from the path.

"Oh no, Victoria," she called out, running after her. "I'm sorry, really I am."

Victoria stopped and let her catch up.

"Please believe me," Beryl implored. "I didn't intend to be so harsh. It was such an unexpected shock, coming from you."

Victoria remained silent, so that Beryl could beg her forgiveness for just a little while longer. It would make her more amenable to her request.

"What about all the things we discussed? Equality, independence and a career," Beryl reminded her. "I thought that's what you wanted."

"No Beryl," Victoria informed her gently, "that's what you want. All I want now is to be with Gerald and I don't see how that will stop me pursuing any ambitions I may have."

Beryl didn't share her confidence. "He'll be just like all the rest," she warned. "He'll expect you to give up everything for him."

"I don't think Gerald is that kind of man," Victoria disagreed, not really minding if she was wrong. "Besides, how will I ever find out, if I don't get to know him?"

At last, Beryl realised that there was no point in any further argument. Victoria seemed to have made up her mind.

"I see," she shrugged, apparently resigned to the situation. "Not only do you deny everything I thought you believed in, now you expect me to do the same by assisting you to meet this man."

Victoria didn't see things in quite such a dramatic vein. "I don't want you to give up anything," she insisted. "I'm simply asking for your help. Not as a sister in the cause, but as my friend."

Once Victoria had appealed to her on that level, Beryl felt obligated to comply.

"Shall I have to lie for you as well?" she finally relented, although possibly she entertained the mistaken belief that once Victoria had been allowed to have her fling, she might eventually tire of this Lothario.

"Almost certainly," Victoria confirmed. "We'll be flying in the face of convention and flouting authority."

That helped. At last, Beryl looked as if she were beginning to warm to the idea.

Her plan worked beautifully. With Beryl in collusion, Victoria was allowed almost unlimited access to the outside world whilst her partner in this deception was always available to furnish a convincing alibi if necessary. It was an arrangement that proved advantageous to both of them. Once they were out of sight of the college, they parted company. Beryl was then free to pursue her interests in the suffragette movement, whilst Victoria went on to meet Gerald.

It was to be an unforgettable year - a year of risk and excitement, of secret liaisons, the fear of discovery, of reluctant partings and counting the minutes until they were together again. Victoria had never realised it was possible to feel this way. It was like walking on air. She was as light as a feather, whilst all around her the world seemed wonderfully bright and inexpressibly beautiful. She'd never been so happy. She was so very much in love that she hardly knew where she was, except when she was with him. She'd been right about Gerald; he was all that was best in men. She felt as if she'd been only half alive before she'd met him, whilst every day that passed was a continuing affirmation of their love for each other, from the first tentative kiss to the last passionate embrace.

She hardly ever went home on weekends now, and missed most of the seasonal holidays as well. She often wrote to her mother explaining that the pressure of work, that the demands of her studies kept her at Caufields. If nothing else, she'd be impressed by her daughter's industrious attitude.

It wasn't that Victoria deliberately wanted to deceive anyone. It was precisely because she was so very much in love that she couldn't bear the thought of anything coming between herself and Gerald, not even for a moment. Her feelings had blinded her to the consequences of her actions, consequences that she would inevitably have to face in the future.

By now Victoria was almost nineteen and about to complete her last term at Caufields. Of course, as a woman, she was not allowed to graduate, but she was able to sit and pass her final examinations. It was then that Gerald proposed to her and she accepted him.

Beryl was dumbfounded by the news. A romance was one thing, she could just about tolerate that, but marriage was quite another. Even though she'd been coerced, the fact that she'd been instrumental in bringing about this travesty made it all the worse.

Poor Beryl. Victoria viewed her friend's consternation with amusement. Her head was so full of high ideals and noble sentiments that she never listened to her heart. If she had, it would have told her that the desire for independence, equality and a career was no defence against Cupid's arrow.

Despite Beryl's opinions, Victoria didn't feel that she was slavishly accepting the only option available to her. Or even that she was relinquishing her claims on equality and independence, but rather that this was her first choice amongst many. She had come to know Gerald as a man of conscience and integrity. With him, her life would be enhanced, not diminished.

Nevertheless, Beryl had already begun to treat her like some sort of casualty. One of the walking wounded who, with care, might yet be healed and returned to the cause. Victoria could but wonder how Beryl would behave when her time came, if indeed it ever did, and what manner of man it would be who could capture her heart, if in fact such a creature even existed.

Victoria's happiness was marred only by one thing. Because she was underage, Gerald would have to ask for her parent's permission to marry her; that was mandatory. Now that he'd proposed, she'd have to tell her mother of her illicit affair for without her consent there would be no marriage.. It was now necessary for her to arrange the long overdue introduction. She didn't even dare to imagine what her mother's reaction might be when she came home and presented her, not only with certificates of education, but also news of a prospective son-in-law. It was a daunting prospect, but a just penalty, she realised ruefully, for keeping secrets and telling lies.

Victoria bore this harsh fact clearly in mind as they took tea in the parlour on a pleasant afternoon during the Easter holiday of 1913. She'd taken great pains to scatter the conversation liberally with trivia so as not to alert her mother to the impending news. In spite of her efforts, she had the distinct impression that, far from being distracted, her mother seemed to be expecting her to make just such an announcement. She'd reached this conclusion without realising that, during her last few days at home, the lightness of her step, the colour in her cheeks and the airiness of her disposition might have betrayed her secret long before she intended to reveal it.

Finally, after what seemed like hours of interminable small talk waiting for the right opportunity to bring up the subject of her engagement, the tension had become unbearable, and she could no longer delay the moment of truth.

"Mother," she announced in something of a rush, "I've met someone."

Her mother didn't so much as raise an eyebrow, but continued to sip her tea. "A man?"

Victoria faltered, feeling a pinch of irritation. How did she do that? It was really most frustrating. For all her mother knew, it might have been another girl from university she wanted to bring home. Or even an African pygmy, with a bone through his nose, who had launched himself at her from the trees in the park, demanding an introduction to her family – but no. As usual, her mother had gone unerringly to the point.

"Yes, a man," she confirmed, a little more tersely than she'd intended. "His name is Gerald Avery. He's asked me to marry him and I've accepted."

Her mother barely paused between sips. "What does he do?"

"He read English Literature at university," Victoria attempted to prevaricate.

Her mother set down her cup, dabbed her lips with her napkin, then fixed her daughter with an uncompromising gaze. "Very commendable, but what does he do?"

Victoria sighed inwardly. She knew this would happen. It was invariably the same attitude. Not did he love her, was he kind, but what did he do? What was he worth? What could he provide? It was all so soulless. As much as she loved him and admired his work, at this point she wished that she could say that Gerald was a banker, a lawyer, even a politician, anything that would sound of substance to her mother, but in the end all she had was the bare truth.

"He's a poet," she mumbled.

It was the biggest shock her mother had received since Mr Darwin had suggested that they were all related to monkeys.

"A poet! A poet," she repeated, incredulity dripping from every syllable.

At least Victoria had anticipated this situation. She had one trump card and now she played it. She informed her mother that, for this year alone, Gerald had earned over £150 for his work, adding, for weighty comparison, that a farm labourer, for all his efforts, might only expect to receive £30.

In hindsight, her mother's response was, perhaps, predictable. "Then I'm vastly relieved that you haven't agreed to marry a farm labourer."

Frustrated by her mother's implacable attitude, Victoria was driven to a sudden and ill advised act of recalcitrance. "I love him," she remarked stubbornly, "and I will marry him, whether you like it or not."

"Don't be impertinent," her mother barked, snapping her napkin against the edge of the table with such force that it made Victoria flinch. "That sort of attitude does nothing to impress me."

Suitably admonished for her insolence, Victoria instantly regretted having antagonised her. "Yes mother," she acknowledged dejectedly. "I'm sorry."

Her mother paused only to refold the napkin and return it to the table, before reasserting her uncompromising gaze upon her errant daughter.

"Your poor dear father, God rest his soul, sent you to Caufields so that you might improve your education," she reminded her. "Not so that you could become infatuated with the first young man who turned your head."

Victoria attempted to speak, to defend her actions, but one look at her mother's expression and she fell silent again.

"You carry on these clandestine assignations, in flagrant disregard of all the proprieties, behind my back, denying me my maternal right to judge the suitability of this man for you," her mother continued with a cold analysis of her daughter's behaviour. "Now you sit her before me, a proposal of marriage already in your lap, expecting me to greet this stranger with open arms."

"But I love him," Victoria begged her to understand, "and I know that you will like him as well, if only you'll agree to meet him."

Her mother was having none of it. "I absolutely forbid you to see this man again."

"What?" Victoria had fully expected her to have some reservations, but her decision had been so sudden, so unexpected and final that she could scarcely take it in, before it exploded inside her mind. All her dreams, her hopes, came crashing down. She was cast so abruptly into such a mire of despair, as she saw a whole year's happiness extinguished with a single sentence, that she felt her heart would burst.

"Oh no, please don't say that," she implored as she watched her aspirations evaporate. "Please say you don't mean it."

"I most certainly do," her mother reaffirmed her decision. "Your education is complete. You live here now, under my roof and underage. You will do as you are told. You will write to this gentleman, this poet, and inform him that you are not at liberty to accept his proposal, and that you will not be seeing him again."

Victoria sat there, stunned, staring open mouthed in disbelief as the truth of what had happened sunk in. Then suddenly she leapt up in a storm of angry tears. "I hate you!" she screamed. "You're cruel and insensitive. I hate you!"

"Go to your room," her mother commanded, "and compose yourself. You may not return until you can conduct yourself with a little more decorum."

Victoria didn't have to be told twice; she no longer wanted to be in the same room with her mother. She dashed upstairs, threw herself onto her bed, and cried for hours.

In spite of what Victoria may have thought, her mother was

neither cruel nor insensitive. She was merely a product of the times. In her mind, she endeavoured to protect her daughter, a young, impressionable and emotionally inexperienced teenage girl from what she considered to be an imprudent and unsatisfactory alliance that she would inevitably come to regret in the future. A poet, no matter how romantic a figure he cut, was quite the most unsuitable choice for someone in Victoria's position. It was quite normal for young girls to fall in love, and she anticipated that this would not be the last time she would have to curb her daughter's impetuousness. She would have to learn to get over this man.

Of course Victoria didn't see it that way at all. She was sure she was being punished for keeping her affair a secret, that her mother was motivated entirely by spite and revenge.

After hours of tearful consideration, she came to a drastic decision. She waited until she heard her mother come upstairs and go to bed. Then she packed a bag, left a note on her pillow, sneaked out of the house, and caught the last train to Cambridge. If she couldn't have her mother's consent to marry, then she would marry without it. She was on her way back to Gerald with the intention of eloping!

Chapter Two

Gerald had also completed his education and left university. He now rented rooms in the town from which he pursued his blossoming literary career. It was almost midnight when a gentle tapping at his door roused him from his bed. He put on his dressing gown and slippers, wondering who would want to call at this time of night, hoping it wasn't an old university pal locked out of his digs after a drunken spree. Victoria was the last person he expected to find standing there.

One glance at her expression and the fact that she was there at that hour told him something was badly wrong. He quickly hustled her inside, in case his landlady decided to put in an appearance. Victoria went willingly. She didn't care who saw her. Her reputation probably wasn't worth the price of a tram fare now anyway.

Gerald listened sympathetically as she told him of what had occurred between herself and her mother. She was distraught, her story disjointed, sometimes garbled, often punctuated by floods of tears or bouts of panic and desperation. In spite of that, it was all too easy to understand what had taken place. That her mother had not only refused her consent, but that she'd also forbidden Victoria to see him again. On the face of it, it was a disaster, but Gerald wasn't the type to panic. Nevertheless, it required a supreme effort of will on his part to suppress the urge to take Victoria and catch the next train to Scotland and then to Gretna Green. Fortunately, he was a level-headed man - someone who, even under stress, was able to weigh the consequences before acting. This represented a significant difference in character between himself and Victoria.

He cupped her face in his hands, looked deep into her eyes and told her truthfully, "I will marry you this very morning, at any church that will take us, if that's what you truly want."

Victoria had arrived on his doorstep ready to do anything he asked, anything. She not only loved him above all else, she also trusted him implicitly. He was her strength. What did she truly want? She wanted to be happy. She wanted to be happy with him and have everyone happy around her. That was unlikely now, under the current circumstances.

She'd calmed down now that she was with Gerald, and had begun to think more rationally. "Why is she doing this?" she asked. "Why is she being so mean?"

"I expect she thinks she's protecting you," Gerald suggested. "After all, she knows nothing of me. It's only natural for her to be cautious."

Victoria looked up at him, her large moist eyes full of anxiety and confusion. "What are we going to do?" she asked.

"I told you," he reaffirmed. "I will marry you this morning. I'll take you anywhere you want to go, but if we do that, we will spend the first years of our marriage looking over our shoulders every day."

He was right of course. Victoria knew her mother would immediately fear the worst and wouldn't let her go without a fight. It was that very thought that made her pause and reconsider. Only now did she realise that her mother's actions, no matter how harsh they appeared, had been motivated out of concern for her welfare, not spite. Unhappily, the fact remained that she hadn't given her consent.

"Your mother is your only living relative," Gerald reminded her. "If we do this, you'll be cutting her out of your life forever. Is that what you really want?"

"I don't want to lose you," she replied urgently, "no matter what it costs." But at the same time, she was in two minds about the wisdom of her actions. "What should we do?" she asked again.

"We must go back together," he told her, "and face her."

"No!" Victoria's eyes widened in alarm as she began to panic all over again. "What if she sends you away and locks me up? We won't be able to marry and we'll never see each other again!"

Gerald raised his hand in a calming gesture. "If that happens," he told her, "no matter what she does, no matter where she sends you, I will find you. I swear it," he promised.

Victoria clung to him, her heart pounding. "I'm terrified," she admitted in a tremulous voice.

"Is she that formidable?" Gerald asked.

"She can be," Victoria told him. "She's a very determined woman."

"Just like her daughter," he smiled down at her.

"Must we go back?" she asked, even though she knew what his answer would be.

"I think we should," he advised. "I must have a chance to try and persuade her to change her mind. My new anthology is to be published this month; it's worth £300. That should impress her, if what you tell me of her is correct. If she wants a man of substance, then here I am!"

"It's so unfair," Victoria objected. "Why should you have to prove yourself to her?"

"Because she is your mother," he told her simply, "your legal guardian, and those are her terms. If wealth and position are her criteria, then I must meet them." He put his hand under her chin and tilted her head up so that she looked directly at him. "All I ask of you is that you be brave for me."

Victoria already loved Gerald to distraction, but now, after hearing what he proposed to do, he'd just become her personal hero. As for his request, she hoped she did look brave, but in reality she was quaking in her boots.

Whilst the journey to Cambridge seemed to have taken hours, perversely the trip back to London felt as if it had lasted only minutes. In no time at all, they were standing at the front door of her mother's house. Filled with trepidation, Victoria felt that she would have liked just a little more time to prepare herself, perhaps a decade or two; but they were here now. She knew she could expect a tongue lashing but after that, it was pure speculation. Gerald flashed her a reassuring smile. She smiled back, resisting the urge to be violently sick. Then he grasped the knocker and rapped twice. The sounds boomed out, like the crack of doom, but that wasn't nearly as terrifying as the soft footfall of her approaching mother.

The door opened and there she stood, looking ten feet tall, wearing an expression that would have put the devil to flight. If her nerves hadn't been getting the better of her, Victoria might have noticed that behind the facade was a look of absolute relief now that she saw her daughter had returned safe and sound, not that she was tempted to any outlandish displays of emotion. There was still the matter of her daughter's delinquency to deal with.

She didn't speak, but merely stood aside and allowed them to enter. It was the coldest of frosty receptions. They were directed into the parlour, but not invited to sit down. They stood there, like prisoners awaiting execution, whilst her mother observed them in disdainful silence, with one withering glance after another. She didn't even ask why they'd come back, perhaps only too glad that they had, although her stoic nature prevented her from showing it.

Victoria stood, hands clasped in front of her, staring at the floor, shuffling her feet nervously, waiting for the ordeal to end. It wasn't until her mother had decided that they'd suffered enough in this way that she eventually broke her silence.

"You are a wicked girl!" she snapped suddenly, making Victoria jump. "Wicked and deceitful. You are wilful and disobedient. Were I a younger woman, I would thrash you for it. As it is, I can assure you that you will not be allowed to leave this house unescorted again before you are 21!"

Having vented her spleen upon her wayward daughter, she turned her steely gaze towards Gerald.

"As for you, young man, do you intend to offer some sort of explanation as to why I should not immediately summon the police and have you arrested for abducting my daughter?"

At the time it didn't occur to Victoria that, if her mother had intended to involve the police, she would have done so by now. Instead, her first instinct was to fly to his defence, but the barest glance from him restrained her.

"If by abduction," he responded calmly, "you imply that I have stolen Victoria's heart, then I plead guilty. My only defence is that she has taken mine in return. I also admit that when she came to me with the intention of eloping, I was tempted almost beyond endurance."

"Then what, may I ask, stopped you?" she enquired stonily.

"No matter what it may cost me," Gerald answered honestly, "I refuse to be the cause of a division between a mother and her daughter."

Victoria's mother may have been a woman of advancing years, but she was a woman none the less. Gerald's apparent honesty, natural charm, impeccable manners and good looks were not lost on her.

"Sit down," she invited finally.

There then followed two of the most gruelling hours Victoria had ever experienced, whilst her mother interrogated Gerald on almost every aspect of his life, from how he intended to support a wife, to his religious beliefs. Victoria sat in silence throughout this inquisition, consumed by anxiety and rigid with apprehension. As much as she would have liked to, she was unable to intercede on his behalf, bound by his request to forgo the temptation in case her untimely intervention damaged the delicate balance of the negotiations. He was utterly alone, but Gerald remained calm and polite, tolerantly answering the barrage of probing questions her mother fired at him. She wasn't about to leave any stone unturned in her rigorous examination of this man, especially if she were expected to consign her only child into his keeping.

Eventually, she seemed satisfied with Gerald's account of himself. The fact that he'd done the honourable thing and shown the maturity and common decency to bring her daughter home, instead of eloping with her, had also gone a long way in the defence of his cause.

Finally, to Victoria's unutterable relief, she consented to an engagement on the condition that, whilst they could still see each other, they would not marry until Victoria came of age. It wasn't that she'd changed her opinion of the situation to any great degree, but rather that she'd had time to reconsider. She realised that simply putting her foot down wouldn't diminish her daughter's affection for this man, and not wishing to drive her to any further acts of folly, had decided to employ different tactics. What she'd achieved was, in her opinion, a masterstroke of strategy. As things stood now, Victoria was content to remain safely at home. The mutually agreed postponement of two years was a long time in which anything might happen – and there was a war coming.

When a situation is discussed for a very long time and nothing happens, it is generally safe to assume that nothing ever will. As far as the European war was concerned, this seemed to sum up the prevailing mood of the nation. Indeed, it was their very familiarity with these rumours that had dulled their minds to the reality. It was their overriding complacency that had blinded them to the impending danger. A storm of apocalyptic proportions was coming, and they considered it to be just so much hot air.

Victoria's mother had laid her plans with great care and to the best of her ability to protect her daughter from a hasty commitment. Her insistence on a two year interval might yet have forestalled the chain of events shaping Victoria's life, but shrewd as she was, she couldn't foresee the future. Neither could she be expected to anticipate the devilish twists and turns conjured by fate that would conspire to undo all her work.

Victoria was not so much content as resigned to wait, and whenever she became impatient with her lot, she would always remind herself of how differently the situation might have evolved. She and Gerald were still together; that was the important thing, although now, whenever he called, her mother was always very much in evidence. Sometimes they were reduced to stealing a quick kiss or a cuddle at the front door or under the stairs before they went into the parlour. Even their walks in the park came under the scrutiny of an elderly chaperone; another condition her mother had seen fit to impose, albeit belatedly. Gerald named her Miss Gooseberry, although he was always careful never to call her that to her face. Happily, they very soon discovered that if they walked far enough for long enough, they could wear Miss Gooseberry out. After a great many circuits of the park, they would choose a secluded bench, wait for about ten minutes until she nodded off, then they were free to canoodle as much as they liked, as long as they were quiet about it.

This state of affairs might have continued indefinitely had her mother not died unexpectedly, eight months later, of a sudden heart attack. If she had known of her condition, or even suspected that she was ill, she would never have mentioned it. It was part of her stoic upbringing to endure without complaint. As Victoria stood by the graveside and watched her mother's coffin being lowered into the ground, it seemed to her that with the passing of this staunch old world Victorian, the sun had finally begun to set on the Empire.

In the weeks that followed, she discovered that her mother's reticence had not only included her personal health but also extended to their domestic situation. Her father's fortune had long since dwindled. They'd been living virtually on credit, and there was a mountain of unpaid bills. Eventually, the house and most of its contents were forfeit; there was little money left.

With nothing to stay for and no further obstacles in their way, she and Gerald decided to marry at once. The ceremony took place in January 1914 at a small provincial church in the suburbs of Chelsea. It was a quiet affair with few guests. There was Beryl, as maid of honour, and George Standish, an old university friend of Gerald's, as best man. Victoria carried a bouquet Beryl had made for her, comprising of white and purple daisies tied with a green ribbon - white, purple and green; the colours of the suffragettes. Beryl never gave up.

They spent their honeymoon at Rosebay, a comfortable half-timbered cottage that Gerald had rented a mile or so from the secluded West Sussex village of Staunton Gifford. He was most particular about carrying her over the threshold, informing her that, in bygone days, it was believed that evil spirits lingered there ready to ensnare a new bride and bring misfortune on her. As it was, he'd tripped on the step, forcing him to release her so that her foot touched the stone. They'd laughed about it at the time but, in the future, Victoria would often recall the incident and wonder about that superstition.

They spent a blissful fortnight at Rosebay. Even in the depths of winter, it was quite the most delightful place. The cottage was warm and cosy, whilst outside the hills and valleys, the bare trees and open fields lay cloaked in a thin shroud of snow that glittered under the pale sun, like an enchanted fairyland. Not that they spent much time sightseeing.

They were both reluctant to leave when the time came to return to Gerald's lodgings in Cambridge. It was then that he suggested they might take up permanent residence here, expressing a desire to escape the turmoil of urban life and live in the peace of the country, as so many of his contemporaries had already done. Victoria had no objections to that. She'd seen so much of towns that the idea of a rural existence appealed to her as well, especially if it was to be here.

They returned briefly to Cambridge and once Gerald had concluded his affairs there, he signed an eighteen month lease on Rosebay, and in the March of 1914 they moved in. What had once been only a honeymoon retreat was now to be their home. Victoria loved being there. It was such an idyllic spot, and after all the tribulations of the last year it seemed so safe and tranquil, as if the world were far away and that nothing could touch them here. Their little patch of Eden, Gerald called it, and she agreed. It was a pity she didn't know how short a time they would have to share it together.

For a while it seemed as though nothing would ever spoil Victoria's perfect happiness but, gradually, just as thunder clouds build up on the edge of a summer's day, she began to notice that the stories about a war in Europe were gaining strength. She confided her fears to Gerald, but he made light of them, telling her not to worry, but she could see that he was also concerned and had only adopted that attitude to spare her from anxiety.

In the months that followed, from time to time she began to suspect that there was a great deal more to this European war than just hearsay. A considerable amount of unusual activity and the many strange new sights and sounds that surrounded her seemed to confirm this. In the fields around neighbouring villages, large numbers of soldiers had been out on manoeuvres, and elsewhere horses were being requisitioned by the army. In particular, the government had commandeered the railways and now they were guarded day and night.

She regretted not having paid more attention to the rumours, but the fact that they had endured for so long without consequence had lead her to believe, like so many others did, that nothing would ever come of them. Only now, as she looked back over the last few decades at a Europe of opposing empires, disputed territories, raging nationalism and political intrigue, did she wonder if this war had always been inevitable, and that the rumours were merely a symptom of that inevitability, echoes of battle plans laid down years ago.

Now an unfamiliar sense of urgency had begun to spread throughout the land, an air of haste that pervaded the quiet, well ordered life of English society. The entire country had begun to change, adapt, as if already girding itself for battle.

As spring gave way to summer, Victoria would often lay awake listening to the sound of lorries and trains moving through the night, as men and equipment were transported to secret locations. It was with a mounting sense of dread that she realised something monstrous and irrevocable had been set in motion, something that would ultimately touch them all, changing them forever, and that far from trying to avert this crisis, the nation was running to embrace it.

By late June, all of England sweltered under a heat wave, and the frenzied activity that had dominated the year so far appeared to pause like the lull before a storm. It seemed to Victoria that now the long summer days were filled with a tension that was almost tangible, as if the country waited, poised ready for action. It was like a loaded pistol, hammer cocked, needing only a finger to squeeze the trigger; and on Sunday 28th it came.

It was in every newspaper all over the world. The Archduke Franz Ferdinand, heir to the throne of the Austro-Hungarian Empire, had been assassinated by a young Serb. It began like a row of dominos, one toppling the other. In the weeks that followed, after a series of impossible territorial demands had been made and rejected, as one diplomatic proposal after another failed, Austria-Hungary declared war on Serbia. Russia mobilised in defence of the Serbs and its interests in the Balkans. France mobilised in support of Russia. Germany, allied to Austria-Hungary, responded by declaring war on both Russia and France, pouring over a million men into neutral

Belgium on their way to attack Paris. Britain had signed a pact to protect Belgium's neutrality. On August 4th, having received no response to their demands for the withdrawal of these troops from allied territory, Britain declared war on Germany.

The waiting was over, the rumours had ended. Now there was a palpable enemy in the shape of the German troops to get to grips with. A great wave of patriotic fervour swept the country, consuming the population with a fanaticism bordering on hysteria. People lined the streets, filled the city squares, threw their hats in the air and cheered. Defend Belgium. Uphold Britain's honour. They clamoured for war, but this would be like nothing they'd ever known before. It was to be total war, with millions of casualties, a war that would cost the lives of almost an entire generation.

Anti-German slogans began to appear everywhere, painted on walls or scrawled in chalk on the pavements, whilst shops with names that sounded even remotely German were wrecked by roaming mobs. Victoria read the reports in the newspapers with utter abhorrence. It was the gradual dehumanisation of normally civilised people that she objected to and that alone was enough to make her despise this war.

Britain's strength lay in her large navy, the 'Grand Fleet', but her army was small in comparison to that which the Germans had put into the field. It was a fact that hadn't escaped the attention of Field Marshal Herbert Horatio Kitchener, an experienced and successful soldier, who'd recently been appointed to the post of Secretary of State for War.

Only days after taking office, he made an appeal for men between the ages of nineteen and thirty to enlist and increase the strength of the regular army. Thousands volunteered, the bravest and the best, and Gerald was amongst them.

Victoria's worst fears were realised, and yet she was far from surprised. She'd been expecting him to come to just such a decision for some time now. She had felt it herself. The call to arms had been so compelling that no true patriot could fail to answer it.

They discussed his enlistment long into the night.

"But we've had so little time here together," she told him.

He took her hands in his and squeezed them reassuringly. "I know, my dear," he agreed, "but it won't be for long. The British Expeditionary Force is already in Belgium. Along with the French, they'll defeat the German advance and then it'll just be a matter of mopping up. It'll all be over by Christmas."

"But you're a poet, not a soldier!" she insisted, desperate to find any argument that might make him reconsider.

"My dear, it's not enough to simply write about love and honour," he told her earnestly. "It's not enough to expound on the beauties of one's country, if you're not prepared to defend it."

"But you might be killed!" The very thought of it moved her to tears.

He held her for a moment until she'd recovered. "Germany has broken Belgium's neutrality," he explained. "It's the most direct route to France. If they take Paris, then they'll turn their eyes towards England."

"You think they might invade us?" Victoria had seen enough in the newspapers to understand the ramifications.

"I'm certain of it," he replied. "You see, Victoria, if chaps like me sit on our behinds and do nothing, the next thing we'll know is that the German's are marching up the lane outside. Then I'll certainly be killed, and I dread to think of what they might do to you."

It was as if he felt that by going to France and facing the enemy there that he might somehow prevent them from ever reaching England and her. Victoria had read enough of his poems to know how he felt about his country. Now that war had been declared, he didn't go to fight in defence of some distant foreign land. It was for England, her pastures, her fields of golden corn, her woods and lanes, everything that was England. Often, they were so intense that it seemed as if he were characterising a woman, beautiful and pure, whom he loved beyond life itself. Sometimes, when she could persuade him to recite them to her, it was with such passionate sentiment that she wondered, from the way he looked at her, if it was actually herself he was describing; if, in fact, she and the country were one in his mind.

It was then that she knew that she shouldn't keep him from going; worse, that she was able to stop him but that she should not. His desire to defend his country was a supreme act of love, not only for the land, but for her. It epitomised everything he believed in - love, honour, duty. It was the nature of his character. That was what she'd seen in him when they'd first met. That was why she'd married him.

By the same token, she couldn't deny him now. If she insisted that he remained with her, he would stay and she could keep him safe, as half a man with half a soul and half a heart. Her choice was horribly simple; keep him and crush his spirit, or let him go and risk losing him forever.

For many, it was impossible to resist the tremendous surge of nationalism that had gripped the country. The propaganda, the reports of German atrocities already being committed in Belgium, and the lies of conniving politicians were a potent concoction inclined to arouse the passions of any red blooded Englishman. Others simply followed suit with little or no idea of what they were agreeing to, and even less regard for the consequences. They went in their thousands, laughing and waving, with full hearts and the absolute assurance that it would be a short war, over by Christmas; that Britain would win, and that it would be glorious.

Victoria wondered if, in the future, the people of tomorrow would understand why the people of today had acted as they did. Would they realise that it was the spirit of the age that moved them? That it was their absolute conviction that what they did was right?

Gerald's social status and university education guaranteed him an officer's rank. After what Victoria considered to be a ridiculously short and woefully inadequate period of training, he was commissioned as a second lieutenant in the West Sussex Yeomanry. He had also grown a moustache. When she asked him why he'd done so, he told her that as many of the men under his command outranked him in years, he had been ordered, as had all the other young officers, to grow a moustache to make him look older. She didn't like it at all, and made him promise to shave it off the day the war ended.

He'd come home, briefly, on a few days leave before his regiment left for France. Together, they'd arranged a modest embarkation party in the garden at Rosebay. Several of Victoria's old college friends were there, including Beryl, as well as some of Gerald's university chums, all of them volunteers themselves.

Victoria loitered by a tall stand of Rosebay willow herb, from which the cottage had taken its name, the slender pink spears nodding in the gentle breeze, sending vagrant tufts of downy seeds floating up into the air, like summer snow. She stood gazing listlessly out at the gathering. It seemed strange to her that after having lived with the rumour of war for so long, now that it had actually happened, the very familiarity of it had softened the blow, so that far from coming as a shock, she felt no surprise at all. Apparently, most of the population had reacted to the news in much the same way for much the same reason. People had changed, the country had changed, and all she could do was stand there and wonder how they had come to this.

The heat wave was unremitting and the golden summer persisted, indifferent to the affairs of men. A molten sun beat down from a bronze sky. The garden was a riot of colour and perfume. All the girls looked beautiful, like blossoms themselves, beneath lace parasols, in their summer frocks of striped chiffon and pink silk, their large wide-brimmed hats bedecked with feathers, fruit or flowers, whilst all the men were dashing in their new uniforms.

Most of the guests, although virtual strangers, had now begun to pair off and stroll quietly around the garden, as if clinging to this one last moment of peace and tranquillity before the world tumbled around them. Victoria watched them with a feeling of absolute helplessness. They looked so pure, so blameless that she felt she was witnessing the last vestiges of innocence before the fall from grace. It was hauntingly beautiful, ethereal and tragic. If this was their little patch of Eden, then it was well named, for now, once again, they were destined to be cast out into the wilderness.

"What are you thinking about?" Suddenly Gerald stood before her.

"The war," she responded gloomily. "What else? I was wondering though," she went on, managing a smile for him, "now that all those other men have volunteered. I mean, there must be thousands of them. Is there really any need for you to go?"

"I rather think there is," Gerald replied, amused by her naivety. "I can't very well stay at home and let other men do my fighting for me. That wouldn't be very fair now, would it?"

"No, I suppose not," she conceded grudgingly, well aware that, even now, the right word from her would instantly compel him to resign his commission, endure the stigma of being called a coward and a traitor, and see his literary career in ruins. In essence, she would have to destroy him to save him, but in the end she realised that she could do neither and resigned herself to the inevitable.

"In any case," Gerald continued, "it won't be for long. I'll be back before you know it."

"You told me that before," she reminded him. "Now the British Expeditionary Force has had to retreat and the Germans continue to advance," she recalled what she'd recently read in the newspapers. The report was still searingly fresh in her mind. "Do you still think it will all be over by Christmas?"

"Perhaps not by Christmas," he admitted, "but I am convinced that it will be a short campaign. Mons was just one battle. We're regrouping along the River Marne now; we'll hold them there. Nothing in the history of warfare has yet been able to withstand the might of the entire British army."

"Oh, well said!" George Standish appeared on their right, his round moon face one perpetual smile. He never seemed to have a serious bone in his body. "And now that we have that splendid new British invention, rather unimaginatively called the 'Tank', we should have no trouble in sending the Hun packing. Have you seen one yet, Gerald?"

"No, I can't say I have."

"Then take my word for it, old chap, it's a veritable moving fortress."

"Boys and their toys." Beryl came up on their left.

"Ah, the delightful Miss Whittacker." George was an inveterate tease, and had today discovered an easy target in Beryl who, in spite of herself, never failed to show a reaction. "May I expect a kiss from you when I leave?"

Judging from Beryl's expression, you'd have thought he'd asked her to eat dung. "No," she replied flatly.

"Not one kiss to keep me warm in the trenches?"

"I said, no!"

"Ah well," George shrugged philosophically, "but I digress," he continued quickly. "I am here, today, as the bearer of a deathless piece of prose, or rather a critique of our times, if not ourselves. I saw it in the '*Nation*' last month and clipped it out." He fumbled in his tunic pocket and produced a scrap of paper. "It's a piece written by the notable author, Mr John Galsworthy," he explained, "entitled '*Studies in Extravagance. The latest thing.*' I won't bore you with it all. It refers to, and I quote, '*An age which ran all the time, without any foolish notion of where it was running to*'." He paused, then remarked, "the next passage lampoons our generation as one which '*had been born to dance the moon down to ragtime*', whilst implying it's a generation devoid of a soul."

"That's very unfair," Victoria complained.

"I know," George beamed. "Isn't it priceless?"

"I doubt there'll be much dancing in the months to come," Gerald frowned.

"No, indeed," George grimaced for once. "That's the Establishment for you. Perhaps, after the war, they'll change their opinion of us." Tiring of this particular game, he returned his attention to Beryl. "Miss Whittacker."

"Now George, you really must stop this," Gerald rebuked him.

However, George was incorrigible. "Beryl, if I swear upon my honour that, when I return from the war, I shall put my heart and soul into supporting the cause of women's suffrage, will you take my arm and stroll around the garden with me, and kiss me when I leave; on the lips, mind you?"

It wasn't so much an embarrassed silence that followed, more a thunderous pause. Possibly the prospect of recruiting a man into the cause was more than Beryl could resist, or perhaps it was something else. Suddenly, she lunged forward, snatched the crook of his arm and stalked off with him, leaving Victoria and Gerald staring after them open-mouthed.

"My God!" Gerald exclaimed. "You don't think she actually means to do it?"

"I have no idea," Victoria admitted. "I think Beryl would rather roast men than kiss them!"

With so many other guests to attend to, Victoria forgot all about the incident until several hours later when some of their friends were making ready to leave. "Have you seen Beryl or George?" she asked Gerald.

"Now that you mention it, I haven't noticed them for some time," he replied, glancing around.

"I do hope they haven't got into an argument," Victoria worried. "If George pushes her too far, I wouldn't put it past Beryl to stab him with her hat pin."

"The others are still finishing their drinks," Gerald pointed out. "We have a little time. Let's go and see if we can find them."

Together they searched the grounds until eventually they found themselves at the back of the cottage by an old ivy clad porch where they stumbled upon the pair, apparently oblivious to all else. George had his arm about Beryl's waist, pulling her tightly to him. Her head was tilted upwards, his bent down, her hand resting lightly on his cheek, their lips locked in the most passionate kiss Victoria had ever witnessed. She stood there, stunned, until Gerald whispered in her ear.

"Let's leave them be."

Although sorely tempted, Victoria never asked Beryl what had happened that afternoon. She never even mentioned that she'd seen anything. These were strange times, giving rise to strange emotions. It was better, in the end, to say nothing.

The last few days of Gerald's leave seemed to fly past. If Victoria could have stopped time, if she could have stopped the world from turning, she would have done so. Nothing would ever be as precious to her as these last moments with him.

On the evening of the last day, they went out into the garden to stand amongst the slender pink spears of willow herb and watch the sun go down. There they had exchanged lockets, each containing a portrait of the other. He had fastened hers around her neck himself, and nothing would ever induce her to remove it. It was there, in the dying embers of the day, that he had sworn that no matter how far away he was sent, he would return to her, here at Rosebay. She had given him her solemn promise that she would remain here and wait for him, no matter how long that might be.

Neither of them slept very much, and in the morning when at

last it was time for Gerald to leave, Victoria accompanied him to the garden gate. From there, it was only a short stroll down the lane to the crossroads, where transport would soon arrive to take him to Southampton, there to embark for France and the Western Front. It was a glorious day, warm and still. The air was thick with the scent of honeysuckle and wild roses, whilst all around lay the rolling Sussex countryside, beautiful as ever.

She had one last gift for him - a bracelet of plaited hair, her hair. Something of herself, so that she might always be with him. It was a symbol, long before poppies had any significance. It was her candle in the window to guide the traveller home. It was a token of her faith, her prayer to God for her husband's safe return. Even as she slipped it on his wrist, the distant blast of a motor horn broke the silence. Her heart gave a lurch. She was overwhelmed by a sudden sense of urgency. Now the hour was upon them. This was the moment of their parting.

Her heart ached so much she thought it would crack. She could feel the tears beginning to well up inside her; she struggled to contain them, desperately searching her mind for some reference of fortitude so that she might appear strong in front of him. Hastily, she thought of what her mother might say at a time like this, if Gerald were her husband. She would probably have told him to do his best, wished him good luck and shaken his hand, but she wasn't her mother. She was Victoria and Gerald was the love of her life. Now he was leaving and she didn't know when she would see him again.

She threw herself into his arms, trembling. "I'm so frightened," she confessed. "I don't know what to say."

Gerald eased her back, pressing his palms gently against her cheeks, his hands framing her face, and looked deep into her eyes. "You don't have to say anything," he smiled. "All I ask is that you be brave for me."

Her eyes grew misty as she recalled the last time he'd asked her to do that. She gulped back the salty tears and nodded.

The motor horn beckoned again, more insistently this time. He glanced in the direction it had come from, then back at her with such an expression of finality. Catching her by the nape of the neck, he pulled her head forwards and pressed his lips against hers in one last long lingering kiss, before he broke away, turned and began to stride down the lane.

In that moment, as she watched him go in the last days of that golden summer, she felt her life change. After this, nothing would ever be quite the same again.

Chapter Three

Even though she'd tried to prepare herself, Victoria soon found that the gaping void in her life left by Gerald's absence was often more than she could bear. It wasn't just that he was away; she could have coped with that. It was knowing that he was in a foreign land, facing deadly danger, that would plunge her heart into her boots every time she thought about it. She tried to keep busy, to keep going, to take her mind off the situation, but she just seemed to rattle around the cottage, like the last pea in the pod, and there wasn't a minute that passed when she didn't think about him.

She had his letters; that was something. Gerald wrote nearly every day, and just to be able to hold the paper he'd touched, and read the words he'd written was a lifeline for her.

Gerald had thought it likely that once the war had begun, censorship would be imposed, at least on letters from the front, as a matter of national security. Just in case that happened, they'd invented a simple word code so that he could continue to inform her of where he was and what was happening to him. There was never any intention to pass military secrets – it was just to save her worrying over the limitations of what he could openly write.

She spent a good deal of time writing letters in return; long letters, filled with the trivia of everyday life. It seemed to her the more she wrote, the closer she felt to him.

In her first letter, she told him of how things at home were changing rapidly - that men continued to volunteer in their thousands, and that right across the country makeshift camps were hastily being erected to accommodate and train them. Staunton Gifford was no exception. It seemed that now there was a camp in every field and pasture. Lines of tents would spring up overnight, like random crops of mushrooms, whilst hundreds of new recruits arrived daily to fill them. All the roads and lanes were clogged with marching men, and when it rained they churned the ground into a sticky mire that was impossible for anyone else to negotiate. Every day was filled with the dreadful din of traffic as lorries and trucks as well as horse-drawn wagons and artillery passed in an endless stream through the village, raising choking clouds of dust, and leaving behind a stench of petrol fumes and manure that was absolutely sickening.

Worst of all was target practice - the incessant clatter of rifle fire, punctuated by the pulsing thud of field guns and mortars. Sometimes it was so loud that she could still hear it, even from inside the cottage. She had begun to feel as if the front line had moved from France and arrived here in Staunton Gifford.

Furthermore each time she went out, she was confronted by squads of men in khaki, who whistled at her or called out in one dialect or another; Geordie, Cockney or West Country, until the sergeant told them to shut up and keep marching. Half of them appeared to be no more than boys, and although they had to be at least nineteen to enlist, it looked to her as though many of them had lied about their age.

She also mentioned some local farmhands who, reluctant to leave their harvest ungathered, had been threatened with dismissal if they didn't enlist. It had caused such an almighty uproar that their employer had been forced to retract his statement, leaving his wife to apologise for the 'misunderstanding'. Victoria thought it served him right. It was despicable that men being asked to risk their lives for their country should be forced into doing so, instead of being allowed to make the choice for themselves. She went on to say how hard she thought it must be for some of the more isolated rural communities to come to terms with what was happening.

In other letters she described the hardship caused by mass unemployment. Because of the war, trade routes to other countries had been severed and consequently, many owners had closed their factories down, leaving thousands of men and women without a means of earning a living. The men were able to join up, but it left little for women to do except rely on the support of one of the charities which were being set up to help the unemployed.

She was able to confirm that the rumours he'd heard at the front were true, and that at home the price of food had virtually doubled. There were accusations of profiteering and hoarding, whilst some imported items such as tea and sugar were becoming scarce. She was quite alright, she assured him. She had her separation allowance, and even though that was little enough, he had left her all his savings which, if she were prudent, would last her at least six months, and by then this wretched war would be well and truly over.

When she wasn't writing letters, Victoria read the newspapers. *The Daily Mirror*, *The Sphere*, *The Daily Sketch*; she bought them all and spent hours poring over the reports, meticulously examining every word for any indication of action in Gerald's vicinity. She became, through her own necessity, something of an expert on troop movements, regiments and the battles they fought. It very soon became clear to her from what she read that this war was developing into something far greater and far more deadly than anyone had ever anticipated.

There had already been the retreat from Mons, and now in early November at a place called Ypres in Belgium, there had been hand-to-hand fighting in the woods, resulting in fifty thousand British casualties. Every day, the numbers were staggering. If it hadn't been for their word code telling her that, so far, Gerald was alive and well and nowhere near any of these battles, she felt that she'd probably have gone out of her mind with worry.

It was vitally important to Victoria that she kept in touch with what was happening during the war, but just when she felt she had a really good grasp of what was going on, now that she could follow it at a glance, censorship came into force. 'The Defence of the Realm Act', or D.O.R.A. as it was commonly known, had been passed shortly after the war began. It gave the government the power to change existing laws or create new ones in order to support the war effort. Amendments were added as and when it was deemed necessary, and now in the closing weeks of 1914, just as Gerald had predicted, censorship was imposed on books, newspapers and letters.

During the first few months of the war the newspapers had printed a full account of what was happening. After censorship all that changed. Now the reports tended to concentrate on the identical and increasingly familiar theme of 'Plucky British Resolve'. There were no real facts any more. The horrors of the war had been sanitised. The truth eliminated. It couldn't have been more obvious that now journalists were only writing basically what they were told to. The only thing that didn't change was the ever-lengthening lists of dead and wounded that were published every day. These and Gerald's letters were now her only source of information, but whilst he remained safe, that would suffice.

At home, the once peaceful village of Staunton Gifford had begun to resemble one enormous barracks. The recruits, in the main, were well behaved, concentrating chiefly on the business of training for war. The constant disruption of daily routine, as regiments of infantry and cavalry passed through the village, could easily be forgiven. They made altogether such a splendid sight that crowds of people would gather in the street just to wave as they went by.

The spinsters of the parish were particularly keen to show their patriotic support of the army, and were well aware that a friendly smile and a kind word wouldn't go amiss. They did, after all, epitomise to some extent what these men were fighting for. Previously they'd only ever encountered the village lads; now there were hundreds of new faces to choose from. None of them had ever received so much male attention before. Even the strait-laced Miss Isabelle Langley, who owned the haberdashers, always managed to be outside her shop whenever the East Sussex Artillery rode through. She was inevitably rewarded for her effort with a superbly executed salute from their commanding officer. It wasn't uncommon to see groups of girls cheering the columns of marching men, or running into the ranks to kiss them. Victoria was not adverse to a smile or kind word, but she drew the line at that.

Occasionally, she would stop and chat to one or two of them, the conversation invariably centring around their wives and sweethearts, whilst a gallery of unsolicited photographs would pass before her eyes. She didn't mind, they all looked young and homesick and lonely; besides, it made her feel safe to have so many soldiers around.

The threat of invasion and the rumours of German spies being everywhere had existed since the beginning of the war. In Staunton Gifford, the influx of new recruits, many of them Scots, Welsh or Irish in origin, constantly gave rise to ill-founded reports that German spies were in the vicinity. As yet without uniforms, strangers with a strange accent asking for directions to the nearest military camp were guaranteed to arouse suspicion. The large numbers of Belgian refugees who had been flooding into the country since August only served to exacerbate the situation. They had names like Van Harben and Vanderhousen, and often spoke Flemish which, to the untrained ear and overworked imagination, sounded like German. This particular brand of paranoia reached new heights of absurdity when it was put about, in a neighbouring village, that German spies were camouflaging themselves as scarecrows in order to observe British troop movements. German spies were blamed for everything from crop failure to bad weather, and although Victoria realised that most of the stories were wildly exaggerated and kept an open mind, she locked her doors at night; after all, one could never be too careful.

*

The old year was fading fast; Gerald had been away for almost four months and it was nearly Christmas. Some soldiers had cut down a fir tree and set it up on the green, and the village children came with paper chains and lanterns to decorate its branches, then gathered round to sing carols. The first flurry of snow had fallen. It lay in fleecy drifts across the fields and woods, down lanes and over hedgerows, softening the landscape, bestowing an air of stillness to the countryside, whilst in the village a sharp frost had etched elaborate patterns on the window panes, and every gutter was festooned with clusters of icicles. The gloom of war had lifted a little now at least there was something else to think about and, for a while, the world seemed a brighter, more hopeful place.

There were few, perhaps, who felt this more intensely than Victoria. In his last letter, Gerald had informed her that he'd soon be eligible for leave. Just the idea of it thrilled her. To have him back, if only briefly, would be the greatest gift of all.

His next letter had barely touched the doormat before she snatched it up, ran into the kitchen, tore it open and began to read avidly. In that very instant, all her hopes were crushed, all her expectations vanished as if they'd never existed, everything she'd waited for turned to ashes.

To her utter dismay, Gerald had written to say that he couldn't come home for Christmas. He wrote, 'My dear, I can imagine your disappointment, as I know you will understand mine, but there is no help for it. The regiment is simply in the wrong place at the wrong time and no leave is to be granted'.

Victoria just sat there, staring at the words, overwhelmed by such a profound sense of loss that for a moment she was numb. Suddenly she hated him for writing this letter, then instantly regretted having thought it. This would have been the first Christmas of their marriage; now they'd spend it far apart. It was so unfair. Other men were home on leave; other men with less service to their credit. If other wives could have their husbands home for Christmas, then why couldn't she?

She looked up, gazing tearfully around the kitchen, at the fire crackling cheerfully in the hearth, the bunches of holly and ivy she'd hung on the beams, and the scarf and gloves she'd knitted for him laying neatly folded on a sheet of brown paper she'd saved to wrap them in. Christmas was such a magical time. She'd always viewed its approach with a feeling of wonder and excitement; now all she felt was a sense of cynical indifference. She stood up abruptly, scattering the pages of the letter, crossed the floor and, tearing down the yuletide bunches, returned to the fire and threw them into the flames. She knew it was childish behaviour, but she just couldn't help herself.

This would never do. Her tantrum had done nothing to resolve the situation, except bring her back to her senses. She gathered up the fallen letter and quickly set about writing a reply. She'd never betray her true feelings to Gerald. These unhappy circumstances were no fault of his, and he'd enough to contend with. She put a brave face on it, telling him that, as much as she missed him, she understood and would be patient. All was well with her. He was not to worry, she wouldn't be alone at Christmas and that she'd spend the holiday with Beryl.

Beryl had invited her to visit whenever she liked. She occupied rooms in a small townhouse owned by her parents on the outskirts of Kensington. Beryl was convinced they'd allowed her to use it out of respect for her independence. Victoria rather fancied they were glad to have her out from under foot, although she didn't dare say as much.

If anything, London was worse than she remembered. The crowds seemed larger and in more of a hurry. The roads overflowed with military vehicles and the streets were awash with khaki, whilst the interminable propaganda was plastered on every billboard and every hoarding at every corner. It wasn't different; there was just more of it. Everywhere she looked there was that wretched poster, the one with Kitchener's face on it, whilst beneath his pointing finger, the words '*Your Country Needs You*' blazed out. She wondered coldly how many lives the stupid thing had cost, and it was all she could do to stop herself tearing them down each time she encountered one.

There were other more unpleasant things to see in the capital. A delicatessen in a line of shops was boarded up. Its front window was smashed, the door broken in and the interior ransacked. The remnants of a hastily written sign, '*We are Dutch*', lay amongst the debris. Evidently it had been ignored. On one occasion whilst out shopping for trifles, they witnessed a woman approach a man in civilian clothes and offer him a white feather, the new emblem of cowardice. Recalling the treatment of the farm labourers reluctant to enlist at Staunton Gifford, and still desperately missing Gerald, Victoria was incensed by the injustice of it. She immediately accosted the woman and demanded if she'd do the same thing to her own husband or son.

The woman stared at her as if she were mad, before declaring proudly, 'My brave boys are both at the front,' after which she hurried away, doubtless in search of her next victim.

The woman's attitude wasn't hard to understand. Feelings against those men who refused to fight were running high, especially in the face of the mounting casualties. To make things worse, there was a large body of men and women who actively opposed the war. Their peace crusades and anti-war campaigns were often violently attacked physically, as well as verbally in the newspapers. Their pacifist ideals were drowned out by the roars of nationalistic outrage, and generally they were considered to be traitors, degenerates and cowards. The hatred and division was fuelled by the ever present propaganda and patriotism. If there was a chance for peace without victory then it was not an option that was generally entertained. It was hard not to be patriotic; it was, after all, the natural way to be, even if sometimes it did fly in the face of commonsense. Victoria loved her country, she thought its people were the noblest in the world. She could only pray that the war wouldn't change that.

Beryl was always happy to take her sightseeing. In Hyde Park they went to look at an exhibition trench which had been dug in the interests of public information. It was clean, dry, stoutly shored with fresh planks and lined with new duckboards. As she looked down, Victoria began to suspect, recalling the early uncensored accounts she'd read in the newspapers, that it didn't accurately represent conditions at the front. Here, in this peaceful park, there was an obvious absence of all the sights and sounds of war. She could only imagine the whine of bullets, the crash of exploding shells and the screams of wounded men. Neither was there the smell of death and disease that doubtless went with it - nothing to indicate the awful reality of war. Judging from the comments of those around her, many seemed to prefer it that way.

On a lighter note, they took advantage of a scheme for women being sponsored by a camera manufacturer, who would take their photographs free of charge, and send them to their loved ones at the front. After a good deal of badgering, Victoria finally managed to persuade Beryl to pose for George, but despite the best efforts of the photographer to make her relax, she remained stern faced and as stiff as a dressmaker's dummy.

At length, the poor man remarked, with a degree of exasperation,

'Dear lady, please spare a thought for the young man who's to be the recipient of this picture'.

The change was almost miraculous. Suddenly, Beryl looked softer, so much more girlishly feminine.

'Finally!' the photographer declared with relief, as the flash powder ignited with a great whoosh and the shutter clicked, capturing the moment for posterity.

'I'll never understand how you managed to talk me into that,' Beryl complained as they were leaving.

'Don't fuss so,' Victoria chided. 'It's not as if anyone but George is going to see it. Perhaps you'd have been happier wearing a mask!'

Beryl smiled thinly, choosing to ignore the sarcasm.

That same afternoon, they visited the cinematograph and for the princely sum of sixpence, Victoria had her first taste of 'living pictures'. She stared in amazement as the grainy images flickered silently across the screen. It was quite the modern marvel, but little more than a novelty. As entertainment, she didn't think it would replace the music halls.

One evening Beryl treated her to a variety show at the theatre. Top of the bill was Phyliss Dare, a popular songstress of the time. After the conjurer, acrobats and comedian had finished, she walked onto centre stage dressed as Britannia to a great roar of approval from the audience. After singing several patriotic and sentimental songs, which were so stirring that even some of the men in the audience were crying, she finished with '*Oh we don't want to lose you, but we think you ought to go*'. Even the entertainment was being used as a device to encourage young men to enlist. The applause became deafening as scores of them stood up and made their way out to the recruiting office situated conveniently near the theatre. At the end of the performance, everyone stood up for the national anthem, '*God Save the King*', yet another amendment to D.O.R.A.

On leaving the theatre, Victoria came across a poster she'd never seen before. It was entitled, '*Women of Britain say GO*'. It depicted a woman and a child looking out of the window as a man in uniform, presumably the woman's husband, walked down the street outside. On the face of it, just a piece of harmless propaganda, but as far as Victoria was concerned, there was no such thing. To think that the British government had been reduced to using men's wives and children against them in order to make them volunteer. Or that wives should be expected to quell their husband's fears for the safety of his family so that he might more readily enlist was deeply offensive to her.

As a woman of Britain, she had said go, or at least she hadn't said stay. The very fact of her being here was evidence of that. This time, she didn't employ the same restraint as she had with the portraits of Kitchener and, ripping it down, she tore it into a thousand pieces before scattering it to the wind.

That evening, Victoria proceeded to put together the parcel she was sending to Gerald. There were the scarf and gloves of course; amongst other things, she added three pairs of thick socks, some pipe tobacco, a small flask of whisky and a bag of butter toffees. Noticing Beryl's interest, and ever the matchmaker, she tentatively suggested that 'wouldn't it be nice if' she sent one to George. To her utter surprise, Beryl quickly produced a plethora of comforts she'd previously gathered together, including a large silk handkerchief with his initials embroidered in the corner.

'This is beautiful work,' Victoria told her. 'Did you do this?'

'Yes,' Beryl confirmed reluctantly.

'Do you mean to tell me that you attended Mrs Hewitt's sewing classes?' Victoria remarked in astonishment.

'What of it?' Beryl shrugged.

Victoria recalled that Mrs Hewitt, their history tutor, had been something of a mother hen. When she wasn't moulding the minds of 'bright modern young women', she never missed an opportunity to bestow some of the more traditional feminine attributes upon the girls. However, her classes had been extracurricular. No one had to join.

'As I remember,' she told Beryl suspiciously, 'you despised them, saying it was just another ploy to lure women into domesticity.'

'I did, and I still do,' Beryl confirmed easily.

'Well then?' Victoria held up the handkerchief and raised a questioning eyebrow.

Beryl sighed, aware that Victoria wouldn't be satisfied until she offered an explanation. 'Mrs Hewitt caught me distributing pamphlets one day and threatened to take me to the Dean, who would be expected to expel me, if I didn't join her class and excel. Can you believe that? Excel!' she exclaimed, still astounded by the excessiveness of the penalty.

'Well, judging from this, you certainly did,' Victoria concluded.

'It wouldn't have been so bad,' Beryl volunteered, 'if I hadn't known the Dean was a member of the movement.'

Victoria's jaw dropped. 'The Dean was a suffragette?'

'She still is,' Beryl remarked casually. 'Where do you think I got the pamphlets from?'

'In that case,' Victoria persisted, 'why did you agree to join the class?'

'Because she'd never have expelled me,' Beryl explained further, 'and that would have aroused the suspicions of the rest of the faculty. I couldn't risk exposing her position. I'd never betray a sister of the cause.'

'Well, I hope George appreciates your sacrifice,' Victoria told her.

'His time will come,' Beryl replied. 'Remember his pledge.'

Victoria shook her head in exasperation. As if anyone could believe that all this effort on Beryl's part was just in order to recruit a male member to the cause. Poor Beryl was having a hard time of it. She'd happily announce to the world that she cared for a horse.

She'd cheerfully agree that she was fond of a cat, but she'd rather cut out her own tongue than admit to herself that she might be in love with a man.

On Christmas Day, they sat down to dinner. They'd laid four places and began by toasting the empty seats. After that, they became emotional, and spent the entire evening being soppy. The dinner went uneaten.

Christmas had come and gone, and the war had not ended. All of England listened as the stroke of midnight gave birth to the New Year, but where once there'd been the happy anticipation of new possibilities, now there was only a growing suspicion that this war might not be as short as everyone had expected.

Victoria returned home in the second week of January. By now, the military had begun to organise themselves properly, and after reconsidering their position, had reached the conclusion that Staunton Gifford was too small to meet their requirements. Accordingly the recruits were being moved to a large estate a few miles further on, where permanent huts were being constructed to accommodate them. Thus removed from the mainstream of activity, Staunton Gifford returned to being the backwater it once was.

By the time spring arrived, it was hard to tell from looking at the village that there was a war on at all. Apart from the cards displayed in almost every cottage window indicating that the man or men of the house were away serving King and country, it would have appeared that nothing at all was amiss.

Victoria had finally begun to adjust to this new normality, adapting to the necessary restrictions and routines as if they'd always been there. She'd given up the notion of a short war, and settled in to wait it out. Even though every day was incomplete without him, she'd nearly come to terms with the situation. She felt that she could probably cope for the duration. Then Gerald's letters, which had arrived with such unerring regularity, stopped coming.

Chapter Four

Even though she had always known there was a chance that Gerald could be killed or injured, Victoria had resisted the urge to dwell on it until now. In spite of her attempts to diminish its significance, the effect the absent correspondence had on her was far greater than she cared to admit. At first, she tried not to be unduly concerned. There had been other occasions, a few, when Gerald's letters had been delayed by a day or two, but after a week had elapsed,
 she began to worry. Without his letters, he was lost to her.

She endeavoured to remain rational, insisting to herself that it was all a mistake that would resolve itself in time, but as another week slipped uneventfully by, her mood changed to one of growing apprehension. There were a number of reasons to explain why Gerald had stopped writing, and although she wanted to be positive, only one sprang readily to mind. She'd tried to be strong, to remain resilient in the face of all her fears, but a second week without any word from him had worn her down, making her susceptible to the worse kind of imaginings. The possibility that Gerald might become a casualty of war had stayed with her ever since he'd left for France. Defying all her efforts to dismiss it from her thoughts, it had haunted her every waking hour. Now, reinstated with a vengeance, it rushed to the forefront of her mind, the stark realisation that the worst might have happened wringing a gasp from her lips. She began to tremble uncontrollably, gripped by a moment of sheer panic, followed by a sickening sensation of emptiness and grief, whilst the endless lists of casualties, all the reports she'd read of death and destruction swam terrifyingly before her eyes. It had happened to so many others but she'd never once believed, until now, that it could happen to her. The knock at the door, the dreaded telegram, the short, shocking message.

'We regret to inform you – killed in action – Lord Kitchener sends his

sympathy – .'

Would the next news she had of Gerald come in that form? All she had to hang on to was that no telegram had arrived yet, but from now on, every knock at

the door would make her flinch.

Once the initial shock had abated a little, she began to think about what she should do. She couldn't just sit around and wait; that would drive her insane. She wouldn't stand by, as so many other women had done, and accept the loss of her husband. There were other possibilities yet to explore, and she was determined not to rest until she had investigated them all.

She could hardly have envisaged that the course she was embarking upon would be a rite of passage that would take her from the limitations of all her previous experiences to face the real and personal tragedies of the war.

She began by paying a visit to the Post Office; it seemed the most obvious place to start with. There was a slim chance that Gerald's letters had been held up there. However, Mrs Spragget, the post mistress, a woman of middle years and sour disposition, was less than helpful. She was immediately on the defensive, taking Victoria's innocent enquiry as though it was some sort of personal criticism. She informed her, somewhat officiously, that the Post Office prided itself on its efficiency, and that no item of mail that was properly addressed would ever go astray. Even after Victoria had insisted that she check the dead letter file, nothing came to light. Clearly, the post mistress felt vindicated. Victoria left, hoping that this was the last of the petty bureaucracy she would encounter today. If not, then her task was going to be a lot harder than she'd anticipated.

As she came out of the Post Office she saw Mr Mitchell, the blacksmith, standing across the street. The other day, she'd heard that the postman had given him a bundle of letters, amongst which was an official envelope. He'd thought little of it, believing it to be a Ministry notice about requisitioning his horses. He'd put it in a pocket and hadn't opened it until the end of the working day to discover that his only son, Wilfred, had been killed in France. She felt she couldn't pass him by without offering her condolences, but when she tried to speak to him, he just stood there and cried.

She felt it would be best to leave him be, but the meeting had set the tone for the day. She was soon to discover that Mr Mitchell was not alone in his grief.

She made her way to the village hall where a room had been set aside for a recruiting office. She wasn't sure how they could help, but anything connected with the military was worthy of her attention. Most of the able men hereabouts had already volunteered, so the place was all but empty and the elderly officer in charge, with nothing better to do, was happy to talk to her. She sat opposite his desk, the small room filled with the paraphernalia of war, dominated by a huge poster of Kitchener on the wall in front of her. The pointing finger seemed to direct itself right at her, as if addressing her personally and was so mesmerizingly convincing that, for a moment, it seemed to demand that she join up immediately. She began to understand just how compelling this kind of propaganda was, and it was only the fact of her gender that prevented her from enlisting there and then. Happily, she couldn't foresee a time when women would be accepted into the army as soldiers.

As she began to explain that she hadn't heard from her husband in some time, she noticed the man's aspect change to a look of resignation. It seemed to indicate that he thought it obvious what had happened, but considered it inappropriate to say so. The mere suggestion of it chilled her. There was, so far, no evidence to the contrary, and yet she was so sure. Perhaps it was only a foolish determination not to face the facts, but she felt it in her heart that he was still alive.

'He's not dead!' she blurted out.

Her outburst took him by surprise, and realising that his expression had betrayed his thoughts, he over-compensated, flashing her with an exaggerated smile.

'No,' he agreed too quickly, 'of course not.'

The recruiting officer, although sympathetic, was unable to help her, explaining that he only dealt with new recruits and didn't have access to the information she wanted. He advised her to contact the Red Cross organisation. Their operation extended across the whole of Europe, even to the front line, and they had all the facilities for tracing missing soldiers. There it was. Already in the space of a few hours, her quest had altered radically. She'd begun by searching for a reason to explain why Gerald had stopped writing; now she was looking for a missing husband. Perhaps, in the end, it had always amounted to the same thing.

Acting on the advice she'd been given, Victoria immediately wrote to the Red Cross, and received an acknowledgement within days, assuring her that they were looking into the matter. It was the first positive response she'd received so far. It lifted her spirits a little, but she had no intention of wasting time waiting for something to develop. She continued to search the newspapers, scouring every page for some indication of what might have happened to Gerald. However, censorship had rendered the press impotent. What the papers had to offer now was less than useless. To be without this vital intelligence just when she needed it the most was absolutely galling, and it was with a growing sense of frustration that she found herself reduced to scavenging, like a beggar, for any scrap of information whenever and wherever she could find it.

Occasionally, she came across soldiers home on leave from the front and would press them unreservedly for news of the war, but they were always reluctant to talk about what they'd seen. Their constant prevarication seemed to suggest that they were holding something back. Perhaps the truth would sound unpatriotic, or maybe what they'd witnessed was so appalling that they'd no desire to recall it to mind, let alone recount it to a civilian, and least of all to a woman. They were always polite, and would salute her before moving on, leaving her to wonder if these were the same gallant young men of Kitchener's volunteer army? The patriots and heroes, bright-eyed and eager, full of fearless anticipation who'd marched out to war so bravely less than a year ago.

It was as if a century had passed since then. There was an air of weariness about them; they looked less optimistic, more resigned, and somewhat out of place away from the killing fields of Europe. Clearly all thoughts of honour and glory had been set aside; now only the business of war remained. They were men who no longer recognised hearth and home, and for whom the only reality was the Western Front.

Regrettably, Victoria had reached the point where she finally had to admit to herself that in spite of all her efforts, her plan was losing momentum. Although she'd been prevented from moving any faster than the circumstances allowed, she'd hoped to have made some progress by now. Instead, a good deal of time had passed with precious little in the way of results to show for it. She couldn't even be sure if she was going about it in the right way, assuming there was a right way, whilst lately her mind had been plagued by the thought that she might have inadvertently overlooked some vital area of investigation. Then again, her attempts to ascertain that Gerald was still alive and well might equally serve to prove that just the opposite was true. Whether she liked it or not, that was a risk she'd have to accept if she wished to continue. Nevertheless, it felt better to be doing something, even if it didn't amount to much. It had been the loss of contact that had instigated her search. It was the not knowing that drove her on. Sometimes recklessly and often without regard for the consequences, either to herself or others.

With her options dwindling, all Victoria could think of now was to talk to her neighbours. Everyone in the village had husbands, sons and brothers in the Forces, and there might yet be some vestige of news that she could glean from them. In her headlong pursuit of information, she was soon to discover that behind the peaceful facade of quiet rural life, every home in the village was a battleground, where wars of hope against adversity were fought daily. The protagonists were invariably women, their faces tired and drawn, who were sick at heart with waiting and worrying. An unsung army of wives and mothers who suffered alone and in silence, and for whose names no memorial would ever be raised.

Her reception varied from house to house. Often, there was a long pause after she'd knocked before the door opened ajar and an ashen face, wide-eyed with anxiety, would peer out. Then there was that brief moment of utter relief when they saw her, or rather when they saw that it wasn't the postman with a telegram in his hand. Sometimes there was no answer; she saw a curtain twitch momentarily, but that was all. There were other occasions when she was summarily dismissed from the doorstep with a silent flick of the hand and a dismal shake of the head; many couldn't bring themselves to discuss the war. At other times, she found herself giving more information than she received. She met many kindred spirits that day, but no one seemed to know very much, except what they'd read in the newspapers.

It was late in the afternoon when she arrived, footsore and weary, at Edith Johnson's house. She and her husband Percy had been among some of the first people they'd met when she and Gerald had come to live in Staunton Gifford, although she'd seen little of them since. She recalled that Percy had been a ploughman - a great robust figure of a man, powerful yet gentle in his manner. A true son of the soil who loved the land. He had been born and brought up in the village and knew nothing else, but when the war came he'd been the first to volunteer. When someone had asked him what he was fighting for, he'd reached down, scooped up a handful of earth and, letting the loam trickle through his fingers, replied, 'This.' He said that he could think of no greater honour than to fight for England, and that no man could rightly call the country his unless he was prepared to die for it - sentiments which Victoria was all too familiar with. All he knew of England was here in Staunton Gifford, and yet the spirit of the country burned so fiercely in his rustic heart that he'd travelled half a continent away to defend it.

Edith recognised Victoria at once, and after she'd explained her reasons for being there, invited her in, saying that Percy was here now at home and that she could see him if she liked. It was more than Victoria had hoped for. Not only a soldier home on leave, but one who knew her and Gerald, and who might be willing to divulge some accurate information.

Edith ushered her into the parlour. The rays of the afternoon sun glanced through the partially drawn curtains, dappling the little room with patches of light and shade. The tranquil silence was punctured by the steady tick of the clock on the mantle. Percy was sitting in a chair by the empty grate. He smiled as she came in, glad of the company, but he didn't get up. The livid scars on his face had barely healed, partly obscured by the thick black spectacles he wore. He rested his white stick against his remaining leg, and held out his hand in greeting, asking her to sit next to him.

When she saw him sitting there, that ruined shell of a man, of all the emotions she felt the worst was shame. How small and mean her errand seemed now compared to his great sacrifice. If this was the price demanded she could but ask herself, was England worth it? And if it was, then how much more was there to pay?

They talked at great length about many things, but always his concern was for the land, and that there were now only old men and boys to cultivate it. Who among them knew how to make the land yield up her bounty, lest England starve? Who could harness a team and plough a straight furrow, sow and reap and bring the harvest home? The ancient wisdom, the skill of generations, and the men and horses it needed lay scattered, dead and dying, across the battlefields of France. There was never one scrap of pity for himself, not a single word of regret that he'd never see his beloved countryside again or stroll its dusty lanes in summer.

He made no mention of the war, and she hadn't the heart to question him. Instead she told him that he was a hero, that she admired him, that everyone did. She told him that it was because of his courage and the courage of men like him that she felt safer in the world. With that, she bent forward and kissed his scarred brow. He smiled, bemused by her behaviour. What was there to thank him for? He'd only done his duty.

There was nothing more to do, nothing left to say. Victoria excused herself and Edith saw her out. As she left, their eyes met but she couldn't bring herself to speak, not even to say goodbye.

She couldn't go on with it, not today. She'd started out in search of news, but all she'd found was sadness and death. All that she'd learned was that she was but one of many and that, for now, her circumstances were better than most. Slowly, she made her way home, sobbing quietly to herself, wishing that she could take the entire world by the scruff of the neck and shake some sense into it.

Having done all she could for now, her best chance lay with the Red Cross, and whilst she waited to hear from them, Victoria lived in constant dread of receiving the one message that would end her search forever. Although she still hadn't heard from Gerald, so far the telegram hadn't come either, and for that reason she remained optimistic. Even though it was the only piece of information she didn't want, there were days when Percy Johnson came to mind and she wondered if a telegram might not be preferable.

Just when she thought she'd explored every avenue of inquiry and that Staunton Gifford had nothing more to offer, an unexpected opportunity came her way. Fleeing from the German occupation, thousands of Belgian refugees continued to escape through France and were still flooding into Britain, bringing with them eye-witness accounts of the war in Europe. Some had lately passed through the village, and Victoria had managed to speak to one of them. As she picked her way through the broken English, thick with accent, she at last heard something of the truth about conditions at the front.

Apparently during some battles, whole battalions had been decimated in a matter of hours; hardly a man was left. Others were scattered so far across the battlefield there seemed no chance of their ever regrouping, and thus divided they would inevitably fall prey to the enemy. Many of the dead were unrecovered and remained unburied. It was impossible to identify them all. Not all prisoners were accounted for; in the chaos of battle it was impossible to keep accurate records. There it was; her first glimpse of the truth the press had been ordered to withhold, that which the propaganda conveniently overlooked, and which the sanitised lists of casualties failed to reveal. Nothing she'd read, nothing she'd heard before had even remotely prepared her for this. She'd had no idea that the war was being fought on such an unprecedented scale. It beggared belief and staggered the imagination. More to the point, if whole battalions could be lost, what of one man?

It all seemed so hopeless, her efforts so futile, but she wouldn't allow herself the luxury of giving up. She carried on, sometimes hopeful, sometimes despairing. The anxiety and suspense wore her out, but she wouldn't abandon him. She wouldn't allow Gerald to drift into oblivion, not until she'd absolute proof that he was dead and until that time came, if it ever did, he was, as far as she was concerned, still alive.

She found that mundane jobs such as housework and shopping helped relieve the stress, even though she had to force herself along, but there was no relief from the war. It was all around her. Staunton Gifford wasn't all that far from the south coast. From there, barely thirty miles of English Channel separated Britain from France, which meant that much of the war in Europe was being fought less than a hundred miles from Victoria's doorstep. Almost every day, she could clearly hear the sound of heavy guns being fired along the Western Front. The steady rhythmic pulse of massed artillery was like a long low rumble of thunder constantly repeating far away. Sometimes the barrage was so heavy that at night she could see the shell flashes flickering eerily against the distant skyline. It was hard to believe that from the relative safety of a secluded country village what she was witnessing were battles of monumental proportions that would ultimately decide the fate of the whole of Europe, and perhaps even Britain as well.

Air raids had become frequent in the south east, but so far her only experience of them was when she awoke one night to the sound of a zeppelin passing overhead, the roar of its engines making the glass of water on her bedside table vibrate. She'd run to the window and stared out into the darkness, but had seen nothing. Next morning, she heard that it had bombed a town in the next county. There had been a great many civilian casualties, and although the Royal Flying Corps had been despatched to intercept, the perpetrator had made a clean getaway.

Nearly three months had passed before she received a reply from the Red Cross. As if in answer to all her prayers, they'd found Gerald.

He'd been wounded, although not seriously, and was now recovering in a hospital in France. As much as it distressed her to hear that he'd been hurt, she was overjoyed to know that he was safe. After all she'd been through, all the doubt and uncertainty she'd endured these many months, and the tyranny of suspense that that had dominated her life, discovering that he was alive was almost more than she could immediately deal with. The sudden explosion of relief made her feel faint; she flopped into a chair, rocking gently back and forth, clutching the letter to her breast, laughing and crying all at the same time.

The day after, she received another letter from the Red Cross, apologising for their error. It had been a matter of mistaken identity. The man they'd found in France wasn't Gerald. In the meantime, they would continue to search.

It was a devastating blow. All her anxieties flooded back tenfold. To be toppled from such giddy heights of euphoria and to be plunged into the limitless depths of despair in one and the same moment was more cruel than if she'd never heard anything at all. It was a damaging experience that left a lasting scar on her subconscious, giving rise to an underlying scepticism of any official information. From now on, she'd only truly believe the evidence of her own eyes. She'd have to see Gerald standing before her in person, or be presented with his dead body before she accepted either verdict. Nevertheless, she'd often recall how she'd felt on that day when she believed he'd been found, and hoped with all her heart that at some time in the future she might experience it again.

Barely able to contain the panic and frustration that was gradually consuming her, she wrote directly to the War Office. She'd deferred doing so until now, hoping that her contact with the Red Cross would be enough to secure the information she wanted, but with her confidence in that organisation on the wane, there was no further reason to postpone it. She was careful to include details of Gerald's regiment, rank and serial number, just to make sure that this time there would be no mistake. If anyone knew where Gerald was, it would be those who'd sent him there.

It took them six agonising weeks to reply, and then it was only to inform her that with more than a million men on active service, it was impossible for them to examine individual cases. The brief message ended with them referring her to the Red Cross.

Victoria was at her wits' end. It had taken precious months of laborious letter writing and anxiously awaiting replies, only to find herself back where she'd started from. All she'd encountered was confusion, misinformation and indifference. How could she possibly find her way through it all? No matter how daunting the task appeared to be, she was nothing if not tenacious, and more than ever she was determined that if there was a way, then she would find it.

The unremitting cycle of failure had made her desperate and inclined to any kind of action, no matter how imprudent it might be. She wrote a letter to 'The Times' complaining about the conspiracy of silence and the indifference to the relatives of serving soldiers she'd experienced. She was deliberately contentious, her aim being to try anything that would provoke a response and gain the attention of the authorities and the press. The letter wasn't published and neither did she receive a reply. She tried again with other newspapers, but always with the same result; they didn't answer and her letters were never published. Clearly, the press had closed ranks doubtless due to censorship, and under those conditions it was pointless to continue.

Convinced that she'd exhausted every source of information Staunton Gifford had to offer, and that remaining in the isolation of the village would impede any future progress she might wish to make, Victoria decided to return to London. At least in the capital, she'd be at the centre of things, and she'd be close to the War Office. She was certain that if she went there in person, she could achieve far more than any letter. She intended to go there every day, and sit there all day if necessary, until they gave her the information she wanted, even if it was only a telegram.

She wrote to Beryl informing her of all that had happened, whilst enlisting her aid and explaining what she intended to do. Anything that smacked of challenging the established order was meat and drink to Beryl, who replied telling her to come at once.

Knowing that if somehow Gerald returned to England, he would come directly to the cottage, she left a letter for him clearly visible on the kitchen table, detailing where she was and what she was doing, asking him to contact her immediately so that she could return at once. With that, she left for London, quite unaware that her previous attempts to gain the attention of the authorities had, in fact, succeeded and that the consequences for doing so would be like nothing she'd ever imagined.

Chapter Five

Victoria barely took time to unpack before setting out for the War Office. A long tram ride and a brisk walk brought her to the granite-clad steps of an imposing stone building. Its tall oak doors set between two enormous marble columns were open, flanked on either side by armed soldiers standing at attention. Having taken such pains to get here and travelling half way across London to reach this spot, she now hesitated. The ranks of granite steps rising up before her looked impossibly steep, whilst the formidable edifice reeked of power and authority and was in every aspect quite daunting, not to mention the soldiers and their guns. Shrugging off the momentary attack of nerves, she took a deep breath, picked up her skirts and began to climb the steps.

She ascended, preoccupied with all the questions she wanted to ask, certain that she'd done the right thing in coming here, but as she reached the top, the soldier on her left broke from his stance and barred her way with an upraised hand.

'You can't go in there, Miss,' he told her flatly.

'Why not?' Victoria asked, taken aback.

'Only authorised personnel are allowed,' he informed her.

'What does that mean?'

The sentry remained unforthcoming. 'It means you can't go in there,' he repeated.

'But I've come a very long way and it's very important,' she insisted.

'I'm sorry, Miss,' the soldier was adamant. 'This is a secure building and it's off limits to the public.'

'Isn't there anyone else I can ask?' she persisted. 'An officer, perhaps?'

The mere suggestion that she wished to defer to a higher rank appeared to irritate him. 'It's more than my neck's worth to let you through,' he refused to compromise. 'I have my orders. You'll have to go.'

Victoria was beginning to feel distinctly annoyed by the stubbornness of this unhelpful soldier. It had been the same unyielding bureaucracy and entrenched officialdom of the authorities that had already caused her to waste so much time pursuing dead ends and waiting for information that never materialised. This was her last hope, and the prospect of being turned away without even being given so much as a hearing was intolerable, inclining her to be somewhat bloody-minded about the entire situation.

She turned, as if to leave, but as the guard resumed his position, she dodged past him and ran into the building, without having really considered what she would do once she was inside. She managed to get about ten yards down the corridor before she was apprehended by a burly Sergeant Major who gripped her by the arm and escorted her bodily back to the front steps, remonstrating all the way.

'This is disgraceful,' she protested vehemently. 'You can't treat me like this. I am a British subject. I have every right to be here.'

Seething with indignation at having been so rudely evicted, she attempted to conceal her embarrassment with a further storm of complaint.

'I never dreamed I'd see the day when a British soldier would behave so shamefully towards an English woman. You're nothing but a bully and a coward. I shall report you to your superiors.'

Being sure of his ground, the Sergeant Major was unperturbed. Doubtless, in his time having stood toe to toe with the enemies of the Empire, one truculent young woman didn't present much of a problem and he was clearly unimpressed by her tirade.

'This country is under martial law,' he informed her sternly, once she'd calmed down. His voice was louder than the average man's, as if from years of barking orders it was fixed at the volume of command. 'You don't have the right to go inside, and you can't see anyone without an appointment.'

'Very well,' Victoria acknowledged stiffly, endeavouring to salvage the remnants of her dignity. 'How may I obtain an appointment?'

'You put in a written request,' he advised her. 'Once it's been processed through normal channels and if your application is approved, you'll be given an appointment.'

'But that could take weeks!' Victoria realised, speaking from bitter experience.

'That's the procedure,' the Sergeant Major pointed out. 'Everyone is very busy. There's a war on, you know.'

Having failed to persuade him with bluster and threats, Victoria decided on a softer approach, in an effort to appeal to his better nature. 'Please, you must let me in,' she implored. 'My husband is an officer serving in France. I've had no word of him in months, and no matter what I do I can find out nothing about him. No one seems to be able to tell me what's happened to him. Surely someone here must know? If only I could speak to them?'

'I'm sorry to hear that,' the Sergeant Major offered a brief commiseration. 'If it was up to me, I wouldn't hesitate to let you in, but...'

'You have your orders,' Victoria anticipated him.

'I'm sorry, but there it is,' he confirmed. 'It's a matter of protocol. You'll have to follow the same procedure as everyone else.'

Victoria was still in something of a petulant mood and the feeling of being constantly forestalled only served to aggravate her temper. 'I think I'd do better if I just waited for you to leave and took my chances evading the guards again,' she remarked provocatively.

The Sergeant Major advanced, forcing her to retreat and take a step down, until he loomed over her. He was a man who was used to being obeyed; he took it for granted and yet, in the face of such blatant effrontery, his tone didn't alter by so much as an octave. His loud voice retained the same patient restraint throughout, as though he were talking to a disobedient child or perhaps a particularly obtuse soldier.

'In that case, Madam, I would have to put you in the cells until you decided to behave.'

Victoria's eyes widened in alarm. 'You wouldn't dare,' she faltered. Not that she intended, judging from his expression, to put him to the test.

Faced with a man twice her age, weight and build, Victoria couldn't help but feel intimidated. Not that she was concerned for herself, but the threat of incarceration represented yet another delay she felt she couldn't afford. However, it was obvious that she wasn't going to get anywhere today, and as the Sergeant Major seemed incapable of speaking in anything lower than a shout, she feared that any further conversation with him would make her deaf.

'It would appear that I have no choice,' she conceded at last. 'To whom do I address my application?'

'That would be Colonel Bass,' he told her.

'I shall bring it in person first thing tomorrow morning,' she finished with a last act of defiance.

'As you wish, Madam,' he nodded. 'If you give it to me, I'll see he gets it as soon as possible.'

There was a note of dismissal in his statement. Exhausted, she took the hint, thanked him and withdrew. Her efforts had gained her almost nothing but now, at least, she had a name - someone in authority to whom she could address her letter, hopefully preventing it from being passed to some anonymous clerk, resulting in the usual perfunctory response.

As good as her word, Victoria returned the next morning, application in hand. As the Sergeant Major took the letter from her, she couldn't help but glance past him into the building. Aware that she might be contemplating another athletic intrusion, he stepped aside, as if daring her to try.

'The cells are at the end of the corridor,' he remarked pointedly. 'First door on the left, two flights down.'

The guards began to snigger.

'As you were,' he barked, so suddenly it made Victoria jump.

Resisting any further impulse to enter uninvited, she contented herself with a baleful glare and departed.

*

Whilst she awaited a decision from the War Office concerning her application for an interview, Victoria continued to study the newspapers. Ignoring the propaganda infested accounts of the war, she concentrated on the casualty lists. It was a grim but necessary task, constantly fraught with the danger of success. There was never any shortage of fresh names, and she was always relieved when she came to the end, having found no mention of Gerald.

Lately, something new had been added. It was connected with the scheme Victoria and Beryl had taken advantage of last Christmas. The project, run by a camera manufacturer, had processed, free of charge, pictures of wives and sweethearts to be sent to men at the front. Many of these photographs were now being found on the bodies of dead soldiers. Often with no other means of identifying them, the photographs were being returned to England and published in the newspapers which, in essence, meant that if you saw yourself, the man to whom you'd sent the picture was dead, the idea being that you would report his identity to the authorities. It presented a bizarre task, examining this 'obituary' of living women, whilst always hoping that you'd never discover your own picture.

It was early in the afternoon of her third day in London. Victoria had spent the last two hours sifting through the morbid photo gallery. Suddenly, she let out a little cry; she hadn't meant to but she couldn't help it. Instantly, Beryl was by her side and before Victoria could stop her, she'd pulled the paper from her hand and begun to scan the page. Halfway through, she stopped abruptly, the colour draining from her face. It wasn't Victoria's picture she saw looking back at her; it was her own.

Victoria would never forget this moment. She'd never seen a look of such profound sadness on anyone's face before.

'Beryl, I'm so very sorry,' she began.

Beryl cut her off with a shake of her head, and went to the window where she stood staring out into the gathering twilight.

'We only had one day together,' she said to herself, studying the reflection in the window pane, caressing the image with her hand, as if it was his face she could see, 'but it was like a lifetime.' She sighed deeply and, touching her fingertips to her lips, she pressed them against the cold glass. 'Goodbye, my dear. God bless you.'

*

That was the last thing that Beryl ever said about George. After that, she never spoke of him again. She behaved as if nothing had happened, at least towards Victoria, and although she still entertained the same radical views as she'd always done, in herself she'd become cold, hardened to the point where she began to take risks in her activities with the suffragettes, becoming careless of her own safety. This was never more evident than on one stormy night, a week after they'd discovered that George was dead.

Beryl had gone to a suffragette meeting, and Victoria was alone in the sitting room, reading, when an almighty commotion ensued outside the front door. A key scraped the lock, engaged, then the door burst open and in flew Beryl accompanied by two other women.

One was a striking individual, almost as tall as Beryl, well dressed with dark hair, whom Beryl introduced merely as Sylvia. The other was also dark, a small woman who kept glancing furtively about, called Jane. All of them looked dishevelled and out of breath.

'What on earth's happened?' Victoria cried in alarm.

'Two men are chasing us,' Beryl panted. 'We only just managed to get away.'

'This is terrible,' Victoria was horrified. 'We must call the police!'

'They are the police,' Beryl told her flatly.

Suddenly, there came a pounding at the front door. 'Open up,' a voice demanded. 'It's the police.'

'What have you done?' Victoria fretted. 'What's going on?'

'I'll explain later,' Beryl waved her concern aside. 'Now we need your help.'

'What can I do?'

'Delay them. You have to hold them off whilst these two escape down the back stairs.'

Victoria hesitated.

'There's no time to think,' Beryl insisted urgently. 'You must do this for me.'

'Alright, alright,' Victoria felt that she had no choice but to agree, 'but hurry up. It sounds as if they're ready to break the door down.'

'I'll be back in a minute,' Beryl assured her.

The tall woman, Sylvia, put her hand on Victoria's shoulder. 'Bravely done, sister,' she commended her.

The smaller woman, Jane, merely nodded her appreciation and hurried after Sylvia, leaving Victoria to ponder the vague familiarity of those parting words.

A fist hammered on the door once again. At least Victoria hoped it was that and not her heart pounding. She composed herself, took a deep breath and opened it.

Before she could say anything, two men pushed past her and began to prowl around the room as if searching for something or someone. The first was tall and thin with a sallow complexion and dour countenance. He wore a bowler hat and a long grey overcoat that was unbuttoned, revealing a dark suit beneath. His appearance and behaviour reminded her of an old bloodhound. The other, red in the face, shorter and more stocky in build, wore the uniform of a police sergeant.

'Wait a minute,' Victoria objected. 'You can't just barge in here like that. Who are you?'

The man in the overcoat stopped pacing and produced a warrant card. 'I'm Detective Inspector Corby of Scotland Yard,' he identified himself, 'and this is Sergeant Wells,' he indicated the uniformed officer, 'also of Scotland Yard.'

'What are you doing here?' Victoria asked. Even though she knew the reason, she thought it better to keep up the pretence of innocence.

Removing his hat, the inspector began to mop his brow with a large handkerchief. 'We're in pursuit of three female suspects,' he told her. 'They were seen coming into these premises and this is the only suite of rooms accessible from that entrance.'

'Be that as it may,' Victoria dismissed the implication, 'there are only two of us here - myself and my friend, Miss Beryl Whittacker. This is her apartment.'

'And you are?' Inspector Corby enquired.

'Mrs Victoria Avery,' she replied. 'I'm Beryl's guest for the time being.'

Much to her consternation, Victoria noticed that the sergeant had taken a small black notebook from his tunic pocket and was writing down everything she said.

'Is Miss Whittacker at home?' the inspector asked.

Before Victoria could answer, Beryl returned to the sitting room, still looking flushed and breathless.

'Ah, Miss Whittacker, I take it?' he assumed.

Once Beryl had confirmed her identity, Corby glanced at the sergeant, who proceeded to flick back through several pages of his notebook, which he then held out so that his superior could read it. After a moment, they both glanced at Beryl, then nodded to each other.

'Miss Whittacker,' Inspector Corby continued. 'May I ask where you have been this evening?'

'I've been here all night,' Beryl lied. 'My friend Mrs Avery will vouch for that.'

'Is that true?' the inspector asked, as if he already knew what the answer would be.

'Certainly it is,' Victoria corroborated, wondering why he hadn't asked her the same question, but the reason would very soon become apparent. 'What's this all about?'

Inspector Corby's gaze flitted around the room, as if he hoped to discover some vital piece of evidence overlooked by his suspects, before returning his eyes to Victoria. 'We're investigating an incident that occurred outside the Houses of Parliament earlier this evening,' he told her. 'It appears that the carriage of the Secretary of State for War was surrounded by a group of suffragettes and as Lord Kitchener attempted to alight and enter the house, a brick was thrown at him.'

'Good grief!' she gasped. 'Was he hurt?'

'No,' Corby shook his head. 'Happily it missed him. Nevertheless, it still constitutes a very serious crime. Given the status of the individual concerned, and the fact that we're at war, it could be construed as an act of treason.'

'Dear God,' Victoria sighed, wondering just how bad this was going to get. 'Do you know who was involved?'

'Only one person was clearly identified,' Corby answered, 'and that was Sylvia Pankhurst.'

'Sylvia Pankhurst,' Victoria repeated in astonishment, glaring at Beryl, who wisely elected to remain silent.

'Do you know her?' Inspector Corby instantly pounced on her reaction. 'Have you seen her lately?' he continued to chivvy.

The situation was growing worse by the minute and thanks to Beryl, Victoria found herself embroiled in the middle of it, but she wasn't about to be harassed into giving anything away. After all the trouble she'd had trying to find out about Gerald, she was only too willing to prove that she could be just as close with information as the rest.

'I know of her,' was all she would admit to, 'but I thought Mrs Pankhurst had postponed her activities in order to support the war effort?'

'That's her mother, Mrs Emmeline Pankhurst,' he corrected her. 'She's been patriotic enough to desist for the duration, but her daughter Sylvia remains militant.'

'Oh, I see,' Victoria acknowledged. 'But what has all this got to do with us?'

'With you, Madam,' Corby shrugged, 'nothing, for the moment. However, Miss Pankhurst escaped in the company of two accomplices. A partial description of one of them closely fits Miss Whittacker, who is already known to us. Do you still maintain that she was here all night?' he asked, apparently offering her the opportunity to change her mind and save herself from becoming an accessory.

Victoria glared at Beryl again. If she'd known how deeply she was involved in these criminal activities, she might have thought twice about helping her. Indeed, she was sorely tempted to turn her in there and then. It would serve her right. However, realising that if he'd possessed one shred of hard evidence, Corby would have arrested

Beryl already, she felt disinclined to accept his offer, especially if it was to come at the cost of her friend's liberty.

'I most certainly do,' she assured him, using the anger she felt towards Beryl to add credence to her statement. 'Obviously, there's been a mistake.'

'It would appear so,' the inspector sounded unconvinced.

Desperate for this affair to end, Victoria pursued her slim advantage. 'Then I can see no purpose in your remaining,' she remarked dismissively, holding the door open, 'and if my memory serves me correctly, you have no invitation to be here.'

Having only superficial evidence to work with, Inspector Corby was in no position to argue, especially now that his chief suspect had been furnished with an alibi. 'As you say, Madam,' he glowered. 'Let's go, Wells,' he addressed the sergeant. 'I believe our bird has flown.'

He made as if to leave, then turned abruptly, facing Victoria again. 'Obstructing a police enquiry is a very serious offence,' he warned. 'I hope you're aware of that?'

Victoria was tired of being intimidated by men of authority. The attitude of latent threat no longer alarmed her. 'I am,' she confirmed, unperturbed. 'I'm also aware that making unsubstantiated accusations against members of the public can also have serious consequences.'

'As you wish,' the inspector concluded menacingly, 'but should we have occasion to meet again, I assure you things will go very differently.'

As soon as the door had closed and Victoria was satisfied that the inspector had left the building, she rounded on Beryl. 'What have you done?' she demanded angrily.

'Only that which needed to be done,' Beryl was unapologetic.

Victoria thrust a pointing finger in the direction that the inspector had left. 'That was no ordinary policeman. He was a Scotland Yard detective.'

Beryl appeared to be distinctly unimpressed.

'That woman you came in with,' Victoria continued to pursue her point. 'It was Sylvia Pankhurst.'

'What of it?'

'She's notorious!'

'She's a guiding light, an inspiration to the movement,' Beryl countered airily. 'By the way, she greatly admired your actions tonight. She told me so personally.'

'Think what you're doing,' Victoria urged in exasperation. 'You attacked Lord Kitchener. He's a field marshal, the Secretary of State for War, a hero of the people. What if the brick had hit him? What if you'd killed him? They'd have hanged you for it!'

'Every great cause has its martyrs,' Beryl replied, matter-of-factly.

'For God's sake, Beryl, listen to what you're saying!' Victoria cried in dismay.

'No, you listen!' Beryl interrupted sharply. 'You're so innocent...'

'Naive, you mean.'

'No, I do mean innocent. You've always believed that the only way to solve an issue is through peaceful negotiation. This war should have shown you how wrong you are. The only time anyone negotiates is when they know they can't defeat you in any other way. We'll only achieve equality through direct action, not words!'

'That sounds like Sylvia Pankhurst talking,' Victoria observed heatedly.

'Those soldiers, the other day, who made such sport of you?' Beryl reminded her. 'Do you think they'd have done that if you were a man? Kitchener has the ear of the king; he influences the government and sends thousands of men daily to their deaths. Do you think he could do that if he were a woman?'

'I worry for you Beryl. One day, you'll go too far.'

'In my opinion, we've not gone half far enough!'

Victoria could see that there was no point in arguing with Beryl;

her mind was set. She wondered if her choice of target had more to do with the loss of George than the cause of the suffragettes, but wisely she didn't say so.

'Please Beryl,' she implored. 'You know why I'm here, what I'm up against. If anything goes wrong, I could lose my chance of finding out what's happened to Gerald.'

Her fury spent, Beryl's belligerent mood began to soften a little. 'I'm sorry,' she sighed. 'I didn't think, but from now on, I'll try not to involve you again.'

*

Apparently, her encounter with the police didn't seem to have damaged her chances with the War Office. Two days later, she received a letter from them giving her an appointment. At last, Victoria felt as if she'd finally achieved something, that all the months of arduous enquiry were now finally coming to fruition.

This time, when she stood in front of the War Office, the austere pile looked far less imposing. The sentries no longer represented an obstacle to her. Now she had permission to be here. She was expected and, bearing this in mind, she climbed the steps with renewed confidence. Having shown the sentry her letter of appointment, she found to her great satisfaction that it was the same Sergeant Major who had previously taken such pains to keep her out, who now invited her inside and, offering her a seat in the corridor, asked if she wouldn't mind waiting for just a moment.

Victoria couldn't help feeling just a little smug. She waited patiently, watching the droves of clerical staff hurry back and forth, bubbling over with anticipation, rehearsing in her mind all the questions she would ask until the Sergeant Major returned to tell her that Colonel Bass would see her now.

Leaving the bustle of the busy corridor and stepping into the unbroken silence of Colonel Bass's office was like entering a different domain. The room she found herself in was vast and empty, like a great cavern and as featureless and as sterile as a tomb. At the end of the room was a large oak desk behind which sat Colonel Bass, and behind him were two enormous union jacks arranged in a huge cross on the wall. It all looked very spartan, martial and somewhat dehumanised.

The appearance of it made her a trifle ill at ease. If this was indeed the opportunity she'd worked so hard for, then why did it seem to her that something wasn't quite right? She was just about to dismiss this sense of foreboding as last minute nerves when suddenly the doors slammed shut behind her, making her jump. They closed with such an ominous finality, as if trapping her inside. The sound they made echoed round the blank walls, reinforcing her concept of incarceration. She was reminded of Orpheus, who had left the land of the living behind and followed his lost love into the underworld.

'Sit down,' Colonel Bass ordered without looking up.

Victoria walked down the length of the room to find that a single chair had been placed a good ten feet from the desk. Sitting in it gave her a profound sense of isolation. The oppressive silence was like a vacuum that weighed down on her. The slightest movement created noise which appeared to be magnified by the stillness of the room, making her feel self-conscious.

The colonel continued to add notes to a file that was open in front of him for some minutes. The sound of his pen scratching at the paper was like the incisors of a rodent gnawing through floorboards. Finally, he laid the pen down and looked up, fixing her with a disparaging glare.

'You are Mrs Victoria Avery,' his voice seemed to boom in her ears. It wasn't a question, more a statement of fact.

'Yes, that's right,' she confirmed, taking it as her cue to speak. 'I'm here today because my husband Gerald seems to have gone missing...'

'It seems you don't approve of this war, Mrs Avery,' Colonel Bass interrupted, paying no attention to what she was saying.

'I'm sorry, I don't understand!' Victoria exclaimed in surprise. It was as if he had another agenda entirely.

The colonel's expression was unchanging. His face was hard, his eyes flinty, there wasn't one glimmer of emotion in them. He studied her dispassionately, his cold gaze fixing her as if she were his sworn enemy. He didn't repeat the question; returning his attention to the open file, he continued to sift through it.

Suddenly, Victoria recognised the notepaper he was holding. 'Excuse me,' she ventured tentatively, 'those are my letters, the ones I wrote to '*The Times*' and the other newspapers. They were never published. How did you get them?'

'Are you acquainted with a Miss Beryl Whittacker?' Colonel Bass enquired, ignoring her question.

Victoria had a feeling he already knew the answer, but she replied anyway. 'Yes. She's my best friend. I'm staying with her at the moment.'

'Are you aware,' the colonel continued, his voice detached and authoritative, 'that she's an active member of the Women's Social and Political Union?'

Again, Victoria felt he already knew the answer, but before she could say anything, he spoke again.

'I see that you're also a suffragette.'

Victoria sighed inwardly; that old chestnut had come back to haunt her again. Beryl had persuaded her to join, but she'd never taken part in anything. 'Not really,' she attempted to answer honestly.

'Yes, actually,' Colonel Bass contradicted forcefully, a hint of aggression in his voice.

Victoria cringed, clenching her hands into her lap until her knuckles whitened, beginning to feel vulnerable. This interview wasn't going at all in the way she'd expected.

'I have a report before me,' Colonel Bass went on, 'from a Detective Inspector Corby of Scotland Yard, concerning an attempt on the life of Lord Kitchener.'

'I had absolutely nothing to do with that,' Victoria insisted, before he had a chance to make any further accusations.

Colonel Bass fixed her again with that same unfeeling stare, apparently indifferent to her assurances. 'Obstructing a police inquiry is a very serious offence,' he pointed out, 'especially under these circumstances.' In this area at least his evidence seemed to suggest that she was culpable.

Victoria chewed her lip in anguish, unable at this stage to deny her complicity. 'Yes,' she agreed in a tiny voice, feeling obliged to respond.

'You were a Caufield's academician?' The Colonel suddenly seemed to digress.

'That's right, I was.' Victoria confirmed, wondering where this line of questioning would lead. 'I attended Caufields Ladies College.'

'I see you were proficient in languages,' he observed, consulting the file again.

'Yes,' Victoria was glad of a question she could answer easily. 'I can speak French and Latin...'

'You speak German fluently.' Again, it wasn't a question.

'Yes, I can,' she agreed without thinking. 'It was part of the curriculum. All the girls...'

'You also appear to be taking an inordinate interest in British troop movements.' He persisted in interrupting her.

'Well, yes, of course. I keep telling you. I'm trying to discover what's happened to my...' She broke off. Suddenly it dawned on her. This wasn't an interview. It was an interrogation. 'I'm not a spy!' she shrieked.

Bass's eyes narrowed almost imperceptibly. He laid his hands on the file, his penetrating gaze burning into her. 'Now why should you say that?' he asked, as if closing a trap.

'Isn't that what you're implying?' She began in panic. 'Please, you must believe me. This is all a terrible mistake!'

'In my opinion, Madam,' Colonel Bass remarked, 'the only mistake here is yours.'

Letting her stew for a while, he removed a cigarette case from his tunic pocket and took time to light a cigarette before moving on. 'Earlier this week, you caused an affray on the steps of this very building, and then attempted to force an entry. What did you hope to gain, Mrs Avery? What were you looking for?'

'Nothing,' Victoria insisted, wringing her hands. 'I told you, I'm trying to find out about my husband. This is ludicrous. Good God, if I were a spy, do you really think I'd try to break in here in broad daylight?'

Colonel Bass exhaled a cloud of acrid blue smoke, then stubbed out the cigarette, pausing to re-examine the file. 'You belong to an organisation that actively opposes the rule of British Government in a time of war,' he began to summarise. 'You have been implicated in an assassination attempt on the Secretary of State for War.' He held up her letters. 'You have personally and publicly criticised our handling of the war. You speak fluent German, and you have admitted here today that you have an interest in British troop movements. Add to that your attempts to break into the War Office, and I would say it's a fairly convincing picture. Indeed, the evidence is damning!'

Victoria felt herself shrinking, like Alice, dwindling away until she was very small and the colonel was a giant. She was completely at his mercy. The chair she perched on was a barren island that offered no protection. She felt abandoned and alone. 'I'm not a spy,' she begged him to believe her, 'I'm not!'

The Colonel was unrelenting. 'Mrs Avery, I'm obliged to inform you that the penalty for espionage is death by firing squad.'

Victoria felt herself go cold, her mouth dried. This was madness. How had she come to be in this position? Too terrified even to cry, all she could do was continue to protest her innocence. 'I'm not a spy.'

Colonel Bass remained unmoved. Without the slightest hint of compassion, he slid his hand across the file until his fingers reached beneath the lip of the desk to press a concealed button.

Somewhere, out in the dim recesses of the corridor, Victoria heard a bell ring faintly. After a minute, the doors behind her opened. Someone entered, their booted footsteps echoing around the room. Victoria shrank further into the chair and closed her eyes, expecting at any moment to feel a hand on her shoulder. In her mind's eye, she could see herself being marched out to the nearest courtyard, put up against a wall and shot.

Chapter Six

Victoria heard someone pass close by, approach the desk and stop. After a moment, not having felt a hand on her shoulder, she opened her eyes to see a young officer standing in front of her. He bore such a striking resemblance to Gerald that for a moment she thought that it was actually he.

'This is Lieutenant Fairchild,' Colonel Bass informed her bluntly, 'temporarily assigned to this department. I've put him in charge of investigating your husband's case. In future, you'll direct all your questions to him.' Closing the file, he handed it to the lieutenant. 'Carry on, Fairchild.'

The lieutenant took the file, turned to her, smiled and gestured that she should follow him.

Victoria was only too glad to do so, but as she rose to leave, Colonel Bass had one last word of warning.

'In future, young woman, I suggest that you confine your activities to the appropriate channels. If you persist in pursuing your original course, you may discover that this department is no longer disposed to offer you the leniency it's shown today.' With that, he looked down and began writing again.

With an outstretched hand, Lieutenant Fairchild reaffirmed his invitation for her to follow him. Victoria couldn't wait to get out of the room. She was shaking from head to toe and in such a state that, by the time she reached the corridor, she was desperate to confide her feelings to just about anyone.

'That man,' she told the lieutenant, her voice wavering with emotion, 'that awful man is overbearing, rude and insensitive!'

'He's a colonel in the British army,' Lieutenant Fairchild pointed out. 'He's supposed to be.'

His candour did nothing to alleviate her distress. 'Do you know, he accused me of being a spy?'

The gravity of her statement merely seemed to amuse him. 'My dear Mrs Avery, if he'd ever once thought that you were actually a spy, then you'd never have been allowed into this building. At this moment, you'd be languishing in His Majesty's Prison Holloway, awaiting execution.'

Victoria drew a huge gasp, her eyes widening with incredulity; she could hardly believe her ears. 'You mean to say that he put me through all that, knowing all the time that I wasn't a spy?'

'Believe it or not, he did you a favour,' Lieutenant Fairchild told her. 'It could have been far more serious had he wished to make it so.'

Victoria was incensed. She felt completely humiliated. Disregarding his remarks, her agitation began to boil over. 'That's despicable!' she fumed.

'I don't think the corridor is the best place for this conversation,' he advised. 'I'm certain we'll be much more comfortable in my office.'

The lieutenant's office was tiny in comparison to the baronial hall occupied by Colonel Bass, but it was far more inviting. It was hardly bigger than a cupboard, lined with filing cabinets and cluttered with stacks of paper that further reduced its size.

'Sorry about the mess,' he apologised, 'but lowly lieutenants don't rate a lot of space.' He paused, studying her for a moment. 'May I offer you some tea?' he asked. 'You look as though you need it.'

When the tea arrived, Victoria was grateful to receive a cup. Her ordeal had left her parched, and it was all she could do to stop herself from gulping it. Nevertheless, to her acute embarrassment, each time she tried to replace the cup back onto the saucer, her trembling hand made it rattle conspicuously, and in spite of trying not to, she slurped when she drank.

Lieutenant Fairchild waited patiently for her to recover enough to continue. Eventually, Victoria put the cup down and eyed him warily. Despite his good looks and easy charm, she was still paranoid about military conspiracies.

'It won't work, you know,' she told him.

The lieutenant folded his hands on the desk top and smiled indulgently. 'What won't work?' he asked.

She was certain that he knew exactly what she was talking about, but if he insisted on continuing this silly charade, then she would tell him anyway. 'I've made a nuisance of myself, and after frightening the life out of me, that colonel of yours thinks to distract me by putting a pretty face in my way.'

It took him some moments to comprehend what she was alluding to. Then suddenly, his eyes widened in surprise. 'Oh, I see. You mean me. I can honestly say that I've never thought of myself in quite those terms before,' he admitted, still somewhat bemused by her remark. 'Do you suppose Colonel Bass sees me that way?'

Victoria was only too well aware that his amusement was entirely at her expense, and was determined not to be the butt of the joke. 'You know precisely what I mean, Lieutenant,' she remarked coldly.

'Please, call me Alan,' he invited, taking her by surprise, 'and may I call you Victoria?'

He had a beguiling way about him that easily disarmed her caution, and after an appropriate pause required by formality, she nodded her consent.

'Excellent,' he beamed. 'I'm sure we're going to be great friends.'

Under any other circumstances, his remark might have been

considered presumptuous. Perhaps the harrowing events of the last few hours had tired her, wearing down her resistance, making her susceptible to his overtures. In any event, Victoria found the suggestion not altogether unattractive. Maybe Colonel Bass was a better judge of character than she'd given him credit for.

'Yes, I understand what you're trying to say,' Alan acknowledged soberly, 'but whatever Colonel Bass's motives might be, I've been ordered to investigate your husband's disappearance. He is, after all, a brother officer and I shall do everything in my power to try and trace him. I can't *expect* you to trust me. I can only hope that you will.'

His apparent sincerity enhanced by his close resemblance to Gerald went further in eroding her resistance. She could see no point in remaining antagonistic, and eventually she relented. 'Very well,' she agreed. 'I believe you.'

He seemed relieved to hear it. 'Then I must ask you now, how far are you willing to go?' he continued earnestly.

'What do you mean?'

'With an investigation of this kind,' he explained solemnly, 'whilst obviously we hope to find that your husband is alive and well, it's also quite possible that we may discover that he has, in fact, been killed. Are you prepared to hear that?'

Of course, she had always been aware of the possibility, but having come this far, she realised disturbingly that she had never truly faced up to the prospect of losing Gerald. Nevertheless, there was no turning back now. 'If I must,' she told him flatly. 'But he's not dead,' she added, her unassailable belief that he was still alive reasserting itself.

'How can you be so sure?' he wondered at her conviction.

'I feel it in my heart,' Victoria told him simply. 'I just know he's still alive.'

Concerned by her reluctance to accept the possibility, Alan felt obliged to enter a note of caution. 'Are you quite certain that you wish to continue?' he asked, as if hoping that she might be persuaded to reconsider. 'The answers you get might not be those you so clearly hope for.'

'You think I'm clutching at straws,' she interpreted his remarks, 'but if you knew how I felt, you'd understand. I'll not desert my husband now simply because the truth may be inconvenient,' she continued resolutely. 'For better or worse, I must go on.'

Despite her apparent inability to face the facts, Alan couldn't help but admire her spirit. 'As you wish,' he conceded. 'I sincerely hope that your faith is rewarded.' He paused to leaf through the file. 'I've only just been assigned to this case,' he admitted. 'I'm afraid that I haven't a great deal to go on at the moment. I've tried to contact your husband's commanding officer, but communications are proving difficult. I fear information will be hard to come by.'

'How hard can it be?' Victoria asked anxiously. 'Surely there are records, accounts of his movements?'

'Up to a point,' Alan stopped her. 'You must try to understand,' he urged, 'that we're engaged in the biggest war in the history of the world. It's like nothing we've ever known before. It's being fought across half of Europe and involves millions of men. Tracing just one isn't going to be easy.'

His reference to the war only served to revive her old habit of scavenging for information. 'Have you been out there?' she asked. 'Were you in France?'

'Yes,' he confirmed, as if he'd been expecting just such a question. 'I've been at the Western Front.'

'What's it like?' Her next question must have been equally as obvious. 'What's really happening?'

'I thought Colonel Bass warned you not to ask those kinds of questions,' he reminded her gently.

'Oh please,' she entreated. 'I'm not after secrets. If I could form a mental picture of what conditions are like out there,' she went on to explain, 'I might be able to understand what Gerald has gone through, how he might have reacted, what might have happened to him.'

'I very much doubt it,' Alan objected mildly. 'Your suppositions based on my observations of the war are unlikely to shed any light on your husband's disappearance. Besides, coercing me into giving you sensitive information will only land us both in trouble.'

Doubtless, Alan was bound by the same laws of censorship that had thwarted her so often in the past. Or perhaps he was merely trying to spare her from the unsavoury truth, but whatever it was, Victoria could draw only one conclusion from his reluctance to answer her questions about the war.

'It's just as I suspected,' she told him. 'It's far worse than anyone will admit to. All the stories I've heard must be true.'

'What stories are these?' he asked suspiciously.

Victoria went on to tell him of her meeting with the Belgian refugee and his accounts of the carnage and confusion he'd witnessed.

'Ah, our friends the Belgians,' Alan remarked, as if his suspicions had been confirmed. 'No wonder you're upset, but it's your own fault for listening to tales like those,' he chided her. 'These people aren't military personnel. They don't view the war objectively, only emotionally. They're civilians fleeing in terror from a ruthless aggressor. What they see and the accounts they offer are wildly exaggerated.'

'But the casualty lists in the papers,' Victoria persisted, convinced that there was more to it than that. 'The pictures of wives and sweethearts from the bodies of unidentified men would all seem to bear out what he said.'

'Yes, we have sustained some heavy casualties,' Alan was finally forced to admit, 'but we've also inflicted serious damage on the enemy. We have it contained, Victoria. We will win.'

'Yes, but at what cost?' She thought only of Gerald.

'That,' he responded frankly, 'can only be calculated once the war is over.'

'When will that be?' she asked plaintively.

Alan looked grim. 'I only wish I knew.'

Having finally gained access to the War Office and personally enlisted their help, Victoria had been under the impression that information concerning her husband would be readily available. Having endured so much to get here only to discover that they were, for the time being, as much in the dark as she was came as a monumental disappointment. Nothing, it seemed, was ever going to be easy. Clearly, her despondency must have shown.

'You look exhausted,' Alan observed solicitously. 'You really should go home and rest. There's nothing more I can tell you at the moment. Give me a week and I'll see what I can do.'

He was right on both counts. She was desperately tired and there was little point in remaining if there was nothing new to learn.

'That would probably be best,' she agreed.

Alan smiled in approval. 'I'll make you another appointment,' he told her, whilst consulting his diary. 'Will next Thursday at two o'clock suit you?'

Victoria nodded. She would have accepted any time and place.

'Good,' he concluded, smiling again. 'I'll write you out a pass,' he offered. 'It will allow you access to this office, but nowhere else,' he added pointedly. 'In the mean time, if anything comes up I'll contact you. Are you still at this address?' He motioned to the file.

'Yes,' Victoria confirmed, 'that's where I'm staying with my friend Beryl. It's her house.'

'Ah, the intractable Miss Whittacker,' he sighed. 'Isn't there anywhere else you could go?'

'No,' Victoria frowned. 'Why would I want to?'

Alan paused, as if considering what to say, then answered with a question. 'Did you know that she's being watched by the police?'

'No, I didn't,' Victoria admitted, suspecting that the information was intended to influence her decision, 'but now that I do, I shall certainly tell her,' she finished stubbornly.

Far from being irritated, her obstinate response seemed to fulfil his purpose. 'I hope so,' he prompted unexpectedly. 'That's why I mentioned it. You see,' he explained his motive, 'investigations like this are far from usual. We have neither the time nor the resources to make an individual search for every missing soldier. This exception has been made for you because you have, let us say, asserted yourself, but your association with Miss Whittacker could compromise your position which is, at best, tenuous.'

Victoria wondered if that was just a polite way of saying she'd been a pest, but wisely chose not to question it. 'In spite of Colonel Bass's assumption,' she informed him, 'I'm not an active suffragette. However, having met him, I could very easily change my mind!'

'Yes, well, the less said about that, the better,' he cautioned her quickly.

'I've nowhere else to go,' she told him truthfully, 'and Beryl has promised not to involve me in her activities again.'

'I suppose that will have to do,' he accepted grudgingly, 'but please be careful, and tell Beryl to do the same.'

'I'll do my best,' she promised as she rose to leave wondering, as far as Beryl was concerned, how that might be achieved.

He was gracious enough to escort her back to the main entrance, offering his arm in a gallant gesture of support. It had been a long time since Victoria had been shown such consideration by a man, and she was both pleased and flattered.

Once they were outside, she thanked him for his efforts. Placing a hand on his shoulder, she stood on tiptoe and dropped a chaste kiss lightly on his cheek. It was, she felt, an appropriate reward for his chivalry towards her. He responded to her gratitude with a salute, reminding her yet again of how much like Gerald he was. When she reached the bottom of the steps, she turned and waved goodbye. It was merely the polite thing to do. As she walked away, she was aware that he was watching her, but even as a married woman, she could find no offence in it.

It had been an eventful few hours but despite all that had happened, she had learned nothing more today except that progress, if any, could be painfully slow and with no guarantee of what might be discovered. Her traumatic experience had left her badly shaken, and she could only speculate as to how close she'd come to disaster, but be that as it may, at least she'd found a champion for her cause.

The following week, she arrived promptly at Alan's office, only to have him admit to her that even after making a rigorous search of such records as were available, he'd been unable to find anything. Although he himself had warned her to expect delays, he seemed a little puzzled, as if he'd been confident that with all the resources of the War Office at his disposal, he would have found something by now. Unbeknown to Victoria, the loss of an opportunity to impress her irritated him.

Victoria wasn't altogether surprised. From her previous experience, she knew that Alan had entered the same dark maze that she'd been fighting her way around these past months. She couldn't help but feel sorry for him. Clearly, his failure was something of an embarrassment to him. When he offered to take her to lunch by way of compensation for her wasted journey, she accepted as much to salve his ego as anything else. She couldn't afford to have him disheartened, or reach the early conclusion that there was nothing further he could do. She took comfort from the idea that if his character was as much like Gerald's as were his looks then he wouldn't easily give up.

As the weeks wore on, her regular visits to the War Office became ever more like luncheon engagements. Alan had drawn a complete blank. None of the enquiries he'd sent out had been answered and he was finding it all most perplexing.

It hadn't occurred to Victoria that it might be easier to remain at home and let Alan contact her if and when he'd found something. If it had occurred to Alan at any time then he had failed to mention it. Her visits to the War Office gave Victoria a sense of purpose. She felt that she was still doing something, little as it was, and besides there was Alan. Whilst being of vital assistance, he was also pleasant, often amusing company - an occasional welcome distraction from the grim task that occupied her. The search for Gerald had brought them together. She trusted him and, as he'd predicted, they'd become close friends. His growing familiarity towards her was merely an indication of that friendship. She'd become accustomed to it and was happy to reciprocate.

It wasn't that she actively encouraged his attentions, it was more that she did nothing to prevent them. Even though Gerald had only been missing for seven months, she'd been alone for nearly a year - alone, bewildered and often afraid. Perversely, having Alan near her made her feel closer to Gerald. Alan was Gerald and Gerald was Alan; the two had become indivisible to her. It was an unconscious association that answered a longing in her heart, and if at any point the similarity was found wanting, she augmented it with her imagination. In the end, her mind saw what it wanted to see.

*

It seemed that hardly any time had passed at all but already there was a hint of autumn in the air, and the trees in the avenue were beginning to turn colour as Victoria made her usual Thursday excursion to visit Alan. As she approached his office, she found him standing outside in the corridor, as if he'd been waiting for her to arrive. He appeared to be a trifle ill at ease and she began to fear the worst.

'I've finally found something,' he told her as he ushered her inside. 'It's not very much, I'm afraid, only fragmentary at best,' he continued distractedly, as she made herself comfortable. 'Part of it I found purely by chance.'

'Is he dead?' Victoria came straight to the point, suspecting that his mood might have been caused by the discovery of that information.

'Ah,' Alan glanced up from the sheaf of papers he'd been shuffling. Realising that his restless behaviour had instigated her question, he made a conscious effort to relax whilst endeavouring to reassure her as best he could. 'Not that I'm aware of,' he replied, 'but only because in spite of what I've found, his status remains unknown. I must also warn you,' he added gravely, 'that you may find some of this information disturbing.'

Whilst she appreciated his concern for her feelings, Victoria felt bound to hear what he had to say. It was, after all, the reason why she'd come here in the first place. 'Please go on,' she urged him.

'I have here a portion of a field report from your husband's commanding officer,' Alan began using the page in front of him as a memory aid. 'It states that Gerald was ordered to take a reconnaissance party, a squad of five men, into no-man's land and assess the enemy's strength on its northern flank. That was at the end of March,' he concluded for the moment.

'That would coincide with the time his letters stopped coming,' Victoria confirmed. 'What happened after that?'

'That's all there is, I'm afraid,' Alan frowned. 'There's only a record of the orders. There's no mention of your husband ever returning - nothing to say that he might have been captured, or even killed.'

This type of dead end sounded so familiar to Victoria. 'You said you had other information,' she reminded him.

'Yes, that's right,' he agreed. 'As you may know, we regularly receive lists of prisoners taken by the Germans. Earlier this week I came across just such a list. It was an old one. It had been misfiled.

It was only a matter of luck that I found it. If I hadn't been dealing with your husband's case, I would never have recognised the names. On it were three of the men from your husband's squad, but there was still no mention of Gerald.'

'I see.' Victoria gained no comfort from the knowledge, only a vague sense of relief that he might still be alive.

'At this point,' Alan warned her, 'the news becomes somewhat grim.'

She braced herself for what he was about to say. 'Please, tell me everything,' she insisted.

'This morning I was correlating casualty reports. It's a duty unrelated to our search,' he explained. 'Among the dead were the other two men from your husband's command.'

Victoria found it a chilling revelation. 'Are you quite certain of that?' She was keen to eliminate any doubt.

'Yes, quite sure,' he confirmed. 'I checked back. Apparently, in June the regiment advanced and occupied the ground that had once been no-man's land. It was only then that they discovered the bodies. That's why the names took so long to appear on the casualty lists.'

'The dead lying unrecovered on the battlefield,' Victoria recalled what the Belgian refugee had said.

'So it would seem,' Alan had no choice but to agree, 'but I have made a thorough examination of the casualty lists and I'm positive that Gerald's name doesn't appear on them.'

'Could he have been buried in an unmarked grave?' Victoria wondered. It was a morbid notion, but the question had to be asked.

'It's possible,' Alan admitted, 'but he would have been wearing his identity discs; there should have been some kind of record.'

'Have you tried contacting his commanding officer again?' she suggested.

Alan merely shook his head. 'I'm afraid he was killed in the advance. His papers have only just reached this office. That's how I came by the report; it led me to find everything else.'

'Is it possible,' she asked, it hardly seemed credible, 'that a man could vanish so completely?'

'Yes,' Alan sighed dismally, 'I'm afraid it is.'

He'd read the reports, recognised what the evidence suggested and the familiar pattern that was emerging. It was what had made him uneasy from the beginning. He'd come to admire Victoria as a woman of courage and resilience and he didn't have it in him to stand by and watch her flounder in ignorance. Regardless of the law of censorship, he could no longer withhold the awful truth from her. Better she heard it from him than from some lesser source and think him false for not having told her.

'I'd hoped to spare you this,' he confessed. 'I tried to tell you at the beginning that it would be difficult, but like yourself, I believed we might discover something more positive.' He paused, then drew a deep breath. 'When a war is fought on this scale, there are a hundred different ways for a man to disappear without a trace. The truth is, Victoria, it's been happening every day since the war began. There are now thousands of men who are unaccounted for.'

'But I'm only looking for one,' she reminded him resolutely.

Although this news was profoundly shocking, it hardly came as a surprise. She'd all but guessed as much from what had been left unsaid. Learning that Gerald was but one among many offered no consolation. This was the closest she'd ever come to tracing his movements, but she wondered if these tantalising fragments would be the last she ever heard of him.

Alan clenched his hands together on the desk top. 'I'm sorry, Victoria,' he apologised, clearly frustrated that he hadn't done better for her. 'I'm afraid I haven't been of much help.'

Instinctively, she reached out and put her hand over his as an illustration of her continuing confidence in him. 'That's not true,' she disagreed. 'If it hadn't been for you, I'd still be completely in the dark.'

He cupped her outstretched hand in both of his and held it gently. 'And what about you?' he enquired earnestly. 'How are you bearing up?'

'Oh, you know,' she replied vaguely, neglecting to withdraw her hand, 'I'm quite alright.'

'Tell me,' he continued tentatively, 'when was the last time anyone took you dancing?'

'Really, Alan,' she laughed self-consciously, 'what kind of a question is that?'

'A serious one,' he replied. 'I mean it. Tell me.'

She thought about it for a moment. 'Do you know,' she admitted, 'I really can't remember.'

'That's a terrible confession to have to make,' he chided, 'and for once, it's a situation I can do something about. There's a dance at the Vauxhall Ballroom tomorrow night. I'd be delighted to take you.'

'But that's impossible,' she protested. 'I'm a married woman. It would be improper,' she blustered on, as if allowing him enough time to find a reason that might overturn her objection.

'My dear Victoria, it's not my intention to kidnap you,' he made light of her opposition. 'It's just a dance, you know, bright lights and music, for the officers home on leave and their ladies.'

'But my husband,' she continued to hesitate. 'What about Gerald?'

'There's nothing more you can do for now,' he told her frankly. 'Driving yourself to a standstill won't help Gerald.' Seeing that she remained undecided, he continued. 'From what you've told me of him, I believe he would want you to go. He would want you to be happy. You've been through a great deal. You deserve a break. Besides,' he added, as a further inducement, 'there'll be a lot of officers there fresh from the front. Think what you might learn.'

Victoria imagined that she was still considering what he'd said when suddenly she heard herself accept the invitation.

'That's the ticket!' Alan applauded. 'I'll come for you at seven.'

It was only as she made her way home that Victoria had time to reconsider her actions. Her plans had not allowed for meeting Alan, or his similarity to Gerald, or her reaction to that similarity. Now that she'd agreed to accompany him to the dance, she found herself sinking into a crisis of conscience.

She was a married woman with a duty to her husband. She'd spent the best part of a year trying to discover what had become of him. It was her only reason for being there. It was why she had come in the first place. It consumed her, preoccupied every minute of every day that had passed since he'd gone missing. The search had been long, arduous and all but fruitless, but the thought of seeing him again drove her on relentlessly, regardless of the cost or risk to herself. Her loyalty to Gerald was beyond reproach and, war or no war, she would do anything to have him back. Her determination was without parallel and whilst the task remained unfulfilled, nothing in the world would shake her from her purpose.

For all of that, there was a part of her that wanted to go to the dance. It was a creature of weakness and indulgence, born of loneliness and fatigue, soft and insistent, that craved her attention, whispering all manner of convenient excuses that she might listen to it and do its bidding. In defiance of all her good intentions, it preyed upon her desire, enticing her to submit, to spare some time for herself, to pause, to rest from the rigours of the search. Going to the dance would offer her some semblance of normality. All about her was gloom and death. Now she longed to embrace life, to let it wash over her, through her, to know happiness again, if only for a few hours. It was hard to resist. It would be easy to give in, to capitulate, to yield herself up to temptation, for just one night.

Finally, she persuaded herself, her perception clouded by her infatuation for this facsimile, that if she went to the dance with Alan there was a chance, as he had said, that she might learn something new concerning the whereabouts of her husband. It was the most compelling argument of all, and by employing this thin rationalisation, she was able to quell the conflict in her mind and bring about a fragile truce. After that she settled down and began to look forward to the event.

Victoria spent most of the next day in a fluster. She wanted to look her best for the occasion, but she hadn't come equipped for dancing. Happily Beryl's skill with a needle came to the rescue and she was able to alter some of her own extensive wardrobe in a matter of hours.

As evening approached, she stood before the mirror, adjusting her ensemble until it met with her approval. It had been some time since she'd been allowed to exercise her vanity and she was enjoying every minute of it. She felt like a schoolgirl again, embarking on her first adventure, complete with butterflies in the stomach. The whole affair had bestowed upon her a delicious sense of excitement, heightened by a twinge of guilt.

Beryl came up behind her as she preened. 'You're positively glowing,' she observed. 'I don't think I've ever seen you look quite so radiant, except on your wedding day.'

Beryl's passing remark gave Victoria pause for thought. Suddenly, her conscience began to trouble her again. 'Perhaps I'm acting inappropriately,' she fretted. 'After all, I'm a married woman.'

'Be that as it may, you're still entitled to a life of your own,' Beryl pointed out.

'Nevertheless,' Victoria insisted, 'I should be thinking of my husband.'

'You've done precious little else this past year,' Beryl reminded her. 'Accepting this invitation isn't going to change anything. It's about time you thought of yourself for once.'

'By going out with another man?' Once again, Victoria began to question the morality of her intentions.

'You're being escorted to a formal dance by an acquaintance,' Beryl replied, endeavouring to put the affair into perspective for her, 'not leaping from your bedroom window into the arms of your lover!'

'You're right, of course,' Victoria agreed, completely susceptible to the least persuasion. Alan and I are merely friends. It was generous of him to offer me this invitation, and it would be churlish of me to change my mind now.'

'Exactly,' Beryl concurred. 'In any case, at this type of function you'll doubtless be asked to dance by all sorts of different men,' she continued to bolster her confidence. 'In that respect, it doesn't much matter who you go with.'

Subconsciously, Beryl's pragmatic approach to the situation was exactly what Victoria had wanted to hear. It assuaged all the troublesome contradictions, and made it seem as if her own commonsense had prevailed. By the time Alan came to collect her, she had dispelled the last of her doubts, suppressed all of her guilt, and was bubbling over with anticipation.

Alan entered the room, his attention briefly focused on Beryl, who had let him in. He took off his cap, placed it on the table, dropped his gloves inside, turned and stopped short as he saw Victoria standing there. For a moment, words failed him. Instead, he let out a long low whistle, his appreciation of her looks making her blush with pleasure.

'Forgive me,' he apologised, almost at once. 'I'm forgetting myself. But you look simply stunning.'

He'd been thoughtful enough to buy her a corsage of orchids. In an attempt to redeem himself, he stepped forwards without thinking, apparently with the intention of pinning it on her personally, only to be confronted by the dilemma of more bare flesh than material.

'I can do that for you,' Beryl intervened prudishly, fearing he might be spoiled for choice.

'Ah, yes,' he stammered a little, 'that would probably be best.'

Beryl stepped past him with the merest glance of disapproval and began to attach the flowers.

'You'll be the envy of every woman at the ball,' he remarked admiringly, as Beryl finished and stood aside.

'You look very dashing yourself,' she responded, his blandishments making her blush again.

'Are you two actually going to this dance?' Beryl enquired tactlessly, 'or do you intend to stand here all night and flatter each other to death?'

Alan flinched, as if starting from a trance. 'Yes, of course, you're quite right,' he agreed, retrieving his cap and gloves. 'We should go.'

Unaware of Victoria's frame of mind, Beryl could only judge the situation for what it appeared to be. Of all the people in the world, possibly she would be the last to assume the role of matchmaker, but the war had changed her a little. Knowing George and losing him had changed her a little. Privately, she didn't share Victoria's faith in her husband's return. Perhaps she felt that one broken heart was enough and if another could be mended, then so much the better. What were a few white lies compared to that? As Alan whisked Victoria off and she glanced in her direction, she merely smiled and sent her on her way with a last nod of encouragement.

As they stepped into the street, Victoria was both surprised and delighted to discover that Alan intended to drive them to the dance in his motorcar.

'My goodness!' she exclaimed. 'I never imagined.'

'What, this old heap?' he remarked casually. 'It's just a second hand Bullnosed Morris that has a tendency to overheat.'

Victoria hadn't the slightest idea what he was talking about. Nevertheless, she was immensely impressed. She'd never been in a motorcar before and racing through the busy London streets with the wind rushing past her ears and plucking at her hair was an entirely new experience for her. As they gathered speed, the buildings on either side began to flash past, melting into a giddy blur until at last they'd reached a breathtaking forty five miles an hour. Victoria found it all quite thrilling.

By the time they arrived, the dance was already in full swing and as the doors opened to admit them, a deluge of music and laughter rushed out, bursting upon her ears, assaulting her senses and making her heart leap. As she entered, Victoria gasped, catching her breath in wonder, instantly captivated; she'd never expected anything quite so grand as this.

The entire ballroom had undergone the new electrification. Its vaulted ceiling supported six massive crystal chandeliers, each one wired for power, so that every tier burned bright with elemental radiance. Their myriad facets scintillated, glinted, flashed and flared, sending garish incandescent shards cascading down the mirrored walls. They glittered like stardust that shimmered on the marble statuary standing sentinel around the hall, sparkled on the dewy garlands that adorned the gilded galleries and speckled the flags and miles of bunting with vivid points of rainbow brilliance, until everything blazed with light and colour. It was dazzling.

The orchestra began to play a waltz as elegant looking couples began to gather on the dance floor, whilst others pondered their choice at an immense buffet, or toasted each other's health with brimming glasses. It was as though she'd stepped back in time. If it hadn't been for the uniforms, she wouldn't have known that there was a war on at all.

Alan proved to be a considerate and attentive companion. He made a point of introducing her to all sorts of interesting people; personal friends, fellow officers, as well as various dignitaries and their wives. From the moment she stepped into the room, she never seemed to be off her feet. She danced half the night away with Alan, and the other half with the rest of the young officers, and some of the older ones as well. She'd never felt so popular before. The evening passed in a haze of delight. The atmosphere was intoxicating, seductive. She surrendered to it completely and let it carry her away.

She never did get a chance to ask about Gerald. Everyone seemed to make a point of not talking about the war. They were living for the moment, and the subject was not conducive to the occasion. The opportunity for such questions never arose.

It was to be a night of 'firsts'. It was the first time she had ever ridden in a motorcar. It was the first time she'd ever drunk champagne. The second glass tasted even better, but by the time she'd finished her third she was beginning to get a little dizzy. Feeling the need for some fresh air, she asked Alan to take her out onto the balcony so that she might clear her head.

It was the brightest of starry nights, she felt light-hearted and happy, everything seemed so perfect. She was entranced by it all. 'Thank you, Alan,' she smiled. 'Thank you for this.'

As she spoke, the orchestra began to play another waltz. Alan stepped forwards and gathered her into his arms. For a moment, she thought that he was going to dance with her, right there on the balcony, but instead he pulled her close and bent forward to kiss her.

She allowed it. Putting her arms about his neck, she clung to him, a victim of her own deception, unaware that what she so happily embraced was only the disembodied memories of her husband, frozen in time, that she'd resurrected to clothe a living man that they might walk and breathe and talk again. It was the alchemy of her own mind that had transformed him. He looked like Gerald, he behaved like Gerald, but as they kissed, the cold, bleak voice of reason began to murmur, reminding her against all her longings, that this wasn't the man she'd married, that this charade had gone on long enough, and that now it was time to return to reality. Resist as she might, the truth she'd shunned these many months would no longer be denied.

'No Alan, please, stop.' Pulling herself free, she turned away, gripping the edge of the balcony for support. 'Dear God,' she breathed, 'what am I doing?'

Alan came up behind her and placed his hands lightly on her shoulders. 'It's Gerald, isn't it?' he guessed.

She nodded. She'd never intended to mislead him, but only to remind herself of her husband. 'Poor Alan. What have I done to you?'

'You've bewitched my soul,' he breathed. It was the gentlest of accusations.

She closed her eyes, her hand flew to her mouth, stifling a gasp of dismay. It was just a harmless fantasy. She'd never meant it to be anything else. Obviously, she'd seriously underestimated the consequences.

'I'm sorry,' she sighed. 'I'm so very sorry. I should never have allowed this to happen.'

'No,' he objected forcefully. 'It's entirely my fault. Somehow, I always knew what you were doing, what you were going through. You were vulnerable. I took advantage.'

Victoria spared herself a wan smile. How like him that was, to accept all of the blame when so much of it was hers. 'You should hate me,' she told him. 'I made you into Gerald for my own selfish reasons. I can't even tell you that I kissed you for yourself.'

His hands tensed on her shoulders. 'I could never hate you,' he replied softly. 'I can't bear to see you this way. You must face up to it, Victoria,' he urged. 'Gerald is dead. You have to let him go.'

'He's not dead.' She refused to listen, tears beginning to spill down her cheeks. 'He's my husband, and he's out there in France, fighting for King and country, justice and liberty, and for me. How can I turn my back on him; how can I possibly do that?'

'You're destroying yourself,' Alan's voice rose in frustration, 'and I refuse to stand by and allow it to happen.'

She faced him defiantly, brushing the tears roughly from her face. 'You, sir, are in no position to do anything,' she reminded him abruptly, instantly refuting the suggestion of any claim he might have laid upon her. 'It's getting late. Please take me home.'

'You're right, of course,' he conceded patiently. He was prepared to wait, to give her all the time she needed. When she came to her senses, he would be there for her.

The drive home gave Victoria time to think about what she'd done. She'd all but betrayed Gerald's trust. She'd let herself down merely for some foolish fancy, and furthermore, she'd used Alan disgracefully. For his friendship and kindness, he'd deserved so much better from her, and as if she wasn't ashamed enough, his magnanimous acceptance of her rejection of him only made it worse. So much so that once he'd seen her safely to her door, she wanted to apologise all over again, but he wouldn't hear of it, still insisting that the responsibility lay with him.

'Until now, I didn't believe that there was another man in all the world with a character to equal Gerald's,' she told him, anxious to prove that she too was capable of a generous gesture. 'I'm sorry I snapped at you. It was uncalled for.'

'On the contrary,' he disagreed mildly. 'You had every right. I deserved it.'

'What you deserve,' she advised him seriously, 'is a far better woman than myself.'

'Allow me to be the judge of that,' he answered with a smile.

Perversely, even though she couldn't bear the thought of his being angry with her, she still felt that she deserved some word of censure from him, if only to salve her conscience, but nothing she could say or do would provoke it. That was punishment in itself. In the end, she gave up trying.

'Thank you for taking me to the dance,' she offered her appreciation in conclusion. 'It was a wonderful evening, particularly for having spent it in your company.'

Her sentiments only served to reinforce his opinion of her. 'You're the most remarkable creature,' he declared. 'I think that if I'd been Gerald, I'd have gone to war solely for you, and King and country be dammed!'

'I'm glad you still think so,' she confessed, relieved to hear it, 'but don't let Colonel Bass hear you say that.'

'I suspect that Colonel Bass has a lot to answer for,' Alan frowned, the mention of his superior officer reminding him of why they'd met in the first place. 'I'll continue to search,' he assured her, in case she feared the events of the evening might have cooled his enthusiasm. 'I'll do everything I can to find out about Gerald for you.' He paused thoughtfully, 'and if, under the circumstances, you choose not to visit my office in future, I will understand. If I find anything, anything at all, I'll send word to you immediately.' With that, he raised her hand and brushed his lips lightly against it.

After all his consideration and chivalry, she wasn't about to let him leave with so mean a farewell. At the risk of appearing capricious, she grabbed his lapels, pulled his head down and pressed her lips against his cheek, in an impulse of feminine gratitude. 'And before you ask,' she anticipated sternly, 'that was for you, not Gerald, and I would have done it even if he were standing here.'

Alan nodded, his admiration for her undimmed. He saluted and after a last lingering look, he left.

Victoria watched him go, sighing. She wondered if, in another reality, things might have been very different.

Alan had provided her with an opportunity to withdraw gracefully from an awkward situation. She decided it would be prudent to take advantage of his gesture, and although she chaffed on the inactivity, she refrained from any further visits to his office.

Her original plan had been to come to London, gain access to the War Office and discover what had happened to her husband. A few days, perhaps a week was all the time she'd allowed for it. Now months had passed, and she was no further forward. She needed to reassess her position. She felt she couldn't impose on Beryl's hospitality indefinitely; neither could she wait here forever for news of Gerald. For the moment, she remained undecided as to how much more time she could afford for the plan, unaware that shortly the decision would be taken out of her hands.

Barely a week had elapsed since the night of the ball. Beryl had left early to attend a suffragette meeting, whilst Victoria had spent the best part of the day shopping for essentials. When she returned, she found the door ajar. Remembering that she had locked it when she left, she tipped the doormat back with the toe of the boot and saw that the key Beryl kept there for emergencies had gone. Fearing they might have been burgled, she pushed the door open a little further and peered cautiously inside. Suddenly, Alan stood up from the chair he'd been sitting in.

'Alan!' she exclaimed in surprise. 'What are you doing here? Have you news of Gerald?'

'I'm afraid not,' he returned gravely. 'It's Beryl. She's been arrested.'

'Oh no!' she cried, afraid that it might be another incident like the one with Lord Kitchener. 'What happened?'

Alan shrugged. 'There was some sort of a scuffle,' he explained briefly. 'Apparently, she bit the officer who was trying to detain her. Nothing too serious, but it constitutes an assault on a policeman. I'm afraid she'll go to prison for it. She telephoned my office from the police station. She wanted you to know.'

'Are they coming for me?' Victoria asked, recalling her previous involvement.

'No,' he assured her, 'but there's no point in your staying here now.'

'Why do you say that?' she asked, suspicious of his tone.

'I've been recalled to active service,' he informed her flatly. 'I leave for France within the week. I'm afraid our search for Gerald is over.'

'I'm sorry to hear that.' Victoria couldn't decide which part of his news upset her the most.

'I'm worried about you, Victoria,' he confessed. 'This latest episode is bound to raise old issues in which your name figures largely.'

'But I thought all that had been sorted out?' she protested. 'They know I'm not a spy.'

'It's not only about that,' he reminded her. 'They also know that you obstructed a police investigation involving Sylvia Pankhurst.'

'I had no choice but to help Beryl,' she told him defensively. 'She's my friend.'

'I admire your loyalty,' he commended her, 'but I doubt if they'll see it that way. We're at war, Victoria. The country's under martial law. There are powerful dangerous forces at large in the land. If you were to become involved in another incident with Beryl, no matter how innocently, Colonel Bass or someone worse might not be so tolerant next time, and I won't be there to help you.'

'But this is England,' she stared in disbelief.

'England at war,' he corrected her.

'I'd no idea that things had changed so much.'

'That's what I was afraid of,' he confided. 'Now listen. Because of the shortage of men, the National Registration Act will soon come into force.'

'I've never heard of it,' she interrupted.

'Not many people have yet,' he told her. 'It will require all women between the ages of sixteen and sixty five to register their personal details. It's to let the government know who's available for work. You'll have to carry a certificate with you at all times. After that, they'll know exactly where you are and exactly what you're doing.' Aware that she hadn't fully comprehended the danger, he continued.

'Be advised by me, Victoria. Go home, back to Staunton Gifford. If you have to work, get a job locally. Avoid all government positions, anything they might consider to be worthy of suffragette attention, any of the Forces, nursing, the Land Army, munitions factories, anything that might be thought of as sensitive or contentious. Live quietly, discreetly, and you'll be perfectly safe. Please, Victoria,' he implored. 'If you won't do it for me, do it for Gerald.'

What he suggested more or less fell in line with what she intended to do anyway. 'Very well, Alan,' she agreed. 'I'll do as you ask.'

'Thank goodness,' he sighed heavily, obviously relieved. 'If you wish, once you've settled your affairs here, I could take you to the station with me on Friday.' He paused, as the thought struck him. 'It'll be our last chance to say goodbye.'

Victoria had already realised that. 'Yes,' she responded gloomily, 'I know.'

In the few days that were left to her, Victoria tried to see Beryl, only to discover that whilst in police custody she wasn't being allowed any visitors, except close relatives. Instead, she wrote a long letter to her, thanking her for all her help and support, and wishing her well for the future. This, with a duplicate set of keys to her rooms, she handed in to Beryl's parents, who received the parcel with the kind of resignation that could only have been exhibited by parents with a daughter like Beryl.

On Friday morning, she picked her suitcase up, locked the door behind her and pushed the remaining set of keys through the letterbox, and in no time at all, it seemed, she was standing on the cold stone of the platform looking at Alan.

He'd gone with her to purchase her ticket, and seen her safely onto the right platform, whilst carrying her bags for her. Her train didn't leave for another half an hour, his in only fifteen minutes; that was all the time they had.

The noise and clamour of the station echoed around them. The occasional piercing shriek of an engine whistle mingled with the solid rattle of baggage trolleys, whilst soldiers milled about everywhere and civilians scurried back and forth in ever increasing droves, but they were oblivious to it all.

For a moment, neither of them spoke.

'I won't write,' Alan said at last. 'You might think it's a letter from Gerald. It would only confuse things.'

'That would probably be best,' Victoria agreed, feeling a pang of melancholy stab at her heart. Delving into her handbag, she produced a photograph of herself and offered it to him. 'I thought you might like this.' It was something of herself, all that she had left to give.

Although he might have considered it small compensation for what he was leaving behind, he accepted it graciously, then, stepping closer, he gazed down at her. 'When I'm in France, I shall think of you every day,' he said, 'and when the war is over, I shall look for you. If I find that you're still alone, I shall approach you again, and this time,' he told her assertively, 'I won't take no for an answer.'

Victoria lowered her eyes submissively. 'Yes, Alan,' she responded in a soft voice.

'If not,' he concluded dismally, 'then I'll leave you both in peace and you'll never see me again.'

She put her hand on his arm. 'Please don't say that,' she begged. 'If Gerald and I are together again, I will already have told him of you, that you were a friend when I needed one. He's bound to want to meet you.'

'Perhaps,' Alan responded doubtfully, 'but I fear I'd only arrive as a complication. It's best we leave it as it is.'

He was probably right, but it didn't make Victoria any happier to hear him say it.

Alan glanced at his watch. 'Damn,' he grimaced. 'I have to go now. My train leaves in five minutes.'

She'd hoped that she might have become used to this by now, but sadly it wasn't the case. She still experienced the same acute sense of loss she'd felt when Gerald had departed. It was all too poignantly similar. Only now, as Alan was leaving, did she feel it, trapped between what she wanted most and what stood before her. Unable to retrieve one, or hold the other, and powerless to alter any of it. How her heart ached with the impossibility of it all.

There was so much she wanted to say but there was no time left to say it. Summoning all her thoughts and feelings into one swift and decisive action, she reached forward, cupped his face in her hands and kissed him full on the lips, long and hard. This time, she was under no illusion. She knew exactly who he was and exactly what she was doing. 'Take that to France with you,' she told him, her voice wavering with emotion, 'but above all, come back safe. Do you understand? You come back safe.'

A tear trickled, unheeded, down her cheek as she watched him drift away through the smoke and steam. Turning once, he pressed the photograph to his lips, waved and then was gone.

It was as if she'd lost Gerald all over again. It seemed to her that there'd been too many goodbyes and not enough reunions. What she felt was too bitter for words.

In a few hours, Victoria would be back in Staunton Gifford, facing what was to be conceivably the hardest time in her life. In a few days, Alan would be in France.

A week later, his bunker received a direct hit from a German artillery shell, killing him instantly and burying him under yards of soil. He vanished without a trace. Nearly a century would pass before a French plough turned up his remains, and by then the thin alloy of his identity discs had corroded illegibly. All that he was, his hopes and aspirations, had been lost to the passage of time. Although he was buried with full military honours, there was no one left who could even say who he was.

Chapter Seven

Yet again, Victoria found herself right back where she'd started from, and hardly any the wiser for her journey. As she hauled her heavy suitcase through the familiar streets of Staunton Gifford, she began to wonder if she was destined to forever go round in aimless circles.

This homecoming, however, was different from all the rest. Her brush with the police, and the more serious encounter with the military authorities culminating in Alan's advice that she should leave London for her own safety, made her feel like an exile, an outcast. She'd been abandoned; everyone she knew was gone. Gerald was still missing, Alan had left for France, and Beryl was in prison. Gerald's parents had long since passed away, and her own were also dead. There was no one. She recalled from her college days how Beryl had set such store by personal freedom. Now Victoria knew that the price of such freedom often meant being alone. What was worse, she felt that by her mismanagement of her affairs in London, she'd squandered her last best chance of finding Gerald.

*

As she pushed the cottage door open, she was greeted by a pile of letters, representing several months' worth of correspondence. Gathering them up, she continued into the kitchen. There on the table, beneath a thick layer of dust, was the letter she'd written to her husband, just where she'd left it, quite undisturbed. Collecting some kindling, she used it to light the stove. There was, after all, no point in lingering over stale hopes. As the kettle boiled, she cleaned the table, swept up and dusted around, then sat down to read the accumulated post. There was nothing from Gerald, of course; she'd noticed that the moment she'd retrieved the envelopes from the mat, but then she hardly expected there would be. Most of the rest were merely public information leaflets from one official body or another, but one, although remarkably ordinary in itself, was to have a profound impact on her life. It was a notice of renewal for the lease on the cottage, and as soon as she saw the sum involved, she knew she couldn't afford it.

Gerald had left her well provided for, but that had been based on the short term, whilst her efforts to trace him had further drained her funds. Now all that money was gone, all she had left was her separation allowance which, thankfully, hadn't yet turned into a pension, but that was barely enough to live on. The notice was over a month old. The option to renew had all but expired. She had little more than a week to find the money or vacate the premises. Now her struggle had taken on an entirely new dimension, one of self survival.

Early the next morning, she dressed in her best, gathered together the necessary documents that would prove the standard of her education, and set out to find a job. She never imagined that she'd have to recall Alan's warning quite so soon, but faced with such dire circumstances, she had no choice but to seek employment.

From the very beginning, she found herself facing a dilemma. Finding another source of income was absolutely essential; she couldn't subsist on her separation allowance alone. The task in itself presented no great difficulties. Since the first year of the war, not only were there plenty of jobs available to women, the government actively encouraged them to work. However, her circumstances were somewhat different to the average woman's. There was Alan's warning to consider. Whether he'd been correct in his assessment of the situation or was merely being over-protective, Victoria would adhere to his advice, no matter how detrimental to her circumstances.

Then there was her promise to Gerald. That was paramount. She'd sworn to remain here and wait for him, no matter how long that might be. She knew now that she couldn't remain at Rosebay, as she'd hoped, but her tenacity was such that she intended to stay as near to it as possible. It would severely restrict her choice of work and how far she could travel, but her promise was sacred to her, and nothing in heaven or on earth would compel her to break it. Her loyalty, although commendable, was to become something of an obstacle in the future.

Initially, she intended to avoid shop jobs; they were generally low paid and she felt sure that with her education she could do far better. She was aiming at clerical work, and spent the next few days approaching every office, bank, solicitors, auction house and land agents within a radius of four villages. Despite the limitations of the rural environment, there were a surprising number of places to try. As with the towns, here also the pen and the ledger held sway, and so much more now that there was a war. However, it soon became apparent that she'd overlooked one major deficiency – she had no experience. She'd never needed to work before. Clearly, it counted against her. And the fact that her education was usually superior to those who interviewed her didn't help either.

Inevitably she met with the same old-fashioned narrow minded bigotry that had existed before the war. The social intolerance she found herself facing might well have relaxed in the cities and towns, but here in this rustic backwater it had, if anything, grown worse. The only people they were willing to employ were men, and because of the war, mature men. Even though she had the aptitude, the ability and the education, she was unsuitable for the position because she was a woman, and a young one at that. She was offered a variety of excuses, but whichever way it was said, the answer was always no. She began to realise that, here at least, Beryl's radical opinions of a male dominated society hadn't been so farfetched after all.

Lowering her sights, Victoria tried all the shops she'd passed on her way out, even public houses warranted her attention, but every position from salesgirl to barmaid that was expected to be done by a woman was already occupied by a woman. With so many husbands in France, there were a lot of wives, many with children to support, who needed extra money.

At the end of her third day of searching, she was dusty and thirsty and tired and back in Staunton Gifford again. She'd no idea of what to do next, except buy herself a cup of tea.

It was late in the afternoon, and the tearoom was all but empty. She ordered one cup of tea and declined the offer of cake, which she would have liked, but decided frugally that it didn't fall within the limits of her newly imposed budget. The tea was brought to her by an ample, friendly looking woman who introduced herself as Rose, and who remarked in a thick rural accent common to the region, as she placed the cup in front of her, 'My goodness dear, you look fair done in! What on earth have you been up to?'

Having nothing better to do and glad of someone to talk to, Victoria gave a brief account of the more pertinent events of her life that had brought her to this moment.

'That's a shame and no mistake,' Rose frowned, when she'd finished. 'It's a rum do, this war. Everything's topsy-turvy, but a fit young woman like you shouldn't have much trouble finding a place,' she told her helpfully. 'There's lots of war work about. You could go to the city and try a factory, or there's the V.A.D.s, you know, nursing, or the Land Army; you could make your way with them.'

Victoria found it remarkable that everything she suggested was exactly the same as that which Alan had warned her against, whilst the Voluntary Aid Detachment, as its name implied, was unpaid. Besides, any one of these jobs might take her far from Staunton Gifford, and that would mean breaking her promise to Gerald. Had she still been in contact with him, it might have made a difference. At least she could have told him what was happening and, if necessary, released herself from her pledge, but under the circumstances that was impossible. As far as she was concerned, she had no choice but to stay.

'I'm afraid I have to remain near the village,' she explained. 'It's for personal reasons.'

Rose scratched her head, not entirely sure what that meant. 'That do limit it some.' For a moment, it looked as if she were about to say more, then thought better of it.

'No, please,' Victoria urged. 'Go on.'

'Oh, I don't know,' Rose hesitated. 'There is a place, but you might not thank me for telling you.'

'I've no options left,' Victoria admitted frankly. 'I'd be grateful for anything you can suggest.'

'Well,' Rose continued reluctantly, 'I was going to say, there is Orchardlea.'

Victoria recognised the name. 'Isn't that the big farm a few miles south of the village?'

'That's it,' Rose confirmed. 'Since her husband died, old Mrs Fisher's been running it with a foreman. Her old man were good at it, but she ain't so clever. It's gone to seed a bit these last few years. Funny thing,' she mused, 'other farms hereabouts gets soldiers to work the land, if they're short-handed, prisoners of war even, but Mrs Fisher don't get nothing. I imagine it's because she's falling short on her quotas. They'll have the place off her if she ain't careful.'

'But is she hiring?' Victoria asked.

'Oh yes,' Rose assured her. 'Old men, women and boys. She can't afford to be fussy, begging your pardon.'

'Neither can I,' Victoria concluded. 'I'll try there.'

'Oh don't do that,' Rose began to moan. 'Think again, my dear. It's terrible hard work. I'm sorry I mentioned it.'

'On the contrary, I'm glad you did,' Victoria remarked decisively, rummaging in her purse for some coins.

'No.' Rose refused her money. 'You have that on me. It's the least I can do, and good luck to you.'

Wasting no more time, Victoria trudged the weary miles to Orchardlea. It was a great sprawling rundown pile of a place. The farmyard was on the edge of the road, lined with tall buildings. Barns, stables and storehouses, heavy beamed and timber clad, all showing signs of rot and decay with missing tiles and broken lintels. As she entered the yard she was greeted by the fruity aroma of manure and many a quizzical glance from passing workers as if to say, 'Who is this dove in the henhouse?' Having enquired of an ancient-looking farmhand as to the whereabouts of Mrs Fisher, her attention was directed to the farmhouse door which stood ajar. She was told to knock and go in.

Victoria did that and found herself in a large stone-flagged kitchen dominated by a huge range that hadn't seen a dab of blacklead in years. It remained unlit. Hams, strings of sausages and bunches of herbs hung from the low beams like festive decorations whilst bottles and casks lined the walls, heavily festooned with cobwebs. In the centre of the room stood a broad ash table laden with ledgers, piles of loose paper and bottles of ink. Behind the table hunched a figure swathed in threadbare woollens, a shawl and scarf. It appeared as if someone had dumped a heap of old clothes there, but it was a woman.

Mrs Fisher sat, her grey hair piled loosely on her head, her face ruddy from years of outdoor work, a pair of tiny spectacles perched on her nose, muttering to herself in irritation. As she heard Victoria come in she paused, peering owlishly at her through the gloom of the kitchen.

'What can I do for you, my dear?' she enquired. 'I'm sorry, but I've no eggs to spare.'

'That's quite alright,' Victoria assured her, 'I don't need any eggs. I've come looking for work.'

Mrs Fisher had begun to rifle through the papers again, but Victoria's remark made her stop short and stare even more closely at her. 'I'm sorry,' she squinted, 'but I haven't any use for a lady's maid.'

'No. I meant farm work,' Victoria elaborated.

'What, you!' Mrs Fisher scowled doubtfully, looking her up and down. 'Why would a woman of quality want to do farm work?'

In answer to this question, Victoria had nothing to offer but the plain unvarnished truth. Stepping forward, she pulled herself up as straight as she could and stated with as much dignity as she could muster, 'I've just travelled the length and breadth of four villages looking for employment, only to be told that because I'm a woman, I can't do the work of a man. Therefore I've come here today to ask if I may be allowed to do the work of a horse.'

Mrs Fisher scratched her chin, the hint of a smile playing about her lips, a twinkle in her rheumy old eyes. 'Careful what you say, gel,' she chuckled. 'The way the army's requisitioning horses these days, you may get your wish.' She waved Victoria over. 'Sit down.'

Although she'd received a less than enthusiastic reception, at least now she'd been asked to sit down. Victoria hoped that it was a positive sign.

Mrs Fisher studied her even more intently, squinting through her tiny spectacles until her eyes were mere slits. 'I dare say you've never done any kind of farm work before?'

'I'm afraid not,' Victoria confirmed.

'Any kind of work at all?'

'No.'

Mrs Fisher sighed heavily. Clearly Victoria's answers, although entirely honest, had only served to illustrate her limitations. She began to shake her head again, as if she were about to refuse after all.

Victoria felt a twinge of alarm. She'd already lowered her standards as far as they would go. She'd just spent the entire week being refused for every position of skill and responsibility she'd applied for. As if that wasn't depressing enough, now it seemed she was about to suffer the ignominy of being rejected for a humble labourer's job, suggesting that her class and gender made her virtually good for nothing. Anxious to prevent the situation from deteriorating any further, she became more insistent. 'Oh, please,' she entreated, 'I learn very quickly and I promise I'll work very hard. Besides,' she confessed, 'no one else will employ me, my husband's missing in France, I'm about to lose my home and I haven't anywhere else to go.'

Mrs Fisher exhaled sharply, feeling the full weight of the moral dilemma that had suddenly landed unsolicited in her lap. 'But you'll never stand it. You won't last a week,' she objected. 'Look at you, you're all pink and soft. What am I going to do with you? As if I didn't have enough troubles.' She returned her attention to the stack of documents on the table, which appeared to be a constant distraction to her. 'Look at it all,' she complained, 'requisitions, quotas, demands. Gaffer was good at it, but it fair makes my head spin.'

'Perhaps I can help?' Victoria offered spontaneously.

Mrs Fisher paused from her complaining to regard her sharply. 'You understand this sort of thing?' She jabbed a pointing finger at the pile of papers.

'I should be able to,' Victoria replied. 'I've a university education. I was first in my year for mathematics. May I see something?'

Mrs Fisher considered her suggestion for a moment, then selected a document which she passed over to her. 'Potato yields,' she declared. 'They're asking for seventeen and a half percent more next season. Seventeen and a half percent! What on earth does that mean?'

Victoria suspected that the woman had chosen the item which she considered to be hardest to understand. Nevertheless, once she'd had a chance to look at it, the problem didn't appear to be too difficult. 'Yes, you see, they want you to produce that much more than last year,' Victoria informed her. 'Do you have a record of last year's crop?'

'Here it is.' Mrs Fisher swept aside a mountain of paper to produce a battered ledger.

It didn't take Victoria long to calculate the necessary equations. 'Yes, you see,' she explained, pointing at a column of scrawled figures. 'The farm produced almost one hundred tons of potatoes last year on that much ground. So, let's see. Seventeen and a half per cent more, that would mean... yes, that's right. You'll have to use an extra twelve acres next year.'

Mrs Fisher had followed Victoria's progress with her mouth hanging open. 'Twelve acres?' she snapped. 'Good grief!' She held her head. 'More pasture under the plough.' Suddenly, she stopped ranting. A shrewd glint came into her eye and she began to study Victoria all over again, as if reassessing her potential. 'You didn't write nothing down,' she observed.

'It was a relatively simple sum,' Victoria felt bound to admit.

'You didn't count on your fingers.' Mrs Fisher made it sound as if she'd employed witchcraft. 'You mean to tell me you did all that in your head?'

'As I said,' Victoria reminded her, 'I've a university education.' Taking advantage of the situation, she continued. 'If you were to give me a job, I would be happy to help with these accounts. Not in working hours, of course,' she was quick to assure her, 'just in my spare time. That is, if I get any.'

Mrs Fisher rubbed her chin again, weighing up the pros and cons. 'Alright,' she announced at last, her decision influenced not so much by altruism, but more by a desire to rid herself of the troublesome paperwork. 'I'll give you a chance, mostly labouring, but some of this,' she indicated the accounts. 'But mind me, if you can't keep it up, if you fall by the wayside, I'll have to let you go. I can't afford to keep no strays.'

'That seems fair,' Victoria agreed. She'd have said the same, even if it wasn't.

'I'll get the foreman, Mr Moss, to keep an eye on you,' Mrs Fisher told her. 'He'll report back to me. As you've no experience, I'll start you at the boy's rate. That's ten bob a week and found.'

It was a miserable pittance, but Victoria was in no position to negotiate. At least she'd have her food and a place to sleep, and most of all she'd be near Staunton Gifford.

'I've three girls living in the loft above the hay barn,' Mrs Fisher went on. 'You can share with them.'

'Thank you. You won't regret it,' Victoria told her.

Mrs Fisher didn't look so sure. 'Maybe I won't, but you might,' she remarked doubtfully. 'I suppose you got possessions, bits and bobs, you want to bring with you?'

'A few,' Victoria wildly understated, not daring to press her luck any further.

'When've you got to leave your lodgings?' Mrs Fisher enquired.

'Monday morning,' Victoria informed her.

The old woman nodded. 'Pack up early. I'll send a cart down Sunday afternoon. That'll give you half a day to settle in. Then we'll see.'

Victoria realised that for all her bluff exterior, Mrs Fisher had made an effort to be generous by considering her possessions and sending a cart to collect her and them. All she had to do now was prove that she was equal to the job.

All the household utensils, china and furniture went with the cottage. Everything else, all that she and Gerald owned, Victoria managed to pack into a suitcase, a valise and one large trunk. They hadn't really lived here long enough to accumulate very much. As she locked up the cottage, she felt as if she were shutting the door on an entire chapter of her life. The life she had hoped for and envisaged spending here with Gerald when she married him. Before the war came and stole it all from her.

She'd informed Mrs Spragget, the post mistress, of her change of address, but as an added precaution she'd also left a letter on the mantelpiece. It was addressed to the new tenants, should there be any, asking them that if Gerald Avery should come looking for her, would they kindly tell him where she was. As she waited by the gate she noticed the little garland of plaited hair, a duplicate of the one she'd given to Gerald, that she'd hung there on the day that he'd left. It was somewhat weather-worn now, but still serving its purpose. She had to go but it would remain. It was her symbol - her candle in the window to guide the traveller home; a token of her faith; her prayer to God for her husband's safe return.

*

The cart arrived, as promised, driven by a rangy looking lad of about twelve or fourteen who, in spite of his youth and small stature, managed to manhandle the trunk into the back of the cart. The place next to him on the driver's seat was already occupied by a large dog that seemed disinclined to relinquish its position, so Victoria sat in the back of the cart with the trunk, her legs dangling over the tailboard. As they pulled away and she watched the cottage dwindle into the distance, she wondered if she'd ever come back here, if she'd ever have the chance to resume her life with Gerald, if anything would ever be the same again? Although never a day would pass when she didn't think of him, she knew now that, for the time being at least, she must concentrate on looking after herself.

Sharing accommodation with three other women didn't bother her. She made friends easily, and her life at college had taught her how to share and interact with other people. It was just as well because her arrival was hardly subtle.

She followed the boy into the hay barn, a great wooden structure just off the main farmyard past the stacked sheaves, the sweet aroma of dried grass offering a sharp contrast to the fruity smell of the yard, to a long flight of wooden steps. She ascended first; the boy followed dragging the trunk behind him, managing to bash it on every step as he went. A person would have to be deaf or dead to be unaware of her approach.

Once she'd reached the last step, Victoria paused to find herself inside the roof, its apex sloping down on either side forming a long triangular room. She took it in at a glance. It was all old wood and weathered boards. In places where the tiles had dislodged on the outside, there were chinks that let in thin slivers of sunlight. Some of the bigger gaps had been stuffed with rags, and a window opposite her, its pane cracked diagonally across its length, was fastened shut with string.

In spite of its rundown appearance, she very quickly noticed that it was all scrupulously clean and well ordered, clearly indicating that female hands had been at work. There were four beds, each in its own generous portion of space, each with its own small cupboard fashioned from an upturned crate. In each space, a rope had been tied between the beams to hang clothes on. It was both inventive and practical. In the centre of the attic, an iron pot-bellied stove crackled cheerfully, its chimney protruding through a neat hole cut in the roof. Nearby was a washstand with a big bowl and jug, whilst a large copper pan filled with water heated on the stove. A rough wooden table stood opposite, in the centre of which had been placed an old stone marmalade pot filled with dried flowers.

Having done his duty, the boy had left her trunk at the top of the stairs and disappeared, leaving Victoria alone facing the three young women she was to share with. 'Hello,' she smiled nervously, 'I'm Victoria.'

The person nearest her advanced, hand outstretched. 'Hello, love,' she smiled broadly, 'I'm Ella; welcome to Orchardlea.'

She appeared to be an amiable young woman of about twenty five, attractive in a garish sort of way. Her hair was bleached blonde, whilst her clothes and makeup seemed to reflect her effusive manner. 'We were told to expect you. We've all been looking forward to it,' she presumed to speak for everyone. Taking Victoria by the arm, she proceeded to introduce her to the others. 'This is Maisie,' she indicated a very plump, round faced young girl, possibly in her mid teens, sitting on one of the beds, who smiled self-consciously.

'Ello,' was as much as she could manage.

'And that's Jen,' she pointed to a tall lean-limbed individual who looked about thirty, although she might have been younger, with dark eyes and long black hair that hung loose about her shoulders. She stood by a window, her arm resting on the sill, apparently intent on staring outside. She paused from her gazing to send a short sharp nod in Victoria's direction. Her manner was reserved and somewhat guarded.

'Well,' Ella gushed, 'Now that we all know each other, let's see about getting you settled in. Good grief! What's that?' she asked, noticing the trunk.

Victoria glanced down at it. 'That's my entire life,' she sighed.

'Oh, right then,' Ella frowned, the drama of the statement lost on her. 'Anyway, it won't do any good to leave it there. Come on, I'll help you move it over to your bed.'

Together they dragged the trunk to the end of one of the beds.

'It'll be safe there,' Ella told her. 'As you're new, we've given you the bed under the bit of roof that don't leak.'

'You're all very kind,' Victoria smiled her appreciation, privately wondering just how primitive conditions here were. She didn't have very long to wait before she found out.

Moving round to the side of the bed, she put her valise and suitcase down ready to unpack. As she did so, the toe of her boot knocked against an object underneath it that made a sound like a small gong.

'That's just your chamber pot,' Ella explained unabashed, 'in case you get caught short in the night.'

'Isn't there a water closet?' Victoria asked hopefully.

'There's an earth closet in the yard,' Jen volunteered offhandedly. 'It's alright in the daytime, but at night the rats come out. They're as big as rabbits; even the farm cats won't face 'em.'

'Oh, I see,' Victoria acknowledged, making a mental note not to drink too much before she went to bed.

Picking her suitcase up, she laid it on the bed and began to unpack. Ella was happy to help, and soon even Maisie, eaten up with curiosity, had overcome her shyness and was lending a hand, whilst Jen looked on from a distance, maintaining her reserve but just as curious.

'You've some lovely things,' Ella remarked admiringly.

'Remnants of a former life,' Victoria told her glumly. 'I don't know why I kept them. I doubt if I'll get much chance to wear them here.'

'Oh, you mustn't say that,' Ella objected. 'We have our moments, don't we girls? You'd be surprised.'

'All the same,' Victoria continued, 'I've brought some hardwearing skirts, two pairs of stout boots and a weatherproof coat.'

'You're wearing a corset, aren't you?' Jen observed bluntly.

'Yes, of course,' Victoria replied, taken aback by her tactless remark.

'Take my advice,' she went on, indifferent to her reaction, 'leave it off. You'll never do any farm work wearing a corset.'

'Stop picking on her, Jen,' Ella intervened. 'Give the poor girl a chance to unpack. You seem to have thought of everything,' she went on quickly. 'But tell me, Victoria, what brings a woman like you to a place like this?'

Doubtless it was a question that had crossed all their minds. It was easy enough to answer. Victoria explained her circumstances to them. In short, she had no choice. She was an impoverished gentlewoman who'd just lost her home, and whose husband was missing in France. She finished with her usual declaration, 'My husband's not dead, he's just missing.'

The three of them glanced awkwardly at each other. They might be living in a backwater, but the tragedy of the war had touched every corner of the country. Now there wasn't a town or village anywhere that didn't have its share of dead or injured men. When it came to the war, everyone was equal.

'Of course not, dear,' Ella smiled rather too broadly. 'He'll turn up; they always do. It's typical of men; just when you think you've seen the last of them, back they come.'

'I wouldn't be too sure,' Jen glared darkly.

'It reminds me of an old tom cat I had once,' Maisie recalled. 'He was out for weeks. Just when I thought he'd gone for good, there he was, large as life and twice as ugly.'

Victoria had never thought of the situation quite like that before. It was a novel way of looking at things, and somehow it made her feel a little more hopeful. 'Are any of you married?' she asked, looking around.

'Us?' Ella stared. 'God, no! We're all still fancy-free. Mind you,' she confided, 'Maisie's got an admirer.'

'No, I haven't,' Maisie objected. 'Cedric's just friendly.'

'Nonsense,' Ella disagreed. 'Cedric Hardacre is smitten by you.'

Victoria thought the name sounded familiar. 'Isn't he the man who owns the ironmongers in the village?'

'That's him,' Ella confirmed proudly. 'He fair dotes on our Maisie.'

'But he looks to be in his forties,' Victoria recalled.

'Age don't matter when you're in love,' Ella told her airily. 'Besides,' she continued in a more practical vein, 'he's always good for some free candles or a bar of soap.'

'She's right,' Maisie agreed. 'He's too old for me.'

'What are you being so bloody fussy about?' Jen scowled across the room. 'It's not as if anyone else is going to look at you.'

'Don't be like that, Jen,' Maisie sulked. 'My mam says I'm a catch.'

'Is that the same woman that told the police the Kaiser was living under her bed?'

'Nah, that was a mistake.'

'Stop teasing, Jen,' Ella scolded. 'We don't have any regular young men,' she returned her attention to Victoria. 'Maisie and me send letters to the boys at the front, of course, like they said we should - the ones without wives or sweethearts, just to cheer them up. It's our patriotic duty,' she pointed out, with only the merest suggestion of self-interest. 'Jen there has three brothers all in the same regiment.'

'You get letters from the front?' Victoria's interest peaked. 'Would you mind if I ask, do they say anything about what's going on out there?'

Curiously, an unexpected silence descended on the gathering. Even Ella quietened down.

'Of course, if it's personal,' Victoria added quickly, 'I quite understand.'

'It's nothing like that,' Ella assured her eventually. 'We all got letters this week, but we have to wait until Friday to find out what they say.'

Victoria was completely confounded by this response. 'Why wait until Friday?'

'It's pay day,' Jen remarked flatly.

Victoria still looked puzzled.

Finally, Jen cut right through the confusion by employing the down to earth, no nonsense attitude that so accurately defined her character. 'None of us can read.'

'I'm so sorry,' Victoria apologised, 'I didn't mean to pry.'

'You weren't to know,' Ella excused her. 'Most of us have been working on the land since we could walk. You don't need no book learning to pick cabbages or milk cows. It's the wage that counts. At least, that's what my dad used to say.'

As a person who took education for granted, this information came as something of a surprise to Victoria. Compulsory education for children up to the age of eight had been in force for nearly forty years, whilst children from the age of twelve had been required to attend since the turn of the century. It would appear that the rules governing this law were lax at best, particularly in the more remote working class areas.

She was disturbed to learn that whilst most villages had a school, many of the poorer rural families withheld their children from attending classes for the sake of the income they could provide from working in the fields, thus depriving them of even the most basic tuition. Any skills they might require in life were handed down from one generation to another, and that was generally considered to be enough.

'What happens on pay day?' she asked. It seemed the next logical question.

'We take our letters to Mrs Spragget,' Maisie told her.

'The post mistress.' Victoria wasn't likely to forget that name in a hurry.

'She charges tuppence to read a letter, and sixpence to write one,' Ella explained.

'Plus the stamp,' Maisie added.

'That's outrageous!' Victoria cried, incensed by what she'd heard. 'It's blatant exploitation! The woman should be reported.'

'That's the way of the world,' Jen shrugged.

'Isn't there anyone else you could ask; Mrs Fisher, perhaps?'

'God, no!' Ella gasped, 'we wouldn't dare bother the boss with something like that. As for the rest, most of them are like us.'

'What about me?' Victoria suggested, determined to reform this disgraceful situation. Her intention was to leave absolutely no doubt of her ability to help them. In her desire to make that quite clear, she may have overdone it a little. 'I can read and write. I also speak French, Italian,' she left out German, 'and Latin.'

'That's good,' Jen remarked with a hint of sarcasm. 'If I ever get a letter written in Latin, I'll know who to come to.'

'What I mean is,' Victoria elaborated, 'I can read your letters for you.'

Ella looked at Maisie. 'That would save us a long walk to the post office.' She turned back to Victoria. 'How much were you thinking of charging?'

'Nothing,' Victoria emphasised. 'I'd be happy to read them to you for nothing, and I'll write them for you as well,' she added, only too glad of the chance to put a dent in Mrs Spragget's nefarious trade.

Even Jen looked surprised.

'You see, Jen,' Ella snapped at her, 'I told you she'd be a gem.'

Jen just glowered.

It was as if a floodgate had been opened. Ella and Maisie scurried about, gathering up their unread mail which they duly presented to Victoria.

Now that she'd volunteered to read their letters to them, Victoria soon discovered that she'd done so without realising the degree of illiteracy she'd have to contend with. The letters were invariably scrawled almost illegibly in pencil, and whilst being grammatically inaccurate almost to the point of nonsense, they were also wildly mis-spelt. It was like trying to translate a foreign language.

This was never more evident than in the first letter she was given, one addressed to Ella from a Private in the East Sussex infantry. She began to fear that she might have overreached herself.

Happily, as the others couldn't read at all, they were entirely unaware of the difficulty she was having. Eventually, she overcame the problem by devising a method of quickly reading ahead by one line, correlating all the relevant details and then offering back her own interpretation. It worked very well, so much so that Ella was moved to remark, 'He's never written a letter as good as that before.'

Clearly, for all her exorbitant fees, Mrs Spragget had only ever read them 'as is'.

The rest weren't very much better, but Victoria continued gamely until Ella and Maisie had nothing more to offer.

'You're next, Jen,' Ella called to her.

Up until now, Jen had stayed mainly in the background, preferring to remain apart from the proceedings. 'I didn't get a letter,' she remarked tersely.

'I thought I saw you with one,' Ella frowned, obviously convinced that she had.

'Well, you didn't!' Jen snapped dismissively. 'Anyway, I can't be doing with all this nonsense. I'm going out.' She made as if to leave, then turned sharply, jabbing a pointing finger at Victoria. 'Just because she can read and write and talks fine,' she told the other two angrily, 'it doesn't mean she's any better than us.' With that, she stormed out.

'Take no notice of her,' Ella advised. 'She has her moods. Don't worry, she'll come round.'

Victoria chatted for another ten minutes before excusing herself, saying that she needed a breath of fresh air. Leaving Ella and Maisie to gossip over the contents of their letters, she made her way down into the yard.

It didn't require much perception on Victoria's part to realise that whilst Jen's attitude seemed to indicate that she was wary of strangers, she was especially resentful of those who flaunted their abilities in front of her and bruised her ego by making her admit to her limitations. Clearly, she wasn't someone who gave her trust easily, even under the best of circumstances, but she suspected that once it was earned, she could be the most loyal of friends.

After a few minutes of searching, she found Jen leaning against the wall of a farm building, staring at the pages of a letter, as if trying to decipher the words by a sheer effort of will. She began to wonder if Jen's personality wasn't a lot like her own, her stubborn pride often forcing her into a course of action that was detrimental to her best interests. She was so engrossed with what she was doing that she didn't see Victoria until she was standing in front of her. She flinched back, glaring at her defensively.

'I'm sorry if I startled you,' Victoria offered her most disarming smile. 'I suppose I must have seemed quite brash just now. I mean, coming into your home and bragging about my education,' she began to apologise unnecessarily. 'I didn't mean it to sound that way. I only wanted to help. I still do.'

Jen studied her suspiciously, grasping the sheets of notepaper as if they were gold leaf.

'Letters from loved ones can be such intensely personal things,' Victoria persisted with her olive branch, 'that they're not always something one wants read out in public, even in front of one's friends.'

She hadn't taken any offence over Jen's behaviour. Indeed, she blamed herself to some extent for not having considered the finer feelings of others before making a vulgar display of her talents. She wanted to give Jen a chance to change her mind by pretending that privacy was the only reason that had brought them both out here, and that she still might benefit from her ability.

She glanced around. 'As there are only the two of us here,' she pointed out, 'if you like, I could read that letter for you now.'

Jen hesitated, still uncertain. She glanced at the letter, then back at Victoria. Eventually, her desire to know its contents overcame both her caution and her pride, and finally she handed it over.

By now, the war had become so familiar that it was easy to become detached from the inhumanity of it, and whilst Ella and Maisie had received letters from men they barely knew, the contents of Jen's correspondence was very different.

Victoria began to read slowly. It was far better written than the others she'd had to contend with. It was from Jen's eldest brother, Tom, and was in many ways the very epitome of what England had become. It intimated a story of a large close-knit rural family that had been wrenched apart by war, and of their struggle to remain united in the face of this adversity. With simple sentiments and honest emotions, he spoke of a fierce pride in what they did, edged with a deep concern for those they'd left behind. Of the war and his comrades, he wrote:

'Ours is a just cause. It is a privilege to serve with men such as these, to know such fearless companions. They are the very backbone of England. There is not one of them who would hesitate to lay down his life in defence of his country.'

He told Jen not to worry, because he and her other two brothers, Jack and Arthur, were in good health and high spirits. They looked out for each other, in the certain knowledge that she looked out for everyone at home.

As Victoria continued to read, Jen's defensive posture began to soften. She listened intently, interrupting now and again to clarify some point of family history, and when at last the letter ended...

'Our thoughts are always with you and although we are honoured to fight for our country, we live for the day when, God willing, we shall all be together again.'

The letter, the news of her family, had easily breached Jen's tough exterior, so that now she seemed close to tears. Come to that, so was Victoria. She offered the letter back.

'I'll leave you to your thoughts then,' she suggested, moving away.

'Why is this happening?' Jen asked suddenly. 'Why are they out there, my brothers, your husband?'

Victoria thought about it for a moment. 'Because they're men of honour,' she replied eventually, 'fighting a war created by men without honour.'

Jen seemed to understand implicitly. 'Yes, you're right,' she agreed, carefully folding the letter and slipping it into the pocket of her skirt. 'You didn't get much of a welcome from me back there.' It sounded something like an apology.

'I'll survive,' Victoria assured her.

'What I said about the corset,' Jen went on, 'I wasn't making fun of you. If you want to survive here, get rid of it.' She managed a smile. 'Come on, let's go in. The others will be wondering where we've got to.'

As the evening began to draw in, the four of them shared a simple supper of bread and cheese, then talked for hours exchanging information about themselves until Victoria began to feel as if she'd known them all her life. As the last illusory barriers of class and background melted away, she could hardly believe that she'd lived within this community for the best part of two years without ever really understanding it. Those she'd so recently come to know were young women, just like herself, with all the desires and aspirations she felt. The only difference between them was that they'd been channelled into a life without privilege or opportunity - one of unremitting toil and privation. They were shackled by a lack of education and trapped in an oppressive society whose ingrained prejudice and bigotry only served to exacerbate their situation. Recalling the attitudes she'd encountered when seeking employment, Victoria could relate to that. All it required was the right stimulation and they would flourish.

It was then that she hit upon the idea of teaching them to read and write. Having quickly learned from her previous mistake, she was careful how she phrased the offer, in case it sounded like charity, but she needn't have worried. Although at first they expressed some doubts, that they were too old for such an enterprise, once she'd assured them that age was no barrier, they fell upon the proposition with enthusiasm. Even Maisie, clearly not the brightest among them, appeared keen to take part.

Their bodies may have been bound to the land but their minds were still free, sharp and alert, ready to seize any opportunity if and when it came along. A chance to improve themselves, to gain a portion of independence, their share of freedom had previously only been something to imagine rather than expect. Now that it was actually on offer, they were eager to take full advantage of it. They may have been uneducated but they weren't stupid; even they could recognise the possibilities. Victoria's fortuitous arrival heralded a new era for them.

As their acceptance of her strengthened, their familiarity grew, and it wasn't long before they'd abbreviated – no, decapitated – her name down to Vix or Vixy, whichever way the mood took them. As for herself, Victoria was left in no doubt that their austere existence had in no way dulled their appetite for life; neither had it curbed their capacity for fun.

Their sense of humour was broad and unreservedly earthy. They thought nothing of speaking their minds in the most uninhibited fashion. They'd spent their entire lives in the country and on farms surrounded by the endless cycle of birth, life and death, observing nature in the raw. All the grittier aspects of the human condition, subjects which although undeniably present in Victoria's world she'd been brought up to believe weren't suitable topics of conversation, if indeed she'd been told of them at all, they took for granted.

The spartan nature of their lives, the practicalities of simply surviving, left little room to support most of the taboos of the age.

They were comfortable with their sexuality; they saw no shame in it. Their opinions were uncompromisingly frank, sometimes embarrassingly so, especially when it came to men. Victoria may have thought that she'd completed her education, but she certainly learned a thing or two that night.

Her naivety was a constant source of entertainment for them. The more she blushed, the funnier they found it. In fact, she seemed to amuse them in all sorts of ways. It wasn't just the coarser side of their natures her innocence affected.

It was only when they decided that it was time to retire for the night that Victoria caught her first glimpse of the direction in which her new life was moving.

'But it's barely eight o'clock,' she pointed out, after consulting a small watch she always wore pinned to her blouse.

'You're a farm girl now,' Ella reminded her, 'and we have to be up with the dawn.'

'That's just a country expression, isn't it?' Victoria suggested optimistically. 'You know, a figure of speech?'

'Sorry,' Jen shook her head. 'It's a matter of fact. It's nearly the end of September. The days are short and there's a lot to do. We have to get started before the sun rises. We're lifting potatoes tomorrow.'

'You mean we have to dig them up?' Victoria asked, imagining herself standing there, spade in hand.

Again, peals of laughter echoed around the loft.

'I can see having you here is going to be a lot of fun,' Ella chuckled. 'No. The harrow's already been through. The potatoes are laying on top of the field. All we've to do is pick them up and put them into baskets. Now, take my advice and get your head down; it's an early start.'

As Victoria lay in her bed waiting to fall asleep, she could only wonder at what the future would bring, but whatever it was, she would meet it with a stout heart. She needed this job. She had to prove herself worthy of it. Picking potatoes off the ground and putting them into baskets, how hard could that be?

She was new here, inexperienced in her surroundings and without any real concept of what was expected of her. After tomorrow, all that would have changed.

Chapter Eight

It was hideously early. Victoria found herself shaken awake, and peering bleary eyed through the window opposite, she saw that it was still dark outside, the merest hint of colour on the horizon suggesting that the sun would rise eventually. Everything looked grey and bleak and raw.

The others were already dressed.

'We let you lay in for a while, seeing as how it's your first day,' Ella told her. 'The water's hot. Best get washed and dressed. We have to get down to breakfast.'

She followed their lead without question. She might have been of a higher class and better education, but they had all the experience. She was on unfamiliar territory and they knew their way around.

They filed down the stairs, Victoria feeling half-naked without her corset, out of the hay barn and across the yard to a stable block. One stable, long since emptied of horses, had been furnished with broad trestle tables and benches, most of which were already occupied by an assortment of farm workers. Many of them called out a greeting above the babble of mixed voices. Jen, Ella and Maisie acknowledged them all whilst adding the identity of the newcomer in their midst. It represented Victoria's one and only introduction to the inhabitants of Orchardlea but, surprisingly, after that everyone seemed to know her name.

Breakfast, all twenty minutes of it, comprised of a big bowl of porridge, liberally laced with thick yellow cream and a mug of sweet tea. It was actually very good. Afterwards the company began to disperse, breaking up into smaller groups that moved off independently, each going to attend to their various duties.

Victoria followed the others out of the yard and down a rough track towards the back of the farm. The path was littered with cow pats and, as she attempted to pick her way daintily through them, she noticed that the stuff was everywhere. It was spattered up doors and windows, across walls and water butts, it clogged the verges on either side, and stuck to the soles of her boots like glue. All around her, mountainous manure heaps steamed in the chill autumn air, oozing pools of thick oily black liquid. It was a kingdom of dung.

'In a couple of days, you won't even notice it,' Jen told her, 'and don't you go turning your nose up at it. This is the stuff of life. It goes back on the land, feeds the fields and makes a good harvest.'

As far as Victoria was concerned, it just smelt bad.

Eventually, they came upon a great wooden wagon to which was harnessed Dicken, one of only two heavy horses remaining on the farm, and he'd only escaped requisition because he was too old for war. They all piled into the wagon which took them the two miles out to the potato harvest.

The sun had only just begun to rise, casting a veil of watery light across the land. The field was vast, bigger than anything she'd ever seen before. September rain and constant activity had churned the ground into thick cloying mud.

Gangs of people were already at work scattered across the field in broken lines, gathering the strewn potatoes in wicker baskets which they eventually emptied into a second cart pulled by Bess, Dicken's mare. Taking a basket from the stack, Victoria followed the others out onto the field where they formed their own line and began to pick up potatoes. That was all there was to it; that, and the next nine hours.

The first mistake that Victoria made was to fill her basket right to the top, only to find that she couldn't lift it out of the mud. Then she had to suffer the humiliation of having Jen help her thin it down, just as Mr Moss strode by. He glanced at the proceedings, rolled his eyes, shook his head and walked on. After that, she developed a mild paranoia, fancying that every time she looked up, the foreman was there watching her; not that it was actually happening but it didn't make things any easier. Even half full, the baskets were too heavy for one person. They carried them in pairs and emptied them into the waiting cart. Once the cart was full, it moved off back to the farm to be replaced by the second cart. So it went on, hour after hour.

With only this menial task to occupy her, the monotony became inescapable, and after a while her mind began to wander. Eventually, as she stared endlessly at the featureless ground, the potatoes seemed to take on personalities of their own. Their rough skins and knobbly surfaces appeared to possess human characteristics, so that they became little brown faces that grinned, glared or gaped at her, depending on which way the bumps went. No one else seemed to be affected by this malady. Possibly, years of this drudgery had taught them to close their minds to the tedium. As for herself, Victoria felt that she'd very soon go completely mad. By way of a distraction, she offered to teach the others to spell a few simple words as a prelude to their reading lessons. They were more than happy to join in, and after that the time seemed to pass a little less slowly.

Victoria soon discovered that there were certain fundamental differences when it came to working in the countryside. For example, if you wished to relieve yourself when out in the fields with no toilets for miles, the only place to do so was behind the nearest hedge. It was common practice amongst all the farmhands, male and female alike. It was doubtful that she'd have adopted this method herself had it not been for the inescapable fact that the only alternative would be to stand there and wet herself. She never did fully adjust to the situation. In the summertime, it wasn't so bad; there were only stinging nettles to beware of. But in the winter, when the frost hugged the ground in icy sheets, squatting there with her skirts and petticoats bundled up about her waist and her drawers around her ankles, she felt exposed and vulnerable, which indeed she was whilst the keen winter winds blew sharply and with scant regard for comfort or dignity. It was a singular experience and one which she felt had probably scarred her for life.

After what seemed like an eternity had passed, a shout went up that the replacement cart had brought the midday meal with it. Everyone began to file off the field to where a makeshift canteen was being set up. Everyone, except Victoria; she remained where she was, still bending down.

Realising that she hadn't joined them, the three of them returned, looking puzzled by her behaviour.

'Come on Vix,' Jen urged. 'It's dinner time.'

Victoria waved them down to her level. 'I can't stand up,' she told them in a strained voice.

They thought that was terribly funny too, but after their less than sympathetic response, they set about helping her up.

'Isn't she a scream?' Ella laughed, putting the heel of her hand into the small of Victoria's back.

'I haven't laughed so much for ages,' Jen admitted, taking her by the shoulders and easing her into a standing position.

'Well, I'm glad you're enjoying yourselves,' Victoria winced, as a splinter of excruciating pain shot up her spine.

'It's only a bit of fun,' Jen assured her as she and Maisie dragged her out of the mud, offering support until she could walk by herself again.

Victoria was all for a bit of fun but not when it was always at her expense. She fancied however that until she learned to deal with her new position, that would generally be the case.

When they arrived at the canteen, straw boxes were being unloaded. Some were already open, revealing large cast iron pots, brimming with thick tasty stew, still piping hot from the insulation of the straw. There was fresh baked bread, wedges of tangy cheese, huge lumps of sticky fruitcake and gallons of tea. In a land of rising prices and food shortages, there were at least some advantages to working on a farm.

Victoria was ravenous. 'I didn't realise how hungry I was,' she admitted to the others, 'but if I go on eating like this, I'll end up with a figure like a cow.'

'You get it down yer,' Jen advised seriously. 'You'll soon burn it off. Look at Ella and me.'

'I don't seem to do that,' Maisie remarked through a mouthful of cake.

'Trust you to be different,' Jen shook her head.

'You know that in America, they have machines for doing this job,' Victoria told them.

They all stared at her.

'Let's hope they keep 'em there,' Jen frowned finally, 'or else we'll all be out of work.'

It was then that Victoria understood that even though the work was backbreaking, it was still work. Without it, you didn't get paid, and if you didn't get paid, you starved. It was a part of life she'd never had to consider before.

The midday meal was the only rest break they got. After that, they continued to work until it became too dark to see, at which point Mr Moss called a halt and everyone piled back into the half-filled cart, sitting uncomfortably on top of the potato crop as it carried them back to the farm.

Victoria was only too glad to stop. She was exhausted. Her hands were raw and chapped, she was chilled to the bone and spattered from head to foot with mud; at least, she hoped it was mud. She was also beginning to regret having taught her companions to spell. They'd become so enamoured of their new skills that they'd taken to repeating their particular word incessantly.

There was Jen with 'D.O.G. Dog.'

And Ella with 'C.A.T. Cat.'

Whilst Maisie continued to drone, 'B.O.Y. Boy.'

In her present state, Victoria found it all very irritating. Even as they negotiated the unlit path through the heaps of manure, it didn't vary.

Suddenly Jen stopped short, pointing. 'D.O.G. Dog!' she exclaimed triumphantly, as the creature barked at them.

Not to be outdone, Ella pointed in another direction. 'C.A.T. Cat!' she cried excitedly, as the animal, perched on a nearby window sill, hissed at the dog.

'B.O.Y. Boy,' Maisie joined in.

Jen stared at her. 'That's a woman.'

'I know,' Maisie agreed, 'but I can only spell 'boy' and there ain't one about.'

Victoria had had quite enough. 'Yes, yes, your efforts are most impressive,' she remarked tetchily, 'but it would be just as well not to overdo things.'

Far from taking offence at her manner, they merely accepted it as part of the learning process and did as she suggested. In any event, they shut up.

Once she'd returned to the loft, Victoria pulled off her coat and, letting it fall to the floor, slumped down on the edge of her bed, a position she felt that was unlikely to change until morning, if at all. At this point, she recalled how enthusiastic she'd been about adopting a rural way of life. How often she'd extolled the virtues of the countryside - its quaint little villages, its sprawling farms, its simple rustic inhabitants, the perfect peace and tranquillity of it all. It had come as something of a rude awakening now that she'd discovered just how hard it actually was to eke a living out of it. Somehow, she didn't think she'd ever look at it in quite the same way again.

It had been a punishing nine hours, and now she was beginning to fade. She'd never imagined that it was possible to feel quite so tired. She ached all over. Her entire body was drained to the point where her arms and legs barely answered her commands. Funny as it might have appeared to the others, she was desperately worried about her condition and her ability to continue. This had only been her first day, and yet she was virtually paralysed with fatigue. She couldn't move another inch, whilst her companions, who'd done twice the work she had, still seemed to have energy to spare.

Having boiled up a large quantity of hot water, they each proceeded to strip off in turn and wash themselves from head to foot before dressing again in clean clothes. Victoria found the whole spectacle somewhat disconcerting. Only two people had ever seen her naked in her entire life. One was her mother and the other was Gerald. In the first place, she'd only been a child, and in the second, it had been her wedding night and it had seemed only right and natural. Eventually, she concluded that their uninhibited behaviour had been born of necessity, of large families and small houses, of cramped conditions and a lack of facilities. Nevertheless, that didn't make her feel any better about it.

'Your turn Vixy,' Ella announced, motioning to the freshly filled bowl.

When she didn't move, Jen approached. 'Are you alright?' she asked with an expression of concern. 'I mean, if you're shy, don't worry, we won't look.'

'Come on Vix,' Ella urged. 'We've all got the same things.'

Be that as it may, Victoria didn't see it as an excuse to put what she had on display. Even so, that wasn't the real reason for her reluctance. She was almost at the point of collapse.

'I'm sorry,' she told them, determined not to be seen as a sissy.' 'You're all very considerate. I'm not being awkward, really I'm not. It's just that I'm so tired, I can hardly move. I'll just go to bed now and wash in the morning.'

Suddenly, they were all standing around her, studying her intently. They looked at each other, then back at Victoria.

Finally Ella reached forwards and, grasping one of her wrists, lifted it up. 'Look at them dirty little hands,' she observed.

'Hmm,' Jen nodded thoughtfully. 'That grubby face.'

'If she leaves it long enough,' Maisie chimed in, 'she'll start to stink.'

'I'm not putting up with that,' Jen declared.

Before she realised what was happening, Victoria found herself being conveyed bodily towards the washstand. Too weak to resist, they began to strip off her clothes, indifferent to her protestations, after which they set to work with washcloth and soap.

'It's just like looking after a baby,' Ella grinned.

'Yeh,' Jen agreed. 'I've got five sisters at home, all younger than me. I've washed 'em all at one time or another. This ain't no different.'

They were unconscionably thorough, whilst there was a certain gratuitous roughness about what they did. Victoria had the distinct impression that they were enjoying themselves. After a brisk towelling down with what felt like the coarsest towel they could lay their hands on, her nightdress was rammed over her head with no more reverence than if they were pulling a skin onto a sausage, culminating in her being dumped unceremoniously into her bed, the covers pulled right up under her chin and tucked in so tightly that she was pinned to the mattress.

'Sweet dreams,' Ella gave her a peck on the cheek before joining the others, and they all walked off chortling to themselves.

Too tired to complain, Victoria put it all down to rustic humour whilst making a mental note always to be sure of washing herself, no matter how tired she was.

When she awoke the next morning, Victoria was immediately aware of two things. One, she felt as if she hadn't slept at all, and two, she could hardly move. All the muscles that had ached the day before had now seized up entirely. No matter how hard she tried, no matter how much force she attempted to exert, her limbs would barely respond. It was a disaster.

Eventually she managed to struggle out of bed. The others, already up and about, didn't appear to notice the difficulty she was having.

'Better get a move on, Vix,' Jen warned. 'We have to get down for breakfast.'

'You go ahead,' Victoria flashed them a brave smile. 'I don't feel like any breakfast.'

'Are you sure?' Ella asked. 'You missed supper last night.'

'Oh yes, quite sure,' Victoria attempted to sound nonchalant. 'You go on; I'll meet you down there.'

They didn't question her motives any further but only nodded their agreement before leaving.

It took Victoria all of her time just to dress. It was a supreme effort, the stiffness of her joints impeding every move she made. Her actions were like those of an automaton, rigid and ungainly. She tried desperately to hurry, constantly worried as to how she'd appear to the others.

She managed to reach the cart with only minutes to spare, expecting to hear some comment about her tardiness, but none came. As the cart moved off, the others chatted happily between themselves, apparently unaware that she'd fallen silent, preoccupied as she was with her predicament. Once they'd arrived, Victoria managed to alight, collect a basket, go out onto the field and bend down. That was all. It was over. She knew then that she could go no further. It was with a rush of intense disappointment that she finally had to concede defeat. Now all that remained was to stand up and walk away.

Before she could do anything, Jen and Ella glided up on either side of her with Maisie bringing up the rear. They didn't speak, they didn't look at her, but as she watched, every second potato they lifted went into her basket. All she had to do was move along with them. As the basket filled, the three of them would take it in turns to convey it to the wagon, whilst whichever of them was left would stay by her to shield her from the foreman's scrutiny. At noon, they bunched around her and assisted her off the field.

In all that time, none of them had spoken; there'd been no attempt at mischief and not one word of criticism. They may have been a rough and ready bunch but they knew the value of discretion. Victoria was overcome with emotion. She'd never known such fellowship, and even when she tried to express her gratitude, they wouldn't hear of it.

Jen merely winked and said, 'D.O.G. Dog.'

Ella put a comforting arm around her shoulders. 'C.A.T. Cat,' she smiled.

Maisie swallowed a large lump of bread she'd been noisily chewing and opened her mouth to speak.

'You can be quiet,' Jen told her.

By the end of the afternoon, Victoria had managed to regain some of her mobility and she felt better for that, but the others stayed in attendance, as they would every day from now on until her body became accustomed to its new way of life.

Ultimately, Victoria's future here would be decided not by a matter of brute strength but by an effort of pure will. Even with the assistance of her friends, she faced a Herculean challenge. She'd not been born to a life on the land; neither had she been given the chance to acclimatise to the conditions gradually. The work was gruelling and the hours were long. She barely had time to recover from the effects of one day's toil before another began. Unable to gain any advantage over the situation, she existed in a state of constant exhaustion that not only drained her body but sapped her spirit, undermining her natural inclination to fend for herself, and robbing her of that vital spark of determination that might have seen her through.

As the weeks passed, failing to recognise the problem for what it was, she came to rely more and more heavily on the support of her friends until, unwittingly, she'd become dependent upon it. Deprived of the energy and willpower to save herself, she was gradually slipping beyond their ability to help her. Eventually, even the combined efforts of her erstwhile companions to protect her from dismissal might have been in vain, had it not been for the letter...

It was late one Wednesday afternoon, a few weeks before Christmas, when Maisie came shrieking up the stairs as though the devil himself were in pursuit. The reason for her excitement very soon became clear. Amongst the letters she'd been sent to collect from the farmhouse was one for Victoria. Yes, Victoria, she who read all their letters for them, but never, ever, received any herself. Now, apparently, that had changed.

'Is it from him?' Maisie panted, red-faced and breathless. 'Is it from Gerald?'

'Is it? Is it?' they all chorused, crowding excitedly around her.

Victoria immediately saw that it wasn't. 'I'm afraid not,' she told them. 'I doubt that Gerald would use a pink envelope. Besides,' she continued, glancing at the address, 'this is a woman's handwriting, and it's postmarked Kensington.'

They all seemed to be a good deal more disappointed than she was. Nevertheless, it was with a growing sense of curiosity that she opened the envelope and unfolded a large sheet of pink notepaper.

Her three friends waited in expectant silence as Victoria began to read the brief note. It was always her habit to read a few lines first, just to become acquainted with the message before reading it out loud. Only on this occasion she read the entire letter in silence and when she'd finished, she screwed it into a tight ball and let it fall to the floor.

Howls of dismay broke from her companions.

'Don't do that,' Jen stooped for the ball of paper. 'It's your letter.'

'Leave it alone.' Victoria's expression and tone was such that they fell back, perplexed and worried.

'What is it, Vix?' Ella asked at length. 'What was in that letter?'

'What's happened?' Jen frowned. 'What did it say?'

Victoria considered it remarkable that she felt nothing at all, no emotion whatsoever, just empty and cold. 'It was from Mrs Agnes Whittacker,' she told them eventually. 'She's the mother of an old friend of mine, Beryl. Beryl was a suffragette.'

'Good for her,' Jen applauded.

'Beryl was sentenced to six months in prison,' Victoria went on tonelessly, recalling what she'd read, 'for biting a policeman. She immediately went on hunger strike and was released after only three weeks under something called 'The Temporary Discharge for Health Act'. According to Mrs Whittacker, it's a common practice with suffragettes who starve themselves. Once she'd recovered, she'd have had to return to complete her sentence. However, even though she was weak and ill, instead of going home Beryl went straight to another demonstration. When the police attempted to disperse the crowd, she was pushed into the road and run over by a motorbus. Apparently there was nothing anyone could do. She was dead before she reached the hospital. They buried her six weeks ago. It was only when her parents went through her effects that they discovered my address. See the envelope here? It's been redirected from the cottage. That's probably what caused the delay.'

The others looked on in stunned silence.

Victoria didn't cry. She didn't become angry. She just sat there until finally she said to them, 'If you wouldn't mind, I'd like to be on my own for a while.'

In deference to her wishes, they all withdrew to their own spaces and remained there. After that, Victoria didn't speak again. She mourned in silence. She didn't speak the next morning, or all through breakfast. Neither did she speak when she went out onto the potato field. She knew the others were watching her, not knowing what to say or do, but she ignored them.

All that she could think of was that Beryl had died in pursuit of her beliefs – equal rights for women everywhere – whilst all she'd managed was to labour like a beast of burden in a wretched potato field and with precious little success at that. At last, she realised that she'd achieved nothing here, and never would in her present state of mind. Beryl's sacrifice had opened her eyes and stirred her from her apathy. In that moment, all the grief she'd managed to suppress, all the pain and the anguish she'd endeavoured to contain suddenly burst forth in a bitter torrent, coursing through her veins like fire, rekindling her spirit. The anger and frustration she felt endowed her with a new-found strength. It was then that she changed, took charge of herself and reversed her fortunes.

Standing up, she surprised them all by hefting half a basket of potatoes onto her hip and carrying it, alone, to the waiting wagon. The effort almost killed her but as she marched triumphantly back onto the field, to the uproarious cheers of her companions, even the foreman was unable to resist of grin of admiration.

Reunited with her friends, she spoke for the first time in eighteen hours. 'Nothing is impossible for those who try,' she told them.

Beryl would have been proud. After that, she never looked back.

The foreman, Mr Moss, must have been impressed with her demonstration because shortly after that Mrs Fisher asked her to begin helping with the accounts. Obviously, the wily old bird had waited to see if Victoria could cope with the manual labour before engaging her on the lighter clerical duties. Victoria was happy to oblige. She saw it as an opportunity to consolidate her position. Besides, the occasional afternoon in the farmhouse came as a welcome interlude from the daily grind, even though she had to endure constant teasing from her friends, who dubbed her 'the boss's pet'.

As she began to feel less and less inclined to go straight to bed after coming in from the fields, Victoria decided to dispense with the petty spelling game, and introduced proper reading lessons as she'd promised. She felt that she owed the three of them a huge debt of gratitude. They'd protected her in a time of crisis. Without their help, she wouldn't have survived her first few weeks at Orchardlea. It was only their initial intervention that had made it possible for her to remain here in the first place. Because of that, she was determined that they would receive the best she could offer. She arranged a programme that not only included reading and writing, but simple mathematics as well. It would mean a lot of work for all of them, but it would help to while away the long winter evenings, now that she wasn't sleeping through them all.

A lack of space in her luggage had meant that she'd been unable to bring any books with her. Instead, she'd hoped to obtain some newspapers to use as a teaching aid. Buying new ones was completely out of the question; it was simply an extravagance none of them could afford. Old ones would do just as well, not only for the others to read from but also for her own use. Since her arrival here, she'd been starved for news of the war, subsisting only on rumour and hearsay and the little she gleaned from her companions' letters. It was a most unsatisfactory state of affairs and one she fully intended to change as soon as the opportunity presented itself. Unfortunately, the others were quick to inform her that newspapers were scarce around the farm. The people here, mostly being unable to read, had little use for them, whilst the few that did occasionally turn up were usually consigned to the earth closet. Nevertheless, now that they all had a vested interest, they promised to see what they could scrounge.

The potato harvest came to an end just as Victoria was finally getting used to the work. Even though she felt as if she'd been cheated, she didn't care if she ever saw another potato again. No sooner, it seemed, had she surmounted one obstacle than she found herself facing a new challenge.

Apparently, the four of them had been reassigned to milking. Judging from her friends' reactions, Victoria concluded that as far as farming went, this was a choice job. According to them, there was no heavy lifting, lots of sitting down, it was indoors and always warm. Early the next morning, equipped with a bucket and stool, she joined the others in the cowshed.

Along the entire length of the narrow building, two rows of cattle had been tethered so that their hindquarters faced outwards on each side of the central walkway. Steam rose in hazy tendrils from the backs of the waiting animals, filling the humid air with the pungent smell of fresh grass as the rumble of their lowing rose and fell, vibrating in the sultry atmosphere.

'You can start with this one,' Jen pointed.

Victoria found herself confronted by a huge black and white creature that turned its head lethargically as she approached to regard her with large liquid brown eyes.

She took a step back. 'It's rather large.'

'It's a cow,' Jen told her. 'They're always large.'

It wasn't as if Victoria had never seen a cow before. She'd seen hundreds, but they'd all been in fields and some distance away. Having one this close was a very different matter.

'There's no need to be frightened,' Jen assured her. 'This is Maude. She's as gentle as a lamb. You've still got soft hands; she'll appreciate that.'

The three of them gathered round, offering advice and encouragement, as Victoria made her first attempt at milking.

'Tuck yourself well in,' Ella advised. 'That's it. Now take a teat in each hand, then squeeze and pull down gently at the same time.'

Victoria did as she was told and immediately Maude flicked out her hind leg and sent her sprawling flat on her back. Of course, it was hilarious; everyone seemed to think so, except Victoria.

'I thought you said she was gentle?' she reminded them indignantly, scrambling to her feet.

'She is,' Jen confirmed.

'But she kicked!'

'So would you, if someone grabbed your tits that way. Try again.'

It took a little persuading to get her to go near the animal again, but finally she was tucked back into its flank. Putting her hands over Victoria's, Jen demonstrated the correct method to her until finally she got the rhythm right, after which both she and Maude seemed reasonably content, allowing the others to deal with their own animals. She found that her newly acquired skills worked just as well on other cows as they had on Maude and she was able to work her way along the line, keeping pace with the others.

Victoria discovered that there was something wonderfully therapeutic about milking. It was slow and peaceful and she felt herself being lulled into a sense of complete calm, until a jet of warm milk struck her on the cheek. Inevitably, there was the usual horseplay and from time to time, Victoria found herself being squirted from one direction or another as Ella or Jen handled a well-aimed teat.

'Very good for the complexion, cow's milk,' Jen called out before squirting her once again.

Finding a task that she'd been able to master so quickly did wonders for Victoria's confidence. She gained a real sense of satisfaction from what she'd achieved, even though by the end of the session, thanks to Ella and Jen, she felt that more milk had gone down her neck than into the buckets.

It would all be over by Christmas. That's was they'd said in 1914. Now more than a year had passed and still the war hadn't ended. Neither was there any indication that it might do so in the foreseeable future. As the festive season approached, it was overshadowed by a pervading sense of uncertainty and apprehension. It touched every soul in the land, coloured every aspect of their lives, and affected everything they did. By now, everyone knew someone who'd been killed or injured, and it was not so much with joyous hearts as with minds chastened by the knowledge that they now faced an indeterminately long war that the population prepared to welcome the yuletide in.

It was to be a Christmas of lost friends, dead husbands, sons and brothers - a time to reflect, to remember, a time to pray.

There was still no word from Gerald, no word from anyone. Since that dreadful message from Beryl's mother, Victoria had received no letters at all. All her friends had; Jen, Ella and Maisie; she'd read them all. It put her in mind of the previous Christmas when Gerald had written to tell her that he couldn't come home on leave, and how poorly she'd reacted to it. Now she'd have given anything to have a letter like that, some sign that he was still out there and thinking of her.

Christmas Day at Orchardlea began much the same as any other day. The land could be left to fend for itself, but not the animals. There was stock to be fed and watered and cows to be driven in for milking. Once Victoria and the others had finished the milking and scrubbed down the byre, they dressed in their best and joined the rest of the farm workers in the waiting carts that took them into Staunton Gifford and on to the parish church.

Sitting in the pew, surrounded by all those saints and angels, almost all of Victoria's prayers were for Gerald. She kept back only three. One was for Beryl and the other was for Alan. The third she shared with the rest of the congregation, who put their hands together and asked God to end the war and brings the boys back home.

In the afternoon, she exchanged gifts with her friends - simple things, handmade mostly, but somehow all the more precious for that.

For the rest of the day, they'd been recruited with so many others to prepare the great barn for the evening celebrations. At six o'clock, as did every man and woman there, they put on their brightest clothes, put their sorrows and fears behind them and went to join the party.

Inside the barn, the sheaves had been arranged to form a large circular arena, illuminated by dozens of oil lamps. The eaves were strewn with gaily coloured paper streamers and boughs of holly, fresh cut, had been nailed to the beams.

There was food a-plenty. Trestles groaned under the weight of the feast. There was a whole roast pig, ribs of beef, assorted fowl, rounds of cheese and crusty bread, cold ham, pickles and cider brewed on the farm. Victoria had tasted cider before but nothing like this. It was strong and golden and bitter. The face she pulled as it went down made the others laugh. One mug wasn't enough and two was too many. Forgetting all the lessons she'd learned about alcohol, she was soon quite tipsy, but it didn't matter; everyone was. They ate too much and drank too much and no one cared. They'd endured a year of unremitting toil and now they celebrated with a vengeance.

There were party games to join in - hunt the favour, blind man's bluff and robin-in-the-middle. Bunches of mistletoe had been hung everywhere and it became a game in itself trying to avoid the inebriated attentions of lusty farmhands who prowled about, ready to steal a kiss from any hapless female who happened to stray beneath one, either by chance – or design.

There was also a makeshift band - a man with a fiddle, one with a flute, another with a drum, whilst a woman played an accordion. They didn't look like much but once they began to play, not a foot was idle. They were country tunes and country dances where everyone held hands and pranced around in a circle, turned about, clapped, held hands again and circled once more. There were jigs and reels, even waltzes were not beyond their repertoire, and when one reveller fell out exhausted there was always another to take their place. The merriment continued late into the night, but in the morning it was business as usual.

As 1916 dawned, it found that a new Victoria had emerged. Fit and healthy, a stronger and more capable woman, ready and able to deal with whatever her circumstances might demand of her.

It wasn't only Victoria who had begun to improve. Jen, Ella and Maisie had taken to their lessons like scholars born. Their voracious appetite for knowledge was insatiable. Their minds were like sponges that soaked up information. Even Maisie, whose mind was not quite so sponge-like, plodded along and with a little extra coaching managed to keep up.

The absence of books had always been a drawback, and as winter turned to spring their rapacious demand for newspapers with which to fuel their education became so great that foraging for them became something of an obsession with them all. It seemed they'd go to any lengths to find them and it was surprising what they could come up with once they put their minds to it.

Sometimes it was only a single page or two, months out of date. Occasionally, it was a crumpled wad that had been used for packing. Often a whole paper was brought in and more rarely, one only a few days old. For a while, Maisie seemed to have come across a regular source. Every day, she brought in neatly torn squares, sometimes as many as twenty at once. It was all well and good until a rumour began to circulate around the farm that someone was taking all the paper from the earth closet and no one could understand why. Not only was it extremely perplexing, it was also downright inconvenient. Fortunately, it was a mystery that would forever remain unsolved.

The papers they found served a dual purpose for them all. Whilst the others learned to read and write, Victoria was once again able to keep abreast of the war. Even though it was still little more than propaganda, there were some items worthy of note.

'What does 'conscription' mean?' Maisie asked, after Victoria had read a paragraph off one of her squares.

'It means that the government aren't waiting for men to volunteer anymore,' Victoria replied gravely. 'They're going to force them to fight whether they want to or not.'

'I've never heard the like,' Jen remarked. 'What does it mean?'

'Yes,' Ella joined in. 'What does it mean? Haven't they enough volunteers?'

'Apparently not,' Victoria sighed.

'But there must be millions of 'em by now,' Ella insisted.

'Not if they're all dead,' Jen pointed out grimly.

'Don't talk daft,' Ella began to argue. 'How can you kill a million men?'

'Jen could be right,' Victoria interceded. 'Perhaps our losses are higher than they're willing to admit. It looks as though things are getting worse.'

'What if the Germans win?' Maisie began to panic. 'They'll invade for sure. What'll we do then?'

Jen took it upon herself to sum up their options. Her martial attitude left no room for doubt or compromise. 'Go down to the yard,' she growled, 'pick up a pitchfork, put your back against the wall and prepare to sell your life dear.'

It was a harrowing thought and a real possibility. The outcome of this war was by no means as certain as it had once been. Rumours proliferated describing the awful atrocities the Germans would commit if they occupied the country, including their intention to put every first born male child to death. Hopefully, what Jen suggested would come as a last resort. Nevertheless, the very idea of Germans standing on English soil, walking through English towns and murdering helpless children was enough to unite them in total agreement. If the Germans wanted England, they'd have to take it in blood – theirs – if need be.

It was a sunny afternoon in late March, one of those occasions when Mrs Fisher had asked Victoria to take over the accounts. She'd only just completed the work before her employer returned to the kitchen.

'Finished already?' She observed the neatly stacked piles of paper, admiring the order Victoria had created out of the chaos she'd found. 'I've been talking to Mr Moss about you. He says you ain't the best he's seen.'

Victoria tensed, her throat went dry and she could feel her heart beginning to pound inside her chest.

Mrs Fisher let her dangle for a moment. 'But you'll do,' she finished with a grin.

Victoria heaved a sigh of relief. Now that she'd become used to life at Orchardlea, it would have been a wrench to leave.

'You done well,' Mrs Fisher told her. 'Better than I thought. Then there's the accounts. You could have spun that job out, made heavy weather of it, but you didn't. I like that. You're an honest girl. I like that too.'

'Thank you,' Victoria smiled. It was praise indeed coming from someone who'd once thought she wouldn't last a week, not that she'd any intention of telling her how close she'd come to being right.

'Seein' as how you ain't a beginner no more,' Mrs Fisher went on, 'I'm going to raise your wages to fifteen shillings a week. Don't let it go to your head mind, you still got plenty to learn.' She picked up a large wicker trug from a nearby shelf. 'Seein' as you're finished here, we got some hens laying adrift in the big barn. Take this basket and go and see what you can find.'

Still glowing over her permanent acceptance into the Orchardlea community, Victoria stood in the great barn, listening to all the scratching and scurrying of the rats and mice in the straw underfoot. She'd always found it unnerving, but not so much now as when she'd first arrived. Looping the handle of the basket over her left arm, she bunched the edge of her skirt in her left hand, drawing the hem closer around her ankles to prevent any verminous intrusion, before proceeding to search among the piled sheaves.

She'd been doing this for some time, finding the odd egg here, a nest full there, before she became aware of voices outside. Ever curious, she moved quietly to the barn door and peered through a gap in the boards.

Mrs Fisher was standing in the yard, confronted by two soldiers wearing the armbands of the military police. She watched and waited, hoping for a chance, when Mrs Fisher had gone, to talk to the men. It was an old habit she'd never managed to break. These days, with valid news of the war ever more scarce, she didn't intend to miss a chance for information.

At last, Mrs Fisher walked away. Victoria had her hand on the barn door ready to pull it open when, suddenly, from behind her an arm closed about her waist and a hand clamped roughly over her mouth.

'Don't scream,' a voice, thick with accent, rasped in her ear, 'I won't hurt you.'

Chapter Nine

It all happened so quickly that Victoria was taken completely by surprise. She was petrified. Having caught a trace of accent she wondered if, unbeknown to her, the dreaded invasion had already taken place and now she was about to become a victim of German atrocity.

'If you promise not to scream, I'll take my hand away,' the voice hissed again.

Under the circumstances, she felt she had no alternative but to accept the condition. She nodded her head in agreement and once she'd been released, she turned to face her assailant.

She found herself confronted by a young man, no more than a youth, who appeared to be every bit as nervous as she was. He was dressed in the remnants of a British army uniform; just the boots, the trousers and the shirt, the latter of which had been wrenched open at some time, tearing off all the buttons. His clothes were crumpled and spattered with mud. His face, arms and hands were equally dirty as well as being scratched and bloody. His dark hair was matted and filthy, whilst a large purple bruise swelled his right cheek just under the eye. It looked as though he'd been living rough for some time.

'What's the meaning of this?' she demanded, now more indignant than afraid. 'What are you doing here?'

He pointed past her. 'Hiding from them.'

She glanced over her shoulder to see that the two military

policemen were still standing in the yard. From the way they gestured and nodded to each other, she gathered that they were preparing to make a search.

'Why are they looking for you?' she asked.

'I've run away from the army,' he told her, his Scots accent now clearly discernible. 'I'm a deserter.'

'Oh.' Victoria retreated a little, wondering if he might be dangerous after all. He certainly looked pretty desperate. Now she was in two minds as to whether or not she should stay still, or try to make a run for it. 'What will they do if they catch you?' she asked, hoping to ascertain just how desperate he was and how much of a threat he posed to her.

'They'll shoot me,' he replied with conviction, still keeping an eye on the men outside.

'Then wouldn't it be better to give yourself up?' she suggested; her assumption being that surrender might offer some form of clemency.

He seemed to find some humour in her remark, the swelling on his cheek making his grin lopsided. 'Not really. You see, they'll still shoot me.'

'But surely you're entitled to a fair trial?' she continued to reason with him.

Again the grin was lopsided. 'Oh aye. No doubt they'll conduct it under rule 303.' As he spoke he made a mime with his hands, as if pulling back the bolt of a rifle, loading a 303 cartridge and closing the breech. 'They like to make an example of deserters.' Suddenly, he flinched back. 'One of them's coming this way!'

Glancing over her shoulder again, she saw that whilst one of the men had gone off in the opposite direction, the other was heading straight for the barn. Victoria had to think quickly. The deserter was plainly terrified. She felt herself to be in no danger from him, whilst the real threat approached from outside, rifle in hand.

Setting aside any thought of her own safety, she stepped forward and, putting her hand against the young Scot's chest, she shoved him back. 'Quickly,' she ordered, pointing to a large pile of straw, 'get under that.' With only seconds to spare, she heaped the straw over him until he was completely concealed, then stood up, basket in hand, as though still innocently searching for eggs.

As the barn door banged open she turned, feigning surprise. 'My goodness,' she cried, clasping a hand to her breast.

'Sorry, Miss,' the soldier paused, glancing around, 'didn't mean to startle you.'

'Oh, one of our brave boys! How nice.' She advanced, fluttering her eyelashes girlishly, trying to make herself as much of a distraction to him as possible.

The man responded instantly. Pulling his shoulders back, he snapped off a salute. 'Happy to be of service, Ma'am,' he smiled. 'May I ask how long you've been in here?'

'Oh, I've been here for hours,' she lied blatantly. 'Why? Is there anything wrong?'

The soldier moved further into the barn and began to poke around in the corners with the muzzle of his rifle. 'We're looking for a man seen heading in this direction earlier,' he told her, continuing to search. 'Dark haired, scruffy looking. He's a jock, eh... a Scotsman.' He moved towards the piled sheaves. 'Have you seen anyone like that recently? Any strangers hanging around the farm buildings?'

'No, I haven't.' Victoria went up to him and put her hand on his arm. 'Oh dear, is he dangerous?' she asked, wide-eyed.

The soldier stopped searching and patted her hand reassuringly. 'No, Miss, nothing for you to worry about. This one's a bloody coward, pardon my French, a deserter. He left his mates and his regiment and scarpered, but never fear, he won't get far. We'll catch him.'

'And what will you do with him then?' Victoria asked casually.

'We'll execute him, Miss,' the soldier was adamant. 'We'll put him up against a wall and shoot him. That's the only way to deal with cowards.'

Victoria realised that the young Scot had been telling her the truth and even though it was a British soldier that stood before her, she found his presence faintly disturbing. For a moment, it appeared as if he was about to resume his search.

'I feel so much safer knowing that someone like you is about,' she flirted shamelessly, appealing directly to his vanity. Her ploy worked perfectly. The man was completely susceptible to her flattery.

His chest swelled. 'Never fear, Miss,' he told her masterfully, 'you're safe with us.' He slung his rifle on his shoulder and prepared to leave. 'If you do see any strangers, tell Mrs Fisher. She'll send a boy for us. There'll be a patrol in the lanes for the next few days.' He saluted again and left in time to meet his partner coming back from the other direction. After a moment's consultation and some shaking of heads, they walked off out of sight.

'He's gone,' Victoria announced in a low voice.

He began to emerge, glancing furtively about.

'Who are you?' she asked, once he'd clambered out from under the straw.

'My name is Alistaire,' he replied, brushing himself down. 'Alistaire McInnis, late of His Majesty's Armed Forces. And you are?'

'Victoria Avery.'

'Thank you, Miss Avery, for not giving me up.'

'It's Mrs Avery,' she corrected him. 'What will you do now?'

'I'll make my way to Inverness,' he told her. 'My uncle has a farm there. He'll hide me.'

'But that's hundreds of miles away!' she exclaimed. 'How on earth do you intend to get there?'

He seemed unconcerned by the distance. 'I'll travel by night, hide by day, maybe jump a goods train. Aye, I'll be fine. But I'm done in now,' he confessed. 'I've been on the go for days. I need to rest and something to eat.'

Victoria looked around. 'Well, you can't stay in the middle of the barn. Anyone might walk in. Come with me.'

As she made to move, he put his hand against her arm and stopped her. 'Do you have any idea what will happen to you if they catch you helping me?' he asked ominously.

Victoria looked him straight in the eye. 'Actually, no, I don't,' she told him flatly, although she could guess from his tone that it wasn't likely to stop at a slap on the wrist. 'But I don't intend to stand by and let them shoot you out of hand. The Germans have done enough of that already.'

She led him towards the back of the barn where the sheaves were piled highest. Behind them in one corner was a heap of empty wooden packing crates. Victoria had come across them whilst searching for eggs. By the look of them, they'd been there for years and were long forgotten. It took them barely twenty minutes to construct a makeshift shelter and once it had been covered with straw, it was indistinguishable from the rest of the stack. Then they returned to the centre of the barn, just to make sure that the hiding place remained invisible from that angle as well.

'I'll come back tonight,' Victoria told him, 'when it gets dark. I'll try and bring some food.'

'We'll need a signal,' he pointed out, 'just so I'll know it's you. I have it... whistle three times.'

'I don't think I can whistle,' Victoria frowned. She tried in any case, just to be sure. Her feeble attempt at blowing through her lips was enough to convince him that she was right.

Looking around, he stooped and picked up a rusty trowel. 'Use this,' he suggested. 'Tap this beam three times and then I'll know it's you.'

Victoria spent the rest of the day on tenterhooks, expecting to hear the alarm raised at any moment, but nothing happened. When the day's work was over and supper was finished, she set Jen, Ella and Maisie a spelling task that would take them a good hour to complete. It was something she knew they could get on with by themselves. Then she complained of a mild headache and told them she'd try walking it off in the yard.

Slipping out into the darkness, she crept stealthily over to the farmhouse. It was never locked and people were used to seeing her go in and out. Nevertheless, Mrs Fisher was bound to be somewhere in the building and if she was caught taking food, she'd have some explaining to do.

Fortunately for her, her pilfering went undetected, and with the provisions in her possession, she made her way back to the barn. She couldn't possibly risk showing a light, and after a few minutes of scrabbling about in the gloom and vermin-infested straw, she found the trowel. Tapping three times, she was answered by a loud rustling, then Alistaire appeared.

'Mother of God,' he swore, falling on the food like a starving animal, stuffing large chunks of bread and cheese into his mouth and gulping long draughts from the bottle of water she'd brought.

As he continued to eat, she told him something of herself and about Gerald. It wasn't mere conversation; she had her reasons for doing so.

Taking a last swig from the bottle, he pulled his arm roughly across his mouth and eyed her warily. 'I suppose I must disgust you,' he guessed, 'what with your husband missing in France, me being a deserter and all those brave men dying in my place.'

'I don't have the right to judge you,' she replied honestly. 'But tell me, why did you run away?'

He shook his head, as if the memories she'd asked him to recall were all painful ones. 'I had a kind of breakdown,' he explained, as if he didn't quite understand it all himself. 'Oh yes, I was out there, in France, at the Western Front, and what I saw there made me lose my mind. So they sent me back home to hospital, and when I'd recovered they told me that they were going to send me back. Apparently, it's Field Marshall Haig's personal order. 'We shall fight to the last man...' I couldna' stand the thought of it, so I cut and ran.'

'Is that all?' Victoria recalled the vengeful attitude of the military policeman. 'Is that really all you did?'

'Oh aye,' he confirmed. 'You see, I had no physical injury, no obvious wounds. That made me fit for service. You know, the French call it shellshock. Even those German bastards call it shellshock, but the English call it cowardice, and if you run, they shoot you. Are you aware,' he continued, 'that when they catch a spy, I mean someone who's deliberately trying to harm the country, they put them in front of a firing squad?'

'Er, yes, I've heard something of the sort,' Victoria confirmed.

'Well, it seems I'm no better than that,' he concluded. 'Once I was a hero. Now I'm an enemy of the state.'

Gradually, Victoria's eyes had become accustomed to the darkness and now that Alistaire had finished eating and drinking, she used the last of the water to wash the cuts on his face and hands, finally applying some salve she'd brought with her.

'You're a good woman,' he thanked her.

'Sometimes I think I'm a very stupid woman,' she told him.

'Why, because you're helping me?'

'No, because I let my husband go to war in the first place.'

'Could you have stopped him, back then?'

'No, probably not, but I certainly could now.'

'That's why you're doing this, isn't it?' he deduced. 'You hope that if your husband's out there, someone might be helping him.'

'Perhaps,' she answered noncommittally, 'but as I'm helping you, you can do something for me in return.'

'What's that?'

'Tell me the truth about the war. Tell me what you saw at the front.'

'For God's sake, woman,' he gasped, 'why would you want to know such a thing?'

'I want to know what he saw,' Victoria explained. 'I want to know what Gerald's going through. Not a single soldier I've asked would tell me, past vague propaganda. So I'm not going to ask you. I'm demanding that you tell me.'

She could hear him sigh in the darkness. 'Do you go to church?'

'Yes, of course.'

'And read the Bible?'

'Certainly.'

'Then you must have an impression of hell.'

Victoria used her imagination and brought to mind the awful vision of purgatory - the flames, the smell of sulphur, the terrible wailing of the damned. 'Yes,' she answered at length.

'If you're ever offered the choice between going to hell or to the front,' he told her, 'choose hell.'

'That isn't what I asked,' Victoria objected. 'Tell me what I want to know.'

'When you look out on this farm,' he began, realising that she wasn't going to be put off, 'you see rolling hills, green fields, trees and woods. It was like that in France once. Now it's in ruins. In some places, it's all gone, completely erased by artillery fire. The ground's been bombarded over and over again, until there's no point of reference anywhere. Not a tree, not a fence, not a road; just acres of stinking mud and duckboards to walk on. Everywhere there are shell craters filled with stagnant water, black with blood, and the bloated carcases of men and horses floating in them.' He paused only to lick his dry lips. 'I was in Belgium at Ypres in 1914. We lost fifty thousand men there. The year after that, it was Loos in France. The

Germans fired phosgene gas at us. It looks just like cigarette smoke floating on the air, but in twenty four hours, those that inhaled it began to vomit. Then their lungs filled with a thick yellow liquid and they just died where they stood.'

He was getting into his stride now, as a tide of painful memories of the sights that had crippled his mind came flooding back. 'I've seen men take shelter in a shell crater only to have an artillery shell explode next to it, burying them alive. You wouldn't even know they'd been there. I've seen men drown in pools of liquid mud that were strong enough to drag a horse down. There are corpses everywhere. Layer upon layer of mangled bodies, and each new barrage sends showers of rotted flesh and loose entrails up into the air. The stench of it never leaves your nostrils. And there are rats, thousands of them, feeding on the dead and the living. Men with their arms and legs blown off, eaten up with gangrene, too weak to move. The sound of gunfire never stops; neither do the screams of dying men. Those that aren't killed by a bullet can fall prey to disease; trench fever, foot rot, dysentery. They say it'll be the war to end all wars. Aye, they're right enough. There'll be no one left to fight another war.'

When he stopped speaking, the silence was deafening.

Victoria felt slightly sick. 'I've never imagined it could be anything like that,' she admitted, swallowing hard.

'I don't think any sane person could imagine such a thing,' he told her. 'You'd have to see it to believe it, and even then, you wouldna' believe it.'

'Do you know if we're winning?' she asked.

'I couldna' tell you,' he admitted. 'I don't believe the generals know themselves. I think it'll just be a matter of who runs out of men first.'

At last, she'd heard the truth she'd sought for so long, but now that she had, she wished she'd never asked.

She'd always rejected the popular conception that this war was some sort of splendid spree. A duel between gentlemen, conducted to a strict code of ethics, suspecting that it was purely propaganda or merely wishful thinking. Nevertheless, the scenes of brutal horror he'd described were staggering. They soared beyond the very worst she'd ever dared to contemplate. To think that Gerald was involved in that almost robbed her of her sanity. 'I have to get back,' she said at last. 'I'll come again tomorrow night.'

'Aye, that'll do fine,' he agreed. 'I'll rest during the day and be on my way after you've been. I canna' afford to linger in one place for too long.'

Subdued by what Alistaire had told her, Victoria spent the whole of the next day preoccupied with the situation. Every time she heard someone shout, her heart was in her mouth. She was glad that the days were still short and the nights came early. She didn't think she could endure the stress much longer.

Setting her friends another long learning exercise, she complained of yet another headache and excused herself again. Sneaking into the farm kitchen, she gathered enough food for one more meal and stuffed an old canvas bag she'd found with as much as she could. On her way back to the barn, she stopped off at a utility shed used to store old clothes and linen. Nothing was wasted on the farm, and these items generally went to make cleaning cloths. The garments were rough and ragged, but at least they were clean and civilian in appearance.

Alistaire seemed to be much improved. 'You've thought of everything,' he observed, as she presented him with the clothes. 'Perhaps they should put you in charge of the war. I reckon you'd make a better job of it than they have.'

Once he'd eaten the evening meal, he changed into the clothes Victoria had brought.

'I didn't realise they'd be quite so tattered,' she remarked critically. 'I should have known. No one here throws anything decent away.'

'No, they'll be fine,' Alistaire assured her. 'I'll let my hair and beard grow. With any luck, folks will think I'm just some old tramp and let me be.'

Together they dismantled the camp and put the crates back the way they'd been before so that no one would know anyone had ever been there. Finally, dressed in what he'd begun to call his 'disguise' and with the bag of food on his shoulder, the time had come for him to leave.

'Inverness seems so very far away,' Victoria fretted, 'and there are so many looking for you.'

'Aye, well, there it is,' he acknowledged stoically, 'but I found a friend in you and that will take me a lot further than I might have managed on my own.'

It was then that she offered him the few shillings she'd managed to scrape together from her meagre wages.

'On no, lass,' he sighed. 'I thank you for the food, but I canna' take your money.'

'Don't be ridiculous!' Victoria insisted. 'I can manage without it and you may be on the road for weeks. That food won't last long.'

Reluctantly he took it. 'I wonder if I could possibly sink any lower than I have?' he thought aloud.

'That kind of attitude won't get you very far,' Victoria warned him. 'You just concentrate on getting home, that's what's important.'

'The French are fine people,' he volunteered suddenly, 'brave and noble. If your husband is still alive and he's out there, they will help him.'

'I pray that's so,' she sighed.

Alistaire took her hands in his. 'In spite of all I've told you,' he said, 'I have seen men come through. I've seen men survive the bloodiest confrontations and come back when all else had counted them lost. Never give up hope, lass. Never give up hope; he'll come back.'

There was that moment of silence when they both knew he must go.

He smiled, sighing. 'My bonnie Victoria, I'll no forget ye, and if you ever think of me, be generous. I was just a man who went mad one day and ran away.'

As she crept out into the yard to make sure that the coast was clear, Victoria considered it an odd twist of fate that after having waited so long for a man to return from the front, when he had, it wasn't the one she'd hoped for. Nonetheless, she had felt bound to assist him, and regretted nothing.

Seeing that there was no one about, she waved Alistaire into the yard and then proceeded to guide him through the range of dung hills and out onto open farmland. 'That way is north,' she pointed, 'and may God keep and protect you.'

With only a nod, he turned and slipped away. As she watched him melt into the darkness, she knew that his assessment of her motives had only been partially correct. Yes, of course she hoped that if Gerald was wandering somewhere in Europe, someone would be kind enough to help him as she'd helped Alistaire, but there was more to it than that. She felt above all that, no matter what the circumstances, at least she'd saved one young man from all the carnage. One man who might now have the chance to live out the life he'd been given, instead of having it brutally snatched from him, as so many had before. As she stood there alone in the night, she hoped that God would smile on her compassion and send her husband home.

*

When she returned to the loft, she found the others apparently still hard at work over their writing exercise.

'You're back early tonight,' Jen remarked innocently. 'Headache gone is it?'

Maisie began to snigger, then Ella joined in.

'What's this all about?' Victoria demanded suspiciously.

'Nothing.' Maisie sniggered all the more.

' 'As he gone then?' Jen enquired, as they all grinned at each other.

Victoria stiffened, suddenly fearful that she'd been discovered. 'What do you mean?' she asked defensively.

'Got what you wanted and sent him home?' Jen replied, still enigmatic.

Now they were all giggling and nudging each other.

'I don't know what you're talking about,' Victoria remarked dismissively.

'Jen reckons you been seeing one of them farm lads,' Maisie finally revealed the reason for their antics.

'A farm boy?' she stared at them in disbelief. 'The oldest one here can't be more than fourteen!'

'Any port in a storm,' Ella winked as the nudging and giggling continued. 'I might try it myself.'

So that was it. They thought she'd been going out to meet one of the farm lads. She began to relax and then suddenly realised what it was they were actually referring to. 'That's disgusting,' she cried with the utmost indignation.

They fell about. There was nothing that delighted them more than taking the rise out of Victoria, especially if it was to do with something risqué. There was no stopping them now, and a torrent of vulgar innuendos showered down upon her.

'He may have started out as a boy, but I bet Vix has made a man of him!' Ella laughed loudly.

'Some of those lads are pretty nimble when it comes to slipping in and out of tight spaces,' Jen commented.

That had them in stitches. Victoria tolerated it, as she always did, blushing furiously, which was exactly what they wanted. Better they thought that she'd been engaged in some sordid affair than ever they guessed the truth.

In May, the government made yet another amendment to D.O.R.A. and introduced the '*British Summertime Act*' which required all clocks to be put forward by one hour, thus lengthening the day and allowing farmers more time to produce more food. The first day of summer was now officially the 21st of May. It was a decision that didn't suit everyone in the rural community.

'That's bloody ridiculous,' Ella shook her head in disgust. 'I've never heard anything like it. They'll be expecting us to work by candlelight next.'

'It's not as if we don't work long enough hours as it is,' Jen complained. 'They can't really do that, can they? I mean, change time?'

'Apparently they can,' Victoria offered up the scrap of newspaper she'd been reading from as evidence, 'and they have.'

'I thought it was summer already.' Maisie looked confused, but then she always did.

To be honest, it made little difference to any of them. They'd always risen at first light and worked until it was too dark to see. In that sense, nothing had changed.

Victoria mulled this new information over in her mind. It seemed to her that nothing would ever stop this war. They would even turn night into day just to keep it going.

As the months passed, Victoria often wondered what had become of Alistaire. There had been no report of his capture, no report of him at all. Until one day in the middle of July, Maisie returned from the farmhouse with a clutch of letters and a postcard.

'That's daft,' she mumbled to herself, staring at the card.

'What's that?' Jen held out her hand for it.

'There's no message,' Maisie told her, handing it over.

Jen looked at the card. 'Yeh, she's right,' she agreed, offering it to Ella.

Ella made a thorough examination of the card. 'What a waste,' she remarked. 'A penny for the card, a ha'penny for the stamp, and they haven't even bothered to write on it. That's silly.'

'What is it?' Victoria asked, attracted to the discussion.

'It's a postcard,' Ella told her, 'but there's no message on it.'

'Who's it addressed to?'

Ella began to exercise her new reading skills, working her way slowly through the block capitals. 'It's for you.'

'Well, may I have it then?' Victoria enquired testily. 'That is if you're all quite finished with it.'

Ella gave it to her. She was right, it was addressed to her: Victoria Avery, care of Orchardlea Farm, Staunton Gifford, West Sussex. There was no message, but when she turned it over, the picture was a scene of Inverness. She smiled to herself.

'Anyone you know?' Jen enquired casually.

'I've no idea,' she replied, fixing the card above her bed. 'Probably one of the farm boys playing a joke.'

*

Summer had reached its height and the farm was busier than ever. The new daylight saving rule meant that the days were longer now and there was far more work to do, but time had a different meaning here. A year wasn't counted in days and months; it was reckoned in seasons. A time to plough, a time to plant, a time to harvest. A day wasn't measured in minutes and hours, but from dawn to dusk. They were either long or short, hot or cold, wet or dry. They were days of patched petticoats and darned stockings, of making do with what you had, but they were good days.

Victoria had already been forced to let out the belt of her skirt by a notch, and now she was having difficulty buttoning her liberty bodice. 'This can't be right,' she complained irritably. 'I've washed this thing dozens of times and it's never shrunk before.' She continued to fiddle with the garment, grumbling all the time, muttering to herself in annoyance, frustrated with her failure to secure the button.

Finally tired of listening to her, Ella came over. Tapping Victoria's hands aside, she dealt deftly with the offending item, then stepped back, eyeing the taut material suspiciously. Suddenly, she put both her hands on Victoria's breasts and jiggled them about. 'It's not the bodice, dear,' she declared with a grin, as Victoria flinched back, 'it's just that there's more of you!'

'She's right,' Jen observed, as Victoria glanced down at herself. 'You've begun to fill out. I noticed it before. It's the life. Lots of good food, plenty of exercise.'

'You've begun to blossom,' Ella added. 'Take my word for it, the boys'll love it!'

Victoria wasn't sure she liked the idea of that.

To make matters worse, Ella continued. 'Just think, when Gerald gets home, you'll be able to grab him, throw him over your shoulder, carry him off and have your wicked way with him. Poor devil won't know what's hit him!'

Victoria laughed along with the rest, but privately she didn't think it sounded altogether very ladylike. She decided to go on a diet immediately. She didn't want Gerald coming home to discover an Amazon in place of the trim wife he'd left behind. In the meantime, unable to afford new clothes, she'd just have to squeeze her extra curves into the ones she had.

Sitting down on the edge of her bed, she began to lace her boots only to have one of the laces snap. 'Oh, now look at that!' she cried in frustration. 'These laces are brand new. I'm never going to be ready in time for breakfast.'

'It's what we've been telling you,' Jen insisted. 'When were you ever able to snap a new lace using only your hands?' She rummaged in her cupboard. 'Here, I've got a spare. Use that, and be careful.'

'When Gerald comes home,' Victoria continued to fuss, re-lacing the boot, 'all he'll see is some red-faced buxom farm wench. He'll probably go straight back to the front.'

'You never know,' Maisie offered innocently, 'he may like you better that way.'

Victoria cast her a telling glance.

'Just a thought,' Maisie shrugged.

Jen had continued to examine the contents of her cupboard after giving Victoria the bootlace. She clicked her tongue, frowning. 'I seem to be running short of a few things,' she observed, looking at Ella.

'So am I,' Ella noticed. 'We're low on candles and soap as well.'

They looked at each other again, then at Maisie.

'Oh no,' the girl squirmed. 'Do I have to?'

'I thought you liked Cedric?' Ella reminded her. 'You know he likes you.'

'He's nice and everything,' Maisie agreed, 'but every time I see 'im, he asks me to marry 'im. I don't know what to say.'

'Say you'll think about it,' Jen advised, 'at least until the war's over. That way, we'll never run out of soap or candles.'

'I always say that,' Maisie complained.

'Then bloody well keep saying it,' Jen argued. 'He'll be more grateful in the end.'

'What's going on?' Victoria asked, concerned at Maisie's discomfort.

'We're going shopping, Sunday afternoon,' Ella told her.

'But all the shops are closed on Sunday,' Victoria pointed out.

'Not the ironmongers,' Jen replied.

'Not Cedric Hardacre's,' Ella joined in. 'Not when Maisie's about.'

Now that the all important harvest was fast approaching, it took precedence over everything else, and with the increased pace of activity on the farm, no one was allowed any time off. Only the sick or injured were excused from work but, as Victoria soon found out, with a little ingenuity, there was always a way to find some time for yourself.

Church on Sunday morning was something that neither the war nor the imminent harvest could change. Following the example of her friends, Victoria sat in the very last pew right at the back of the building. In the heat of the summer, the doors of the church had been left open for ventilation, and when the Vicar announced, 'Now let us pray', and everyone closed their eyes and bowed their heads, they sneaked out.

Like a gaggle of geese escaped from the pen, the four truants hurried noisily through the dusty all-but-deserted streets of Staunton Gifford towards the ironmongers. As Victoria had predicted, all the shops were closed, and in any case none of them had any money besides the ha'penny they'd each brought for the collection plate. Notwithstanding, the others were already discussing the items they needed to collect once they'd reached their destination, but without the means to purchase, Victoria was still in some doubt as to how this would be achieved.

'Surely he'll still be at church?' she suggested, as she saw the ironmonger's sign hanging out over the street.

'He always goes to the early service,' Jen told her knowledgeably. 'Then he comes back to the shop to re-stock. Cedric's a man of regular habits.'

She was right of course. They'd barely reached the front door before it flew open, the bell above it clanking loudly, as Cedric Hardacre, a short thickset middle-aged man, stumbled into the street, almost tripping over his own feet in his haste to greet them.

'Maisie, dear Maisie,' he cried, wiping his hands on the long brown apron he was wearing, clearly delighted to see her. 'What a wonderful surprise.'

From the moment he appeared, it was obvious that Cedric Hardacre was besotted with Maisie. It was the way he gazed longingly at her to the exclusion of all else. His normally sober nature cast into confusion, he'd become awkward and tongue-tied. The very sight of her robbed him of any eloquence he may have possessed and compounded the dilemma that faced him. Having already made his proposal in the best way he knew how and exhausted his meagre repertoire, all he could do now was to go on repeating himself, with precious little idea of how to improve the offer.

Eventually collecting his wits, he made an effort to redress his all too apparent eagerness. With no customers to serve, he had discarded his jacket, his tie and the collar of his shirt, which was open at the neck with the sleeves rolled up to the elbows.

'Dear me, I must look a sight,' he remarked, offering a self-conscious smile that revealed a tombstone-like set of brilliant white teeth, half obscured beneath a large cavalry-style moustache. 'Please excuse my appearance,' he wittered on, pulling the front of his shirt together and hastily rolling down the sleeves in a vain attempt to appear casual. 'I had no idea you were coming today.' He finished by making a token gesture of smoothing his dark hair, which was already slick with pomade and parted down the middle.

After that, his attention began to wander again and he just stood there, staring at Maisie in fascination, until Ella made a point of coughing loudly. 'Oh,' he flinched, starting from his trance. 'I see you've brought your friends with you,' he observed courteously, doubtless wishing that she'd come alone. 'So many lovely ladies, my goodness, what's a man to do?'

'You could start by letting us in,' Jen suggested tonelessly.

'Of course, yes, of course,' he dithered. 'Where are my manners, keeping you all standing out here? Come in, come in.'

They all trooped inside with Cedric bringing up the rear, the others exhibiting such familiarity of their surroundings that Victoria felt certain they'd done this several times before.

Inside, the shop reeked of polish and detergent, edged with the sharp tang of paraffin and turpentine. It was stacked from floor to ceiling with all manner of hardware and dry goods, leaving only narrow corridors to move up and down in. There were, in some places, an odd assortment of wares. Mops and besoms were stacked together with a collection of fishing rods, whilst a column of galvanised buckets nestled against a pile of stone hot water bottles. Elsewhere, china chamber pots, arranged in a pyramid, were filled with tins of boot polish and black lead. Not an inch of space was wasted. Apparently, Cedric's establishment catered for a good deal more than merely ironmongery.

Ella went off by herself and Victoria followed Jen, who seemed to know exactly where she was going, whilst Maisie lingered by the counter with Cedric in constant attendance. As she made her way through the clutter of merchandise, Victoria could still hear him speaking in hushed tones.

'Well Maisie, have you thought any more about what I asked you?' he enquired hopefully.

'Yes, I have been thinking about it, Cedric,' Maisie hedged, 'but what with the war...'

'Yes, yes, of course,' obviously Cedric had heard all that before, 'but please tell me I might have a chance?'

'There's no one else at the moment,' Maisie responded evasively.

Cedric seemed not to notice. 'You know you're the only girl in the world for me, Maisie,' he told her wistfully. 'Everything I have is yours, if you will only say yes.'

'That's very kind of you, Cedric,' Maisie continued to prevaricate, 'but I must have more time to think.'

'Take all the time you need,' Cedric agreed, always ready to comply with her wishes. 'I wouldn't want to rush you.'

In the meantime, indifferent to the proprietor's inarticulate protestations of love, Ella and Jen began to call out to each other as they continued to move around the shop.

'I've found the hairpins, Jen.'

'Get a packet for each of us. Oh, and while you're over there, we need some more matches.'

Jen picked up a bundle of boot laces from the shelf in front of her and gave them to Victoria to hold whilst she gathered two handfuls of candles, passing them over as well. She continued in this way for some time until Victoria's arms were full. Eventually, they came upon a large display of soap. Surging ahead, Jen picked out a delicate little pink tablet and held it up so that Victoria, without a free hand, could smell it.

'Hmm, that's lovely,' she smiled appreciatively. '*Vinolia Otto toilet soap*,' she read from the label.

'As used by the gentry,' Jen assured her.

Then Victoria noticed the price. 'They're a shilling each, Jen,' she warned. 'We can't possibly afford it. Come to that, how are we going to pay for any of this? Do you have some sort of credit arrangement?'

Jen cast her a pained expression, suggesting she should know better. 'Cedric never charges us for anything,' she explained anyway.

Finally, Victoria understood what was going on. 'This is disgraceful,' she objected. 'That poor man is clearly infatuated. We can't possibly take advantage of him.'

'Suit yourself,' Jen shrugged, picking up a chunk of thick waxy yellow soap about the size of a cobblestone, marked as '*Galvin & Pratts Carbolic Marvel*', at only a ha'penny a bar. 'This is what we can afford. Take a sniff.'

Victoria did so, then flinched back, her eyes watering. 'Oh, well, perhaps just this once,' she conceded, as Jen piled the Vinolia into her arms, the moral high ground she'd so recently adopted dissolving, like some inconvenient stain, under the remarkable influence of Galvin & Pratt's Carbolic Marvel.

Victoria could only look on in astonishment at the dispassionate way in which Jen and Ella operated. With complete detachment, they continued to loot the shelves, indifferent to the more sensitive issues taking place at the front of the shop. It wasn't like them to be callous. It was more as if they simply didn't take Cedric very seriously. As for herself, still able to hear his stumbling courtship, his sincerity only added to her growing sense of guilt.

By the time they returned to the counter, Cedric had become bold enough to hold Maisie's hand, but when he saw them approaching, he quickly let it go, just in case there might be some suggestion of impropriety. 'Ladies,' he forced a smile, frustrated by the untimely interruption. 'Back so soon?'

'We can't hang around, Cedric,' Ella explained, selecting a large brown paper bag and filling it with their spoils. 'The wagon's due to leave for the farm soon.'

Jen had likewise filled a bag. 'What do we owe you, Cedric?' she asked, as if she already knew what the answer would be.

'Not another word, ladies.' Apparently unable to influence the object of his desire in any other way, as usual he hoped his generosity would impress her. 'Please be my guests.'

'Well,' they both chorused, looking at Maisie, 'aren't you going to say thank you to Cedric?'

Cedric offered up his cheek in what appeared to be a time-honoured fashion and, blushing, Maisie deposited a kiss upon it.

So did Ella. 'You're a dear, Cedric. See you again soon.'

Unbelievably, even Jen kissed him. 'Bye for now, Cedric.'

Then Victoria felt an elbow nudge her in the ribs. 'What, me as well?' she whispered reluctantly. This time, the elbow was more insistent and she knew she was expected to follow suit, and she gave him a quick peck on the cheek.

They left Cedric standing forlornly in the street watching them depart, his face framed in an expression of regret and disappointment, of dashed hopes and lost opportunities. Bedevilled by fears of younger and more vigorous men who might easily steal Maisie's heart, but could not love her so well as he.

'That was simply awful,' Victoria complained. 'I've never been involved in anything quite so despicable as that in my life! That man is so in love. How could we have abused him like that?'

'We only take what we need,' Ella offered as justification, 'and besides, he gets to see Maisie. What's a few trifles compared to that?'

'Nevertheless, it seems cruel,' Victoria persisted, dissatisfied with the explanation.

'You wasn't so fussy when it came to a choice of soap,' Jen reminded her.

'I know,' Victoria admitted shamefully, regretting her part in the subterfuge. 'I feel so cheap.'

'Just remember Galvin & Pratts Carbolic Marvel,' Jen cautioned. 'That really was cheap. Be grateful you don't have to wash with it.'

Exploiting poor Cedric's feelings for Maisie was only one of the ways in which they made the most of what life had to offer, but their efforts were not always directed solely towards acquisition. Sometimes it was merely a matter of comfort.

By now, they were all quite familiar with the war. It was a fundamental part of their lives, albeit an unwelcome one, but all they knew of it was only what they'd read, or what they'd heard. None of them had ever had any personal experience of it. How could they? However, a nocturnal excursion into the sleepy Sussex countryside, in pursuit of relief from the oppressive summer heat, was due to change that and bring them face to face with the enemy.

Chapter Ten

The annual wheat harvest was of national importance. The German submarine blockade, which began early in 1915, had cost Britain thousands of tons of merchant shipping, most of it vital supply vessels. With the ever present threat of starvation looming, it was imperative that the country grew as much food for itself as possible. Wheat was crucial to Britain's survival, whilst it was generally considered that a turnip or a potato was worth as much as a bullet or a cannon shell. Once this essential lifeline had been successfully gathered in, it made way for another more localised yet far more celebrated harvest. Apples.

The orchard, from whence the farm had derived its name, lay to the west of the property, covering many acres of gently sweeping Sussex downland. The cider produced from the apples that grew there had, in its heyday, made the farm prosperous, and the *Amber Oblivion* was to this day renowned throughout five counties. Such was its reputation that, when the call went out, every man, woman and child not otherwise engaged who could run, walk or crawl came to Orchardlea to pick apples. The lack of horsepower didn't deter them. Anything in private hands with four legs and four wheels was pressed into service. The caravans grew larger as they moved from village to village picking up anyone bound for the farm.

These willing volunteers were not paid. Instead they received a percentage of the cider which they could easily sell for a good profit, or drink themselves. Most of them drank it themselves.

Amongst the army of migrants that descended on the farm were the remnants of Jen's family, those of them who had no work elsewhere or who were not fighting in the war. They lived over forty miles away. Jen's search for work had taken her far from home, and then the war had closed in, so to speak, behind her. She seldom had the chance to visit them; the last time had been nearly a year ago. It was a tearful reunion.

There was her mother who looked very much like the old Queen Victoria, but much less dour and without the grim '*We are not amused*' expression. She was friendly and kind and always smiling, the more so for seeing her eldest daughter. She had brought with her the three youngest of Jen's five sisters, and the four youngest of her seven brothers, which of course included Harry.

Victoria fell in love with him the moment she saw him. Come to that, so did Ella and Maisie. Harry was just five years old, blonde, blue-eyed and as bright as a button. He was, every inch of him, an angel.

Although Jen paid equal attention to all her siblings, it was quite obvious that Harry was far and away her favourite. As he played amongst the lines of pickers, waist deep in flower-strewn meadow grass, she would find any excuse to break from gathering apples to catch him up in her arms and swing him high above her head, or cuddle him up to her, kissing and caressing him. He never strayed far from her, even though there were other small children to play with, and whenever he was afraid or suffered some minor scrap in a rough and tumble, it was always Jen and not his mother he would run to for comfort.

Victoria found the rapport they exhibited captivating, but it was the change in Jen that amazed her the most. It was still Jen, but not the same. Not Jen being strong for everyone. Not Jen hard-edged and cynical. Under Harry's influence, she'd been transformed. She'd become softer, more gentle, happy. She looked years younger, as if the weight of the world had dropped from her shoulders, freeing her to love this beautiful child.

The multitude here was enough to rival the hop gangs of Kent. There was no chance of accommodating them all, but the weather remained kind, and makeshift camps were erected all around the perimeter of the orchard. Some had brought tents with them, others set up oilcloth shelters, whilst many simply slept in the open.

Jen quit the loft at this time, electing to stay with her family. Victoria and the others often went to visit her, to sit around the camp fires and talk the evening away. Most often, Jen would sit with Harry cradled in her lap, singing softly to him until he fell asleep. Jen had never looked more radiant. Harry, it appeared, was her whole world, and finally, when the last apple was sent to the press and everyone went home, she was inconsolable for days.

'I've never seen Jen behave in this way before,' Victoria confided to Ella one morning as they walked across the yard together, casting handfuls of corn to a large flock of chickens that scurried hungrily about their feet.

'Well, it's that Harry, isn't it.' Ella immediately isolated the reason for Jen's mood. 'She always goes off like that when she has to leave him. Mind you, I don't blame her. I could have gobbled him up myself.'

'Yes, he is a beautiful boy,' Victoria agreed wistfully.

Ella caught the note of longing in her voice. 'I suppose you might have had children yourself by now,' she surmised, 'if it wasn't for the war, if Gerald hadn't had to go away.'

'I would like to have children,' she confessed, feeling a twinge of regret that she'd not already done so. Meeting Harry had made her feel somewhat broody, and she felt the absence of a child in her life more keenly than ever before. The worst of it was that if, by some mischance, Gerald never returned, the prospect of children would become remote. Doubtless, she could always remarry, but even though a child of her own would be nice, Gerald's child would be so much better.

Ella seemed to know what she was thinking. 'Don't worry, Vix,' she told her, offering a smile of encouragement. 'You're still young, there's plenty of time. He'll come back and then you can start a family of your own. Mind you,' she added jokingly, 'don't end up like Jen's mum. Draw the line at a dozen!'

Victoria's mood lightened. As much as she wanted children, two or three would be quite enough. 'What about you, Ella?' she asked. 'I haven't heard you say much about your family. Have you any brothers or sisters?'

The handful of corn that Ella held fell back, uncast, into the basket. She went quiet for a moment, but she wasn't one for keeping much back. 'I have two sisters,' she replied eventually, 'both younger than me. One's in service in London, the other's married and lives in Lincolnshire. I nearly had a brother as well, but mum died trying to give birth to him, and he died a few days later.'

'Oh, I'm sorry,' Victoria began to commiserate. It was many a large family that had lost a sickly child and many a woman who had died in childbirth. It was the times they lived in. It was a fact of life and one which Victoria hoped would improve in the future.

'It's alright,' Ella shrugged dismissively. 'It was a long time ago, I was only fourteen.'

'What about your father?' Victoria went on to ask. 'Is he still alive?'

'Maybe,' Ella shrugged again. 'I haven't seen him for years.' She had the strangest look in her eyes, as if she were being asked to recall events that she felt were best forgotten, but knowing all the same that until she answered the questions, they wouldn't stop. 'Dad was a good man, but when mum died he changed. You see, I looked a lot like mum when she was young, and after she was gone, he wanted me to take over from her.'

'Oh, yes, I see,' Victoria acknowledged. 'Keeping house and looking after your sisters - a lot of work for a young girl.'

'No, Vix.' The tone of Ella's voice commanded her to listen, aware that she'd completely misunderstood, and knowing Victoria as she did, she wondered if she ever would. 'He wanted me to replace his wife in his bed.'

For a moment, Victoria wasn't sure that she'd heard her correctly, but when she realised that she had, she was stunned. Suddenly, images of her own father sprang into her mind. He'd been strong, powerful, wise and kind. She'd loved him as a father, and he'd loved her as a daughter. He'd been her protector, her guardian, and with the aid of her mother he'd sought only the best for her. Until the day he died, she'd entrusted her life to him, and that trust had never been betrayed. A daughter's trust in her father was sacred. The thought that he or that any other father might abuse his own daughter shocked her to the core. 'What did you do?' she hardly dared ask.

'I was fourteen years old,' Ella reminded her. 'I did what I was told.'

'Oh.' Victoria's hand flew involuntarily to her mouth, a chill sweeping through her. She might have been naive in the ways of the world, but Ella's explanation left little room for doubt.

'When I was old enough to understand how wrong it all was, I ran away,' Ella volunteered. 'I did all sorts of different jobs, mostly farming. Finally, I ended up here, then the war came along.' Suddenly Ella was her old self again - the big smile, the brash disposition. 'Now I'm learning to read and write, who knows what will happen once the war's over? I might move on, try something else.'

Victoria hardly knew what to say.

'You'd think I'd hate men, wouldn't you?' Ella remarked, observing her expression, 'but I don't. I love 'em, I always have. I love 'em all. It seems to me the older they get, the sillier they are, bless 'em.'

It was a curious moment. Victoria stood there, studying her friend. Ella was so vivacious, so outgoing; who could ever have guessed at the tragedy of her life. Yet, strangely, far from pitying her, all Victoria could feel was admiration.

*

The weather continued warm, then it grew hot. Beneath the eaves of the hay barn, the loft was stifling. Even with all the windows open, there was no relief from the oppressive heat.

Ella had gone down to the back of the barn to peg out the evening's laundry, and had not yet returned. Jen, now apparently fully recovered from Harry's departure and back to her old self, sat in a chair next to Victoria's bed, practising her reading from a week-old newspaper they'd recently discovered. Maisie sat at the table, busy with needle and thread, repairing her stockings.

Having just washed and dried her hair, Victoria was engaged in the marathon of brushing out the waist-length tresses. Since childhood, she'd been taught that nothing less than a hundred brush strokes would do, and even though she knew it was a necessary task, she'd always felt herself to be a slave to the tyranny of this arduous routine. It was an attitude which was soon made manifest to those around her by her continual mutterings of exasperation.

'You should have joined the Land Army.' Jen folded the paper and held it up, tapping a photograph in the centre of the page.

Victoria parted her damp locks and peered out at the picture Jen had indicated. It depicted five young women of the Land Army, posing cheerfully against a rustic fence. Most of them, she quickly noticed, had their hair bobbed short. 'Cut my hair?' she frowned at

Jen. The idea was preposterous. 'No self-respecting woman would ever consider it.'

'And they're wearing breeches,' Jen drew her attention to what she'd missed.

Victoria looked again. 'That seems indecent,' she declared, beginning to roll her hair up and setting to work with an arsenal of pins.

'Times are changing,' Jen remarked, 'faster than you think.'

'Well, I don't see dressing as a man and cutting your hair like one as much of an advance,' Victoria objected, still struggling with the weight of her own 'crowning glory'.

'Even so,' Jen wondered, 'don't you wish you'd joined the Land Army? You'd have had proper training, better conditions and it says here they're paid twenty shillings a week!'

'Where does it say that?' Victoria surged forwards, losing her grip on one particularly awkward strand that immediately unravelled and fell back into her lap. 'My goodness, you're right, twenty shillings!'

'You could still join,' Jen pointed out.

'It's not about the money,' Victoria told her. 'Oh yes, sometimes I think I'm being foolish, or selfish, even unpatriotic, but if I joined this, or any other organisation, I could be sent anywhere in the country. Staunton Gifford is where Gerald and I agreed to spend our lives together. If... when,' she corrected herself quickly, 'he returns, this is the first place he'll come to. I'd never forgive myself if anything happened and I wasn't here.'

'You'd be amongst people you were used to,' Jen persisted. 'If I'm reading this story right, they're all the daughters of clergymen, lawyers and bankers.'

'If by that you mean women of my class,' Victoria interpreted, 'I've come to believe that there's only one class of women in Britain, and that's the one without equal opportunities and no right to vote.'

She paused to consider what she'd just said. 'Oh dear,' she sighed eventually, 'now I'm beginning to sound like Beryl.'

'Nothing wrong with that,' Jen agreed with interest.

'What about you?' Victoria asked her. 'Your reading and writing is improving all the time. You could enlist in the Land Army.'

'Not me,' Jen declined. 'I'm like you. I'm far enough away from my family as it is. If I was to go any further, I'd never see them at all.'

'Then it looks as though we're stuck with each other, doesn't it?' Victoria concluded, well aware that by family, Jen meant Harry, of course.

Jen grinned, threw down the paper and began to assist her in her battle with her hair.

Just then, Ella appeared looking hot and flustered.

'What's the matter, Ella?' Maisie asked. 'You look vexed.'

Ella exhaled between clenched teeth. 'I ran into that Berty Thomas just now,' she told them all. 'You know, that red-headed lad who looks after the pigs. How old would you say he was?'

Jen thought about it for a moment. 'I don't know exactly,' she mused. 'Twelve, thirteen maybe?'

'That's what I thought,' Ella frowned. 'Anyway, I'm hanging out the washing, then he passes by and starts to get saucy about our underwear. Instead of cuffing his ear, like I should've done, the next thing I know I'm flirting with him! I couldn't help it. I don't know what's come over me.'

'It's this bloody war,' Jen was sure of it. 'Any male comes your way these days, it's either false teeth or pimples. There ain't a decent man around.'

'That's the truth and no mistake,' Ella agreed. 'Look at us all, just a bunch of frustrated hens and not a rooster in sight.'

'It's the heat,' Victoria pointed out, a little less graphically. 'It has us all on edge.'

'Not much we can do about that,' Jen remarked gloomily.

Maisie paused from darning her stockings, having stuck the needle in her finger. 'What about the blind pool?' she suggested, sucking noisily at the injured digit.

Jen looked genuinely impressed. 'That girl's a genius,' she declared, causing Maisie to grin all over her face.

'What's the blind pool?' Victoria asked, not having heard it mentioned before.

'It's the pond up at Threepenny Wood,' Ella explained. 'It ain't fed by a stream, the water comes up from underground. It's as clear as glass, as cold as ice and deep enough to swim in. We ain't been there for ages.'

'Think of it, Vix,' Jen tapped her arm. 'Cold, clear water, enough to take your breath away.'

'Oh,' Victoria sighed, a tingle running down her spine at the mere thought of it. Then suddenly she remembered. 'I'm afraid I don't have a bathing dress.'

They all stood and stared at her in the way they'd come to do each time she made some innocent but pointless remark, illustrating that once again she'd completely failed to grasp their meaning.

'Let me guess,' she sighed resignedly, noticing their expressions. 'You don't have bathing dresses either. You never have had, and going to this pool means swimming in the nude.'

Once again, Jen looked impressed. 'You know,' she told the others, 'I think she's beginning to get the hang of us!'

'Come on, Vixy,' Ella urged, 'it's nothing to be ashamed of. Besides, we've already seen you in the buff.'

'That wasn't by my choice,' Victoria disputed, 'and in any case, that was in here. What you're suggesting now is that we take our clothes off in a public place.'

'It's hardly public,' Jen disagreed. 'If we go tonight, it'll be dark. The moon don't rise till late and we'll be inside the woods; no one will see us.'

'She's right,' Ella agreed. 'We've done it lots of times before. We've never been caught out.'

'I suppose I could keep my petticoat and liberty bodice on,' Victoria thought aloud.

'No, that'd be like eating an orange with the skin on,' Maisie objected.

'She's right,' Ella told her. 'It won't be half as refreshing that way.'

Victoria continued to hesitate. It was fiendishly hot, and a cold swim would be nice, but her modesty was getting in the way of it. She also felt a tad hypocritical; having only just criticised the Land Army girls for wearing breeches in public, she was now contemplating wearing nothing in public.

'If you don't go,' Jen announced stubbornly, 'none of us will.'

'That's not fair,' Victoria protested, feeling the duress.

'I agree,' Ella joined in. 'If you're going to sit here and boil, then we'll all boil with you.'

'What, me n'all?' Maisie asked.

'All of us means you n'all,' Ella told her.

'Oh yes, that's right.'

'Yes, yes, alright, I'll go,' Victoria relented finally, imagining that by morning she'd be appearing in the dock of the local magistrate's court, clad in nothing but a policeman's jacket, to answer charges of indecent exposure.

They waited until it was almost dark, then slipped quietly out of the farmyard and set off for Threepenny Woods. It was barely a mile away, but trying to find it in the dark, across open country, was proving more difficult than they'd anticipated. Without a path to guide them, or a light to see by, negotiating the rough terrain was hazardous at best.

'I thought you said you remembered the way,' Ella reminded Jen, as they blundered into yet another clump of brambles.

'I thought I did,' Jen didn't sound so sure now. 'It's been a while.'

'Perhaps they've moved it, 'cos of the war,' Maisie suggested, in an attempt at wit.

'If you don't shut up,' Ella responded irritably, 'I'm going to leave you here for the goblins.'

'They wouldn't want her,' Jen remarked, casting about. 'I think I've got my bearings now.'

After another fifteen minutes, a five-barred gate that wouldn't open but had fallen over when they tried to climb it and a tree stump none of them noticed until Victoria barked her shin on it, Threepenny Wood finally appeared on the horizon, silhouetted against the afterglow of the sky. By this time, they were all hot, tired, perspiring heavily and looking forward to a swim.

'When you get in there,' Jen warned Victoria as they walked along together, 'you'll feel as though you're being watched. Take my word for it, we all get that feeling, but it's nothing to worry about. The woods are full of badgers and foxes, things moving about, but there's nobody else there, just us.'

Inside the wood, it was appreciably cooler than in the open fields. That in itself was a relief. After a short walk, they found themselves in a clearing standing before the blind pool. The pond was a mirror to the sky, its still waters, speckled with reflected starlight, beckoned invitingly.

The others didn't waste a second. Tearing off their clothes they plunged in, shrieking with delight as the cold water closed over them. Victoria, still cautious, took her time. She began to undress slowly, her imagination running riot. She fancied that every old man and boy from the village was hiding in the bushes, leering at her. Taking comfort from Jen's warning that it was a common illusion brought about by the circumstances, she continued until she'd divested herself of her last garment. Simply removing her clothes cooled her down. It felt odd, standing there naked. Of course, she'd undressed before, in her bedroom or bathroom, but never in the open air. There was the strangest sensation of freedom, mixed with a hint of wickedness and risk. In spite of her attempt to elope, her brush with the police, military intelligence and giving assistance to a deserter, she considered this to be the most daring thing she'd ever done.

'Come on slowcoach,' Jen called out. 'It'll be morning before you get in.'

Victoria walked to the bank and dipped her toes in the water to test the temperature. 'Oh, it really is cold!' she giggled, quickly pulling her foot back.

'Jump straight in, it's the only way!' Ella told her.

Without any further hesitation, Victoria leapt from the bank and plunged waist deep into the pond, letting out a huge gasp of pleasure as the icy liquid enveloped her. After the initial shock, she began to swim. It was wonderful to feel the cool water moving against her bare skin. At the farm, she'd had to make do with a strip wash from a bowl. It had been years since she'd been able to immerse her entire body. It felt so sensual, so decadent; she was having the time of her life.

They frolicked in the pool for hours, like so many carefree water nymphs, all thoughts of anyone seeing them having fled away. Laughing and shrieking, diving and splashing, or just floating lazily on their backs in the water. Until, at last, exhausted, they pulled themselves out and lay on the bank, staring up at the stars, allowing the warm breeze to dry them.

'The moon's beginning to rise,' Jen noticed. 'We should think about going home.'

Victoria lay on her back, arms folded behind her head, looking up at the sky through the canopy of leaves. She hadn't felt this cool for weeks. 'Oh, just a little while longer,' she pleaded.

Ella, who likewise had been lying on her back, raised herself up on one elbow. 'What's that noise?' she enquired vaguely.

Victoria jerked into a sitting position, covering herself with her arms, wondering if it was footsteps Ella had heard, fearful of an intruder.

'I can't hear anything,' Jen answered, looking around.

'Listen,' Ella insisted, 'it's getting nearer.'

They all sat on the grass in silence, straining their ears for any telltale sound.

'Now I can hear it,' Jen said after a moment. 'It sounds like a railway engine.'

'It can't be,' Ella dismissed her suggestion. 'The lines are miles away.'

Maisie was next to speak. By now the fast approaching sound was clearly audible to them all. 'It sounds like one of them new motor bicycles.'

The noise was getting louder all the time. It was like the propeller of a great ship turning, a deep throbbing pulse that was now almost deafening. Suddenly, to her horror, Victoria recognised the sound. 'It's a zeppelin!' she shouted, jumping to her feet.

As they bunched together by the edge of the pool, a great black shape suddenly loomed above the tree tops, obliterating the low crescent of the moon, the roar of its engines pounding on their ears and making the very ground shake.

'It seems awfully low,' Victoria screamed to make herself heard.

'No wonder,' Ella shouted back, pointing upwards. 'One of the fins on the tail has collapsed.'

Even as she spoke, the nearside engine, the one they could see, began to stall. The motor backfired, blasting a shower of sparks into the night sky with a noise like a cannon shot.

'It must have been attacked,' Jen bawled at the top of her voice. 'Serves 'em bloody right.' She waved a clenched fist at the huge cigar shaped craft.

'Don't!' Victoria screeched. 'They'll see us.'

'Are there really Germans up there?' Maisie gaped, awestruck.

'Well, it ain't Santa Claus!' Jen continued to shake her fist.

'They have machine guns,' Victoria screamed a warning. 'If they see us, they'll fire. Quick, take cover under that tree.'

They cowered beneath the branches of an oak, the zeppelin hovering directly above them. Terrified, they clung to each other, trembling; the awful din making the ground quake beneath their feet.

Maisie began to cry. 'We're all going to die,' she panicked.

'I'm not waiting here to be shot,' Jen yelled. 'Let's make a run for it.'

'We haven't got any clothes on,' Victoria yelled back.

'Getting caught naked is better than being shot,' Jen argued above the thunder of the engines.

'That's not what I meant,' Victoria yelled. 'If we break cover, the moonlight will reflect off our skin and they'll see us. Stay where you are!'

Any further argument was abruptly curtailed when something heavy crashed through the branches of a nearby tree.

'They're bombing us!' Ella threw her arms about Victoria's waist in a rib-cracking embrace.

Something hit the ground nearby with a heavy thud, making them all scream again.

'They're dropping bombs!' Jen joined the huddle, pulling Maisie in with her.

As the zeppelin began to move sluggishly away from their position, they could hear other objects falling through the canopy of the wood further off.

'It can't be.' Victoria lowered her voice as the sound of the engines began to fade. 'There aren't any explosions. What on earth's happening?'

They continued to cower beneath the tree; four entirely naked young women, huddled together in sheer terror, as the zeppelin began to move slowly away. They didn't leave the cover of the tree until it had passed completely beyond the wood. Only then did they come out into the open to stand and watch, mouths agape, as the enormous airship drifted out of sight, still trailing smoke and sparks.

'I nearly shit myself,' Jen remarked eventually, encapsulating all their emotions in a single sentence.

'I think we were all in danger of doing that,' Victoria didn't mind admitting.

'What was all that about?' Ella wondered, venturing forward. Suddenly she gave a cry of alarm, falling headlong into the grass.

'Are you alright?' Victoria ran forward to assist.

'Yes,' Ella struggled to her feet. 'I must have tripped over a broken branch.'

'No, you didn't.' Victoria held up the offending object. 'It's a wicker chair. Perhaps an angler left it?'

'No,' Maisie pointed. 'There's other things over here.' She walked forward and picked something up. 'It's a loaf of bread!'

'There's something floating in the pool,' Jen noticed. 'I can see it glinting in the moonlight.'

'Be careful,' Victoria warned, 'it could be dangerous.'

Jen was already wading back into the pool to retrieve whatever was floating there. 'It's a bottle of beer,' she waved it above her head, 'and there's another one.'

Suddenly, Victoria realised what had taken place. 'The airship was damaged,' she explained her theory to them. 'The crew weren't able to maintain altitude; that would account for how low it was. They were trying to get rid of excess weight, anything that wasn't essential.'

'Lucky for us,' Jen clinked the two beer bottles together. 'Let's get dressed and see what else we can find.'

'Please be careful,' Victoria insisted, as they began to dress hurriedly. 'You don't know what you might come across.'

Using their towels as makeshift bags, they began to search the ground for more salvage, moving ever deeper into the woods. What they discovered was a treasure trove of valuable souvenirs and comestibles. There were more bottles of beer, as well as chunks of salty bacon, foot-long sausages wrapped in muslin, pieces of burnt silk and sections of aluminium rigging, whilst great lengths of rope lay coiled in the branches above them like lianas. They'd almost reached the point where they couldn't carry much more when Maisie let out a shriek of dismay. Dropping everything, they hurried over to see what was wrong.

They found her standing in a little clearing, sobbing quietly to herself. 'He was just lying there,' she sniffed as they came up.

Spread-eagled on his back was a figure of a man in uniform.

'Is it a German?' Jen asked in a hushed voice.

'I can't see,' Victoria said, peering closer.

'I've got some matches,' Jen volunteered, reaching into her skirt pocket.

Collecting some of the loose paper that was littered all around them, they fashioned a rudimentary torch and lit it. In the ragged orange light, the man's stark face, eyes and mouth wide-open, stared back at them.

They gasped, cringing back. So this was the face of the enemy, the monster of Europe, the brutal invader, he that would subjugate and enslave them all.

'I thought they'd look fiercer than that,' Maisie sounded surprised.

'Dear God,' Victoria dropped to her knees beside the body, 'he's only a boy.'

'Is he dead?' Ella asked.

'Of course he's dead,' Jen scowled. 'You don't fall from that height and live.'

'He was dead before he fell.' Victoria observed the bullet wounds that peppered the front of the uniform. 'That's why he was thrown out.' She touched her fingertips to the cold eyelids and pressed them shut. 'To have died so young,' she murmured.

'What of it,' Jen spat. 'He's a German, just like all those other bastards that bomb English towns. If it had been his finger on the trigger up there, we'd all be lying there now, not him.'

'Anyway, that's torn it,' Ella told them. 'We'll have to report this. They'll know where we've been.'

'Why?' Jen snorted. 'Leave him there. There'll be a patrol through here sooner or later.'

'We can't leave him to the foxes and flies,' Ella objected. 'It might be days before a patrol searches these woods.'

'What do I care?' Jen shrugged. 'Our boys are dying every day fighting this scum. You've heard of the atrocities they commit. Do you think my brothers would get any pity if they were captured?'

Emotions were running high. 'You're right, of course, Jen,' Victoria endeavoured to calm her down, 'but just because the Germans are cruel and spiteful, it doesn't mean that we have to behave in the same way. Besides, if we don't report this body and somehow they find out we've been here, it will look suspicious.'

Even Jen could see the logic in that. 'Alright,' she relented, 'but I'm keeping the beer.'

Discarding everything they'd found, except the beer, they hurried back across the fields, but even before they'd reached the farm, they could see that patrols were already moving up and down the lanes, the long yellow beams of the headlamps preceding the vehicles along the narrow winding roadways. They flagged down a truck and imparted the news of their grim find to the soldiers in it. In the commotion, no one thought to ask their names or where they were from or what they were doing out here. Relieved that their anonymity hadn't been compromised, they returned to the hayloft and drank the beer to steady their nerves, if nothing else.

Over the next few days, the army placed a cordon around Threepenny Wood, recovered the body and cleared the debris, so that one might never have known that anything had ever happened there.

News began to circulate that the zeppelin had reached the coast at dawn, where it had been intercepted by a squadron of the Royal Flying Corps, and shot down in flames. The entire crew had been incinerated; none survived, much to the approbation of the watching crowds. It was the war, Victoria concluded, that made such callous beasts out of normally rational, civilised people. Those that cheered as the zeppelin crew burned had been victims of air raids themselves. It was the spectacle of the aggressor brought low that gave them hope and raised their spirits. At least she hoped that was the reason for it.

The body of the young German airman was moved to the cold store at the back of the local dairy, and when the authorities had finished examining it, it was taken to the parish church for burial.

The funeral was poorly attended. Just one police officer and two soldiers stood in as witnesses. Except for them, Victoria and her fellow nymphs, no one else from the village came. As the funeral proceeded, Victoria noticed that the vicar had altered the text of the service. Instead of saying ' our brother' here departed, he changed it to ' this man' here departed. It seemed that even in death, the young German was still the enemy.

They buried him in an out of the way corner of the cemetery and forgot about him, all except Victoria. She returned, alone, a few weeks later, to lay a bunch of wild flowers on the grave, before the weeds grew tall and obliterated it. Standing back, she pondered if, somewhere in Germany, there was a mother or a sister, a wife or a sweetheart, who would forever wonder what had become of him.

The incident with the zeppelin and the discovery of the dead

German airman had come as a considerable shock to them all. Until then, the war had been a familiar but distant event. Now it had reached out and touched them. That it had occurred at all was bad enough, but to have it happen on English soil, where they'd supposed themselves to be least vulnerable, was traumatic to say the least. It was doubtful that any of them would ever feel entirely safe again. Although they'd all experienced the same thing, it affected each of them differently, and as time passed, they each found a different way of dealing with it.

Jen faced it with a defiant patriotic justification. It was either them or us. For her, there were no grey areas. It was either black or white.

Ella adopted a more philosophical approach. In war, there would inevitably be casualties. The man they'd found was but one of those. The loss of life, although regrettable, was only to be expected.

It was hard to say in what way Maisie had been affected. She was the youngest, the most impressionable. She'd been first to discover the body. She'd never seen a dead human before, much less one that had met its demise in the way of the young German. It was doubtful that she fully understood all the implications of what had happened, but lately she'd become a little withdrawn, more introspective, if that was possible for Maisie, so that her friends could only guess as to what was on her mind. Ultimately, she would feel the need to confide her feelings, with the most unexpected repercussions.

As for herself, Victoria had become preoccupied with thoughts of the woman in Germany who waited in vain for a man who would never return. The similarity to her own situation came a little too close for comfort. She drew strength from her belief that Gerald was still alive, and no matter how many men died, he would not be among them, but the face of the dead airman and the element of mortality it forced her to acknowledge continued to haunt her.

Almost everything she'd done up to now had revolved around her vigil for Gerald. No matter what the risk, or how great the hardship, against all the evidence and opinion, she had waited and would continue to wait. Indeed, there was little else she could do, apart from remain here where Gerald could find her. Without relevant information or the means to obtain any, and with censorship cloaking every aspect of the war, all that was left to her was the waiting. She had cast off vain hope and wishful thinking. For her it was, as it had always been, entirely an act of faith, but in the months to come, that faith would be tested more severely than ever before, even to breaking point.

Chapter Eleven

1917 ushered in a new era of austerity. The German submarine blockade had now reached its height in an attempt to gain a stranglehold on the country and starve Britain into submission. To make matters worse, the winter rains and late spring frosts of the two preceding years had lead to two consecutively diminished harvests. It was rumoured that England had less than six weeks of grain left. Even though rationing had been imposed, it had little effect on the rapidly diminishing food stocks, and the threat of famine loomed closer every day.

The majority of the population had, in spite of all the hardships, sustained itself with the hope that this war would eventually be over, and that once it was, things would quickly return to the way they'd been before, or something very like it - that the quintessential English way of life of afternoon tea and church on Sunday, of pleasant strolls in the park or leafy country lanes would continue unchanged.

However, it was clear that Britain was facing a clever and powerful enemy, equally if not more determined than itself. Now, after more than two years of savage fighting, the Germans were actually closer to Paris than they'd been in 1914. It had become a war of attrition that offered no swift victory. It might go on for another year, or another ten years. Already, the names of ferocious and colossal battles, names that would stand the test of time – Ypres, the Somme, Flanders and Passiondale – were well known and would remain throughout history like milestones pointing the way to the bloodiest conflict of the twentieth century. The once widely held opinion that '*of course*' Britain would win this war was no longer so widely held.

For the first time since hostilities began, a note of pessimism concerning the outcome of this war began to creep into the minds of the people and with it the fear that perhaps England might never return to what it had once been - that the golden summer of 1914 would be the last; that the country they knew and loved might cease to be; its wealth and history plundered by a barbarous invader and its people reduced to little more than slaves under the iron heel of a ruthless dictatorship. The nightmare they now endured might be one they would never wake from.

Likewise, Victoria had also made a point of keeping her old life in sight, remembering what it had been like, with the intention of returning to it some day. Now, due to the protracted nature of the war, she too had begun to fret about the future. What if Gerald didn't return for another decade; would they even know each other? The war went on interminably. She was conscious of time running out; the best years were slipping by. Then again, if he never came back at all, the chance of resuming her former existence would have died with him.

Although she was relatively happy at Orchardlea, she'd only ever intended it to be a temporary position. What if, by waiting too long, she'd condemned herself to be marooned on this farm, ending her days alone, forgotten by the world, as a worn-out old labourer, without ever having found that for which she'd set sail? By forsaking all other options, she'd made a wager with destiny, putting all her hopes on one cast of the dice, never once believing that she would lose, until now. It was then, once that thought had occurred to her, that something inside her, very small, very private and deep down, began to scream and couldn't stop.

Even in these dark times, there were bright spots. Jen's three brothers, Tom, Arthur and Jack, had come home on a rare leave together. There wasn't much Jen could do about seeing them. Since the army had requisitioned every worthwhile animal in the country, there was far less horsepower available now, virtually no transport for civilians and definitely no money for fares even if there had been. It was a long journey on foot. Getting home had always been difficult. Now, if anything, it was even harder.

Besides, the increasing demands of the farm prevented Jen from leaving. Although they were all allowed a few hours rest on the Sabbath, no one could be spared for any length of time, no matter how compassionate the reason.

Knowing this, her brothers had saved her the disappointment and came to visit her, bringing Harry with them as a bonus. Their status as serving soldiers had made it easy for them to borrow a pony and trap to drive the forty miles and surprise her one Sunday afternoon.

Jen was ecstatic, as she always was with Harry about. She hadn't seen him for nearly six months, since the time of the apple harvest. She clung to the boy as though their lives depended upon it, showering him with kisses, tears of joy streaming down her cheeks, whilst her brothers looked on as if they'd expected nothing less.

Victoria had never witnessed such devotion towards a younger sibling before. There seemed to be a special bond between Jen and Harry, one which the prolonged absences did nothing to diminish, but for the moment she couldn't think what it might be.

The brothers' arrival came as a surprise to them all and whilst Maisie was always happy to have company, Ella was delighted. 'I do love a man in uniform,' she confessed. Now three of them, all reasonably handsome and of a viable age, had turned up out of the blue. It was like Christmas for her. She spent the entire time flirting outrageously.

Although she'd never met them before, Victoria felt that she already knew them from everything she'd read in Jen's letters. In person, she found them to be good humoured and polite, solid and dependable, the kind of men a woman could feel safe with.

Clearly, they felt the same familiarity towards her, having learned all about her from the same source. Towards the end of the afternoon, they took her to one side and thanked her for what she'd done for Jen, for teaching their sister to read and write. Obviously, they considered it to be an act of great generosity. In such a close-knit family, to help one of them was to help them all.

They went on to discuss Gerald's disappearance. Ever since Jen had informed them of Victoria's situation in one of her letters, they'd continued to ask questions and spread his name far and wide along the battle lines, but so far to no avail. They assured her that they would go on searching but, in the meantime, if she needed a man's help, she should consider herself free to call upon any one of them at any time.

Victoria had never encountered this kind of male behaviour before. They were talking to her like a sister, exhibiting the same consideration and concern that they would show to a female relative. It was a very sudden transition from only child to having three big brothers, but Victoria was touched by their thoughtfulness, and more than happy to accept the change.

When the time came for them to leave, Ella and Maisie volunteered to clear up the remains of the lunch they'd provided, whilst Victoria elected to accompany Jen and her brothers down to the paddock nearby where the pony had been left to graze. Once the animal had been harnessed to the trap, she followed them down to the gate at the end of the lane.

Trying to prise Harry from Jen's arms was something like attempting to scrape a barnacle off a rock using only your fingers. It was then that Victoria began to think that she knew what the bond between them might be. Jen looked distraught, but with a good deal of coaxing from her brothers, she finally relinquished him and they were on their way home.

Even after the trap had vanished around a bend in the road, Jen climbed the gate and perched precariously on top, still waving vigorously until there was nothing left to see. Finally she descended, breathless and tearful, to find Victoria studying her intently.

'What?' she asked at length.

'Will you ever tell him?' Victoria asked.

Jen's familiar defensive posture returned. 'Tell who?'

'Harry,' Victoria became specific. 'Will you ever tell him?'

'Tell him what?' Apparently Jen was determined to make hard work of this.

'That you're his mother and not his sister.'

'Who told you?' Jen crumbled, without the least attempt at denial.

'No one,' Victoria replied. 'I saw it for myself.'

'Have the others guessed?' Jen asked, obviously fearful of discovery.

'I don't think so,' Victoria answered honestly.

'Please,' Jen begged, 'don't tell them. Don't tell anyone.'

Victoria concluded from Jen's behaviour that, even though the rural community was broadminded about so many things, their tolerance did not extend to the unmarried mother and her child. 'Of course I won't,' she assured her, 'but don't you think you should tell him?'

'How can I tell him something like that?' Jen began to cry. 'I loved his father and I thought he loved me, but as soon as he knew I was pregnant he vanished, left the district. I've never seen him since.'

'I'm so sorry,' Victoria told her truthfully.

This sad story answered so many questions about Jen. Now, at last, Victoria understood why she was so cynical, so defensive, slow to trust and quick to condemn.

'Mum and Dad were good about it,' Jen volunteered, as if she was glad of the chance to finally get it off her chest. 'I went to stay with an aunt in Leicester and they put the story about that Mum was expecting again. She even went about with a cushion stuffed up her dress. When Harry was born, I smuggled him back and Mum took him over. Then I came here. It was further away than I wanted to be, but it was all I could find at the time. I needed to work to support him. I used to visit every weekend; then the war came and put a stop to it.'

'At least you know where he is,' Victoria pointed out.

'He might as well be on the other side of the world.' Jen found little comfort in her words. 'If I'd known what was going to happen, I'd never have let him go. Now every day without him claws at my insides.'

'Then why don't you go and get him?' Victoria suggested firmly.

'I can't,' Jen was adamant. 'I'm not being selfish, Vix,' she was quick to point out. 'I don't care about myself. I'm not worried about a scandal. It's just the way they'd treat my boy, if they knew. The names they'd call him. He doesn't deserve that.'

'But surely he deserves to know who his mother is?' Victoria insisted. 'Imagine what he'd think, once he becomes a man and only then found out?'

Jen couldn't answer that. She looked confused.

Victoria stepped forward and put a comforting hand on Jen's arm. 'I come from a section of society which spends all of its time worrying about what other people think. Believe me, it isn't worth it.'

Jen still looked undecided.

'Take my word for it,' Victoria told her. 'It's just as well to tell the ones you love how you feel about them whenever you can,' she spoke from bitter experience, 'because you never know if it's the last time you'll be able to do so.'

*

When war had been declared, the Foreign Secretary, Sir Edward Grey, had said, 'The lamps are going out all over Europe!' They'd certainly gone out in the hayloft. There was no more oil left. A half inch of candle represented all the illumination they had. Victoria was attempting to repair the torn hem of a skirt whilst Ella endeavoured to read from a newly discovered paper, only a week old, by the faint glow of the stub. They had both been reduced to hunching over the table in an effort to share what little light there was. Jen and Maisie lay on their beds in the dark, listening to what Ella was saying. They were all now quite proficient with their reading, taking it in turns whenever a newspaper came to hand, but occasionally there were hiccups.

'It says here,' Ella announced, squinting at the small typeface, 'that the Russians are having a re-evaluation.'

'Is that some sort of a sale then?' Maisie asked from the shadows.

'I suppose it must be,' Ella concluded.

'No. That doesn't sound right.' Victoria put her mending aside and took charge of the newspaper. She went pale as she read the headlines. 'No,' she corrected Ella, 'the word is revolution.'

'Is that like what the French had?' Jen asked. 'You know, when they took over the country and cut the King's head off?'

'That's exactly what it is,' Victoria confirmed.

'That's mad.' Ella stared at her across the guttering candle. 'How can you kill a King?'

'That won't happen here, will it?' Maisie sounded worried.

'Certainly not,' Victoria objected vehemently. 'This is England! No one would dream of harming our dear King.'

'That's the trouble with foreigners,' Jen remarked. 'They do a lot of strange things. You can never trust them.'

'It's worse than that,' Victoria pointed out. 'It means Russia will leave the war. That'll give the Germans more men to throw against our troops.'

Exclamations of dismay issued all around from in the darkness and, as if to illustrate the magnitude of the calamity, a light flared up in the room. It wasn't an omen; Victoria had merely leaned too close to the candle and the edge of the newspaper had caught fire. They managed to save most of it by throwing a towel over the burning pages and stamping on it.

No matter what was happening in the world, it was still necessary to keep body and soul together. The remnant of the candle had been squashed under foot leaving them completely in the dark, but even there, one thing was now quite clear. It was high time they paid another visit to the ironmongers.

Victoria refused to go unless the others promised to restrict their foraging to the absolute bare essentials. She would no longer be a party to their petty larceny, for that was all it amounted to, and whilst expensive necessities such as candles and decent soap were items she couldn't bring herself to go without, she drew the line at that.

Maisie, on the other hand, expressed none of her usual reservations about returning to the shop. Indeed, when the time came, she appeared quite anxious to go.

Having once again absconded from church for which, no doubt, their souls were well and truly damned, they hurried off to Cedric's shop. His welcome was just as effusive as before, if not more so, and as usual he hovered around Maisie at the front of the premises whilst the rest of them went to gather provisions.

Tempted as they might have been, Jen and Ella adhered to the restrictions Victoria had imposed. Consequently, it didn't take them very long to find what they needed, and they returned to the counter earlier than usual to discover Cedric and Maisie engaged in a very curious conversation.

'I saw him,' Maisie was saying.

'Saw who?' Cedric asked.

'The German,' Maisie told him, 'the one from the zeppelin.'

For one awful moment, Victoria and her co-conspirators thought that Maisie was about to betray their secret. So far, it seemed, she'd managed to avoid doing that.

Apparently, the incident in the woods had made her realise that not only was the enemy capable of reaching England, but also the very village in which she lived. This had given rise to flights of unbridled imagination, spurred on by the graphic reports of German atrocities she was now able to read in the newspapers. Lately, she'd begun to entertain the worse kind of fears that prey exclusively on the minds of young girls concerning certain aspects of an occupation. Her anxieties had escalated to such a degree that she now felt compelled to seek the advice of the only man she knew and trusted, without realising the passion it would invoke.

'But he was dead, my dear,' Cedric pointed out reassuringly.

'Yes, I know,' Maisie replied, 'but the next one might not be and could have his friends with him.'

She paused, fidgeting with her hands, wondering how to phrase the question she'd come here specifically to ask without offending his sensibilities. It was a difficult and delicate subject, and one she would not have dreamed of broaching except under the most extreme of circumstances. It was a question about the behaviour of men, soldiers to be precise, who conquered foreign lands. One which she felt only another man could answer. Someone she viewed as a man of the world, a man of experience, someone like Cedric.

'I want you to answer a question,' she continued nervously, 'and I hope you won't think badly of me for mentioning such things, but you must be honest.'

'Of course I will, my dear,' Cedric agreed at once. 'Anything. You can ask me anything.'

Satisfied with his assurance, Maisie glanced hesitantly at the others, but even their presence didn't inhibit her from wanting to know the answer to this most disturbing question. 'If the Germans do get here and if they catch me,' she proceeded deliberately, 'once they've raped me, will they let me go, or will they kill me? I hope you say they'll kill me, because I don't think I'd want to live after something like that.'

There was a moment of stunned silence. None of them had ever imagined that Maisie's concerns about an invasion had reached this level. She'd always seemed so blissfully unaware of worldly matters. It wasn't that she was naive, not in the way Victoria was, as her hearty appreciation of Jen and Ella's cruder bouts of humour tended to prove. Neither was she simple. It was more that her mind was not agile enough to make much use of complicated facts. Yet here she was, asking this question. She'd never indicated the degree of her anxiety, not even to her friends, perhaps for fear of appearing foolish. After all, they'd never really taken her very seriously.

Even at her tender age, she had doubtless stumbled upon innumerable hay meadow seductions so that the act of copulation between humans as well as animals was no mystery to her, and presented no terrors in itself.

However, it would be one thing to surrender her maidenhood behind a hedge to some muscular country lad, and quite another to have it torn from her by some foreign invader. Perhaps it was the element of brutality and danger that had made her so conscious of the threat. On the other hand, it might have been the little extra learning that Victoria had bestowed upon her that had raised the threshold of her awareness. It was insufficient to enable her to take a balanced view of the situation, but just enough to make her worry.

Cedric's face turned ashen, his features assuming an entirely new aspect, uncharacteristically hard and aggressive. 'It'll never happen.' He began to shake his head, staggered by her remarks. He put his arms protectively around her, rocking her gently back and forth. 'Oh Maisie, it'll never happen,' he almost sobbed with anger, 'not whilst I'm alive.'

Releasing her, he took a step back to regard them all, glancing from one to the other as if somewhat surprised and a little disappointed that they'd not confided in him earlier. Clearly, he was labouring under the assumption that this was a fate they all lived in dread of.

'To think that you were worried all this time, whilst I remained ignorant of the fact.' His voice trembled with fierce emotion. His tone expressed the kind of anger a man reserves for the times when all that he holds most dear is threatened. It was not directed at them, only at the situation. 'Whilst I've no doubt that the wretched Hun is no match for the British army,' he continued gravely, 'let me assure you that before a German lays a hand on any one of you, he'll have to step over my dead body.'

'Cedric,' Maisie began in alarm, but there was no holding him now.

'If, by some fiendish mischance, they do get past our troops, then you may depend upon me to come to your defence.'

Normally, it would have been difficult to accept Cedric as a man of action. Under those circumstances, his offer might have sounded ludicrous, but in his present state of mind, he was entirely convincing, ready to do murder and more than a match for any German.

'But they'll have guns, Cedric,' Maisie fretted. 'You'll be killed.'

'Better me than you,' he insisted loudly, dismissing her fears with a wave of his hand. 'This is our country and I'll not stand to hear of any woman on British soil being afraid in her own home.' The thought of it clearly incensed him.

They listened aghast, overawed by this unexpected outburst. None of them dared to interrupt. He prowled up and down in front of them, like an aging lion before his pride, ready to do battle to the death so they might live, and live free.

'I may be too old to fight in this war, but I'm not too old to defend those I love,' he continued, glancing at Maisie. 'I swear to protect you all to the last drop of my blood. You need never be afraid whilst I have breath in my body.' His voice reached a crescendo. 'Do you understand?' he finished forcefully.

They stood there, like a row of schoolgirls, subdued in the presence of their headmaster. 'Yes, Cedric,' they chorused obediently. 'Thank you.'

Cedric nodded, apparently satisfied that he'd got his message across. He seemed an unlikely champion, but his devotion was beyond question. Clearly, it had been a mistake to take him at face value. Possibly it had crossed all their minds that, if Maisie ever accepted his proposal, she would be consenting not just to an old man, but to a brave one.

Astonished and bewildered, Victoria glanced at Jen and Ella. They looked back at her, then down at the armfuls of merchandise they were holding. One by one, they came forward and piled the items onto the counter.

'We can't afford this,' Victoria admitted, shamefaced. 'We never intended to pay for it,' she felt bound to confess for them all. 'We'll put it back.'

'You'll do no such thing,' Cedric informed them, taking an empty bag from behind the counter and filling it with one sweep of his arm. 'You've never taken anything I didn't want you to have.' It was as if he'd always known why they came, and he forgave them and always would, for Maisie's sake.

Noticing how little there was in the bag, he went to a jar of barley sugar twists he kept for the children of his customers, filled a large paper cone and added it to the collection. 'I won't see you leave empty-handed,' he told them, disregarding the fact that he'd already offered his life in their service, 'and I look forward to seeing you all again soon,' he made a point of saying.

'No,' Maisie stepped in front of him, turning her back on the others. 'They won't be coming any more,' she informed him with unexpected assertiveness, 'unless they want to *buy* something,' she remarked meaningfully, glaring over her shoulder at them.

Although Maisie had been startled at first by Cedric's initial reaction to her question, what he'd said after that had impressed her more than all his protestations of love, or any act of generosity. It had inspired her to defend him in return, at least from the attentions of her light-fingered companions.

'But I'd like to come back from time to time, on my own,' she smiled shyly, 'if that would suit you?'

'Certainly it would, my dear,' Cedric nodded appreciatively, suspecting that his cause might have advanced a little. 'Anything you say.'

Leaning forward, she planted a rough kiss on his mouth, making everyone gasp in surprise. It seemed that this was to be a day of revelations.

Indifferent to their reactions, she turned to face them, thrusting a pointing finger at the door. Without a single word of dissent, they all shuffled out somewhat contritely and moved off together in silence, astounded by what had happened.

'What was all that about?' Jen demanded eventually, after she'd had time to recover from the episode. 'Why didn't you talk to us if you were that worried?'

'What would you have said?' Maisie asked.

'I'd have told you not to be so stupid,' Jen replied. 'What German in his right mind would want to rape you?'

'That's why I didn't ask you the question,' Maisie retorted. 'I wanted a sensible answer.'

Maisie had never stood up to anyone before, let alone Jen.

'Oh, I see,' Jen acknowledged, justly reproved. 'Well, if you admire him that much,' she continued, a trifle subdued, 'why didn't you just agree to marry him instead of stopping us from going back to the shop? You didn't have to go that far,' she finished plaintively.

'What you were doing was dishonest and cruel,' Maisie remained adamant, 'and it's not going to happen again.'

'Hark at her,' Ella stared. 'That bloody zeppelin's got a lot to answer for.'

'You're right there,' Jen grumbled. 'If they hadn't buried that German, I'd kill him.'

Victoria tended to agree with Maisie, even though she knew she was going to miss a decent bar of soap. Their bickering amused her, but there was something more. A new truth had emerged. Apparently this war was capable of bringing out not only what was worst in people, but also what was best.

*

Working in the fields was the better part of farm life. The four of them had been sent to join a gang of pea pickers in the ten acre field. There they walked between the long rows of shrubby plants, gathering the ripened pods and putting them into the big canvas bags they had slung across their shoulders. They'd been working for almost half a day when Mr Moss walked onto the field and, Victoria being the nearest to hand, he collared her.

Apparently, a passerby had noticed that the gate to the sheep pasture had come open and some of the animals had escaped. Whilst this helpful individual had been good enough to close the gate, he'd done nothing about the strays. Now Mr Moss wanted Victoria to take herself off to the fallen oak, round them up and get them back into the field.

She set out with reasonable confidence. Sheep were far smaller than cows and she'd already herded them successfully enough. It was an attitude that only served to illustrate her ignorance concerning the contrary nature of sheep.

She crossed four big fields and went through half a dozen different gates until she'd reached the place of the fallen oak. The great tree had blown down in the fierce gales of 1916 and now lay its length across a hazel copse just outside the sheep pasture, its bare branches jutting like skeletal fingers against the open sky. With no signposts to speak of, it had become a point of reference in an otherwise uniform sea of greenery.

Entering the lane, she immediately came across the object of her search. Three sheep were standing along the dusty track, munching at the hedgerow. As soon as she appeared, they stopped chewing to regard her suspiciously. She began to swing her arms and make shooing noises in an effort to get them moving, but that didn't work. They just stood there, staring indolently at her as if daring her to advance, and when she did, they scattered, all in different directions. She pursued the nearest animal up the steep bank, scrambling through a gap in the hedge, where sinuous coils of brambles plucked at her clothes and pulled off her hat, teasing out long strands of hair from her head that dropped in front of her face, blinding her for a moment. Pulling herself free from the tangle, she plunged into a tall stand of thistles. The thistles hereabouts were of such a height and robust nature that they managed to penetrate all the layers of her skirts and petticoats, making her yelp. Having survived this gauntlet, she continued to chase the woolly blighter around the entire length of the oak, through the hazel copse and back into the lane, where it rejoined its two companions who had resumed browsing at the wayside.

Each time she tried to approach, they moved off a little, which took her further away from the gate. She couldn't believe the trouble she was having. She had a university education; surely she could outwit a few sheep? She tried pulling up bunches of grass in an attempt to lure them back to the gate, but they showed no interest in her offering, preferring to nibble at the hedgerow. She tried calling them, as one might summon a dog, but with no result. She endeavoured to manoeuvre her way around and get behind them, but again, they kept just out of reach. Nothing she did seemed to work. By now, thoroughly frustrated, she felt that this contest was becoming personal.

Returning to the hazel copse, she found herself a stout pole which she intended to use as a goad to prod the animals along, but instead they stampeded off, leaving her no option but to follow. She dashed after them and, in fits and starts, they continued a good mile down the lane, through muddy puddles and piled cowpats, until eventually, hot and breathless, she managed to corner them at the very opposite end of the field to which she'd intended.

Fortunately for her, big fields have more than one gate. The lane had skirted the entire pasture round to another entrance. She couldn't believe her luck. The sheep had come to rest bunched together against the bank. Exercising the utmost caution, she crept stealthily past without disturbing her errant charges. The timbers of the gate were old and creaked agonisingly, making her cringe as she opened it. Finally, putting the stick to good use, she managed to herd them back into the field, slamming the gate behind them. She threw the stick aside, making a great show of brushing the dirt from her hands. She felt pleased with what she'd achieved, although she had to admit to herself that by then, the sheep appeared to have tired of the game and seemed only too willing to rejoin the flock.

She recalled ruefully that Gerald had penned many a long verse eulogising the tranquillity of sheep grazing in meadowland. She wondered, if he'd been forced to chase the stupid smelly creatures across miles of English countryside, through muck and mire, whether he'd have waxed quite so lyrical.

She was hot and tired, her hair was full of bits of twig, whilst her right hand and wrist tingled uncomfortably from nettle rash. The way back was all uphill, and in her present state she felt disinclined to return in that direction. She could just see the roofs of the taller farm buildings, far off in the distance from where she stood and, like the roads that led to Rome, all the lanes hereabouts generally ended up at Orchardlea. All she had to do was follow this one, and it would take her back. It was a sound idea, but after a good twenty minutes walking, she discovered that she was completely lost.

Although she'd lived in the vicinity for the best part of two years, she'd never been here before. She didn't recognise this place. Here the hedgerows were taller and more dense. The lanes were deeper, darker and more overgrown. She couldn't get her bearings and for all she knew, she might have wandered off the farm altogether. There was nothing else to do but keep going. She quickened her pace, hoping to walk her way out of this dilemma all the sooner. As she turned a bend, the lane opened out. The hedge continued along on her left, the bank rose up on her right. On top of it was a gate, and standing behind the gate was a woman.

The unexpected meeting made Victoria jump with surprise. The woman didn't seem to notice her. She stared out across the fields and up and down the lane, as if searching for something. She was a figure of desolation. There was a wild look about her. Her face was gaunt and pale. Her long red hair hung filthy and tangled around her narrow shoulders. Her clothes were grimy and ragged, and the fingernails on the thin hands that gripped the top bar of the gate, like talons, were broken and black with dirt. Suddenly, she looked down at Victoria, making her flinch, fixing her with a hollow stare. Then she spoke. 'Have you seen my husband?'

Victoria was completely taken aback, and before she could answer, the woman had returned to gazing out across the fields. Then, curiously, it was as if she'd noticed Victoria for the very first time and, staring hard at her, she asked, 'Have you seen my husband?'

'No, no, I'm afraid not,' Victoria began to reply. 'There's no one else in the lane.'

Before she'd finished speaking, the woman had already resumed her preoccupation. Then glancing down, she saw Victoria. 'Have you seen my husband?' she asked earnestly.

Finally, Victoria thought she'd grasped what was happening. This woman's husband wasn't in the lane; he was at war. She was trying to find out about him. She could certainly help there. Her extensive knowledge of the armed forces was going to come in handy. At least she could give this woman some idea of where he might be. 'Do you know his regiment?' she asked.

The woman didn't seem to hear her. She continued to search the horizon with her eyes, always searching. Then she saw Victoria. 'Have you seen my husband?'

'That's what I'm trying to ascertain,' Victoria replied, raising her voice a little, in case the woman was deaf. 'Do you know his regiment, his battalion? Can you tell me his name?'

The woman regarded her expressionlessly and then repeated, 'Have you seen my husband?'

Then, at last, Victoria really did understand. There was nothing she could do to help. There was nothing anyone could do. This poor woman was quite without her wits. 'No. I'm sorry. I haven't.' She offered a nervous smile and hurried away. She turned once to look back. The woman was still standing there, staring into the distance, apparently oblivious to all else.

It was a disturbing encounter. It made Victoria uneasy. She hurried, running most of the time, until she found her way back to Orchardea, coming in behind the piggery. From there, it was an easy walk to the pea fields. She was glad to be back in the open, out in the sunlight, with people she knew.

'Good Lord!' Jen exclaimed when she saw her. 'You're as white as a sheet, Vix. What's happened? Did you see a ghost?'

'Quite possibly,' Victoria returned shakily. 'I finally managed to get the sheep back into the field,' she explained, 'then I became lost. Somewhere over there,' she pointed, 'a few miles from the fallen oak. There was a woman standing by a gate. She was so strange.'

'Long red hair?' Jen enquired casually. 'Dirty looking?'

'Yes, that's right,' Victoria agreed. 'She kept asking the same thing, over and over again.

'Have you seen my husband?' Jen finished for her.

'Yes, that's exactly right,' Victoria confirmed. 'Then you know who she is?'

'Maggie O'Connell,' Ella joined in.

'Mad Maggie,' Maisie added.

'That's unkind,' Victoria objected. 'The poor woman can't help being that way. I take it her husband's dead, killed in the war?'

'Maggie's husband, Ralph, drove a cart for the neighbouring farm,' Jen took the trouble to explain. 'They hadn't been married long. Every Friday afternoon, he'd drive past that gate and she'd be there waiting for him with a supper. They'd eat it together, then he'd drive her home. Anyway, this particular Friday, something frightened the horse, no one knows what exactly, but it reared up, the cart went into a ditch and rolled over. Ralph was crushed to death.' Jen paused to consider Victoria's original question. 'It happened four years ago, Vix. Maggie's husband was never in the war.'

'Dear heaven,' Victoria sighed. 'Do you mean to say, she's been there all that time?'

'Every Friday since then,' Ella told her, 'and if anyone passes by, she asks...'

'Have you seen my husband?' Victoria added the last line. 'Why doesn't anyone do anything?'

'Folks tried to help her, years ago,' Jen shrugged, 'but she wouldn't stop going down to that gate.'

It was an awful tale, sad and grim, and the tragedy of it couldn't even be blamed on the war. Suddenly, a terrible thought occurred to Victoria. 'Could that happen to me?' she wondered aloud. 'Could I become like that? Out of my mind, wandering aimlessly, ragged and filthy, waiting for someone who'll never return?'

'No, not you, Vix,' Jen was quick to assure her. 'Maggie O'Connell was just a simple labouring woman. When Ralph was killed, she couldn't cope, but you're strong. You've a good education, a fine mind; you'll manage.'

'Jen's right,' Ella added. 'You're better than that. Besides, Gerald will come back. You wait and see. Everything will turn out for the best.'

'We'll have old Mossy down on our necks if we don't get going,' Maisie warned, 'and it sounds as if the weather's starting to turn.'

Jen looked up. 'What are you talking about?' she frowned. 'There ain't a cloud in the sky.'

'Well, I can hear thunder,' Maisie insisted.

They all stood and listened for a moment, now able to discern a low rumble, far off in the distance.

'No,' Victoria spoke at last, 'it isn't thunder. The wind's blowing from the south. It's the sound of gunfire.'

They listened in silence for another moment, the events of the past banished from their minds as they contemplated the stark reality of the present.

'Anyway,' Jen remarked dispassionately, 'we'd best get to it. These peas won't pick themselves.'

*

In the middle of the year, the news came through that America had entered the war, bringing with it thousands of fresh troops and tons of badly needed equipment. For many, it rekindled the fragile hope that this war might end sooner rather than later.

It couldn't end soon enough for Mrs Fisher. She wasn't getting any younger, and the stress of running the farm at capacity was beginning to tell on her. She'd been under so much pressure lately that she'd inadvertently allowed the paperwork to pile up, and she was in something of a panic by the time she called on Victoria to deal with it.

In spite of the work that carried on here, throughout the war years Orchardlea had constantly fallen below the targets the government had set for it. There was a real risk that Mrs Fisher would have the property confiscated from her, and a more competent manager put in her place. She was only too well aware of the situation, having already received several warnings from various government departments.

Victoria worked all morning, and by mid afternoon she'd managed to sort out the mess. There was some good news, and some bad news. Judging from the way the accounts read now, Orchardlea had finally pulled itself up. Unhappily, there were two vital documents that would corroborate these facts, and which should have been sent off a week ago, but were still here.

When she told Mrs Fisher of her findings, the old lady was beside herself. Her entire workforce was scattered all over the farm. There wasn't a boy available to send to the village, and every horse and cart was fully employed. Finally, she came up with a solution in the shape of an old bicycle. Giving Victoria some money for stamps, she told her to cycle into the village and take the documents to the post office personally, adding generously that there was no need to hurry back.

When she'd first arrived at Orchardlea, Victoria hadn't the slightest idea of how to reap or sow, milk or herd stock, but she'd been able to ride a bicycle ever since she was a child. Relieved that Mrs

Fisher hadn't asked her to walk there and back, she made excellent time through the empty lanes, taking her feet off the pedals and freewheeling down all the hills, until eventually after forty minutes or so, she arrived in Staunton Gifford.

It proved to be an efficient, if somewhat cool reception from Mrs Spragget, whose deplorable letter writing trade had suffered a severe decline thanks to her, and after discharging her duty and seeing the documents safely into the first class post, she returned to the bicycle. Thanks to Mrs Fisher's generosity, she now had some time for herself. She didn't return straight to the farm, but instead went a good deal out of her way and visited the cottage.

She'd been meaning to do so for some time now, as soon as an opportunity presented itself. Lately, she'd become infected with a severe bout of nostalgia, and was anxious to see if anything had changed. To her surprise and delight, nothing was different. The garden was heavily overgrown, but the cottage was exactly the same. No one had occupied it since she'd left. Leaning the bicycle against the fence, she opened the gate and went inside. Peering through the bare window, she could see the kitchen table and chair where she'd sat and read Gerald's letters, and where she'd written her own in return. She went round to the front door through which she'd passed on countless occasions. She put her hand against it and pushed, but this time it wouldn't open for her.

She went into the garden by way of the ivy nook where she'd seen Beryl kissing George, pausing to wonder vainly where their lives might have taken them had events turned out differently. Further on, the lawn stood knee high in thick tussocks, and everywhere there were tall stands of willowherb, the slender pink spears sporting clusters of downy seed heads that shivered in the gentle breeze. In the borders, the cultivated plants struggled to compete with the army of weeds that had invaded the plot, but there was still a good deal of colour and the perfume almost as rich. She closed her eyes and inhaled the fragrance, felt the warmth of the sun on her face and in her mind's eye, she could see it all just as it once was. She remembered that last golden day when everyone had been there, when Gerald had been with her.

It was as much as she could bear, and there was no purpose to be served in what she did. She put her hand against her breast and felt the locket beneath her blouse. She rubbed her fingers gently against it, as if in some vain attempt to resurrect him, like a fairytale genie, but even she thought that would be asking a little too much.

There was one thing left to do, one last ritual to perform. Returning to the gate, she let down a length of her hair and cut it off with a little pair of scissors she'd brought for the purpose. Plaiting the tresses, she fashioned a small garland and hung it on the gatepost. It replaced the one she'd put there when Gerald had left, which had long since succumbed to the elements, as a reaffirmation of her undying devotion. It was her symbol. It was her candle in the window to guide the traveller home. It was a token of her faith, her prayer to God for her husband's safe return. If Gerald should ever pass that way, he would see it hanging there and know that she still waited for him.

Aware that she'd tarried long enough, and not wishing to abuse Mrs Fisher's good will, she realised reluctantly that it was time to leave. With a last backwards glance and a huge sigh, she mounted the bicycle and began the return journey.

Her detour to the cottage had forced her to take a different route back. Not that she minded; she knew all the lanes in this area. She and Gerald had walked every one of them in happier days. It was a glorious July afternoon. The cloudless sky was deep blue, and the hedgerows as she spun along were thick with honeysuckle and wild roses, their scent mingling with the sweet aroma of the clover flowers from the pastures beyond. It would have been idyllic had she not suddenly come upon a scene of such utter destruction that it caused her to break sharply and stare aghast.

A little way down the lane, the hedgerow had been torn up to make way for traction engines and heavy lorries which now plied back and forth across the churned pasture. Beyond that, the woods were being felled; tree after tree had been brought down, sawn up and carried out, whilst bonfires of discarded branches smoked against the skyline. It was the same as far as she could see. The hillsides had been denuded, the hedgerows rooted out and the green fields chewed into an ugly mire. The devastation was so complete that it seemed to soar beyond anything it was rumoured the Germans might do, if they invaded.

She cycled a little further on to where some men were sawing timber at the end of the lane. On making enquiries, she was told that the wood was needed for the war effort, anything from ammunition boxes to shoring boards for the trenches. She couldn't believe her ears. What insanity was this? The beauty that was England, her woods, her fields, her country lanes and hedgerows, everything they were fighting to preserve was being dismantled to fuel the war. As she made her way back to the farm, she wondered if the world would ever become what people in their heart of hearts truly wanted it to be, or if it would remain as it was now, the creation of their greed, anger and stupidity.

She would have little time to dwell on what she'd seen. Only a week later, she came out of the milking shed to find the postman standing in the yard with a telegram in his hand. He looked right at her.

'No,' she breathed, shaking her head. 'Not me. Not now.'

He walked straight up to her and thrust the envelope into her hand. 'I'm sorry,' he mumbled, before hurrying away.

It was a mistake, it had to be. Victoria tore open the envelope, pulled out its contents and read the short, stunning message.

'Regret to inform you. Second lieutenant G. Avery. Serial No 712964. West Sussex Yeomanry. Missing, believed killed in action 7th July. Lord Kitchener sends his sympathy.'

After that, everything went dark.

Chapter Twelve

The first thing Victoria was aware of as she regained consciousness was a dreadful pounding in her ears. Her head ached and as she lifted her hand to touch it, she discovered a damp cloth had been laid across her brow. As her vision cleared, Jen's face swam into view looking down at her and she could hear voices speaking her name. The last thing she recalled was standing in the yard looking at the postman. Now she was lying on her bed, her boots had been removed and the right side of her temple throbbed violently. She tried to sit up.

'Steady girl,' she heard Jen say, 'you've had a fall.'

Jen eased her forward and adjusted the pillow so that she could sit up comfortably. She was surprised to see Mr Moss and Mrs Fisher standing at the back of the loft watching her with concern.

'Is she going to be all right?' Mr Moss asked, seeing that she was awake.

Jen turned. 'Yes, thanks, Mr Moss. We'll look after her now.'

He nodded, glanced at Mrs Fisher and then both of them withdrew.

'Mrs Fisher has left some brandy for you,' Jen told her, filling a small glass and offering it up.

It was strong and pungent and burned her throat as she swallowed, making her cough. Jen immediately refilled the glass and offered it again.

'I don't want any more,' Victoria declined.

Jen ignored her, pressing the glass to her lips and making her drink. After that, the trembling in her arms and legs seemed to ease a little.

'You've got quite a lump there,' Jen observed, as she wrung out the cloth and replaced it on her forehead. 'There'll be a nasty bruise. We'll have to find some witch hazel to put on that.'

Then suddenly Victoria remembered everything. She raised her right hand; the telegram was still there, clenched in the ball of her fist. 'Oh God, Jen,' she howled in panic, 'it's come. The telegram, it's come!'

'Now just you calm down,' Jen advised her soberly. 'Don't go jumping to any conclusions, just because you got a bit of paper.'

'I think it's daft,' Maisie remarked. 'Your husband's been missing for ages. Why send a telegram now?'

'Maisie's got a point, for once,' Jen latched on to the idea, as the others gathered round. 'Read it again; not the personal details, the next bit.'

Victoria stared blearily at the crumpled message. 'Missing,' she read aloud.

'That's a bloody revelation, ain't it,' Jen scoffed. 'You've known that for years. Read the next bit.'

Victoria did as she asked. 'Believed killed in action.'

'Believed,' Jen sneered. 'They're not even sure. Perhaps, maybe. Now they send a telegram and it's official. What you got there is rubbish. It ought to hang in the earth closet.'

'I agree with Jen,' Ella told her. 'When you first came here and told us how long he'd been gone, well, we all thought he was dead.' She stopped short when she saw Victoria's expression. 'Sorry, Vix,' she smiled self-consciously. 'Of course, we don't think that now. We haven't for ages, what with you telling us 'he's not dead', like you always do. What I'm trying to say is those people who sent that telegram, they don't know any more than you do.'

Victoria was well aware of what they were trying to do. To bolster her spirits and make light of these evil tidings, but the fact of the matter remained that it had come. Its absence had been the foundation on which she'd built her hopes. Whilst it remained undelivered, the contest, for that was what she felt it had become, her faith against hard fact, could continue, but what was she to do now that it had arrived?

'I knew a man in London,' she told them. 'His name was Alan Fairchild. He worked at the war office and he found files that had been misplaced, names of dead men who'd gone missing months before.'

'So what?' Jen replied dismissively. 'Remember what happened to Sally Carver.'

Sally Carver was a young woman of the village married to John, with two small children. Her husband had been reported dead at the very beginning of the war, killed in the retreat from Mons. Sally had remained a widow for almost eighteen months until she met Albert, a soldier home on leave with nothing but his knapsack to keep him company. They had fallen in love, married and now Sally was expecting another child. It might have been a happy ending, except that just a few days ago her first husband, John, had come home.

There was much in what Jen intimated. Poor Sally was far from the only woman to be dealt such a perverse blow. This war had a way of twisting lives around. There were many other examples she could call upon, if she wished to restore a measure of hope.

'You're right, all of you. You're absolutely right,' Victoria agreed decisively. 'This means nothing.' She crushed the telegram back into a tight ball and threw it on the floor. 'Nothing's changed and nothing will, until Gerald comes home. Now, let's get back to work.'

'Hold your horses,' Jen put a hand on her shoulder and pushed her back against the pillow. 'You're not going anywhere. You caught a nasty crack on the head when you fainted. Mrs Fisher's given you the rest of the day off. You just lay there quiet and rest. We'll be back later.'

They were good friends. Victoria felt that she was lucky to have them, even though, once they'd left, she slipped off the bed, retrieved the telegram, smoothed it out, folded it twice and put it in her pocket. She'd told them she hoped what they wanted to hear, but there was something she'd not revealed to them. There was a special place in her heart where she'd kept the image of Gerald alive all the time they'd been apart. Each day, she looked there and he smiled back, but now when she looked, he'd gone. The telegram had dealt her a mortal blow.

Even after the bruise on her head had faded and then finally vanished, she remained buoyant. It was important to look good in front of the others. The telegram, in a way, had dispersed so many doubts and provided a sense of closure for her. She was travelling in a new direction now, and her way had been made clear. She practised being happy until it became second nature. Indeed, at times it was so convincing that she almost believed it herself. The deception was necessary. She couldn't risk her new plan being discovered before she'd had time to put it into action. It was the only thing that was important to her now, and to that end she bent all her efforts.

Weeks turned into months, Christmas came and went. It was 1918 and the fourth year of the war. Victoria had kept her secret well. She'd laid her plan with great care and deliberation. Now she was almost ready to carry it out, and no one even suspected what she was about to do.

It had taken her a long time to find the right place, somewhere out of the way, secluded, unfrequented. After a good deal of searching, she'd discovered a derelict mill house, far to the east of the farm by the river. Abandoned and forgotten, bereft of its wheel and its roof, it might have been built with her purpose in mind. It was further proof, as if she needed any, that what she intended was meant to be. Inside, a heavy beam, perhaps twenty feet from the floor, stretched from wall to wall, and leaning against it was an old cherrypicker. It couldn't have been more perfect.

Finding the rope had been easier; it was used all over the farm. Finally, she had selected a good length of inch thick hemp and concealed it in the barn where she'd hidden Alistaire, the deserter. She could retrieve it whenever she liked. Every spare moment, any time she could slip away alone, she would go to the barn and work on it, tying and retying the knot, until she'd got it exactly right. Now the noose slipped up and down wonderfully well. There wasn't the slightest chance of it snagging.

When all was ready and the day came for her to leave, she made a great show of complaining about a stomach ache. Her acting ability surprised even herself and she was left alone in the loft with a dose of cod liver oil. When everyone had gone, she changed out of her work clothes and into her best clothes, taking particular care to dress in clean underwear – that was most important. She didn't know who would undress her body, but whoever it was, she didn't wish to appear shabby in front of them. She decided not to leave a note. It would be quite apparent to everyone why she'd killed herself, and with a last look around the loft, she went down into the yard.

Outside, it was a bright clear crisp January morning. Her breath drifted out into the air like a veil. Strangely, she felt invigorated, light, almost euphoric. She stood there for a moment savouring the sensation. All the pain, all the doubt, all the anguish had vanished. She was as free as air. Free to go. She went to the barn and retrieved the rope and put it in her bag, then trotted off across the fields and down towards the mill.

On the way she saw a robin, a cheery little fellow, who sat upon a branch and watched her as she passed. She had no crumbs for him, but he bowed to her in any case and flew away. Only then did she hesitate, just a fraction, but no, all the robins in the world would not divert her from her chosen course.

Once inside the mill, she took off her hat and coat and her jacket. Taking the locket from inside her blouse, she opened it and took one last look at Gerald's picture. She had not let it leave her person since the day he'd given it to her. She'd always worn it whilst she'd believed him to be alive. Now she removed it and put it in her pocket. After all, there was no sense in allowing the chain to be broken when the noose tightened.

Then she set about with the rope. After a couple of casts, she managed to loop it over the beam and tied it off to a solid iron bracket that had once held the axle of the mill wheel. Everything was in place. The noose hung about fifteen feet from the floor, next to the ladder. She pulled a length of thin twine from her pocket and fashioned a pair of manacles, using slip knots. Once she was in position and the noose was around her neck, she could put her hands behind her back, slip her wrists into the loops and, flexing her arms, pull them closed. There was no point in trying to hang herself if she was going to grab at the rope when she fell.

There was nothing left to do now, except climb the ladder. That would come presently. For now, she went back to the door of the mill and looked out onto the frosty morning. It was all so peaceful, so beautiful; she would miss scenes like this, but her way was set. Returning to the ladder, she put her foot upon the first rung and paused. When they discovered her, people would think that she'd lost her wits, like poor Maggie O'Connell, but she hadn't. She was as sane now as she'd ever been. Her mind was sharp and clear, and she'd considered this course of action for so very long. In the end, all it amounted to was this. It wasn't that she couldn't go on without him. It was just that she didn't want to.

Now she had both feet on the first rung. She climbed to the second, then the third. Another six rungs passed beneath her. The ladder wobbled briefly. She stopped, letting it settle. She didn't want to fall and hurt herself. As she continued to climb, she felt completely at peace. A great sense of calm settled over her; it was wonderful. At last, she stood beside the noose. To think that she'd come to this – not that it mattered any more. Nothing did. She knew that there was a place in heaven for heroes, but that there was none for suicides. She hoped that there might be some middle ground where she could meet with Gerald once more and take him in her arms again and kiss him before she was consigned to damnation. She would suffer it gladly, for all eternity, just for that one brief moment.

She reached out for the noose, her fingertips brushing against the fibres. She stretched a little further.

'What are you doing, Vix?'

The voice seemed to echo around the mill. The ladder lurched, Victoria clung precariously to it, pressing herself against the rungs, the mood of the moment bursting, like a soap bubble.

'Who said that? Who's there?' she demanded, shocked and outraged, straining her head round, trying to see the intruder. It was no good, she couldn't see. She had to shuffle awkwardly around on the ladder until finally she looked down into the mill. Framed in the doorway was the silhouette of a woman. What Victoria had been about to do was so intensely private and personal that to be caught in the act was too embarrassing for words. Her feeling of calm changed to one of agitation. 'Who are you?' she demanded once more. 'Show yourself.'

The figure advanced, and Jen sauntered into the mill.

'Jen,' she breathed in astonishment. 'What did you say?'

'I said,' Jen repeated quite deliberately, 'what are you doing, Vix?'

Victoria glanced at the ladder upon which she stood, and then at the noose that dangled nearby. She felt as she'd done once, very long ago, when her mother had walked unannounced into her room and found her lying on her bed reading a lurid romance. At the time, her mother had asked the same question. Now, all she could come up with was the same answer she'd used then.

'Nothing.'

'Ah well, that's good,' Jen seemed pleased to hear it, 'because I need your help.'

'My help?'

'Yes, your help. Come down for a moment.'

Jen's attitude was becoming irksome. This was so surreal. Apparently, she'd noticed nothing. All she'd come for was to ask a favour. What was the woman thinking of? She picked her way back down the ladder until she stood once again on the stone floor of the mill house. Jen walked over to a large crate and sat down, patting the space beside her with the flat of her hand, indicating that Victoria should join her. Reluctantly, she did so, sitting with her back to her.

'What are you doing here, Jen?' she sighed despondently.

'I want to write a letter,' Jen replied.

'A letter?' Victoria's voice rose in pitch.

'Yes, a letter.' Jen took a sheet of paper from her pocket and smoothed it out on her knee. Then she took a pencil from behind her ear and made a great display of licking the tip, smacking her lips noisily. 'Now, let's see,' she mused, 'Dear...' She spelt out the word in the most irritating fashion, 'D.E.A.R.' Then she paused. 'What's his name?'

'Who?'

'Your husband.'

'My husband?'

'Yes, your husband. What's his name?'

'Gerald.' As soon as she spoke his name, all the pain rushed back and all the grief she'd bottled up started to rise within her as the tears began to trickle down her cheeks.

'Say it again,' Jen insisted, 'louder.'

'Gerald,' Victoria began to sob uncontrollably. 'His name is

Gerald. Why are you writing a letter to my husband?' she sniffed tearfully.

Jen slapped the pencil down on the paper. 'Well, there it is, you see,' she declared relentlessly. 'When Gerald comes home, as we all know he will, and finds that his wife has topped herself, he's going to want to know why. So before it happens, I'd like a few answers to give him.'

All at once, Victoria let out a huge gasp, as if her heart had broken, and collapsed into a flood of tears. 'I'm so ashamed,' she cried.

It was what Jen had been waiting for. It was what she'd been trying to induce. She caught hold of Victoria in a firm embrace. 'Go on girl,' she snarled fiercely, 'get it all out. You think I don't know what shame is?'

Victoria just cried and cried, in choking waves of tears, overwhelmed with remorse for what she'd been about to do. Only now did she realise that the shining sanity which had taken her to this point was nothing but the madness of despair that had driven her slavishly along. She'd truly believed that there was nothing left for her in the world. She'd given up hope and very nearly given up her life. Whilst millions fought and died to defend her world and her existence, she'd sought to throw it all away. Her actions, she felt, were beyond contempt.

Consumed with grief and shame, Victoria poured out all her misery, her body racked by convulsive sobs and gasps. When at length all her tears were spent, she eased herself away from Jen and turned to view with reddened eyes the terrible spectacle of the noose. It was as if she'd fallen into a deep sleep and dreamed a dream of death. Now she was awake again, and only the noose remained in evidence to suggest that once her reason had been driven from her.

She looked back at Jen in horror of what might have been and that so nearly was. 'I can't believe what I was about to do,' she admitted. 'I was actually going to kill myself.'

'Yes, I know,' Jen agreed easily. 'When you get that idea into your head, it all seems so perfectly reasonable.'

'How did you know I was here?' Victoria asked. She'd taken such pains to keep this place a secret.

'I followed you,' Jen remarked casually. 'I've been following you for months, every time you went off by yourself.'

'But why?' Victoria stared in surprise.

'Because I recognised the signs,' Jen told her simply.

In spite of her efforts to the contrary, Victoria realised that she'd given herself away after all. Then another thought occurred to her. 'How did you recognise the signs?'

Jen just looked at her.

Victoria clasped a hand to her mouth. 'Oh no, Jen, not you.'

Jen nodded. 'When I found myself abandoned and pregnant, I didn't want to live either. Nothing seemed to matter any more. Just like you, I started going off by myself, looking for somewhere to do it.' She paused to pull a handkerchief from the sleeve of her blouse and began to wipe the tears from Victoria's face. 'It wasn't around here, of course. It was back home at Melsbury. I found a beautiful glade in the middle of the woods, and a great big oak tree, easy to climb, branches like gallows. I was going to hang myself too.' She made it sound as if it were a regular pastime. 'I had the rope slung out and I was halfway up the tree.'

'What stopped you?' Victoria felt compelled to ask.

'He did,' Jen replied. 'It was Harry. Oh, I didn't care if I lived or died, but he hadn't had a chance of life yet. I couldn't rob him of that just because of the way I felt, so I climbed down, and I've been glad I did every day since.' She took Victoria's face in her hands and looked deep into her swollen eyes. 'And so will you be, Vix,' she assured her. 'Every time tomorrow comes. One way or another, you'll be glad you're here.'

'To think that I was about to abandon him,' Victoria glanced around at the noose again, 'to let his memory vanish with my death.'

Jen put her hand against her cheek and turned her head away. 'With him or without him, Vix,' she told her, 'the world's a better place with you in it.' She finished wiping away the tears and looked hard at Victoria, smiling. 'Now, tell me,' she asked, 'am I going to have to keep following you around?'

Victoria managed to smile back, shaking her head. 'No,' she told her truthfully. 'No, you won't.' Jen need not have worried, for at the very moment of her salvation, she'd forced herself to look deep into her aching heart, and found Gerald there, smiling back at her.

Jen gave her a final hug and stood up. 'Well then,' she continued in a business-like fashion, 'what are we going to do about all this?'

Together they untied the noose and pulled it down, and with a piece of sharp-edged rusted metal, they sawed it into lengths and cast it into the river. Then they hauled the heavy ladder from its resting place against the beam and let it fall. It struck the wall and broke in two, splintering against the stone floor. After that, Victoria took out the locket and put it on again.

'I'd better get you back to the loft and give that puffy face a wash,' Jen remarked in motherly tones. 'It looks as if you've been in a fight.'

She had, and with Jen's help, she'd won. Victoria would never forget her suicide attempt. For as long as she lived, the shock of what she'd intended to do would always remain fresh in her mind. No matter how difficult the circumstances became, no matter how lonely she felt, or how hard the pain was to bear, she would never again try to take her own life. She no longer lived in hope, but only with a grim determination to see it through. It was plain fare, but it sustained her.

*

A month later, in February, the 'Qualification of Women' Act was passed, granting women over the age of thirty the right to vote. Although it came as much by way of thanks from a grateful government to the women of Britain, who'd taken over the many dirty and difficult jobs vacated by the men who'd gone to war as anything else, it still counted as a significant victory for the suffragette movement. Without a doubt, their ceaseless campaigning had played a major role in bringing about this radical change in social and political attitudes.

Sadly, it all came too late for Beryl Whittacker. It was at this time that Victoria particularly felt her absence. So far, she'd not even been able to leave the farm and return to London to visit her grave. It was a pilgrimage she'd vowed to make just as soon as the war was over.

Beryl would have been so proud that her actions had been so completely vindicated. She'd not so much sacrificed her life for the cause, as others had done, as lost it pursuing that which she believed in. Quite possibly, it all came down to the same thing; not that it mattered now. Whichever way you looked at it, the outcome always remained the same. Her death was not as spectacular or symbolic as that of Emily Davidson, who'd thrown herself under the King's horse during the Derby of 1913. To be pushed into the road and run over by a bus seemed such an ignominious end for so noble a character. Doubtless, Beryl would have considered the cause worth the cost. Nevertheless, it still seemed like a waste of a perfectly good life.

Victoria felt that intensely too. She still carried a considerable burden of guilt and shame regarding her aborted suicide attempt. She was only too well aware of the stark contrast between Beryl, who'd lost her life trying to improve the circumstances of all women, and she, who having succumbed to such an unhappy state of mind, had been willing to throw hers away. Jen, the only other person aware of what she'd tried to do, had never raised one word of criticism against her, but it would be a very long time before she forgave herself. Until then, the guilt and shame she endured would serve as a just penance for her wickedness.

The victory for the suffragettes was not the only sweeping change to take place that year. There were many more, and they were moving swiftly. Whilst the war was being fought on the western front, another war was being fought on the home front - the war to wrest every ounce of food possible from the land. Its front line troops were the men and women who ploughed and sowed and reaped in all weathers and at all hours. Farmers had been forced to contend with long hard winters, late cold springs, and unseasonably heavy rain. Conscription and better paid jobs in towns and factories had robbed them of the majority of their skilled labour, leaving them with only school children, women, pacifists and prisoners of war to do the vital work. The former were usually unequal to the task, whilst the latter were often unpredictable, unruly and difficult to handle.

Rationing had already been imposed, and food shortages were commonplace. The only way to counteract the German submarine blockade was to grow more food at home. If that failed, Britain would starve, and the victories that British soldiers had given their lives to win in foreign fields would be wasted. What happened on the farms of England was equally as important as what happened on the battlegrounds of France and Belgium.

A massive 'plough-up' campaign had been in force since the summer of 1917. Now there was more pasture under the plough than there had ever been in the annals of British farming, and England's green and pleasant land was beginning to look more like the battlefields of Europe every day.

Under-equipped and with a vastly inferior and mostly inexperienced workforce, the farmers were beginning to struggle under the burden of increasing government demands. Originally, it had been promised that thousands of soldiers would be taken from active service to help on the farms, but after the battle of Passiondale far fewer could be spared. Fortunately, there was still the Women's Land Army: teams of young women fully trained in current farming methods who could be sent wherever they were needed.

Orchardlea's status had by now so much improved, thanks in part to the accuracy of Victoria's accounting, that Mrs Fisher was now able to call upon some of this extra help. To aid the 'big push' on the land, ten thousand tractors had been imported from America. Two of these were duly delivered to the farm. A week later, a group of Land Army girls appeared with a traction engine and a mechanical thresher, followed a day later by a lone individual from another unit, driving a motor plough.

As news of their arrival spread rapidly throughout the farm, anyone who could came out to have a look, viewing it all with considerable suspicion and a good deal of alarm. No one had ever seen anything like it before. The equipment was strange enough, but it was the girls who raised the most eyebrows.

To Victoria, they looked exactly like the ones she'd seen in the newspaper photograph. They wore stout boots, laced leggings, breeches, a tunic, short-brimmed hats and a smock that covered the breeches to the knee. In the minds of many, the sight of women wearing breeches flew in the face of all decency, whilst for some it bordered on depravity.

The land girls were expected to wear the smock whenever they went out in public, but as the weeks went by, they all decided that the confines of the farm didn't constitute a public place and dispensed with it altogether, further outraging many of the residents.

For once, Victoria was glad that she hadn't after all joined this organisation. She didn't feel she would have been comfortable in such outlandish attire. The land girls, however, seemed perfectly at ease in their uniforms as they sauntered confidently around the farm. In particular, the robust young woman who'd driven in on the motor plough and who seemed keen that Victoria should know her name was Frederica, or Freddie as she preferred to be called, even offered to lend her a spare pair of breeches so that she might try them on. It was quite the most disgusting suggestion that Victoria had ever been called upon to entertain, and she didn't hesitate with her refusal.

To some extent, it was even difficult to hold a conversation with these girls. Their breeches, close-cropped hair and tight fitting caps made it seem as if she were talking to a young man, instead of a young woman. They appeared to be a new breed, an emergent species - independent, self-confident and outgoing. They dressed like men and did the job of a man whilst being ready and able for the task.

Beryl would have labelled it as emancipation. Mrs Fisher, on the other hand, simply encapsulated their looks and behaviour as 'modern' and that term, for most of the rest, seemed to sum up everything they said and did.

There was one occasion when Victoria came across a land girl standing in the yard, smoking a cigarette. It was hardly the type of conduct that could be attributed to the 'best kind' of girl, but eaten up with curiosity, she went across and asked if she could try it. The girl was only too glad to let her have a puff, instructing her to suck on the cigarette and then inhale the smoke. Victoria did as she was advised and spent the next few minutes coughing violently, her eyes streaming, and the rest of the day feeling rather queasy.

Whilst they displayed an obvious confidence in their own ability to do the job for which they'd been sent, the land girls were in no way arrogant. Nevertheless, there remained a suggestion in the minds of all those who saw them that these futuristic she-males had come here to teach the yokels a thing or two about farming - they who'd worked the land for a lifetime. However, there was no escaping the fact that they'd been trained to operate equipment that nobody here could understand, not even the men, and whether anyone liked it or not, they and their machines would ultimately become the spearhead of the workforce at Orchardlea.

Despite all the apparent differences, they were on the whole friendly enough, good natured, gregarious and anxious to fit in, unlike the wretched machines they'd brought with them. They belched black smoke, made a dreadful racket, perpetually stank of petrol fumes and continually dripped oil everywhere. It was a lot harder to wash a single spot of oil from the hem of a petticoat than any amount of cow dung. Unfortunately, there was no denying that they were faster and more efficient than any team of horses. They didn't get tired and they didn't need feeding.

After a lifetime of faithful service, poor old Dicken had been relegated to hauling manure out to the newly turned fields. Whilst engaged in this menial task, he had become lame and was invalided back to the stables.

Victoria had found time to visit him one afternoon with a bag of apples. As he munched his way through the tasty treat, she looked out and across at the distant hillside to where the tractors and the motor plough had taken over from him. The land girls' confidence in their ability to do the job hadn't been misplaced. They were making fast light work of the ploughing, as acre after acre fell easily to their new technology. Whereas once it had taken a man and a team of horses a week to plough that field, now the Land Army girls only needed a day.

Quite suddenly, it seemed, the rural idyll had changed. Instead of gentle birdsong, the aroma of fresh tilled soil and the creak of leather harness as the ploughman and his horses turned a well-placed furrow, now there was the screech and clank of grinding metal and the stench of exhaust fumes.

Dicken nuzzled her shoulder with his velvety nose. She reached up and stroked his broad muzzle. It was true. An old thing always knows when a new thing has arrived. Dicken obviously did. She didn't think that what she saw signified the end of horsepower, but certainly it was the beginning of the end. The machines were here to stay.

In late September, General Ferdinand Foch, Commander in Chief of the allied armies, ordered an all-out assault, the 'big push' on the German positions. In the weeks that followed, hundreds of thousands of British, French and American troops pressed home the attack, finally storming the Siegfried line, the last great stronghold of German resistance.

At home, bedevilled by the caprices of the British climate, a more formidable foe than any German, farmers all over the country were preparing for their own 'big push', mustering every able-bodied individual who would answer the call. It was imperative to move quickly and decisively; the weather threatened to close in at any moment. Torrential rains could come and destroy the vital crops.

To help Orchardlea fulfil its part in the plan, fifty soldiers were drafted onto the farm and billeted in bell tents next to the spinney at the end of the lane. Unlike the land girls and their infernal contraptions, everyone was glad to see them, especially Ella, who thought she'd died and gone to heaven. Not only was their company a pleasant change from the acne-scarred farm lads and the weather beaten old specimens they'd had to contend with, but many of them were experienced farm workers in their own right. In the fight for food, they would make a significant difference.

The wheat and barley stood waist high, golden and ripe. A vast army of labourers had been assembled. Now they were poised, ready to gather the biggest harvest in the history of the nation, knowing that it was by this harvest that England would stand or fall.

It had been many a long year since the farm had seen this much activity, as men, women, horses and machines converged on the land in a united front. As the storm clouds loomed overhead and the autumn mists descended, they worked ceaselessly, making use of every favourable hour to wrest the bounty from the earth.

Victoria and her friends had been assigned to work alongside the threshing machine, which had been placed at the centre of the largest wheat field and was now the focal point of the whole operation. It had been coupled to the traction engine with long leather belts to drive it. The flywheel hummed continuously as the threshing arms rose and fell in a rhythmic clatter, whilst gangs of people scurried to and fro, arms laden with precious sheaves, to keep it fed. It sent great clouds of chaff up into the misty air. It got everywhere; in their hair, their mouths, their eyes, inside their clothes, prickling against their skin, so that everyone seemed to be constantly scratching.

The majority of instructions were given as hand signals. It was virtually impossible to hear yourself speak above the din of the machinery, but nonetheless there was a great sense of purpose and camaraderie among the workers. Victoria had never played a part in anything quite as important as this before. At last, she felt as if she was making a worthwhile contribution to her country, and she delighted in the atmosphere of fellowship and friendliness. In some instances, there was more than she would have liked.

The robust land girl, Freddie, having set aside the motor plough, was now in charge of operating the threshing machine. She'd developed the most disquieting habit of winking at Victoria whenever she passed. Previously, she'd even asked her if she might like to take a walk with her one evening. Victoria hadn't spent the best part of three years in the hay loft, listening to Jen and the others, without learning about some of the less attractive aberrations of female behaviour. Therefore she'd declined, suspecting that the girl had something more on her mind than merely walking. The rest of the land girls were alright, even though at times they spoke and behaved like men, generally they confined themselves to flirting with the soldiers.

With the elements constantly threatening to interrupt the proceedings, the work continued apace until, despite the hindrance of the weather nationwide, the bulk of the harvest had been brought safely in. When taking into account those who'd been instrumental in achieving this success during one of the worse seasons on record, the majority of them being women and inexperienced volunteers, it would come to be considered by many as the greatest victory of the war.

The harvest had been saved, but that didn't mean that work stopped around the farm. There were still routine jobs that needed to be done. It was early November and, having come full circle, so to speak, Victoria found herself once again back in the potato fields. Things were different now. She was no longer the novice she'd once been and the work, although still hard, didn't tax her nearly as grievously as it once had. Many of the soldiers assigned to the farm were still there. They'd remained to 'mop up', and their contribution to the work made life easier for everyone.

It started with a single voice, far off, at the other end of the field. Someone had come running from the farm with urgent news. The one voice became a chorus that rippled out across the field from person to person, advancing like a tide, until finally it erupted into a tumultuous wave of many voices. Victoria and the others looked up, peering into the failing light of the November afternoon, trying to make out what was happening.

People were shouting, waving their arms and running about. In the distance, some women sank to their knees, put their faces in their hands and wept.

'I knew it,' Maisie cringed against Victoria. 'It's happened. The invasion's begun!'

For a moment, it seemed as if she might be right. Then Victoria noticed that some of the soldiers were shaking hands. Several threw their caps in the air and began to cheer. Suddenly, from the next field, the steam whistle of the traction engine pierced the air, followed by the tractor hooters all sounding at once. Then they could hear the church bells ringing right across the valley.

They all stared at each other, not knowing what to think. Out of the gloom, a soldier came racing down the field, heading for a group of his comrades further on.

Jen called out to him. 'Hey, what's going on? What's happened?'

He skidded to a halt in the soft earth, facing them with a huge boyish grin and threw out his arms in a sweeping gesture. 'The Germans have surrendered!' he shouted gleefully. 'The war's over!'

Chapter Thirteen

Naturally, everyone was glad that the war had ended, but the instinct to celebrate the victory, the peace, was entirely subdued by the stark realisation of the appalling cost. In the four years and three months of its duration, almost an entire generation had been consumed by it.

It was in the first few weeks of peace, as those who were left struggled to make sense of what had happened, that the last summer before the war began to assume a special significance. It came to represent a lost age of tranquil beauty and perfection. A time of changeless certainty. A matchless utopia inhabited by finer, stronger, wiser beings. An irreplaceable arcadia, transfixed in the minds of all who remembered. Of an England that once was and would never be again.

The men who had died in the war, no matter what their origins or disposition, were transformed into the immaculate flower of English youth - handsome, brave, bright and bold; flawless heroes whose sacrifice would stand as a shining example of courage and selflessness forever, and whose memory would always be synonymous with the last golden summer of 1914. Such was the mood of the nation that the strength of emotion affected everyone, immaterial of their age, sex or position. Regardless of the truth, or what had actually existed at that time, for all those who looked back on the last few months before the war, the nostalgia was irresistible.

They had won the war, as they'd been certain they would, but it was difficult to feel light-hearted in the face of such poignant loss. Now a war-weary population turned to embrace the peace and all the new problems it would bring with it.

Victoria was not immune to any of the sentiments that surrounded her. Of course, she was relieved that the war was over. For one thing, it eliminated the monstrous threat of invasion and all its attendant horrors, but as the nation drew a breath and prepared itself to face the future, there was only one thing that concerned her.

In her mind, the war had represented a doorway through which Gerald had passed. Whilst it continued, that doorway had remained open. Now it had ended, that door had closed, trapping him behind it. Already the country had begun to move on. All around her people spoke of the future, of progress and change. Soon the war would slip into memory, become a thing of the past, putting that door beyond her reach, beyond her ability to set him free. The tide of life had begun to flow forward again, but she was anchored to the spot.

For now, there were other more immediate issues that she was obliged to take into consideration. Soon the men would be coming home, returning to their wives and families and the jobs they'd left behind. The women who'd occupied these positions throughout the war, and so valiantly supported the nation in its time of trial, were now expected to relinquish them and return to their former roles in society, in the kitchen and the nursery.

Victoria found herself in a similar position. Whilst Jen, Ella and Maisie had worked at the farm for several years before the war and held jobs in their own right, she'd been hired to fill a gap left by men who had volunteered. Soon they would return and she'd have to move on. She'd never realised that it had always been a condition of her employment. At the time, it hadn't occurred to her to ask. Besides, she'd fully expected to be reunited with Gerald long before now.

Apart from that single lapse when the telegram had arrived and she'd briefly lost sight of him, she always firmly believed that he was still alive and out there somewhere. It was nothing she could explain in words. It was just a feeling, something like rapport, when one instinctively knows what another is thinking. She wondered how much longer she would have to wait. He seemed to be taking his time about it, and lately there'd been moments when she felt that if he had turned up, she would probably want to slap him.

So often in the past, Victoria had found herself alone in moments of crisis, but this time she had friends, people who cared about her and were concerned for her welfare. Mrs Fisher had become quite fond of her. She wasn't the kind of woman to discharge anyone without a very good reason, especially if it was a person she could easily have kept on, in spite of the men coming back from war. The truth of the matter was, even though she'd improved beyond all measure, with the best will in the world Victoria wasn't really farming material. Now that an opportunity had arisen, Mrs Fisher had it in mind to steer her in a better direction.

One Friday morning in early December, she summoned her to the farmhouse. She began by thanking her for all she'd done and continued by congratulating her on her many achievements, then finished by asking, 'Now you're sure Jen and Ella can manage these accounts?'

'Yes,' Victoria assured her. 'They've become quite good at it.'

'That's all I wanted to hear,' Mrs Fisher remarked decisively. 'Now, as for you, my gel, go back to the hay loft and get dressed in your very best. I'm sure you have some nice things in that big trunk of yours. Put it on, all your finery, jewellery, makeup, everything. You have to impress!'

'Impress who?' Victoria asked, slightly bewildered.

'Lady Helen Wendesby,' Mrs Fisher told her. 'She's head of the Women's Institute hereabouts, and she's got something going on down at the village hall. I got wind she's looking for an educated woman, and I thought of you straight off.'

This was the first Victoria had heard of it. 'I'm not sure I really want to...'

'No, don't try and thank me,' Mrs Fisher cut her off. 'It's the least I can do. Just you make sure you trick yourself out right smart. You'll be meeting gentry.'

'I would prefer to have more time to think about it,' Victoria replied.

'There's a cart leaving for the village in an hour,' Mrs Fisher seemed not to hear her. 'She's expecting you.'

Still somewhat bemused by the proceedings, Victoria made no further objection, chiefly out of courtesy to Mrs Fisher, and returned to the loft to change for the interview she fancied she'd been shanghaied into. Once, she would have been glad of the opportunity but now, curiously, she felt no enthusiasm for this meeting. She was sorry she had to leave the farm and her friends. For more than three years it had been her home, and they her family, but she consoled herself with the thought that she might not have to leave just yet. If this interview was conducted in the same way as all the others she'd attended, then she'd be back here in no time.

After some meticulous preparations, she finally felt as if she measured up to Mrs Fisher's expectations. She was actually quite pleased with the result. She hadn't worn this outfit for some years, and in spite of the extra pounds she'd gained in that time, she'd still managed to fit into it quite well. Indeed, she hadn't looked this good since she'd accompanied Alan Fairchild to the ball. She paused in recollection. She'd such fond memories of him. She wondered, now that the war was over, if he would return as he'd promised, or if he would merely become another missing man in her life. She'd not waited for him in the way she had waited for Gerald. Nevertheless, she hoped with all her heart that he had survived the war. Unfortunately, her reminiscences would have to wait; she was already pressed for time and, reluctantly putting his image from her mind, she returned to what she'd been doing. Once again, she gathered together the documents that would prove the quality of her education, even though it was doubtful that anyone would be interested in what they stood for, and made her way down to the waiting cart.

As she came out into the yard, an elderly farmhand, a man she'd worked alongside only the other day, tipped his hat and addressed her as 'Ma'am'. Clearly, he hadn't recognised her. When she alighted outside the village hall in Staunton Gifford, men passing by acknowledged her in the same way. It had never happened when she'd dressed as a farm girl. What a difference some clothes made.

She was surprised to find that the generally unfrequented building had now become a veritable hive of activity. Inside, every corridor was filled with members of the W.I. who bustled to and fro, some laden with all manner of equipment whilst others were engaged in arranging furniture, or pinning up freshly printed signs which seemed to indicate that the building was being segregated into different departments. After asking for directions, she made her way to an annex at the side of the building which appeared to be administrative in nature. At one end there was a separate office. The door was ajar. She knocked and waited.

'Come in,' a cultured voice invited.

Victoria entered and was immediately glad she'd made an effort to look decent. Although in her middle years, Lady Helen Wendesby was perhaps quite the most elegant looking woman she'd ever seen, apart from photographs of royalty. She smiled as Victoria came in, rising a little from her chair and offering her hand in greeting. 'How may I help you?' she asked, indicating that she should sit down.

'My name is Victoria Avery,' she introduced herself.

'Ah yes, Victoria. May I call you Victoria?' She seemed to recognise her name. 'I've been expecting you.'

There it was again. Victoria noticed that everything seemed to have been prearranged. It was a pity no one had bothered to tell her about it. 'May I ask how you know of me?' she enquired.

'Oh my dear, you come highly recommended,' Lady Helen replied, selecting a letter from a pile on the desk in front of her. 'I have here a character reference from your employer - a Mrs E. Fisher of Orchardlea Farm, I believe. She is unstinting in her praise. Allow me to read it to you.' Lady Helen proceeded to read the letter just as it had been written, but in impeccable English and with a refined accent. 'Dear your Ladyship, I have here a girl what is honest and clever. She is quick with sums and good with words. She works hard and don't complain. Knowing, as I do, that you are in a bit of a fix, I think as how she will come in handy to you. Yours faithfully, etcetera...' She put down the letter and folded her hands on the desk in front of her. 'Well, as I think you'll agree, it's a glowing testimonial.'

Victoria cringed inside. Perhaps she should have spent some time teaching Mrs Fisher how to write. Now she wondered if Lady Helen had invited her here merely as an object of curiosity. 'What exactly have I been recommended for?' she asked.

'I see that in her eagerness to bring us together, Mrs Fisher has neglected to tell you about us,' Lady Helen smiled. 'Never mind. Now that you are here, permit me to bring you up to date.'

She had an agreeable and somewhat persuasive manner about her, and Victoria felt that the least she could do was hear her out.

'You could say that this organisation was born out of necessity,' she began. 'It was created by women initially to offer moral support and practical advice to other women who were affected by any aspect of the war.'

Hearing that, Victoria felt it was a shame she hadn't known of them before.

'Since then,' Lady Helen was saying, 'we now have almost forty branches nationwide, and have expanded our scope of interest to include women of all ages and backgrounds, so that they might come together and benefit from each other's individual knowledge and experience. At present,' she offered as an example, 'we are primarily engaged in finding new and rewarding outlets for women who've been made redundant by the men returning from war.'

Victoria began to suspect that she might be a part of that programme and that it was the reason for her being here.

'There are a wide variety of activities,' Lady Helen told her, 'including discussion groups, lectures and practical demonstrations, covering almost any topic from politics to pastry making.'

Victoria thought it all sounded like a very good idea, and as Lady Helen paused to be sure she was following, she quickly bade her continue.

'The parish council have been generous enough to loan us this hall,' she explained, 'purely on a temporary basis until we can find permanent premises. Meanwhile, organising it all will be no mean feat,' she warned her, 'and certainly no job for the faint hearted. In the next few months, we shall have to cope with hundreds, if not thousands of women from all the outlying districts, and whilst I have any number of volunteers to offer advice, hang posters and make tea, I no longer have a personal assistant. My previous assistant,' she confided, 'a most delightful and efficient young woman, Mrs Georgina Marshall, recently discovered that she is expecting a child, following her husband's return from France. That reminds me,' she broke off and hurriedly scribbled a note on the pad beside her, 'we really must hold some lectures on family planning,' she muttered, before returning her attention to Victoria. 'As I was saying, even though this is a purely voluntary organisation, I find it expedient to maintain a paid private secretary – someone who can keep me abreast of all my engagements, as well as helping in organising events, and who will be expected to deputise in my absence. Would you consider yourself capable of such a task?' she asked.

In answer to that, Victoria offered her the documents that verified her standard of education. Not only did Lady Helen take the trouble to read them all, she actually seemed to appreciate their significance.

'That is a most comprehensive education, Victoria,' she complimented her, in the meantime glancing at yet another document. 'I see that you have spent the last three years labouring on a farm,' her tone of surprise and slight frown indicating that she had recognised the sharp contrast between her academic ability and the nature of her current employment - a curious choice for a woman of your intellect.'

'Not really,' Victoria disagreed. 'When my husband left for the war, I promised to wait here for his return. I admit I didn't think it would be this long, but I intend to keep my word.'

'And your husband is?' Lady Helen enquired.

'Gerald,' Victoria told her, 'Gerald Avery.'

'The poet,' Lady Helen suddenly realised. 'I thought the name sounded familiar. I take it that electing to remain near the village limited your choice of occupation,' she continued with outstanding astuteness, 'and being a woman in this somewhat backward rural area further reduced the opportunities available to you, hence your career in agriculture.'

'That's an accurate assessment,' Victoria confirmed, suspecting that the woman might be clairvoyant, or at least well informed.

'That was an extremely brave decision,' Lady Helen sounded impressed, 'given the nature of the work.'

'Courage is relative when you have no choice,' Victoria informed her, omitting that her previous involvement with the police and army intelligence might have had something to do with it.

'Just so,' Lady Helen agreed soberly. 'I take it then that your husband has not yet come home?'

Victoria nodded. 'He disappeared six months after the war began. I've had no word of him since then. Although I did receive a telegram the August before last, suggesting he might be dead. I'm still trying to fathom that out.'

'Then you believe he is still alive?'

'Certainly I do,' Victoria responded stubbornly. 'I feel it; he's not dead.'

Helen Wendesby gave her a look of such sympathy. 'How old are you?' she asked.

The question took Victoria completely by surprise. She had to think about it for a moment. She'd missed a couple of birthdays on the farm. There they generally didn't bother with such trifles. She cast her mind back over all that had happened, the calendar of events since Gerald had gone missing. She'd obstructed a Scotland Yard investigation regarding a notorious suffragette. She'd been interrogated as a spy, been tempted to adultery, helped a deserter to escape, stripped naked in a public place, attempted to commit suicide, and all before she was… She made a quick mental calculation. 'Twenty four.' The revelation astounded even her. 'I'm twenty four.'

Helen Wendesby shook her head. 'Only twenty four,' she sighed. 'You have so much in your favour,' she observed. 'Youth, beauty and intelligence, whilst your whole life still lies before you. Do you think it's wise to continue waiting after so long?'

Victoria thought the question somewhat presumptuous, whilst what it suggested was totally unacceptable. 'He's not dead,' she repeated sharply. 'I will not abandon him.'

'But if he is dead,' Lady Helen persisted, 'to waste your life on such a pointless vigil…'

What she said made good sense, but still Victoria found it impossible to agree. 'You wouldn't say that if you knew how I felt.'

'Oh, but I do,' Lady Helen declared. 'When my husband, Sir Henry Wendesby, was killed in the Boer War, unlike you I had not the luxury of hope. His friends and fellow officers saw him die. They recovered his dead body, buried it in South Africa and sent his personal effects to me. We had been married for only a year. The Boer War was small compared to what we have just endured. It did not affect the entire country. I had to mourn alone. There were times when I thought there could have been a mistake, that he might still come home, but in the end I had to learn to give him up.'

'I am so very sorry,' Victoria apologised, feeling that her recent attitude might have appeared rude. 'But tell me,' she asked with sincere interest, 'how do you come to terms with something like that?'

Lady Helen fixed her with a firm but gentle gaze. 'My dear,' she answered quietly, 'if I had ever come to terms with it, I should not be here now.'

Victoria didn't know what to say to that. She understood what was implied, but she could find no answer for it.

Lady Helen studied her for a moment as she sat there in silence. 'I perceive that there is more to it than merely your concern over his disappearance,' she began again, employing that razor-sharp astuteness of hers. Or perhaps she merely utilised her own experience. 'You're afraid, aren't you?'

'Afraid of what?' Victoria demanded defensively, beginning to squirm under this intrusive line of questioning.

'Afraid of what might happen if he actually does come back,' she elaborated.

'I don't know what you mean,' Victoria blustered evasively.

'I think you do,' she interrupted. 'Four years is a very long time. Haven't you already asked yourself if he comes back now, will he still be the same? Will he still be the man you married, the man you said goodbye to? Will he still recognise you as his wife, the woman he left behind?'

Victoria was beginning to feel trapped. Although she hated

to admit it, Lady Helen was right. She'd not always felt this way, and whilst her hopes for Gerald's safe return remained bright, she had lately begun to worry that the passing of the years might have changed them both. That the life she'd waited so long to resume might in fact no longer exist.

It had only just occurred to her, having so recently learned of the W.I.'s agenda, that Lady Helen was applying that process to her. Nevertheless, it wasn't something she felt comfortable with being forced to face. Neither did she care to have anyone prying into her personal affairs, no matter how well intentioned the motive. Under the circumstances, she felt her best course of action would be to leave. 'I'm sorry,' she remarked suddenly, rising from her chair, 'obviously I'm not the person you're looking for.'

'No, please stay,' Lady Helen held up her hand, assuming an authoritative manner that commanded obedience. 'On the contrary, you're exactly the woman I'm looking for,' she smiled. 'Your strength, determination, courage and loyalty speak volumes to me. Please accept this position,' she urged, 'and if, in the future, your plans do not evolve in the way you would have wished, then there are so many opportunities in organisations such as this for someone like you.'

Not only did her offer represent a chance for the future, it also suggested an alternative future without Gerald. Because of that, Victoria hesitated.

'In the meantime,' Lady Helen persevered softly, 'I can offer you comfortable lodgings near the village and a salary of five pounds a week. It would be a life you are more accustomed to, as I believe your friend,' she emphasised, 'Mrs Fisher, knows.'

Having just had it confirmed that she was indeed, as she had suspected, the victim of a contrived plot to bring her here, it made little difference either way. She still hesitated.

Lady Helen allowed her a moment before placing her hands on

the desk and announcing in a business-like fashion, 'Well then, for the sake of an argument, let us say it is settled. I will drive up personally to Orchardlea on Saturday morning and collect you and your possessions. We shall have the whole weekend to settle you into your new accommodation. Then on Monday morning, we shall begin work in earnest.'

Victoria couldn't decide whether she'd been forced, coerced, or simply duped into accepting this position, but whatever had happened, she'd got the job. As she rose to leave for the second time, Lady Helen stopped her. 'There's just one last thing, Victoria,' she added. 'I have found that a happy and friendly atmosphere is so much more conducive to good relations. Now, I have already seen how solemn and serious you can appear, but for the sake of harmony, do you think that you could spare a smile once in a while?' She put her head on one side, a humorous twinkle in her pale blue eyes. 'Would that be too much to ask?'

*

There was no farewell at Orchardlea, only a tearful parting. Her friends refused to say goodbye because, as they reminded her, she was only moving into the village. That wasn't very far away and they could visit her any time they liked.

They helped her pack all her belongings back into the suitcase, valise and enormous trunk. Then Ella helped her drag it out into the centre of the loft. 'It doesn't seem so very long ago since I helped you drag this bloody thing in,' she sighed.

She went quiet for a moment, then sniffed loudly as her eyes glazed with tears. Finally, she made a supreme effort to perk up, to show that she was still the same carefree old Ella. 'You take care of yourself, Vix,' she hugged her. 'Things won't be the same around here without you. Be careful if any soldiers wander into the hall,' she added a warning.

'Some of 'em probably haven't seen a woman in months. If you have any trouble, just let me know.' She sounded hopeful.

Maisie was sitting on the edge of her bed just as Victoria had seen her on the day she'd arrived. She seemed just as shy now as she'd been then. Victoria sat down beside her, putting an arm around her.

'I never had a friend like you before,' she blurted out unhappily. 'Someone who didn't treat me as if I was daft, and now you're leaving.'

'You're not losing me,' Victoria consoled her. 'When I've settled into my new home, I want you to visit me, often.'

'Me, really?'

'Yes, really, and when you can't come in person, you must write to me, long letters, promise?'

Maisie rallied a little. 'I promise,' she smiled.

Victoria kissed Maisie on the cheek, rose and turned. Jen was standing only a few feet away. For a moment, they just looked at one another. Then suddenly they both rushed forward, colliding in an emotional embrace. They clung to each other, more than friends, less than lovers, there was such a special bond between them.

'Thank you,' Victoria whispered to her. 'Thank you for my life.'

Jen gave a huge gulping sob. 'No matter what happens, just be glad,' she whispered back, 'every time tomorrow comes.'

'Kiss Harry for me.'

'I will.'

After an extra hard squeeze, Jen eased Victoria back at arm's length. 'You've done the right thing, Vix,' she assured her. 'This was never the life for you, pulling spuds out of the ground. What kind of a life is that for anyone? Now that you've taught us all to read and write, we're going to think twice about it ourselves.' She stood back and gazed at her as if in admiration. 'You look every inch a lady, Vix,' she remarked proudly. 'My word, you do. We'll have to mind our Ps and Qs from now on!'

'Don't you dare,' Victoria objected. 'As far as any of you are concerned, I'll always be Vixy.'

At that moment, they heard footsteps coming up the stairs and the rangy looking youth she'd first encountered when he'd come to collect her in the cart all those years ago appeared. Incredibly, he hadn't changed. He was still skinny, stoic and silent. Even the dog that accompanied him looked the same. At least he hadn't been swallowed up by the war. He took hold of the trunk by one handle and proceeded to drag it down the stairs, bashing it on every step as he went, and out into the yard.

When Helen Wendesby said she would drive up personally, Victoria had no idea that she'd meant in her own car with her at the wheel. Victoria's arrival at Orchardlea hadn't raised many eyebrows, but she was certainly going to make a grand exit.

The rangy youth loaded the heavy trunk, single handed, into the boot of the car and simply walked away as he'd done before. Suddenly, Victoria realised that she'd never noticed him around the farm, not in all the time she'd been there, not that she'd been looking out for him. She wondered idly if Mrs Fisher kept him in a cupboard somewhere and only let him out when there was heavy lifting to be done.

As they drove away, Victoria looked back to see her three beloved friends waving her off. It was true; she was only moving into the village, but as she watched them dwindle into the distance, she felt as if she were going to the dark side of the moon. She would miss their company, their earthy wit and easy good humour, and they would forever hold a place in her heart, second only to the one occupied by Gerald.

She soon discovered that the comfortable lodgings she'd been promised were a suite of rooms in the old rectory, situated on the outskirts of the village near the church. It was a large Victorian house built in the gothic style that had been succeeded by a smaller, more modern premises in which the resident vicar and his family now made their home. Lately, it had undergone some renovation and been converted into a block of self-contained apartments, mostly occupied by members of the W.I. who'd been seconded from other districts to help open the new branch.

The apartment that she'd been allocated was fully furnished. It consisted of a small bed-sitting room with ample shelf and cupboard space, and a neat little kitchen complete with its own range, wooden sink and water pump. There was also a separate area for bathing which housed a large galvanised bath and, oh thank God, a water closet. She'd almost forgotten they existed. Even in these modern times, decent plumbing remained a scarce commodity throughout the country, whilst it was almost non-existent in Staunton Gifford. She was very surprised and extremely grateful to see it. She could even forgive its hard wooden seat, which was a vast improvement on the nettles and thistles she'd grown used to lowering her bottom onto.

Helen Wendesby took great pains to ensure that she was properly settled in. She was most particular and quite fussy about it all. Victoria imagined that this was what having an older sister must be like. She was helpful, considerate, full of good advice and just a little bossy. At last, when she felt satisfied that Victoria was quite comfortable, she left her in peace, but not before reminding her that it was a seven thirty start on Monday and that she should not forget to smile.

She couldn't have wished for better accommodation. A cheerful fire had been laid in the grate in anticipation of her arrival, and it was warm and cosy even if it did seem a little empty and quiet, but she'd been on her own before, and doubtless she'd get used to it again. Now that she was alone, she was eager to make use of all the facilities she'd been denied for so long. She deployed the bath and filled it right up to the brim with hot water, and lay there soaking for hours, imagining it to be a secluded woodland pool, but without the zeppelin, of course.

During the three weeks leading up to Christmas, Victoria found herself working harder than she had on the farm. Her willingness to engage in any task and tackle any problem that presented itself not only created in her a Jill-of-all-trades, but rapidly made her the focal point for the army of volunteers who now readily deferred to her, whether it was necessary or not. Although she was always happy to help, it didn't prevent her from realising that by employing this conscientious approach, she'd made the proverbial rod for her own back.

At the same time, she encountered more women from such diverse backgrounds than she'd ever met in her entire life. They descended on the hall like a swarm of bees, conducting themselves in a more or less orderly fashion. Some were merely curious, whilst others had far more serious reasons for their visits. There were war widows, struggling to hold their families together, in desperate need of help and advice. There were others whose husbands had returned either blind, limbless, hideously disfigured or insane. It was after listening to their stories in particular that Victoria became aware that, for some, the war would never end.

Many of the situations she found herself confronted with were far less dire, ranging from domestic squabbles and ailing children to the problems of illiteracy, as well as a small group of young spinsters who, having supported the boys home from the front rather too generously, now found themselves in the category of unmarried mothers. Not to mention one indecisive soul who simply couldn't make up her mind which dress to wear for her husband's birthday party. There was also a large contingent of disgruntled and disaffected ladies who, having once occupied a man's job and served their country with full devotion, now found themselves to be discarded. So much of what Victoria saw and heard seemed to touch upon her own experiences, on many occasions rather too closely.

Just as Ella had predicted, a good number of demobbed soldiers also turned up at the hall. Usually, it was only to cadge a cup of tea before resuming their journey home, or merely to ask for directions. Occasionally, Victoria found herself cornered by men with fistfuls of family photographs. Most of them hadn't seen their wives in six months; some had children they'd never seen. All of them were uncertain about the reception they'd get at home. Victoria did her best to reassure them all, admiring every picture of every child, whether it looked like an angel or a chimpanzee, and throughout it all, she kept smiling.

Sometimes it was easy to smile, even with sore feet and a throbbing headache; sometimes it wasn't. Nevertheless she carried on regardless of how she felt, and smiled and smiled and smiled until her face felt numb and she began to fear that it would become permanently fixed in that expression.

In those first few weeks, there was no pause in the intensity of the work. It was barely more than organised chaos, and in the midst of it all floated Lady Helen Wendesby, cool, calm, unflappable and always in control. She was an accomplished administrator, and whatever crisis evolved, she could always sort it out to everyone's satisfaction. Victoria knew that her mother would have put it down to 'breeding', but she decided enviously that the woman had probably made a pact with the devil. Even when the doors closed, they would continue to work late into the evening, sorting out rosters, assigning volunteers, until everything was ready for the next day.

With so many soldiers passing through, Victoria made a point of observing every countenance that came before her with the slim hope that one of them might be Gerald's. It rapidly became a pointless exercise. In the end, with so many faces to look at, they all eventually became a blur, so that she might not have immediately recognised him even if he'd been standing directly in front of her.

He, on the other hand, might have stood a better chance of recognising her. With a radical change of diet, she had quickly begun to regain her figure, and with no heavy work to do, she'd started to lose some of the strength and muscle tone she'd acquired on the farm, making her appear altogether softer and more rounded. Also the substantial increase in salary had allowed her to buy some new clothes. This and the fact that in spite of her years in the hay loft where her innocence had taken a considerable beating and her naiveté had been all but erased, she'd made a conscious effort to retain her gentility and a sense of her origins, which meant that now she was more like the Victoria she'd once been before Orchardlea.

Everything stopped for Christmas. Lady Helen had invited Victoria to join her in the celebrations at her family home on the Sussex-Surrey borders. It was kind of her, but Victoria had declined. She had a far more important engagement to attend. She was going back to Orchardlea.

She arrived early on Christmas eve to be met by Ella and Maisie who informed her, with some concern, that Jen had vanished without a word two days earlier, and they'd not yet heard from her. It was an ill way to start the festivities, especially as it was the first Christmas in four years without a war to contend with.

The great barn was decked out like it had never been before, and this time it thronged not only with women, old men and boys, but also with young men, lots of them, and everyone was happy to have them there. The celebrations had begun; they were in full swing. The noise of the music and the laughter rose to the eaves when suddenly the music stopped abruptly, and everyone fell silent.

Jen was standing on the makeshift platform that had been set aside for the musicians. She'd come back and she'd brought Harry with her. She clutched him to her, facing them all, fiercely, defiantly, and told them in a loud firm voice that he was not her brother, not even her nephew, or some abandoned waif she'd discovered by the wayside. He was her son, her child, her boy and from now on they would never be apart. For a moment, the silence hung like a pall over the gathering, until someone somewhere began to clap. Others joined in, then a sudden burst of applause erupted from the crowd and people began to cheer.

Harry was taken from her and passed around to be kissed by everyone, like some good luck token that by some happy chance had fallen into their hands. Now that the truth was out, now that they knew he was illegitimate, what was the name they called him? Why, it was Harry, of course, and the only bastard on their minds was the one that had let Jen down. It seemed that the war had changed some things for the better. It would be a Christmas to remember, one of joy and hope. One in which the sentiment of peace on earth and good will to all men finally meant something.

With the new year came the announcement that the Women's Institute had found better premises; a new and permanent base from which to conduct their operation. It was larger and more central to the area it served, even though it was several miles outside of Staunton Gifford. As the local population began to make use of the new office, the deluge of women that had once poured into the village hall now dried to a trickle.

By the end of January, Lady Helen had set a date for the closure of the Staunton Gifford branch. She'd already reassigned such volunteers as were left to the new project, and now only she and Victoria remained to finalise the details that would hand the hall back to the parish council.

Although preoccupied with the relocation, Lady Helen had taken some time to try and convince Victoria that she should join her. She'd told her that she was virtually indispensable, and that it was high time she should consider her own future. At one point, she even offered to have public notices printed at her own expense and pasted up around the village, so that if Gerald did return, he would know exactly where to find her, but still Victoria remained indecisive about the move. The thought of advertising her personal affairs to the entire village didn't seem entirely appropriate either. Eventually, Lady Helen appeared to have given up trying to persuade her. Indeed, she seemed quite distant at times, and Victoria began to worry that her constant vacillation might have appeared offensive, and that now she might be reappraising her opinion of her.

On 4th February, the day before the branch was due to be closed down, she approached Victoria with some unexpected news. 'I'm afraid I shan't be able to join you tomorrow,' she informed her apologetically. 'Now that the new branch is officially commissioned, I've been called upon to make a report of its progress. I have to drive to London first thing in the morning.'

'Oh, that's a shame,' Victoria remarked with disappointment. 'It's our last day here as well.'

'Yes, I know. It's regrettable,' Lady Helen sighed. 'I had hoped to share a glass of wine with you to toast the successful conclusion of this venture, but there it is; work before pleasure,' she finished briskly.

'Yes, of course, I quite understand,' Victoria agreed.

'Even though your presence in the hall tomorrow will only be a token gesture, I know that I can rely upon you to make sure that we finish as we began, and that our service here is available to the public right to the end,' Lady Helen continued seriously. 'Remember that the reputation of this organisation will rest with you. So please make sure that everything is in order when you leave. It's only half a day,' she added, less officiously, 'and I don't expect that anyone will bother you. Please open punctually at seven thirty and close precisely at noon.'

Victoria knew from experience that Lady Helen was a stickler for details, and agreed to follow her demands to the letter. She was perfectly capable of running the hall by herself and had no doubts in her ability to close it down.

'Keep the key with you,' Lady Helen insisted, 'and I'll collect it at a later date. I dare say we'll have a good deal to talk about when I return.'

She put her hand on Victoria's shoulder. 'I have every confidence in you, my dear,' she assured her, before kissing her on the cheek and bidding her farewell. She withdrew, sweeping out of the room, only to pause in the doorway and look back at her. 'I do hope that you will give some further thought to pursuing a career in the Women's Institute,' she smiled. 'I would hate to think that you had foregone an opportunity you might later regret not taking.'

Victoria felt she should have known that Lady Helen was not the sort to give up easily. What she said made excellent sense, but somehow the thought of accepting the offer seemed like admitting that Gerald was dead, and there was no longer any power on earth that would convince her of that.

It was one of those dank and dreary February mornings. Leadened grey clouds scudded across a barren sky, occasionally giving way to patches of watery sunlight that vanished almost as quickly as they appeared. Sporadic showers were accompanied by low rumbles of thunder that never really came to anything but continued to roam around the heavens grumbling dismally, and there was that cold damp chill in the air that cut right to the bone.

The first thing that Victoria did after she'd opened the hall was to make herself a cup of tea. Feeling better for that, she busied herself with what little was left to be done. It didn't amount to much. It was just a matter of stacking a few chairs, making sure that everything belonging to the W.I. had been despatched to the new location, and taking down a few posters. She even swept and dusted. At nine o'clock, she made another cup of tea and ate the sandwich she'd brought with her. She spent the next thirty minutes rechecking everything she'd already done. After that, she tended to drift around rather aimlessly for a while. Lady Helen had been right in her assumption that no one would bother her. No one did, not at any time, not even to say hello. It would have been nice if they had, but they didn't.

By eleven o'clock, she was thoroughly bored. She'd done everything twice and some things three times, and there was still a whole hour stretching out in front of her. She regretted not having brought a book to read. She began to wonder if it was really necessary to stay for the entire time. After all, there was nothing to stop her from closing early, except for the fact that she'd given her word.

It was only now, trapped in this vacant moment, that she began to think about the future, but only the future and not what form it might take. In spite of her resistance to the idea, she finally had to admit to herself that if Gerald didn't come back soon, then he wouldn't come back at all. She'd never considered a life without her husband, and each time she forced herself to take him out of the equation, it no longer made any sense. Sitting here alone in this empty room, she was aware that she was poised once again at yet another crossroad in her life, and no matter how hard she tried, a choice of direction still eluded her. In the end, she stopped thinking about it. She'd managed to put it off this long, and there was always tomorrow, and the next day, and the next.

She went to the window and looked outside, but there was nothing to see but the miserable weather. She returned to the desk and sat down, sighing. To relieve the boredom and pass the time, she began fantasising. It was harmless, and having learned from her mistake with Alan, it involved no other living soul but herself and Gerald. It was a daydream, plain and simple. Actually, it was neither plain nor simple, but a daydream nonetheless.

She imagined him walking back up the lane towards the cottage. It was the most marvellous sunny day, and the air was thick with the scent of wild roses and honeysuckle. She saw him coming from where she stood in the garden, and flew out of the gate, dashing down the lane to meet him. He caught her in his arms and lifted her high into the air before smothering her with moist kisses. She liked that part most of all; the more she thought about it, the better it became.

The rain began to beat more insistently against the window pane distracting her, causing the vision to fade. She looked up. There was no cottage, no lane, no Gerald, only this empty room, this empty desk and this empty woman.

At eleven fifty seven, heaving a huge sigh of relief, she put her hat and coat on, collected her handbag and took one last look around the hall before leaving. Stepping outside, she gazed up and down the street. It was utterly deserted; there wasn't a soul about, lending an air of desolation to the village. She felt as if she were stepping into oblivion, into emptiness and nothingness, that whatever happened from now on would be but a pale reflection of her aspirations. She closed the door and locked it, putting the key into her purse, and turning the collar of her coat up against the chill wind, she began to walk away.

She hadn't gone very far before she came to an abrupt halt. She could sense a presence as though someone were standing behind her, a presence that was strangely familiar. She flinched as the shock of recognition sliced through her. For a fleeting moment, she almost believed it. A tiny spark of hope flared briefly and in an instant was gone. She shook her head, clicking her tongue in annoyance. She was being foolish. There was nothing behind her. She was deluding herself again. She'd only just been thinking about him, that was all it was, merely an echo of her fantasy. She shuddered, a little shiver running down her spine, in an attempt to shrug off the feeling, but it persisted and grew stronger.

She sighed, frowning. It wasn't possible, she told herself; surely she only imagined it. Once again, she tried to dislodge the troublesome hallucination, levelling all her strength, all her willpower against it, but it was useless. All her instincts told her to accept what she felt, all her reason denied it, whilst the ever-present voice inside her whispered, 'No, he's not dead'.

Yet still she questioned, still she doubted. It was just a trick of her mind, a desperate whim of her heart. If she turned, if she looked, there would be nothing, only the empty street and the bitter disenchantment of reality. All too often, she'd embraced these emotions only to discover that she'd been mistaken. She wouldn't endure that disappointment again. She wouldn't be taken in as she'd been before. She closed her eyes, drew a deep breath and cleared her mind, but when she opened them again, she could still feel the presence, stronger than ever, more powerful, more insistent. Finally, she could resist no longer.

She spun round, recoiled, a startled cry wrenched from her throat. Her bag fell from her numb fingers, splashing into a puddle at her feet. Occupying the position she'd only just vacated stood the figure of a man, a man wearing an officer's uniform. He stood still and silent, the peak of his cap shading his face. There had been times in the past, a few rare occasions, when she thought she'd seen him standing at a distance, but never this close, on a street corner, at the edge of a field, or in a lane. Her heart had given a lurch; she'd blinked and he was gone. It wasn't lunacy, only loneliness, but the episodes had left her permanently sceptical of her ability to separate fact from fiction, so that even now she hardly dared to trust the evidence of her own eyes.

More curious than alarmed, she took a step forward and then another. It was not so much a bold advance as stalking, one hesitant pace at a time. Her eyes narrowed with uncertainty as she turned her head this way and that in a cautious examination of the features. Surely it was just another illusion, her heart projecting the image her mind most wanted to see. At any moment, the apparition would vanish as it had always done, but the closer she got, the more substantial it seemed.

The man raised his head a little; the shadow fled away. She stopped, gasped, her dry lips soundlessly framing his name. 'Gerald?' He seemed to nod, the hint of a smile tugging at the corners of his mouth. She raised a trembling hand, pressed it against his chest and felt the beating heart pounding beneath his ribs. Reaching forward, she cupped his cheek in her palm. He pressed his face into it; it was warm. He lived, he breathed, but was it her husband? Was it the man she'd said goodbye to? Was it Gerald, the same, or someone else? Only a stranger she'd once known. After four long years, the next few minutes would decide the issue.

Suddenly, he made as if to salute, but she grabbed his arm and held onto it. There had been enough saluting; there had been enough of that. Then she saw it, where the sleeve had slipped back, there, on the exposed wrist, a bracelet of plaited hair, her hair.

In an instant all her doubts evaporated. She gazed up at him through a haze of tears, unable to speak, so happy, so relieved, so grateful for his safe return, that words failed her. She lunged forward, throwing her arms about his waist, gripping him so tightly that he gasped before enfolding her in his.

There was a low rumble of thunder, the clouds parted and a shaft of golden sunlight shone down to envelope them. It was nothing but a vagary of the weather, a manifestation of the climate, merely a shift in the wind but it was as if heaven itself had blessed this reunion.

Chapter Fourteen

At the end of the Great War, once the numbers of British dead and injured had been determined, it was estimated that over half a million men still remained unaccounted for. They had vanished without a trace. Almost certainly, the vast majority of them were dead, but how and where they'd died and what had become of their bodies would always remain a mystery.

Paradoxically, Gerald had been more fortunate. Whilst leading his squad through no-man's land, they'd been ambushed by a German patrol. After an exchange of gunfire, two of his men had been killed, three had been taken prisoner, and he lay unconscious, critically wounded in the chest. Leaving him for dead, the German patrol had departed, taking their captives with them.

Several hours later, a contingent from the German Medical Corps accompanied by stretcher bearers had arrived, searching the area for casualties. Finding none of their own men, they'd stumbled across Gerald. Realising that he was still alive, they'd torn open his tunic to apply a field dressing to the wound, inadvertently pulling the locket and his identity discs off, which had fallen unnoticed to the ground. Once they'd patched him up, they'd taken him back behind their lines to a field hospital where, contrary to British propaganda, German doctors had operated for five hours to remove the bullet from his chest and save his life. Being wounded and captured had probably prevented him from being killed outright, as had been the fate of so many of his contemporaries.

Without any means to identify him, they'd labelled him simply as 'Tommie', a general title for any British soldier, and given him a number. It had been merely a matter of expedience that had set the seal on his anonymity.

For almost a year, he lay incapacitated, his life hanging by a thread. Continually slipping in and out of consciousness, he called Victoria's name every time he came round until the German medical staff were as familiar with it as he was. In his delirium, he would ask the same question over and over again of any woman that passed by his bed, and the exasperated German nurses would always reply, 'Nein, ich bin nicht deine frau'.

By the time he'd recovered his senses and was able to tell them his real name, his capture had long since been reported to the Red Cross. None of the German medical staff had either the time or the inclination to amend the error of his identity, presupposing that they even remembered that there'd been an error in the first place.

It was then that the first seeds of doubt had been sown in Gerald's mind. He'd thought it unlikely at best that they'd given an accurate account without being in possession of his correct name. If, as he suspected, a mistake had been made, it meant that Victoria would have no idea of what had happened to him.

He'd not been permitted to write to her, not even a note to confirm that he was still alive and well. The Germans weren't about to let an enemy soldier send a message, no matter how innocent it might appear, from behind their lines to England. He'd pressed them on this point as far as he dared, but they'd remained adamant, informing him that by now his wife would know that he was alive. Perhaps they were telling the truth as far as they recalled it, but he doubted that they were right. Finally, he was forced to let the matter drop. He was, after all, in no position to make any demands on his captors.

Shocked to learn of how much time had elapsed whilst he'd been unconscious, and that the war was still being fought, he could only speculate as to what Victoria might be thinking. Perhaps she'd already given him up for dead? The thought of that began to torment him, and thereafter it became the engine that drove all his plans.

In June 1916, he was deemed fit enough to be moved and transported to a prisoner of war camp, deep in the heart of Germany. Few of his personal possessions had survived, but one of the German nurses had saved the bracelet of plaited hair and returned it to him before he left.

By now, he'd realised that this war wasn't going to end quickly, and he had no intention of remaining a prisoner indefinitely. He'd already been away from Victoria for far too long. It was imperative that he escape so that he could return to her.

He never reached the camp he was destined for. Ever watchful for an opportunity, and almost within sight of the gates, he'd made his bid for freedom and spent the next eighteen months on the run. Hiding by day, living off the land and moving mostly at night, he'd made his way precariously out of hostile Germany, back through occupied Belgium and on towards France and the western front. Ragged, starving, cold and exhausted, he struggled on alone and on foot across all of war-torn Europe, sustained only by the thought that some day he would see Victoria again.

Barely surviving in the desolation that was Europe, picking his way slowly mile after painful mile through enemy territory, he was constantly aware of the relentless passage of time, of how long they'd been apart, and of what that separation might be doing to Victoria. So often in his despair, he'd prayed that some benevolent force might spirit him more swiftly along to make an end of this agony of delay, and his wild imaginings of what might have befallen his young wife whilst she was unprotected and alone. But his prayers had gone unanswered. He rarely ever managed to travel more than a few miles a day. The months continued to slip by, acting like a goad, spurring him on to even greater risk, so that not a single hour would be wasted, so that not another day might pass before they were together again.

Indifferent to the tribulations of one man, the war had raged on, the rival factions pushing each other backwards and forwards across the same ground, in an insane tug-o'-war. An exploding shell had unearthed Gerald's identity discs over two years after he'd lost them, to be found by British stretcher bearers searching an area once occupied by the Germans. With so many mangled corpses lying around, it was naturally assumed that the discs belonged to one of them, and Lieutenant Gerald Avery was pronounced missing believed dead and a telegram duly despatched to his wife.

After several attempts and some close shaves, in the January of 1918 he'd managed to cross through enemy lines and back into allied territory, where he'd considered himself to be safe. Unfortunately, his complacency proved to be a mistake. Once there, without a uniform or the means to identify himself, he'd been taken prisoner by the British and held, pending investigation. When they discovered that the man he claimed to be was listed as dead, they suspected him of being an enemy agent. Nothing he told them seemed to make any difference, and they placed him under arrest, keeping him incommunicado, pending further investigation. With the war reaching a critical phase, it had been more a matter of convenience than national security.

From the bars of his cell, he'd begged them to send a message to tell his wife that he was there, but they'd ignored him, suspecting it to be some sort of plot. Then he'd cursed them, cursed their stupidity and cursed the name of England.

With the war reaching its climax and all efforts being concentrated on the 'big push', they virtually forgot about him. He languished in prison, counting off the wasted months, contemplating the irony of his incarceration.

It was only after the war had ended when they'd bothered to make a detailed examination of his file, studied the photograph and listened to his testimony that they were eventually convinced of his identity. He was immediately released and reinstated to his former rank.

By this time, Gerald was a driven man, consumed by an overriding sense of urgency. Impatient to get home after all these years, he would brook no further delays. Within the space of two days, he'd embarked on a ship bound for England. There had been no point in writing a letter. By the time it arrived in Staunton Gifford, he would be there.

It was only as the coast of Britain came into sight that he began to think that perhaps it might have been wiser to have written first, and given Victoria time to get used to the idea that he was still alive. Once, he could have been certain of his welcome. As it was, after all this time, there was no way of knowing how she'd react to his unexpected arrival, assuming she was still there. In his haste to get home, he hadn't considered that. Now that he had, the seeds of doubt that he'd nurtured these past two years began to grow in his mind. His sense of anticipation became clouded with apprehension. There was still the sense of urgency, the desperation to get home, but now there was also the fear of what might happen and what he might find when he got there.

He arrived in Southampton in the early hours of the morning on 5th February 1919. Thousands of men were being sent back from France, and there were a good many vehicles leaving the docks. He'd managed to get a lift in a lorry carrying troops bound for Aldershot, which had dropped him off at the station. From there, he'd caught the train to Chichester where he'd changed platforms and been forced to wait an excruciating hour, the mounting anxiety beginning to nag at his mind, for the branch service to Staunton Gifford.

It was a small rural station, and there were no cabs for hire at that time in the morning. It was just as he'd expected. As a man who'd crossed half of Europe on foot, the prospect of walking the remaining few miles to the cottage didn't trouble him at all. By now, the sun was well risen and as he continued his journey, he began to recognise some of his old haunts. He hadn't passed this way in over four years, yet much of it remained familiar. It was good to be back in England once more. There had been times in the past when he'd thought that he might never see this country again.

He was just beginning to take comfort from the thought of how little had altered when suddenly he was confronted by a scene of unimaginable destruction wrought by the war effort. He stared in horror at the denuded landscape, the uprooted hedgerows, fields laid waste and felled woodlands, stretching out mile after devastated mile before him. This was like nothing he remembered, and he began to wonder what else might have changed during his absence.

What he'd seen had come as a profound shock, strengthening his doubts and adding fuel to the embers of his anxiety. The closer to home he got, the worse it became. What if she wasn't there? What if she'd given him up for dead and moved on to live another life that no longer included him? What if she herself was dead, having succumbed to the Spanish flu or fallen foul of an accident? Worst of all was the thought that, whilst none of these things might have happened, she might simply reject him on his return for having left her for so long.

He'd attempted to put himself in a more positive frame of mind, telling himself not to be foolish. He knew this woman. She was faithful and true. Of course she would have waited for him. She would be there, at the cottage. Everything would be alright. Wouldn't it?

Try as he might, his fears didn't abate. What if she'd changed beyond all recognition? What if she no longer recognised him? What if she no longer chose to recognise him? He fretted that his years living rough might have altered him in ways he was unaware of, but that she might notice and be repelled by. The hopes and doubts swirled around in his brain until at last, when he'd finally reached the crossroads, his head felt fit to burst, and there was that feeling again of anticipation clouded by apprehension, whilst something new had been added. Now he was afraid.

He had walked, like a condemned man, along the ravaged lane that would lead him back to the cottage. Now he was close, oh so very close. He'd paused, digging deep into what little courage remained to him. It wasn't the way he'd so often imagined it would be. Yet he'd come so far, endured so much for this moment that he had to find out. Whatever awaited him, one way or the other, he had to know.

As he'd rounded the bend in the lane, the desperate cry of such utter dismay that broke upon his lips might easily have been heard in the village. He could see, even before he'd reached the cottage, that it was empty. The bare windows and overgrown garden told him that it was deserted. All his worst fears were suddenly realised.

Breaking into a run, he'd burst through the gate and rushed up to the door, hammering uselessly on it, shouting her name, but there was no answer. He'd made a hasty circuit of the grounds, still calling out, peering in at the window and the empty rooms beyond, but there was nothing. Crouching down, he'd squinted through the letterbox. There were some envelopes scattered on the floor, only Ministry leaflets by the look of them, but the layer of dust told him that they'd lain there a long time.

He was normally a level headed man, even under stress, but the extreme circumstances had driven him beyond the boundaries of his character. He began to panic. The evidence seemed to suggest that she was long gone by now. He stared aimlessly about, not knowing which way to turn. Then he'd noticed it, the remnants of a garland of plaited hair, weathered and frayed, hanging on the gatepost. It was a match for the one he wore on his wrist. Although the cottage appeared to have been empty for several years, judging from the condition of the bracelet it would have had to have been placed there relatively recently. That meant there was a chance that she was still in the vicinity. If that was so, then he would find her. With renewed hope, he struggled to clear his mind, to think, to plan what to do next.

At that moment, an elderly couple had driven past in a rickety trap pulled by an ancient looking nag. He'd hailed them to stop, and asked if they'd seen the woman who used to live here, if they knew what had become of her.

The old man had thought about it; there was a trace of memory. 'Small, dark?'

'Yes, that's right,' Gerald had urged him to remember.

The old man rubbed his chin, frowning. 'She baint be 'ere now,' he'd stated the obvious at first. ' 'ad to move on, years ago. Couldn't pay the rent, or so I 'eard.'

Gerald shrank inside. It was one more thing he hadn't considered. 'Where did she go?' he asked, growing ever more agitated.

The old man had been quiet for a minute, then the light of recollection burst upon his face. 'Now I remember,' he announced. 'She went labouring at Orchardlea.'

'The farm?' Gerald glanced in that general direction, but no sooner did it seem that he'd discovered her whereabouts than she was gone again.

'No, no,' the old woman had contradicted her husband. 'She baint be there now. She 'ad to leave, 'cos of the men comin' back from war.'

'Where did she go?' Gerald was barely able to contain himself.

'I've seen 'er somewhere,' the old woman frowned. 'Now where was that?'

'Yes, where was that?' Gerald prompted.

'Let me see... of course!' She threw up her hands. 'I'm daft, I am. She were at the Women's Institute. That's where I saw 'er, at the village hall, only t'other day.'

'The village hall?' Gerald had wanted to be sure. It was just as well.

'Yes,' she grinned. 'Oh, but she baint be there now.'

'Oh really, and why is that?' he enquired with great self restraint.

'They've closed it down. Well at least, they're going to,' the old woman told him. 'Come to think of it, today's the last day. I am daft,' she repeated. 'She is there, until it closes.'

Gerald's adrenalin spiked. 'When does it close?' he asked, resisting the urge to agree with her.

'Twelve o'clock,' the old woman answered without hesitation. It was the only thing she had been sure of.

Gerald glanced at his watch. It was eleven twenty seven, and the hall was four miles away. His frustration must been apparent. The old couple had looked at each other and winked.

'You jump up 'ere, boy,' the old man invited. 'I'll get you there in time.'

It was good of him to offer, but Gerald couldn't help glancing at the horse and thinking he'd seen better carcasses rotting on the battlefield. 'It's four miles away,' he told them.

'Never you mind about that, boy,' the old man insisted. 'You climb up; I'll get you there.'

Once Gerald was safely on board, the old man whipped up the horse and they began to career along the rutted cart track. It was the most hair-raising journey he'd ever undertaken, and that included his escape from Germany. He began to wonder, as they pelted along, if in some previous life the old man had been a Roman charioteer. He felt it would be a pity to have crossed half of Europe virtually unscathed through a war, to have returned to England only to die in a Sussex ditch. The fact that the old lady seemed to be relishing the ride didn't do his ego any good either.

They'd reached the outskirts of Staunton Gifford at eleven fifty precisely. The entire journey had only taken twenty three minutes, but Gerald felt as if he'd aged ten years.

'I told you I'd get you 'ere on time,' the old man beamed proudly.

Offering a brief word of thanks, Gerald had jumped off the trap and began to sprint down the street, slowing to a brisk walk as he approached the village hall. He was so close now he fancied he could almost feel her, but at the same time, there was still that nagging sense of doubt. He'd no idea of what to say or do when he saw her; neither could he be certain how she might respond when she saw him.

Unbeknown to him, the situation had begun to take on a momentum of its own. From now on, the circumstances would dictate a course of events he didn't control, but could only react to.

He'd almost reached the door of the village hall when suddenly it began to open. Startled, he'd instinctively ducked into the doorway of the adjacent building where he'd stood, rebuking himself for his stupidity. Under stress, he'd reverted to an old habit, born of his days on the run, where it had become second nature to hide, to take cover if anything unexpected happened. Again, he was gripped by the same irrational fear he'd felt on the road. What on earth was happening to him? He was a man who'd faced German bayonet charges without turning a hair, but now his nerve had failed him. He stood paralysed with doubt and indecision, and all because of a five foot two inch, seven and a half stone woman. Slowly, it began to dawn on him that, up until now, whilst he'd remained uncommitted, the future had been one of limitless possibilities. There'd been a certain degree of safety, a sense of comfort in that, but once he made himself known to her all the possibilities would narrow to one unpredictable and irrevocable conclusion. This was what he faced; that was why he hesitated.

For the time being, he'd remained hidden, gulping in deep breaths in an effort to compose himself. Then he'd heard the key turn in the lock and her footsteps begin to recede down the street. Whether he was ready or not, the moment of truth had arrived.

The mere thought that she was moving away from him again rapidly restored his reason and his resolve. At last, he realised that whilst his confidence in himself had waned, in spite of all his doubts his faith in her remained undiminished. Putting all his trust in that one slim fact, he'd stepped out onto the pavement.

It was the first time he'd set eyes on her since 1914. The feeling of apprehension had vanished instantly to be immediately replaced by a raw impulse. It was all he could do to stop himself from yelling out her name, from dashing down the street, scooping her up and showering her with kisses, but it had been four years. He dare not run the risk of charging blindly in and alarming her. It was almost more than he could endure but he resisted the urge, aware of the need after all his haste for caution. It had been a long time for both of them, but not too long, he hoped.

He'd been about to speak her name when she'd sensed him standing there and stopped. Everything, their lives together, their happiness, their future hung on that one agonising moment.

His final decision had been simply to stand there, to say and do nothing that might deter her. He'd merely presented himself to her again, much in the same way as he'd done on the day he'd first met her. The choice would be hers to make. She would decide the outcome; and decide she did, much in the same way as she'd done on the day she'd first met him.

Eventually, as they began to walk off arm in arm, Victoria couldn't help but notice how wonderfully bright, how absolutely radiant everything appeared. The rain poured down, the sky was the colour of slate and the wind was freezing, but it was the most glorious day she'd ever seen. She even fancied she could smell the scent of wild roses and honeysuckle.

She took Gerald back to her rooms where they spent the rest of the afternoon and the best part of the evening just holding each other. They were both exhausted and emotionally drained. It was as much as they could do to take in the fact that they were back together again. For now, that was enough; the rest would follow in time. They hardly spoke; there was no need for words, not yet, not now. She cried a good deal and he did his best to comfort her, trying not to cry himself.

When at length they could no longer stay awake, there being only one small bed he elected to sleep on the floor. He said he was used to that.

In the morning, now that they were rested and the initial shock of their meeting had subsided, Victoria soon became aware that she had her husband back in body but not in spirit. Today, he seemed awkward and self-conscious around her. It was as if he'd assumed responsibility for their separation, that it was somehow his fault alone, and that if he made the least mistake, no matter how inadvertently, in word or deed, she would abandon him instantly. He was cordial rather than familiar, polite instead of passionate. He treated her as though she were merely a good friend rather than the woman he'd married. It seemed to her that when their shattered lives had joined again as one, a vital fragment had been overlooked.

The second night went much the same as the first. Victoria accepted it. She knew he was unsure of his ground, still a little shy of her. He was not the type of man to impose his will on a woman, even if she was his wife.

On the second day, he remained reserved, undemonstrative, clearly ill at ease and obviously embarrassed by his own diffidence. Victoria understood the conflict that raged within him. She was experiencing some of the same ambivalent emotions herself.

There was a poignant sense of utter relief, of absolute joy and expectation, and of doubt and apprehension; the anticipation of a swift return to normality, to all that was comfortable and familiar, but there was an element of strangeness, of uncertainty about it. Sometimes, it was the oddest thing to look at him and see Gerald, a man she knew intimately, and at one and the same time feel it was only a duplicate of her husband, identical in every detail but an imitation nonetheless. It was both disturbing and perplexing. Judging by his behaviour, Gerald viewed her in much the same way. Individually, they were the same, just as they'd been when they'd parted, but that which had once made them a pair now seemed indistinct.

It was a gulf of four years' absence that had divided and estranged them. How to bridge the gap and bring them both safely back together was a problem that, for the moment, seemed impossible to solve, but as she thought about it, Victoria began to realise that perhaps it was a void only one of them needed to cross.

She knew instinctively from the way he looked at her that his depth of feeling for her remained unaltered, that the old Gerald was still in there somewhere and that all he needed was a little encouragement to reveal himself. She knew that if they were to make any progress, she would have to restore his confidence in her love for him. To convince him once and for all that no matter how long they'd been apart, no matter what they'd seen or done, they were still the same people. That she was still the same woman he remembered, that he was still the same man she'd waited for and wanted now.

She'd been taught that in the physical side of marriage it was appropriate to let the man take the lead. Previously, she'd been content to let that happen. However, during her years in the hay loft living with the likes of Ella and the others, she'd learnt that this didn't necessarily always have to be the case.

Consequently, on the third night, she informed him gently but firmly that if he didn't join her in the bed, she would sleep beside him on the floor.

It was a delightfully snug fit, the two of them together. After that, the situation began to improve rapidly.

As news of Gerald's return began to spread through the village, Jen, Ella and Maisie quickly put in an appearance, expressing a desire to visit her. Victoria felt that she would have liked a little more time alone with him before receiving callers, but Gerald didn't seem to mind, and because of their insistence she felt obliged to invite them.

Ostensibly, they were there to enjoy afternoon tea, but of course it was only an excuse to view the object of all Victoria's vigilance and passion. They were just as frank in their opinions around Gerald as they'd been with Victoria, often discussing him openly as though he were some stray animal she'd recently taken in.

Although Gerald found them to be pleasant and amusing company, as the tea progressed he began to feel as though he was being studied like a specimen under a microscope. Whilst he could appreciate their curiosity, he could only hope that they wouldn't feel the need to dissect him.

As they left, they didn't fail to congratulate Victoria on her good fortune.

'He seems very nice,' Maisie told her, 'just like you said he'd be.'

Ella took a more direct view. 'God, Vix, he was well worth waiting for,' she assured her with a frown of conviction. 'Mind you, if you ever get tired of him...'

'Yes, thank you Ella,' Victoria smiled patiently, 'but I think I'll keep him for the time being.'

Jen paused to glance back at Gerald. 'It looks as though tomorrow's finally come,' she observed with a smile.

'And not a moment too soon,' Victoria didn't mind admitting.

'In that case,' Jen advised, as she hugged her goodbye, 'from now on, be sure to make the most of 'em all.'

At the end of March, they all attended a most important ceremony, the unveiling of the Staunton Gifford war memorial. It had been paid for by public subscription; everyone in the village had contributed to it.

As they gathered round to hear the vicar read the service, it represented all those young men, husbands, sons, brothers and sweethearts, who couldn't be with them on that day. On the column of the white stone cross were carved the names of all those from Staunton Gifford who'd fallen in the Great War. The herdsmen and the plough boys who'd strolled out of this little village one bright summer's morning, never to return, and whose finer clay now enriched the battlefields of Europe.

The death toll was so high that almost everyone in the community had suffered a bereavement. Many a heart ached with the loss of a man whose life, had it continued, might have benefited his family, the village and the country.

The memorial might endure for centuries to come bearing the names for posterity so they might never be forgotten. But the memory of those who had died would never remain so fresh as in the hearts and minds of those who'd known and loved them.

Incredibly, among all the names of the dead was one that yet lived. It was only after the ceremony when the wreaths of poppies, the new emblem of the war dead, had been laid and the crowd began to disperse that Gerald and Victoria, on closer inspection, had discovered that his name had been included on the memorial. The stone had been commissioned at the end of 1918 and had taken months to carve. At that time, Gerald had still been listed as dead. For Victoria, it would be a lasting reminder of how close she'd come to losing him.

A few days later, they moved back into Rosebay. Gerald had wasted no time in leasing the cottage again. It was a mutual agreement; both of them wanted to resume their old way of life as soon as possible, and the familiar surroundings of the cottage would go a long way to achieving that. He made a point of carrying her over the threshold again, only this time he didn't stumble.

There was still an element of strangeness, although not nearly as strong as it had been at first, until they became used to each other again, and grew accustomed to each other's company. There was also the excitement of rediscovery, the thrill of finding that, for all their years apart, the bond between them hadn't weakened but grown stronger.

It was during those first weeks, as they re-established themselves as a married couple, that Victoria succumbed to a curious malady; she couldn't bear to let Gerald out of her sight. In the comparative confines of her rooms, she hadn't felt the need, but in the more spacious surroundings of the cottage, it was different. She began to follow him everywhere as if afraid that he would disappear all over again.

If he went into another room, she would find a reason to be there. If he went out into the garden, there was always a job there that required her attention. Sometimes he would wake at night and find her sitting up beside him, watching him. It was as if she couldn't quite believe that he'd come home at last. Her mood continued for some time until eventually he was grateful that her vigilance didn't extend to his visits to the water closet. He said of her that she was more tenacious than the German guards, and more stubborn than the British.

At times, she would shadow him so closely that he thought to scold her for it, but one look at that pale, serious little face and those large green eyes that regarded him so earnestly, and he would forebear. He'd take her in his arms and hold her, swearing that he would never leave her again. He would keep on telling her that until she believed him, and if she never believed him, then he'd just keep on telling her.

In a little less than six weeks, she'd begun to recover from her over-protectiveness, and after he'd expressed a desire to visit the tobacconists to buy some pipe cleaners, she'd reluctantly agreed to let him go by himself. He remarked that he felt like a small boy who'd been entrusted with his first solo errand, that his liberation was greater than that of Belgium.

Nevertheless, when he returned all of twenty minutes later, she was waiting for him on the doorstep, and as he came through the gate she dashed out and ran into his arms. Two elderly ladies passing by enquired if he'd just returned from France, and were astounded to hear that, no, it was only the tobacconists. They walked on, muttering something about 'newly weds'.

It wasn't long before Gerald returned to his writing, and the money he earned from it would eventually allow him to buy the cottage outright. He and Victoria would spend the rest of their lives there, whilst the woods and hedgerows grew back, the fields became green again, the wounds healed and something of the England they'd once known returned. In the years to come, the poems he would write about the war, his desperate struggle across Europe, but most particularly those about Victoria, her courage, faith and love, would make him one of the most widely read poets of his time.

As for the others, now that she could read and write, Jen left farming and trained to be a teacher. After a period as a probationer at the village school, she was eventually able to take it over when the resident teacher retired. She campaigned tirelessly for improvements in the education of working class children, particularly those from rural backgrounds. She also became a powerful force in the continuing struggle for women's equality, whilst also finding time to put her son through school and then university. She never married.

Neither did Ella who, after a brief spell with the Women's Institute, went on to dedicate her life to the rehabilitation of disabled servicemen, not only from the first but also from the second world war. In 1947, she was awarded the Order of the British Empire in recognition of her services to humanity.

Four months after the war ended, Maisie put her ironmonger out of his misery and married him. A year after that, she gave birth to a daughter whom she called Victoria after the kind lady who'd taught her to read and write and so improved her station in life.

A month after that, Victoria gave birth to a daughter whom she called Jen, after the dear friend who'd saved her life. Five years after that, at the age of thirty, she went to vote for the very first time. As she entered the polling booth, she was asked for her name. She told them, 'Beryl Whittacker'.

And forty years after that...

'Well, why is his name on there, if he isn't dead?' the girl asked irritably.

'I told you before,' the young man replied with a degree of exasperation. 'It was a mistake. He was reported killed, but he wasn't dead.'

'Oh, I see,' she responded with little interest. 'I want to go home. I'm getting cold,' she complained, tugging at the hem of her tiny skirt as if that might somehow help warm her.

Victoria wasn't in the least surprised. She wondered why the girl had bothered to put the garment on at all; she'd owned handkerchiefs that would cover more. Honestly, the girls these days. She paused, smiling to herself, as she recalled some remarks made by an irate farmhand in 1918.

'Honestly, the girls these days, walking around in trousers, smoking cigarettes. Good God, next they'll be expecting to vote. You mark my words, it's the end of civilisation as we know it.'

He was right, of course. Civilisation did end, around about the 1920s when everyone cut loose and went roaring mad, and again in the 1960s with the nation enjoying a new age of prosperity after the ordeal of yet another world war.

Victoria felt an arm slide under hers. She turned her head, smiling up at Gerald. 'That young woman wonders why you're not dead,' she told him, nodding after the receding pair.

'I've often wondered that myself,' Gerald admitted, 'all things considered.'

'The young man thinks that your name being on the memorial is a mistake,' she added.

'The fact that any of those names are there is a mistake,' he answered grimly.

'I can think of a few others that deserve to be there,' Victoria recalled. 'They weren't soldiers, but they died for what they believed in. To think that after all they sacrificed,' she mused, 'it wasn't even the war to end all wars.'

Gerald looked down at her as though her remark had jogged his memory. 'Do you recall, when the second show kicked off, how vehemently opposed you were to my taking any part in it?' he asked.

'What about it?' she acknowledged.

'Well, you were happy to let Jennifer join the Land Army,' he suggested a possible contradiction.

'That was different,' she told him. 'She was young. It was a safe occupation. She was serving her country and I knew it would be a worthwhile experience for her. You'd already done enough. Besides, you were too old and you had me and the rest of the children to consider.'

'Yes, of course, I know that,' he agreed, as if he'd not yet come to the reason for his question. 'But you said that if I tried to join in, you'd break both my legs.'

'Yes, I remember saying that,' Victoria confirmed casually.

'Well,' Gerald pursued his point, 'I've been meaning to ask you all these years. Was that just a figure of speech, or did you actually mean it?'

Victoria reached up and began to straighten his scarf. 'The army took you from me for four years,' she began to explain her motive, 'and when you came back, I felt you were mine to keep. In any case,' she finished with a thin smile, 'I was of the opinion that you'd be more than capable of writing from a wheelchair.'

'Ah yes,' Gerald grimaced, 'I thought you'd say something like that.'

Victoria finished adjusting his scarf and looked back at the memorial. 'There aren't so many wreaths as there used to be,' she observed.

'There aren't that many of us left,' Gerald pointed out. 'Not from the first one at least, but then all things end.'

'Do you think they'll remember us, when we're gone?' Victoria asked. 'The next generation, I mean. What we did, what we saw, how far we've come? Or will it be just another history lesson, a story in a book?'

'Possibly,' Gerald shrugged. 'After all, they've their own lives to live, their own stories to write. Then again, perhaps it's all the same story, it's only the characters that change.'

'I'm not concerned for myself,' she added, gesturing at the memorial, 'only for them.'

'There'll always be someone who remembers,' Gerald assured her. 'But more to the point, let's hope they learn a lesson from our mistakes.'

'Have you laid your wreath?' she asked him.

He nodded. 'Are you ready to go home?'

'No, not yet. Wait here a moment,' she told him.

She went over to the memorial and taking something from her bag, she laid it at its base and stood there for a moment in silent contemplation before returning to Gerald.

'You do the same thing every year,' he remarked with curiosity, 'and you've never said what it is.'

'It's personal,' she told him.

He was silent for a moment, obviously still curious. 'Promise that one day you'll tell me what it is?' he insisted at last.

Smiling, she linked arms with him. 'Yes, alright,' she agreed. 'One day.'

At the base of the memorial as the mist began to roll in, swirling around the tall stone cross so that it appeared to fade away, there between the wreaths of sombre laurels and the scarlet of the poppies, lying in the shadows against the cold stone, was a little garland of plaited hair.

It was her symbol - her candle in the window to guide the traveller home. It was a token of her faith, her prayer, her thanks to God for her husband's safe return.

* * * * *

Lightning Source UK Ltd.
Milton Keynes UK
UKOW031817260112

186131UK00009B/29/P